Mc

MOMENTS

Irish Women Writers in Aid of the Tsunami Victims

———————————

Edited by Ciara Considine

Irish Book Publishers' Association
Cumann Leabharfhoilsitheoirí Éireann

Moments
Irish Women Writers in Aid of the Tsunami Victims
First published April 2005 by
CLÉ – Irish Book Publishers' Association
25 Denzille Lane,
Dublin 2

Moments the collection © copyright CLÉ 2005
Named short story © copyright named writer 2005
(for full copyright details see Copyright Notices page 349)

ISBN 0 904089 04 5

A CIP catalogue record for this title is available from the
British Library

Typeset by Ciara Considine
Cover design by Fidelma Slattery
Cover image Marie O'Malley
Printed in Ireland by ColourBooks Ltd

Contents

9 Editor's Introduction

11 Cecelia Ahern *Twenty-Four Minutes*

20 Catherine Barry *A Colourful Marriage*

30 Sara Berkeley *That Moment, Right There*

39 Maeve Binchy *My Friend Frankie*

50 Clare Boylan *Ordinary Love*

60 Helena Close *Geronimo*

68 Evelyn Conlon *The Sound of Twin*

76 June Considine *Flower Child*

85 Judi Curtin *Jack and Emily*

92 Denise Deegan *Checkout Girl*

102 Martina Devlin *Fortune Cookies*

112 Margaret Dolan *The Long Field*

122 Emma Donoghue *Expecting*

129 Clare Dowling *The Ziegfeld Girl*

137 Rose Doyle *The House of Pleasure*

147 Catherine Dunne *The Four Marys*

153 Christine Dwyer Hickey *Teatro La Fenice*

163 Laura Froom *The Cycle*

171 Karen Gillece *Hair*

180 Tara Heavey *The Winner*

188 Arlene Hunt *Reflection*

197 Cathy Kelly *Pink Lady*

205 Pauline McLynn *This Charming Man*

214 Roisin Meaney *Three Letters*

222 Lia Mills *Leaving the Wedding*

232 Éilís Ní Dhuibhne *Emma Jane*

241 Anita Notaro *Having a Baby*

248 Mary O'Donnell *Come To Me, Maîtresse*

258 Sheila O'Flanagan *Burying Joe*

264 Patricia O'Reilly *Away with the Birds*

272 Julie Parsons *Breaking and Entering*

279 Suzanne Power *One Mile and a Quarter*
285 Deirdre Purcell *Seashell*
292 Trisha Rainsford *We'll Be Away in a Tumbrel*
299 Patricia Scanlan *One Small Step*
305 Mary Stanley *Awakening*
314 Kate Thompson *Dancing*
320 Breda Wall Ryan *One Perfect Day*
329 Sarah Webb *One Moment in Time*
339 Notes on the Authors
349 Acknowledgements
352 Copyright Notices

This collection is made complete by you, the reader. By buying this book, you have not only secured for yourself a great read – one to pick up and put down at your ease – you have also made a €10 contribution, the full cover price, to GOAL, to directly help victims of the tsunamis. We thank you for this.

Ciara Considine and Joseph Hoban
Project Co-ordinators

Introduction

Life can change in an instant, we know it well. That change can come like a speeding train around a bend – sudden, noisy and furious, with a force we can but behold. It can also arrive almost imperceptibly, a slow erosion, until its imprint is exposed, fossil-like. Or arrive with stealth – a burglar of the conscious mind – only fully revealing its presence after it has wreaked havoc. Change can bring us joy and exuberance, as it fulfils our long-held desires – from Lotto wins to lovers; for personal victories or fond wishes for our loved ones; for something new, something good, to come about. Change paints itself onto as broad and diverse a canvas as we can imagine. But whatever form it takes, every change has a moment of beginning.

For the hundreds of thousands of victims of the tsunamis, devastating change came in an instant on the morning of 26 December 2004. In the hours that followed the world looked on helplessly as vast regions of coastal Asia were plunged into devastation, and countless lives were wiped away with terrifying ease.

Moments came about in response to that shocking event. In the spirit of goodwill that gripped the country in the weeks after the disaster – and in some ways as an antidote to a collective sensation of helplessness – the idea for the book was born. Everyone my colleague Joseph Hoban and I approached – from the writers to publishing personnel to distributors to printers to booksellers – responded immediately and generously to our requests for the support required to get this unique charitable venture off the ground (see acknowledgements for further information).

It was agreed that the stories should be united by a theme.

Moments

'Moments of change' seemed to reflect that which is wrenched so forcibly into consciousness in the unhinging aftermath of tragic events: the fragility and, in turn, the preciousness of life.

The stories in *Moments* recognise this, and acknowledge both a world that is beyond our control, and the personal choices that allow us to chart our own paths. They explore change in all its guises – the speeding train, the stealthy burglar, the harbinger of joy – in a series of tales that by turn engage, move, challenge ... and renew. Here are stories of love ending and of new beginnings; of plots hatched and plans foiled; of seemingly innocuous events that shake deep foundations, and of momentous changes that affirm what we know; of unanswerable questions raised, and of answers offered to questions never posed. In almost forty stories, we observe the workings of love, loss and longing; of youthful wisdom and the spontaneity of old age; stories both of thriller-like suspense, and a deceptive simplicity that touches deeply.

Enjoy the moments.

Ciara Considine
March 2005

Twenty-Four Minutes
Cecelia Ahern

Steven awoke to his alarm ringing at seven a.m. Waking up, the first disappointment of every day, was as usual followed by its faithful friend, dread. The alarm was like a siren, a warning bell, *get up or else*. Slowly rolling over, he stretched out his arm and punched down on the clock. Although the room was silenced, the ringing continued in his ear-drums. What he would give to sleep all day, to close his lids and block out the light. Once again he had spent another night glaring unblinkingly at teletext and info-mercials, sleep, as usual, not coming easily.

He looked vacantly at the growing crack in his magnolia ceiling and listened as the kids next door fought to use the bathroom. Walls like cardboard separated their two-bedroom-and-a-boxroom townhouses, stuffed together like shoeboxes in the dusty stockroom of a department-store basement: piled high, packed tight, squeezed in, airtight. Multi-coloured toy-like houses for first-time buyers, pristine and pastel with pretty thresholds to cross, blinding buyers to the realisation they'd just crossed the most expensive toll-bridge they were ever likely to pay. Suburban bliss.

Steven could imagine what all the people looked like from above, lab rats running around the maze of houses, pointlessly, distracted by irrelevant and unnecessary daily routines. Did nobody think, *what is the point*? Did nobody else feel like suddenly stopping what they were doing, looking up to the

Gamesmaster in the sky and refusing to continue playing this stupid game?

He exhaled slowly, counting to three as the screaming next door turned to tears, the knocking on the door turned to bangs and the dog's barking turned to howls. Kicking the covers off, he wearily pulled his body out of bed and began his morning routine: shower, dress – shirt, suit, tie – coffee, alarm, front door, walk to the train station. The monotony. Night out on a Thursday, hangover on a Friday, football on a Sunday. Every week identical.

One thousand five hundred and twenty-seven steps to the train station and he arrived at the platform at exactly 07.42, met by the same tired faces, the same bored expressions, the same coats, briefcases, hairstyles and shoes. Everyone was uniformed up and ready for battle. Nobody spoke, nobody smiled – there was just the occasional cough or beep of a mobile phone and the fuzzy sounds of personal stereos as commuters stared blankly and wearily into space, eyes glassy and sleepy, their previous night's dreams still fresh in their minds, their beds not yet cold.

The sign over the platform declared a three-minute wait, as it always did, when he arrived. The man beside him in the brown suede coat was consistently ahead of him, the woman with the black briefcase, torn at the corner and with a scratch through the middle, always behind him. Everything was done in perfect unison, their lives predictable no matter how much longer they took drinking their coffee in the morning and no matter how many extra minutes they spent closing their eyes under the soothing hot water of the shower, dreaming of somewhere and something else.

Finally the familiar sound forced a few heads to turn and a few eyes to blink out of their trance. The wail of the horn, the vibrations on the tracks, the hiss and squeal as the train prepared to stop: everyone moved forward and took their positions. As the train slowed, dull faces on crammed bodies stared out at them, expressionless. Nobody got off; everybody got on an already crowded train. Steven got on last. He always did.

He stepped through the door and could move no further. He turned his back on the faces staring at him and held his breath as the door slowly shut. He said goodbye to fresh air and looked out the small dirty window at people running to the platform, seconds late, panic and frustration scrawled across their faces. How different their days would be now. A second too late and they were out of the rat race. He watched them as the train pulled away, envying them, while inside the train hot, tired bodies huddled together in the cramped conditions, rocking back and forth with the swaying carriage. Some slept as they stood; music and chat from earphones kept others awake.

The train slowed and stopped at the next station. Doors opened, no one disembarked, more tried to squeeze in. Steven found himself being forced in further, away from the door. The toilet door opened – a distasteful odour emanating into an already stuffy atmosphere – and three students disappeared inside for space.

The doors closed and the train moved on. The atmosphere was tinged with morning breath, coffee and B.O. One person fainted; there was a scuffle to move her forward and help her off at the next stop, where she was left on the bench, flushed, embarrassed and gasping for air.

Sardines in a housing estate; sardines in a train. Everywhere he went Steven was squashed, trapped, his mind cluttered with a million messy thoughts packed together so tightly he thought his head would explode. But he was keeping it together; he was waking up each morning and reminding himself to breathe. But not in this stuffy carriage: he would hold his breath here, as he had been doing over the past few years of his life, waiting for things to get better. Battling with his mind to cheer up and see the positive, losing each time and lying down even more battered and bruised.

But today was different. Today he would be victorious. Today he would receive confirmation of his promotion, a promotion that would allow him to leave the stuffy, cluttered and windowless confines of his basement office, piled high with paperwork and metallic filing cabinets, so uninspiring and so small he didn't even have space to pace. Today he would win the battle and race up those steps like Rocky, dancing at the top with his fists in the air.

But he had to get there first and the train hadn't moved for fifteen minutes. People were beginning to become agitated, feeling the strain of their personal space being invaded. Steven could only move his head – his arm and briefcase were caught behind him. When he turned his head one way he received a mouthful of frizzy hair; the other way left him staring directly into the face of a heavy-breathing, overweight and balding man. He chose the hair.

Without any explanation as to why they hadn't moved, the train moved on again, jerking and spluttering along the track and trying to pick up pace with its heavy load. The next stop spat out six people and sucked in ten more and Steven breathed in the last of the fresh air before the door closed, the frizzy hair tickling his nose as he did so. The newcomers explained that the delay was due to a man jumping in front of a train further along the line. Someone tutted in annoyance and checked his watch. 'He wouldn't have felt a thing,' was the last sentence uttered before the seconds of chat ended and the commuters were once again plunged into silence, leaving the woman who had spoken flushed in the face, as if struck by the silliness of her words.

'How could anyone do that?' another woman had asked in confusion and horror. Steven understood how. He understood what it was like to want to get out of a situation so much you'd do anything. Standing trapped between strange bodies on the connecting joints of a train every morning, then working in a windowless office cell, without any human contact, looking at so many numbers for so many hours that they all began to look the same. Everything felt like it was moving in on him. His world was getting smaller; it was fading away and was forcing him to live only in his head. A head that was pounding, exhausted, fed up and growing tired of listening to itself. When there was nothing holding you up, nothing to show there was a point to all this, when there was no one capable of putting a smile on your face, he understood how a person could do it. He understood it very well.

The train eventually stopped at Tara Street station and the door opened with a hissing sound, like the loosening of a mineral-bottle lid. It had the same effect as a birdcage being opened: out the door they all fluttered, tiredly bumping into one another as they walked at different paces downstairs and out into the fresh air. The sun was rising over O'Connell Bridge, the buildings casting shadows on the pavements. Steven walked in and out of the darkness as he moved with the rolling crowd, just one more body, just another meaningless, overactive mind churning on a crowded city pavement.

Two thousand six hundred and four steps to the bank, they all marched on in full uniform to the beat of a drum. Forty-eight steps downstairs to his office where he took his position in the firing line and awaited the moment when Gerard Rush, his boss, would give him the good news.

Twelve noon sharp, and the door to Steven's office opened, banging against his desk. Gerard popped his head around the door. His face said it all. His complexion was grey and his expression grim.

'I'm sorry, Steven. They decided to go with Andy in the end. I fought for you, I really did.' Gerard sat before him, his back almost touching the door of the small office. His voice was sincere, his apology genuine.

The promotion was the one thing he had had to look forward to, so much so that it had become the solution to every problem. Everything would be all right when he got the job. It was the crutch that had helped him limp along. It wasn't a lifelong ambition, it wasn't his *aim* in life to sit behind padded porridge screens leafing through files, it was just that there was *nothing else*. There were no other distractions, no other goals or interests. It was all there was, every little hope in the world pinned right on the promotion. His crutch had been taken away and now he was falling.

The woman's voice from the train came back to him – *He wouldn't have felt a thing* – and suddenly there was clarity. He had found another crutch, albeit a temporary one.

Gerard watched him – his grey and wrinkled face full of concern – expecting him to scream, shout and fire the stapler at his head. The strip lighting buzzed loudly in the silence that ensued. But Steven smiled, a big broad smile that Gerard hadn't seen for years.

'No worries, Gerard, I understand.' He beamed, his eyes lighting up.

Gerard looked confused. 'You're sure?'

'Yep,' he chirped, leaning back in his bony chair, looking around his closet-sized office proudly, 'absolutely.'

'OK.' Gerard nodded quickly, confused by his reaction. 'Well, that's a great attitude to have, I must say. Do you want to take a break or anything, get a breath of fresh air?' He studied Steven's face closely.

Steven laughed. 'Yes, actually, I will in a while, but in the meantime I'll get back to work on this lot.' He picked up a pile of papers and banged them down in front of him, the dust bouncing up from the old table.

'Right.' Gerard paused. 'OK.' He stood up and got ready to leave. 'I'm very sorry, Steven,' he said sincerely, holding out his hand.

Steven looked up from the stack of papers and took Gerard's hand. 'Thanks, Gerard' – he grasped his hand tighter, holding on that little bit longer – 'thanks for everything.' His voice was gentle.

'No problem, Steven. It's my pleasure.' Gerard gulped lightly, not liking the change in atmosphere. 'It's not the end of the world, remember. It's just a job,' he stressed.

Steven picked up the phone and called his parents.

Twenty minutes later he put on his suit jacket, turned off the buzzing strip lighting and exited his office. He waved at Gerard down the hall, who hesitantly gave him the thumbs up. With a spring in his step he hadn't felt for years, he walked the forty-eight steps to the ground floor and outside into the fresh air.

He walked the 2,604 steps to the train station, the streets quieter now with everyone buried at work. Entering the station his head felt light, no longer heavy and pounding. A haze had lifted from his mind, a weight from his shoulders, and he experienced a sensation of floating he'd never had before. He was happy, clear in his mind about what he wanted to do. He didn't want to worry any more, he didn't want to feel scared and he didn't want his mind to keep torturing him. He knew what he needed to do and *he wouldn't feel a thing*.

He entered his train ticket into the machine and pushed his way through the barrier, relieved that for once in his life his destination was unknown. Anywhere but here. Arriving on the platform, hands trembling and heart pumping with adrenaline, he was glad to see that the station was empty. His mind was focused; there was only one way for him to go. Glancing up at the sign hanging over the platform, he saw that the next train would be in twenty-four minutes; twenty-four minutes was a long time to wait. He needed to do it now. Angrily he kicked a can and sent it flying off the platform and onto the tracks. He watched it lie there, knowing its destiny. He had nothing to do but pace the yellow line he had obediently stayed behind his whole life. Today he would cross it. His skin grew clammy and a chill ran through his body. He could do this.

Twenty minutes. What would Gerard think when he didn't get back to work? He pictured his friendly boss staring down the hall, making sure Steven had returned. Gerard had known something was up; he had felt it in Steven's handshake and seen it in his eyes. It wouldn't be long before he entered Steven's office and saw the note. Steven played out the scene. Gerard would panic, call the Gardaí, and they would immediately set out looking for him. But they wouldn't find him. Not the way they wanted to, anyway.

He glanced up at the sign. Sixteen minutes. He paced the yellow line, clenching and unclenching his fists. What would the lads think when he didn't turn up to football on Sunday? They'd be angry he'd let them down, at having to take Rory Malone off the bench for the first time since he'd scored an own goal at last year's final. He could imagine them all bitching about him over a few pints after the game, blaming their loss on Rory Malone and Steven's no-show. Maybe the next day they'd find out what had happened and hopefully understand.

If only they knew how his days were covered in darkness, like someone had turned off the light switch in his mind; if only they knew how his waking up in the morning was the first disappointment of every day. He was tired; he had nothing left to give, no more ideas to try. If they could understand that, then they could understand his decision.

Nine minutes left. The crowd at the train station. How would they feel? Would they even notice he wasn't there? The lady with the torn briefcase and the man in the brown suede coat, would they notice him missing from the middle of their daily queue? Would they notice that one more person than usual could squeeze on the train? Would they be looking out the dirty window as the train pulled away, waiting for him to run onto the platform, out of breath and panicked at having missed the train? When the platform was empty, would they even notice? Would they remember the previous day's talk about the man jumping in front of the train and would that woman, that same woman, think, *He wouldn't have felt a thing*, just to make herself feel better, so she could sleep well that night and rest easy in her bubble?

Four minutes. His grandad. What would he think? Would he even know what had happened, or understand? Steven could imagine him being told by the nurse that his only grandson had passed away. He could imagine him asking, 'What grandson? Steven who?' and settling down to watch his geraniums blow in the breeze on his window sill. Steven smiled as he walked faster and faster to the end of the platform, his head dizzy with relief. He needed to get off the platform now and move down along the tracks to a point where the train's sudden braking would make no odds. He only wanted to have to do this once.

One minute. He crossed the yellow line and jumped down off the platform. He could see a man on the opposite platform waving frantically but he couldn't hear a word he said. His mind was focused on the sounds of the train as it approached the bridge over the city, the wail of the horn, the vibrations on the tracks, the hiss and squeal of the wheels. His heart beat faster, his throat dried up and he loosened his tie. His parents. What would they think? This would destroy them. He pictured them receiving the news, remembering their last conversation on the phone when he had told them both he loved them, how they had joked and laughed together and how he had sounded happier than they could remember in a long time. As he walked along the edge of the track towards the train, high above the city, the Liffey below him, he thought about what they would be doing now. His father would be out in his garden on this fine day and his mother would be on the phone. She was always on the phone. His father would be calling things to her, giving her a step-by-step narration of the state of the garden while she waved at him wildly, trying to signal to him that she was on the phone. But he'd keep talking anyway.

He noticed he had stopped walking and was midway over the bridge. The train was seconds away; the ground beneath his feet was shaking. It was time to look up to the sky and admit defeat. He had had enough. Now was his time: if he was going to do it, he had to step out now.

His hair blew wildly as he pressed his eyes closed fiercely, holding his breath. His heart beat faster and the blood in his veins pumped violently around his body. He could feel his pulse beating in his throat. The sound was unbearable, a loud thunderous sound, like the sky falling down around him. And then the wind stopped. His hair stopped blowing and his chest relaxed.

Steven opened his eyes, breathed deeply, peeled himself from the side of the bridge and shakily climbed back up onto the platform.

Twenty-four minutes. A long time to have to wait to die. Exactly how long it took him to figure out he didn't want to.

A Colourful Marriage
Catherine Barry

I find Heather upstairs in my bedroom. She is sprawled on her stomach, legs in scissor-like formation. She has the television on full blast as usual. I turn it down slightly. She giggles.

'What's so funny, Het?' I ask.

I know she won't answer me. I am resigning myself to the fact that she might never speak again, resigning myself to her muteness. When was it that she stopped talking altogether? I immediately feel it is my fault. I must have done something wrong. Despite my guilt, I am not about to give up. Not now that the Enfield Child Guidance Clinic has come on board. Thank God.

I don't want to think about it. My hands begin to shake uncontrollably. I need a Valium to think straight. I need a Valium to think about something else. I need a Valium to function. I need …

I tell the thoughts to go away. The thoughts of Miles and Heather, my husband and my daughter. They are supposed to be the two closest people to me in the whole world. Not strangers who pass me on the landing, barely speaking, barely breathing the air around me, and barely exchanging glances over the kitchen table at breakfast.

It isn't long before the tablet takes effect. I can apply my make-up without my hand jerking this way and that. I can talk without feeling the pain in my cheek, where last night Miles thumped me repeatedly. I can pretend I was not thrown across the floor and did not hit the corner of the glass coffee table. I can pretend there wasn't blood on my nightdress. I can pretend he didn't say those horrible words:

'The only thing you're good for is sex.'

I can blot it out, just like I am blotting out the purple-and-yellow bruise that has blossomed overnight. I have had much practice in the art of disguise. I can manage perfectly, as long as I can't *feel*.

I pull in to the Enfield Child Guidance Clinic and find a parking space easily enough. We are early. As we enter through the dull brown doors of the clinic, I feel Heather's tiny hand grip mine just a little bit harder. I squeeze it back without looking at her. I can feel her anxiety. Her cherry lips draw hard into a straight line and her shoulders are rigid and tense, her steps loud and methodical on the polished concrete stairs.

We sit down on a crooked couch that slouches to the right and wait. Heather amuses herself with broken bits of toys. Everything seems broken, secondhand or lopsided. It is strangely comforting. After all, I am all of those things myself.

In the appointment room, I stare hard at the enormous window screen before me. I can't see anything through it. On the wall beside it is a white telephone. Mark Holby, the facilitator, picks it up and begins whispering down the line.

Heather wanders about the room as if searching for something. I pretend not to notice. No one else is making any reference to it anyway. I wish she would just sit down. It is making me nervous.

I can't very well order her to sit down.

What will the panel of psychologists behind the screen think of me then?

I am so anxious and nervous, knowing there are six of them behind there. We are being studied, like some unusual monkey strain threatened by extinction.

Mark Holby ends the mysterious dialogue with the other side. It all feels so absurd. The panel seem to be instructing him. I wait.

Back arched, shoulders up, fingers drumming my locked knees. I try to drop my shoulders and look more relaxed.

'OK, Mrs Corcoran,' he starts.

'It's Clare.' I smile.

'Clare.' He nods towards me and smiles back.

I shouldn't have offered my first name. It has come out rather abruptly. I am not objecting to being called Mrs Corcoran. It isn't like that.

Shit.

I should explain.

Now they are going to assume there is something wrong with my marriage …

Do they know my heart is thumping?

Is there a sound monitor that picks that up?

Nothing guiltier than a racing heartbeat …

Can they see the yellow and purple bruise under my right eye that I have so meticulously covered up with concealers, make-up and eyeshadow?

Heather looks at me accusingly. I can see the question in her eyes. Why am I putting her through this? It isn't like I haven't asked myself the same question over and over.

When Heather was two and a half, I enrolled her in the Montessori school. Initially, she settled in well, but after a time, she began to withdraw. She didn't mix well or join in with the other kids.

At four, she was still wetting the bed at night, but so were some of the other kids. An occasional hit and miss was permissible, wasn't it? Yet Heather was liable to wet herself at any time and she was eight years old now. She was also experiencing difficulties in school. She was simply refusing to participate. The teacher had discreetly enquired if we had been experiencing 'problems' in the home. My response had been an emphatic no. She then suggested I get Heather's eyes, ears and nose checked in the Children's Hospital. Just in case. She wanted to rule out the possibility that her lack of academic progress could be attributed to a physical disability. However, at the Audiology Centre all results came back normal. In the final analysis, we were advised to explore another avenue.

They referred Heather to the Enfield Child Guidance Clinic.

'Clare?' Mark Holby is repeating my name.

I am acutely aware of the psychologists behind the screen.

'Clare, tell me how things have been and what has been happening since our last session.'

'Well … ' I stall.

What exactly does he mean? Am I supposed to describe the housework? The shopping?

'Em … oh … we've been fine,' I smile.

'And you?' he asks.

What does he mean by that?

As far as I am concerned, I have just answered that question.

'It's just that you said "we",' he smiles.

'Yes, I did,' I admit.

Shit.

Is that the wrong answer?

'I'm afraid that is a habit,' I add hastily.

'What is?' he asks, scribbling away in his notepad.

'When someone asks how I am, I always include Heather in my thoughts. It's an automatic thing with me. I don't know why I do it,' I say.

Do I sound mother-hen-ish?

'Sure,' he reassures me. 'This is your third or fourth appointment, yes?'

'It's our fourth,' I confirm.

'Well, the panel feel that it might be a good idea if you and Heather separate for the next few sessions.'

Heather's hand almost crushes mine. I can feel the steeliness of her nails sinking into my palm. Her grip is tenacious.

'What exactly does that mean?' I ask.

'Well, instead of interviewing you together, we were thinking perhaps Heather would like to meet the team. She can watch through the screen while you and I have a talk,' he answers.

Heather looks terrified. I pat her hand reassuringly. She leaves the room reluctantly. Mark Holby returns alone.

'Can Heather see me?' I ask anxiously.

'Yes,' he answers, matter-of-factly.

I look at the camera out of the corner of my eye.

'It's OK,' he says, looking straight at me, 'when the camera is running, the red light goes on; you can see for yourself.'

I am surprised by this remark. I haven't budged my head. I don't have to. I have a gift of knowing what is happening all around me without moving an inch. I have acquired the skill through the unpredictability of Miles's rages. I never know when the next explosion is coming. I have lived my entire life through the corner of my eye.

'Well, Clare, the panel feel they are no closer to understanding the source of Heather's … em … "problems".'

He says the last word quietly.

'Can she hear what's being said?' I ask. 'You know, Het is very sensitive.'

'No, don't worry, Clare, she can't hear us,' he confirms.

'Good. She's very protective of me, you see.'

'Yes. We can see that,' he nods.

'What do you want me to talk about?' I ask hurriedly.

I want the clock on the wall to fast-forward an hour so I can just get the hell out of there.

'How about we talk about you for a while?'

Fuck.

I can't say no.

It will look like I don't care about Heather.

I don't like this: the sudden turn of events. The spotlight is suddenly upon me. I feel like I am strapped up to one of those lie-detector machines.

Can they guess?

The 'thinking' is back.

This has nothing to do with Miles.

This has nothing to do with Miles.

I try to counteract it.

'Well, I am a mother and a housewife,' I stumble, knowing it sounds dumb and bland. 'Look, I'm not very good at this … really, I think—'

'What happened your eye, Clare?' he interrupts me bluntly.

I swallow. Hard.

'This? Oh, it's nothing!' I blurt.

'It looks pretty something to me. What happened?' he presses on.

'I fell over some of Heather's toys. God, I am always doing it. You know the way they leave them all strewn about the floor. I am forever picking them up and asking her to help, but …'

The phone on the wall bursts into life.

Mark Holby picks it up. I can hear a muffled voice at the other end of the line.

'The camera is rolling now, Clare,' Mark Holby confirms – but I already know.

'Can you tell us something about Mr Corcoran? Miles is his name, I believe, yes?' Mark Holby rushes on.

I fall silent. I am acutely aware of Heather, listening and watching from the other side.

'Well, let's see now.' I play for time. 'Miles is forty-three. He's a big golf fan, you know. Plays nearly every day. A real passion he has.' I smile. 'We got married … oh, about … about nine years ago? Miles has worked in his father's business all his life – computers … very successful. Now he has taken a year's leave to take up the position of captain in the golf club. I think he's rather flattered,' I stall.

'A very honoured title,' Mark remarks.

'Yes. I know. Miles is so proud.' I smile.

So far … so good.

'He's a good man, Miles, a successful man. A good catch, as my mam would say. He's worked very hard to give Heather and me the standard of life that we have. I couldn't ask for a better husband, God bless him. You know, he works every hour God sends him. I think the golf club will be good for him.' I laugh nervously.

'A very busy man by the sound of it,' Mark says. 'How is his current relationship with Heather, then? How do you think he feels about the problems Heather has been experiencing?'

I sit very still, twiddling my thumbs, aware of Heather's watchful eyes. It is excruciating not knowing the right answer.

I go over the options in my head. I am pausing too long and I know it. The silence is tangible. The clock on the wall ticks. I watch the phone but nothing happens. It stares back at me, like an accusing finger.

'Well, he's very concerned,' I say. 'He doesn't understand why it's happening. Miles is a truly gifted father, always patient, always kind, loving and attentive. Always willing to listen …' I trail off.

My hands are wringing wet with perspiration. I want to rub them against my thighs, but I know it would be very obvious.

'He always has time for Heather,' I add.

A terrible thumping begins on the other side of the screen.

Mark Holby doesn't flinch.

'Always has time?'

I am not sure if he is asking me to verify this or if he is just having an afterthought – a private reflection that has escaped by accident.

'Oh, yes,' I nod.

'It's just that you said he was very busy and not home much these days.'

The banging and thumping continues on the screen.

It occurs to me that Mark Holby is deliberately ignoring it.

I can't.

'Yes. He is busy. What I meant was, when he is home, he

always finds time to sit with her and talk to her.' This comes out rather clipped and cold.

'Where is Miles today, Clare?' Mark asks, moving forward quite suddenly, and willing me to look him in the eyes.

'He had a very important presentation to attend to in the club, and I didn't really want to bother him about this. I didn't want to upset him.'

I laugh. Nervously.

'I understand.' Mark leans back and proceeds to chew on his pen. Thank God.

Now, fucking back off.

'It just strikes me as a bit odd,' he starts up again.

'What's that?' I ask.

'Just that you claim Miles takes a big interest in Heather's welfare, yet he hasn't attended *any* of the sessions,' he finishes.

The interminable thumping on the screen continues.

'Clare, has Miles ever assaulted you?' His manner is forthright.

My eyes well up.

My throat feels dry and choked.

'No. Never,' I whisper.

As I utter the words, Heather throws her full body weight at the window.

Please, Heather. Please don't. Please, darling. Please don't do it.

'I'm sorry,' I blurt, desperately trying to hold back the tears from spilling down my cheeks.

I can still hear Heather banging and thumping angrily on the screen.

My Het.

My baby.

She is angry with me.

She is angry with me for lying.

'You know, she always does that,' I pounce.

Mark looks up at me, surprised.

'She *always* does that,' I repeat. 'God. You know, it can be *so* embarrassing, but I'm used to it, you see. She hates us being separated in any way. Often she does it in supermarkets, if I go down one aisle and she goes down another and she thinks she's lost. She scares easily. I suppose you could call it a tantrum. Isn't that what you would call it? Yes, I think that's the common term for it: a tantrum. I don't see it as that, though. I … suppose because I am used to her ways. She's not a bad kid, you know? She's very good, really. So good in school, excellent at art and never a minute's trouble …'

As I speak, my throat aches to let out my pain. My tears teeter on the edges of my eyelids.

I hold them wide open, willing them to stay in.

'We know, Clare. We know what's going on,' Mark says gently.

He pats my shoulder.

He lifts my face and examines my bruised eye.

I wince with the pain. 'Please don't. Please … not in front of Heather; she knows nothing,' I beg.

The tears flow freely now.

'Clare, it was Heather who told us,' he says softly.

'No … no … please.' I turn my cheek away.

'Heather told us, Clare,' he repeats. 'Clare, listen to me. The next time you come out of that house, it will be on a slab. Do you understand?' He barely whispers this in my ear.

I nod.

I do understand.

The horror of his words jolts me into reality.

The door opens and Heather steps in. She stares at me. Waves of shame wash over me.

I want to go to her immediately and hold her and tell her I am sorry.

She turns on her heel and marches out of the room; reflecting my thoughts: saying sorry would not be enough.

I bury my face in my hands and weep uncontrollably.

'Leave him,' Mark implores me. 'If only for Heather's sake. Leave him now.'

I rise and follow the sound of Heather's heavy footsteps clattering down the stairs.

I catch up with her and tap her on the shoulder.

I offer her my hand.

I can see the tears in her eyes.

She takes my hand and then reaches up and kisses my stinging cheek.

I cuddle her close as we sit on the steps, her head buried in my chest.

She stares at the poster on the entrance door. It reads: *When home is where the hurt is.*

Neither of us speaks.

I pull out my mobile phone.

I dial Directory Enquiries.

'Hello? Yes, I wonder if you can help me. Can you give me the telephone number of Free Legal Aid, please?'

That Moment, Right There

Sara Berkeley

Ten Sunshine Lane. One of those warm nights you can hear music – out of the houses maybe, or from the cars that kids are cruising round the neighbourhood. In all the whispering of baby's breath and bamboo palm, Andy is playing slack-key guitar. Tea-lights around our door and on the windowsills light the faces of our friends. The talk is of money.

Porter and I smile at each other. The dark runs off his face like laughter. He's handing a plate of chicken around. Barbecued, crispy, I can smell it and I'm hungry.

'What's he going to do all day?' says Lenny comfortably. 'Sit at home and read the paper?'

'I'll help him spend his millions,' says Jim.

'I'd buy a Raphael,' says Judy. 'A Caravaggio. Something with real ultramarine. They made it with powdered lapis lazuli.'

'I'd quit work,' says Jim. He's picking morosely at a thorn that got lodged in his foot during the football game.

Porter comes to me with the chicken. He points to the best bit.

'Wouldn't you want to do something good?' says Marla. Her children are unruly and her husband didn't come with her again. 'Scholarships for bright kids,' she says. There is longing in her voice.

They're talking about Andy. Everyone's sitting round our garden on a summer night trying to work out what they'd do.

'All that good stuff with money?' says Lenny. 'You can keep it.

You'd have everyone clambering up your trouser leg for a piece. That's so, Andy, isn't it?' He grins at Andy, who inclines his head as though there might be some truth to that. He doesn't stop playing.

'What is it about money, though,' says Elaine. 'And affording things? Lenny's brother calls us from Florida, the whole family's going to be there next week except us. His sister's calling us, his mom. "Just come for a week. Five days. Just the two of you if the kids are doing their thing." And we're saying no, 'cause we can't afford it. But we *have* the money. What does affording mean, anyway? That we had the money earmarked for a new water heater?'

'Affording just means whether you want the thing,' says Lenny lazily. He holds his wineglass with his fist loosely around the stem.

'No, but what would you *buy*?' says Judy. 'If you had a lump sum and you wanted to buy just one thing.' She makes a gesture, opening it to the floor.

Andy stops playing. 'I'd buy you,' he says.

Everyone is quiet.

Judy smiles – *You're kidding, right?* – and looks around to see how everyone else is taking it. Nobody is giving.

'Right,' she says, and tilts her head back, looking at him from narrowed eyes.

'Seriously,' says Andy. 'How much are you?'

'An-dy,' says Marla.

'What are you,' says Lenny, 'Robert Redford in *Indecent Proposal*?'

'Sure,' says Andy. 'The guy was right. Everyone can be bought.'

Judy raises her eyebrows, but she says nothing.

'So, how much are you?'

'Not for sale,' says Jim. He doesn't jump in with it. He's still examining his foot and he doesn't look up.

'Isn't that for the lady to decide?' says Andy.

Everyone is looking at Judy except Jim. I catch Porter's eye and frown: *Should we break this up?* But he shakes his head. Porter reads a situation better than I do.

31

Judy picks up her glass and takes a sip of wine.

'Forty thousand,' she says. She puts the wineglass down. 'Before tax.'

Jim looks up at her.

'I'm on special offer,' she says.

Jim's staring at her. It's pretty quiet in the garden. The tea-lights flicker and it's getting too dark to make out the contours of the house properly.

'That's pretty cheap,' says Andy.

'Better make a higher bid, Jimbo,' says Lenny.

'That's my price,' says Judy.

'Won't buy you a Raphael,' says Andy.

'You might get a frame,' says Lenny.

'Shut up, Lenny,' says Jim. 'Here's my counter-offer,' he says to Andy. 'One old toaster and a two-dollar bill. If you want to sell yourself,' he says to his wife, 'at least make the offer attractive.'

Judy starts to laugh. Real laughing. She splutters, becoming helpless like after a really great joke.

'Frankly, I don't see what's so funny,' says Jim. He's looking at his wife.

She's laughing in big sobs now, holding her stomach, tears starting.

'The thing is—' she starts, and then another peal of laughter takes her, 'the thing is, he really *loves* that toaster!'

Marla's laughing now too, and Lenny. Then Jim gets a slow smile. He turns his beer can round on the table, swivelling it on the bottom rim. Then he starts to laugh. Most people are laughing now. Andy doesn't crack a smile. He takes up the guitar and starts to pick out a complicated piece.

'What about you, Porter?' says Lenny as the laughter is dying down. 'You're awful quiet over there, you and Cath.'

'Oh,' says Porter, 'I dunno. I never think about money that much.'

There's a chorus of groans and protests.

'Come on,' says Lenny, 'you can do better than that.'

Porter smiles in the smudge of a tea-light and looks at me.
'OK, then,' he says. 'I'd buy me more of the same.'

It's six months later. Porter comes in from work and he looks like he's trying to figure something out. He takes a beer from the fridge, sits up at the counter where I'm cooking dinner. I wonder if he's having trouble with the floor manager again. The guy means well, but he's new and young and he tries too hard to show who's boss.

'What's up?' I say.

'I talked to Jim today,' he says.

'How's everything?'

He puts his beer down, wipes some froth off his top lip. 'Judy moved out.'

'Moved out?' It's a real surprise, a shocker, but the shock doesn't set in right away. Instead, I start picturing it: Judy moved into a motel room somewhere with lots of suitcases and hatboxes. She's a real hat girl, Judy, likes to wear those broad-brimmed ones with the flowers and the little bits of plastic fruit.

'She moved in with Andy,' Porter says.

I stop chopping okra. The motel room just got wiped out, like with a soft cloth, and there's no picture in its place.

'What?'

Porter knows it's not that I didn't hear him. He says nothing. For a couple of minutes, it seems like there's nothing for either of us to say.

'What about Evan?' I say. I'm incredulous, but I'm trying to feel my way around in this, get a purchase. It's like climbing ice.

'What about him? He's at school. UCLA, isn't it?'

'Phoenix. Somewhere hot, I don't know. What about Jim? Is he ...' I don't finish. I remember every word of it now, the toaster conversation. The two-dollar bill. *If you want to sell yourself,* he told her, *at least make the offer attractive.* Porter and I talked about that night for a while. It seemed like the last night of summer. What about Jim now? I picture him gunning his truck up to Andy's ranch,

33

brandishing something, yelling. I try to fit this new and shocking piece of information into my picture of Jim, my picture of Jim and Judy, our friends for more than fifteen years. We raised our kids together. But it's like a puzzle piece that's too large, the wrong colour, or from another puzzle altogether.

Porter finishes his beer, drinking the last of it in one go.

'I need a shower,' he says. 'Is there time?'

'Sure. Porter?'

He stops at the kitchen door. I can't think how to frame what I want to say, so I shrug and he leaves. I can't do it, though, I can't just keep standing there cooking dinner like everything is pretty much the same as it was when I got the pans out. I go over and stand by the kitchen table, but I can't sit down either; it's a bit too odd to sit down when I'm supposed to be cooking dinner. I stand there, thinking about all that must have happened to get us to this moment, with Porter telling me in the kitchen that Judy Steiner moved in with Andy, in his big house up at Caribou Ranch. Then I go out into our hall and down to the bedroom. Porter's on the bed, just sitting there, not undressed yet. He looks up.

'So what does this say,' I begin, 'about all our friends and their marriages? I mean, we think we know all these people, but do we really? If I had asked you to describe Jim and Judy's marriage yesterday, how would it have looked?'

Porter's not really following me. Or maybe he doesn't want to.

'Say you have a bunch of plates here.' I point to the bed, laying out imaginary plates. 'And each one has the marriage of one of our sets of friends on it. There's Lenny and Elaine. Judy and Jim. Marla and Harris, Andy and Robin, when they were married. Everything you see – that's just the tip, just the tip of the iceberg. Each marriage goes way, way down. There's so much *nobody* knows except the two people.'

'You forgot Porter and Cath,' says Porter.

'Right,' I say. 'There's our plate.' I point. 'Right there.'

34

'Looks pretty tasty,' Porter says, and he has that smile. 'Our plate.'

But this is not something I can laugh about just now. I'm having a lot of things well up over this Judy-moving-out business. How could she fall for the money thing? Give up all those years with Jim and Evan and their house with the back room they built on themselves, the back sun-porch? How could she just *move in* with Andy? And did this make him right, that anyone can be bought? For a moment, I started picturing an *Indecent Proposal* ending to their story: Judy and Andy driving around in limousines, and she's got the white suit on like Demi Moore and the parasol; Jim showing up drunk and falling in the dirt. But this is not a movie. This is part of our life, and I'm starting to feel very sore about something that isn't entirely to do with Judy driving around in a limousine.

'There are tasty bits,' I say. 'And not-so-tasty bits.'

'What does that mean?' says Porter.

'It means,' I say, backtracking a little now from the tone of my previous remark, 'that there are things in any marriage you wouldn't want outsiders to see. That's all.'

'What things?' says Porter. He moves one leg up on the bed, starts unlacing his boot.

I stay standing in the bedroom doorway. This isn't really the direction I meant the conversation to take. So I could let him just take his shower. I could go back to the kitchen and finish chopping the okra.

'What things?' says Porter. He eases his boot off, but he doesn't start on the other one.

I shrug. 'Things we both know about.'

He starts unlacing the other boot. 'What if we don't,' he says, 'both know? Since this marriage thing goes down so deep. What if one of us is seeing less of it than the other?'

Maybe there's a challenge in his tone. Maybe it's just the way he's taking his boots off while we discuss this, like I'm only worth the part of his attention that isn't getting ready for a shower. I don't know. But I started on this thing. It could be called cowardice not to see it through.

'Well, there's things like the way you always fall for those secretaries Ed hires.'

He had been taking off the second boot. He stops.

'What?'

'Come on, Porter. It's maybe not something we talk about, but we both know it's going on.'

'Wait a minute,' he says. 'We *both* know? How is this something we both know, when it's not even true?'

'Oh, Porter, please. There's no need to be that defensive. Cindy? You're telling me you didn't have a crush on Cindy? And that skinny one with the red hair, what was her name? And now the way you can't talk about Annabelle without getting that … look on your face?'

'Goddammit!'

His boot hits the wall pretty hard. It isn't even close to me, wasn't meant to be, but I flinch anyway.

Porter is standing by our bed. There's an expression on his face I've never seen before. I should have gone back to the kitchen, I realise that now. But it's too late. How did a conversation all about somebody else's problem wind up being all about us? I'm not sure I know how to slow this thing down. I feel a bit racy, a bit like I'm running too fast down a hill.

'What is this, Cath?' Porter says. 'What's this about? Are you thinking what you're saying here?'

'Sure I am.' It comes out sounding more sure than I feel. 'You don't have to be defensive. It's pretty normal for people to get crushes on their secretaries, I would've thought.'

He's got that look again. It isn't angry, and it isn't hurt. More sort of bottled up.

'Maybe for some people,' he says, real even, 'it is. But not for me.'

'I can handle it, Porter,' I say. 'As long as you don't do anything about it, I'm cool with it. But just don't tell me it isn't going on. Don't do that.'

He stares at me. Neither of us moves a muscle. The front door slams, then the pounding upstairs, two at a time. Casey or Conor. Lindsey takes the stairs kind of slow and dreamily, like she's in a shampoo ad.

Porter moves to the bathroom door.

'I'm taking a shower,' he says. There's a kind of disgust in his voice.

'Wait,' I say. I follow him into the bathroom. He has started to undress, but it's a small room and I can see he doesn't want to be naked in front of me at this moment.

'Are you accusing me?' he says.

I shake my head, but I don't want him to get in the shower yet. If he gets in the shower, I've lost something I don't know how to get back.

'No,' I say.

'Good. 'Cause there's nothing, I did nothing with any of those women. I didn't even look at them.' His voice is bitter now, he's reaching down inside, pulling up stuff he doesn't really want to talk about. But I started this thing, and now he has to finish. 'There isn't a woman in the world,' he says, 'there's nothing I'd go against my promises with you for. I made those promises seventeen years ago and there's not a single day I haven't stood by them.'

He looks like he might be finished but I know he's not.

'So what it is,' he goes on, slower now, 'is like this. A guy has to have some space, you know? You have to have a shut door you can sit in front of with your head in your hands sometimes, get a bit of peace. Like when you're a kid, you go to the woods, down to the creek, you climb a tree. Nobody can find you there. I just needed a shut door I could be behind sometimes. That's all.'

It's really quiet in the bathroom. I can hear his breathing.

'You come in that door,' he says, 'you follow me into that place, it's never going to be the same again. I can't go back there. You understand?'

37

I nod. I don't trust my voice. I'm wondering if Jim and Judy had a talk like this one day in their bathroom. I wonder exactly how things began to unravel for them. Was it really the forty-thousand-dollars conversation? I think back to that night, and suddenly I hear it real clear again, into the stillness of our garden, the exact way he said it: *I'd buy you.* That was the moment.

I think of my life with Porter and I have this image suddenly that it's like a giant piece of knitting, a big cosy sweater maybe, or an afghan, and I think how I just picked a hole in it and now I have the wool tied round my finger and as I leave this bathroom and go back to the kitchen, as I move around the house and on about our lives, I'll keep unravelling it, bit by bit, on and on till there's maybe nothing left except a big pile of useless crinkly wool.

He's undressing now. He has his back to me, and he leaves his clothes in a neat sort of pile like he always does. Not folded exactly, but neat. He gets in the shower and slides the door shut without looking at me. He turns the water on full.

I stand in the doorway to our bathroom. At least two kids are home now, I can hear music upstairs and one of the boys yelling. Porter's mother never left him alone. Always in his face, in his business. And now here I am, the wife he always trusted to be different. I wonder about that shut door. Once you open doors like that, you can't ever get them closed again. Like I told Lindsey just the other day: once that cherry's popped, honey, there's no opportunity to say, Gee, I think I made a mistake.

I watch my husband in the shower. The glass is that frosted type. I just see a blurred outline. He's washing around his back, up under his arms, like you do in the shower when you think you're alone.

'Sorry,' I say, into the rush of sound.

Samantha. That was her name, the one with the red hair. She was the prettiest of them all.

My Friend Frankie
Maeve Binchy

We were such friends from the very start. From the day that Frankie moved in next door to Number 37, when we were both eleven.

I was an only child, dying for someone to play with.

My mother didn't like Frankie at first because of her accent. But then my mother didn't like *anyone's* accent. People from the North of Ireland had a barking sound, people from Cork had a curious singsong way of talking – more Chinese than Irish – people from Kerry were unintelligible. Frankie had a broad Dublin accent, therefore she was common.

Frankie was great fun from the beginning. She had twin brothers of seven who, according to her, were *desperate*. Her father, Ringo, was a lorry driver and her mother, Lola, worked from four until ten in the morning cleaning offices.

My mother said that Frankie's mother was very flash. Flash was bad. It had to do with not being humble. And who ever heard of adults being called Ringo and Lola? They weren't proper names.

My father said that all credit was due to the family for dragging themselves up in the world. My mother would purse her lips over this.

'You don't want to be telling them all our business,' my mother warned me.

What business? I asked myself. What did we do that couldn't be told?

'Does this mean I can't be her friend?' I asked. I had learned somehow that, if you ask the question that nobody else will ask, you often get away with things.

I realised that they couldn't tell me not to be Frankie's friend. And they didn't.

Ours was a wonderful friendship. I had always been a bit shy, afraid the other girls might not like me, or my parents might not like them. But now it was different.

At school, Frankie and I decided that we were brighter than most of the others, and should do all right if we did a *bit* of work.

With this in mind, we didn't waste too much time acting the eejit and obsessing about rock stars.

We would do our homework together, either in Number 37 or at my house. More often it was mine, since the twins were a terrible nuisance and Frankie's mother would want us to entertain them. She was always exhausted, what with dragging vacuum cleaners and buckets around offices in the middle of the night.

In my house we had a warm room and dictionaries and an atlas. My mother would make us a sandwich and ask Frankie stupid questions, like did her mother play bridge, and what hotels did her father stay in when he went on his travels?

And we did great in our exams. Or, rather, did well, as my mother insisted on saying, correcting what she thought was sloppy grammar I had picked up from Frankie. We both got places in college; I studied languages, Frankie did law.

'Very foolish of her,' my mother sniffed. 'I mean, who does she know? How can she expect to get any work unless she *knows* people?'

I said nothing.

Frankie and I had worked out this policy of not answering back.

My mother was a ludicrous snob, discontented with everything and everyone.

Frankie's mother was a worn-out dishrag, too tired even to go to the pub with her husband at the weekend.

We would not be like our mothers.

And we wouldn't waste time or energy arguing with them.

Our fathers, on the other hand, were no problem.

Frankie's father, Ringo, was on the road more and more, and her mother found the office cleaning harder – more stairs than ever, and what with her veins and everything ...

The awful twins were fourteen now, and compared to most fourteen-year-old hooligans I suppose they weren't too bad.

My own parents hadn't changed much over the years. My father went off peaceably at one minute to eight in the morning and caught the bus to work in the big insurance company. My mother would dab at his shoulders with the horrible clothes-brush shaped like a fox's head. Then she would sigh and have another cup of tea and sigh again that life had dealt her such a disappointing hand.

But we took little notice of them; by now we were off at university, where we studied quite hard and did the rounds of parties. And though I knew that the other students thought I was a bit standoffish and distant, it would all change when Frankie would collect me at the library. We would swing off together with a great crowd of people. We got drunk now and then and even fell in love from time to time. Casually at first and then, in the last year, more seriously.

Frankie fell in love with a drug dealer.

And I fell in love with a miser.

I tried to talk Frankie out of the drug dealer at every available opportunity. I told her about the life that lay ahead. She was going to be a lawyer, for God's sake. She simply could not get involved in his doings.

She kept promising to give him up and not following through.

But one day, as we sat by the canal watching the swans, Frankie said that she would never in her life be able to relax like this with him. And so she finally found the courage and ended it. We went to Venice to celebrate, and that's where she talked me out of the miser.

She said he thought of every single thing in terms of how much it cost and whether he could get it cheaper elsewhere. He even took sugar packets and individual portions of marmalade from cafés.

His only plans for a career in teaching revolved around how much he would earn. She said that he would never buy me flowers as long as I lived. Cut flowers were a waste of money.

And I did give him up. I finally made the decision on the boat trip back from Murano, clutching a lovely red glass vase, which I knew would never hold a single bloom that this man would buy.

Frankie got a job in a big firm of solicitors and I got a job in a school, teaching French and Spanish. We discussed sharing an apartment together, even went so far as to look at places, but in the end we were both happy enough to go on living at home. It wasn't as if they put any restrictions on us.

My mother went on sighing that there were no people of quality around any more; my father continued to take no notice of her whatsoever, just eating what was put in front of him, polishing his shoes as if his life depended on it, watching quiz programmes and telling us nothing about what he did all day at work.

I had given up hoping that either of them would ever be open or confiding, but I had my friend Frankie for all that.

Frankie's parents were also much the same as ever. Nowadays Ringo went to the pub every night, and her mother was the head of the cleaning team and hated the responsibility of it. Frankie gave her mother money to buy some decent clothes, but Lola saved it in the post office in case of an emergency.

With Frankie living next door to me, even if I had wanted to become introverted and melancholy like my parents, I couldn't. Plus Frankie was great at organising holidays. We travelled to Morocco, Crete, then to Budapest. When we were twenty-five we rented a little place in the south of France to celebrate being a quarter of a century old.

And that's where we met Rita.

Rita was great fun altogether. She ran a little crêperie on the beach. Her last job had been as a taxi driver back in Ireland, the one before that in a garden centre. She had made it a rule never to stay anywhere for more than six months because 'your brain started to rot'. Frankie and I felt very dull in comparison.

We talked about her a lot. Where had she got all this independence and courage?

Possibly she didn't have much of a family life. She never spoke to us about her parents. Frankie and I decided that she must have been thrown on her own resources at an early age. Otherwise she would never have struck out like that.

Rita was thinking of going to work in a casino in Atlantic City and asked if we would come with her. For a moment I thought that Frankie was going to say yes. I tried to look enthusiastic, but Frankie must have read my feelings because she patted me on the knee and told me to relax.

That night, as Frankie and I sat outside our little house, sipping wine, we agreed that life was passing us by. By the time we were retiring from our respective professions – another thirty-five years – Rita would have had another seventy careers!

Rita became part of our lives. After that initial meeting, we would holiday wherever she was working. One year, when she was teaching English in Sweden, we took a train journey through forests of Christmas trees and swam in an ice-cold lake. Another year, we visited her in the south of Spain where she worked as a bingo caller, and another on a trip to Turkey where she was giving Belly Dancing for Beginners lessons.

Rita phoned or wrote, and formed an easy part of our friendship, never over-intruding.

*

Our lives ticked along. We often talked about Rita and wondered how someone could be so free. If we ever asked about her home and her background she'd just shrug and say that it was no worse or better than anyone else's.

We didn't tell Rita about our own problems at home.

Frankie's father was by now a complete alcoholic, and had been banned from driving. He lived mainly in the garage they had converted for him, complete with a little shower room and no stairs to stumble on. Lola still cooked his meals and washed his clothes. And, although she was well into her sixties, she still went out to clean offices.

The boys had long left home; one was a sports journalist, the other a minor league footballer. Frankie had given up trying to get her mother to throw Ringo out. Marriage was 'For Better or Worse'. Oddly, the fact that her father now lived in the garage just made things easier because you didn't have to deal with him any more. And the house was much smarter now.

Frankie had spent money having Number 37 redecorated. The upstairs was converted into an apartment for herself; her mother lived in the rooms downstairs.

They all rubbed along reasonably well together. Frankie would raise her eyes to heaven about her parents. But she never considered leaving them, although she could easily have afforded her own place. Maybe she felt they would fall to pieces without her, maybe she wanted to go on living next door to me? Whatever it was, she was able to live with life in Number 37.

And, as long as I had Frankie, I was able to live with the increasingly glacial atmosphere in my home.

My parents seemed to have ceased talking to each other entirely. The sighs and silences were deafening. I mainly stayed out of their way, and watched television in my room or in Frankie's most evenings. Sometimes we went out.

But we weren't having much luck in love.

After the drug dealer, Frankie went out with, in turn, a married man, a hypochondriac and a man who claimed that he, like most people, was bi-sexual and he hoped Frankie would be the same. And I got involved with three men in a row, each relationship progressively more unwise. There was the man who was in love with his mother, the compulsive gambler, and the seriously possessive guy who couldn't stand me as much as speaking to another man.

Rita, meanwhile, continued on her travels, keeping us up to

date on what seemed to us a most exotic life. Then we heard that she was coming to Dublin for a visit and we got very excited.

We agreed she would stay with Frankie, as Frankie had a real flat. We hoped she wouldn't think our lives dull and pathetic: still living at home at our age, with nothing much to show for our thirty-something years on earth.

Rita was just the same as always: full of life and energy.

'Aren't you the wise man to live out here? You can invite in whoever suits you,' she said to Ringo in his garage.

And then she sat down and drank a can of lager with him as if she were in an elegant drawing room.

Frankie was so pleased. I wished I had thought of doing that, it was such a simple thing, but there was something in me that was repelled by him.

Rita asked Lola if there was a chance of any cleaning work, as she needed a bit of spare cash to buy her round of drinks.

I dreaded inviting her to my house, but I felt I had to.

My mother made endless fuss, asking me a dozen times in advance who Rita's people were, and wondering would she like egg or tomato sandwiches. I just kept replying mulishly that I didn't know.

'You don't know very much about her,' my mother said disapprovingly.

Which indeed was true.

I had no idea that Rita would behave like she did.

She discussed the insurance company with my father and he told her abut the various mergers over the years, all of which had conspired to lessen his own position there. These were things he had never relayed to my mother or me. Rita advised him eagerly that, given his love of quiz shows, when he retired he could set up a business running pub quizzes. She even gave him the name of a pub where he could start making enquiries. I hadn't seen him so animated in years.

And as for my mother! Rita listened to the endless stories about the world having sunk to the lowest common denominator, about how there were no longer garden parties or tennis parties or people calling for cocktails. And Rita nodded madly in agreement, saying that it *was* terrible and my mother should throw her own cocktail party, for which Rita herself would make and serve the drinks and canapés. And the hint of a smile came to my mother's sad, discontented face.

True to character, Rita soon embarked on her travels again, and Frankie and I felt as if something big had been taken out of our lives.

That night I said to Frankie, 'For all Rita's great sense of adventure, I think she's probably quite lonely.'

'We're *all* quite lonely,' Frankie said.

This seemed odd in a way. Frankie, the tough lawyer, great fun, always laughing at life, Frankie the firm and loyal friend – when had she time to feel lonely?

Rita's visit had repercussions.

My father did indeed start running table quizzes in a pub.

My mother gave a cocktail party and served Cosmopolitans.

Ringo's drinking, while still a problem, had calmed down considerably. He had even taken to inviting Lola in for a sociable drink some evenings, and actually put glasses on the table for them to drink from.

Lola took on more people and worked less hours.

Only Frankie and I didn't change.

And then one day Rita rang from Scotland and said that she was going to spend the summer building a youth club and a playground on some wasteland in Glasgow. Would we join her?

I was coming to the end of a long, tiring term and needed some sun, sea and wine, so I said I might pass on that one.

'I thought you might,' Rita said cheerfully. 'Frankie was telling me earlier that it wouldn't be your sort of thing.'

'It's not that it's not my sort of thing!' I was a bit indignant at being filed away as someone who wouldn't join in. And why had Frankie answered for me, anyway?

'No, I mean she was saying that, what with your upbringing and everything—'

'Upbringing?' I seemed to be repeating everything as if I weren't all there. What would Rita know about my upbringing?

'You know. With your mother being a bit toffee-nosed and your father a bit far away.' She spoke easily, as if it were no big deal.

I couldn't believe it. 'Frankie told you all this about me?'

Frankie and I *never* told anyone about our home life; it had been that way since day one. Complete solidarity, total secrecy. My life centred around my friendship with Frankie. We knew things about each other that no one knew.

'Sure,' Rita said. 'We were talking about it as a possible scheme, and she said that you'd prefer something a bit more classy. She'd be easy with it herself; I mean, she was only dragged up, like I was. You were brought up. There's a difference, you know!'

I felt like cold water was cascading down inside me, starting at my throat, on through my chest and into my stomach.

Frankie talking about me like this behind my back! It was unthinkable.

I mumbled something to Rita about it being a terrific idea, about calling her later. Then I hung up and went straight to Number 37.

Frankie was delighted to see me. She didn't realise that my whole world had tilted.

'Rita rang,' I said, my voice like doom.

'Did she? I was talking to her earlier; she has this marvellous cracked scheme—'

'You told her about me!' I interrupted.

Frankie seemed unaware of what I was talking about.

'I what?'

'You told her all my business – my secrets, my personal life …'

'But you don't *have* any secrets, any personal life.' She laughed at me easily.

47

'You told Rita about my family, things that only you knew. How on earth could you do that?' There were tears in my eyes and my voice was shaking.

'Jesus, Mary and Holy Saint Joseph,' Frankie said, mystified. 'Are you drunk or something? *What* did I tell Rita? What in God's name are you talking about?'

'You told her all about my mother having notions and my father being silent. You *told* her the kind of house I grew up in.'

Frankie still didn't get it.

'But didn't she see it for herself when she was here?'

'We *never* tell anyone. I didn't tell her about your father being a drunk.'

'Well, you didn't need to couldn't she see *that* the moment she met him?' Frankie was looking at me as if I were having a nervous breakdown.

'And what made you suddenly speak about me and my upbringing to Rita tonight?' I said.

'I've always spoken to Rita about stuff. She's our mate. She was interested. I assumed you told her about my set-up here in this house. You know the way we talk about her; we've often talked to each other about her. It doesn't mean that we like her less. It's what people do.'

'But that's different, Frankie. Rita's just Rita. You and I are special friends,' I heard myself say.

And that was the moment. The moment that I knew we were just *ordinary* friends, and that friendship means different things to different people.

The moment I knew that from now on everything would be different. There was no going back to the way things were, or, more correctly, to the way that I *thought* things were.

Frankie and Rita discussed me casually. I was too loyal to have these kinds of chats. Or, as they might call it, too buttoned up. Too reserved – like her cold, icy parents.

No matter what was said now, nothing would ever be the same.

Frankie told me that what she had actually said was that I was working too hard and that teachers were always nervous wrecks at the end of the school year. And that was the reason why I wouldn't be up for the Glasgow trip.

I heard my own voice, as if from miles away. 'Sure, that must be it.'

And I saw relief come over Frankie's face that things were back to normal. And we talked about the holidays. Maybe we could compromise, spend half the time building the youth club, then go on a cheap cruise across the Mediterranean and back.

And when we got out the atlas and planned it – as we had so often done before – Frankie remained eager as always and I looked out the window at the house and garden where I, like my parents, would grow old and silent, misunderstanding the nature of everything.

Ordinary Love
Clare Boylan

On her way out to church Jane found an old man standing on her doorstep. He said his lover had left him. He stood and cried in the easy, can't-help-it way, like a child pees when he has left it too late to ask for the toilet.

She was trying to think of something to say when he looked directly at her and she realised it was Frank. It was her husband.

'What do you want, Frank?' She held the door as a barrier, to keep him on the outside.

'I want to come home.' His voice was muddy gravel as it waded through tears.

Jane looked away over his shoulder at the perfect, cold, still sky, which was aloof from the shabby business of the earth. She was thinking, *don't make a fuss, he'll be gone in a minute.* 'Frank, you have your own home. Your life is none of my business.'

'I tried to kill myself,' he said. 'My bottle failed.' He hung his head but he loitered.

She forced herself to focus on him, to think of him as something other than a disturbance. The curious thing was that although he looked old and cheap he had not changed in the way the children had. He was still entirely himself. 'Can I come in?' he said. 'I'm cold.'

The house that they had made together forty years before still held, as houses do, the imprint of its origins. People bought those sixties houses meaning to move on. Jane had at first no money and later no reason to change the laminate units in the kitchen, so they remained, along with an old gas cooker. She led the way to a boxy living room with a low ceiling and stunted hearth. She had the unfocused feeling of a person in a nightmare who is being pursued by something at once threatening and familiar. The old man's hovering scrutiny was a cross between a child home from boarding school and an auctioneer's assessor. His eye hung desolately on a rug with an abstract pattern – now fashionable again – which held tenure at the hearth and showed the battle damage of sparks and pets and babies long gone. He went to the window, which showed a small prison of a garden with high concrete walls. An allotment of sky still rose above it, full of nursery promise. He had once told the children that they had bought this piece of sky along with the house. It was their place in heaven. He was smiling again as he turned back into the room. 'So how are you?' he said.

'I'm fine.' Jane was made wary by his smile. 'I was on my way out. I'll make you a cup of tea.'

'Don't you mind living alone?' he said.

'How do you know I'm on my own?'

'It's the smell.' He sniffed. 'The house has that old-house smell the occupants never notice. It says that somewhere, in some peaceful corner, the rot has set in. It's nice.'

'Frank, don't get comfortable.' She rattled the fire with a poker. 'Don't think it's like old times.'

When she went to the kitchen she was surprised to find that her hands were shaking. Whatever you do for the least of my creatures, you do for me, God had said. She put fruit cake on the tray along with the tea.

'I'm sorry about your lover,' she said.

'People can be cruel.'

'You left me,' she said. 'That was cruel.' And then, since it was no longer relevant and he looked so miserable, she tried to soften it. 'You'll find someone else.'

He shook his head. 'You know why?'

She made a gesture to indicate that she did not know nor wish to.

'Because I lost interest in sex.'

'Well, I'm sorry, Frank' – Jane poured the tea and measured in milk – 'but it has nothing to do with me.'

'No, that's the point.' He looked eager. It still lit up his eyes, as in the old days. 'It does concern you. It concerns us, honey.'

'Don't call me that,' Jane said.

'I often thought about you' – when she failed to offer him his cup of tea he reached for it himself – 'I wanted to get in touch but I didn't think you'd want to know. How are the kiddies?'

'They're in their thirties, Frank. They have mortgages and pension plans and children of their own.'

'That little picture of the dancer's gone,' he noticed. 'Were you short of money?'

She shook her head. No need to explain that when the children set up their own homes they had hungrily eyed anything that was of use or value, and she had gladly given things away.

'I never stopped loving you.' He ate his cake and eyed her with a hard and hopeful eye. 'Did you think about me?'

She could not sit with him, talking rubbish like this. 'The fire's going out,' she said. 'I'll fetch some wood.'

'I'll go.' He half rose and looked expectant.

'No, I will.' She did not want him to make free with her territory and she needed to get to the air. She went to the yard. Even out there she felt trapped. She could sense him creeping in on her, infinitely patient, an inch at a time. How was she going to get him to go?

As she turned back into the house she looked up and saw him at her table, munching her cake. He seemed more relaxed now and more familiar. Standing there with a pile of logs in her arms, she had a sensation like the ground opening up beneath her feet. She suddenly remembered a time when they were young and the children were young – hundreds of years ago, it must have been – when she would come in from hanging out the washing, and see him sitting inside, framed by the window. And that frame had seemed the frame of love. She could picture his face as it was then, pale and thin and solemn. *My friend*, she would think. *My love*. He wasn't like other husbands. He loved the babies in the same way she did. They hadn't much money but he made their awful little house a home: flowers from the garden placed in the light of a lamp, a glass of wine poured when she was tired. Music piped out its quiet invitation from the room where he was. And bed. Bed had been such a friendly place – not earth-shattering sex, which she hadn't cared about anyway, but fitting together like pieces of a puzzle and talking and reading out bits of the books they liked and stroking each other when they felt sad. Some awful old ghost of self-pity began to rattle at her cage. She watched the elderly man stand up and begin to wander around. He was looking for something. He located what he was looking for and she saw that it was the whiskey. She watched him slyly helping himself to a drink. She came in and threw the logs down in the hearth, making as much noise as possible.

'Did you always know?' she shouted. 'Did you know even when you met me?'

'Know what?' He looked meek and furtive and hugged his drink.

'That you were queer.'

'Good God,' he muttered. 'Good God.' His voice shook. 'Did we never talk?'

'We talked about nothing. How could we? How could I?'

She found herself unable to speak again. She was appalled at herself and furious. It was ridiculous. She had no feeling for this ridiculous old man. Yet he owned and could animate her past.

It had been a sunny day in spring and she had taken a folding table out to the garden for lunch. The apple tree was in bloom and the garden was full of its green smell. Jane was thinking, as she did not normally do, about sex. Maybe she just wanted another baby. Frank sat down opposite her with his normal vague, caring face. 'I have to talk to you, Janey,' he'd said. 'Something awful's happened.'

She remembered thinking that he'd lost his job and that it was all right, because they could probably even be happy poor. It was odd about him losing his job, though, because he wrote copy for an advertising agency and he was good at it. He looked forlorn and she thought what a female adjective 'forlorn' was. 'What's up, honey?' she said and she touched his face.

It was what happened next that stayed with her most. He flinched. He flinched when she touched him. His forlorn face hardened into misery. 'I've fallen in love,' he said.

'What? With another woman?' She laughed, although she knew he wasn't joking. Frank was a famously faithful husband.

'No…' The single syllable meandered with a curious hide-and-seek quality. 'With another man.'

Her hand had played idly with an apple on a plate and she could still see the too-hearty veins of red on its surface, like the pattern of bloody seepage on cold Carrera marble. She thought that the expression on her face was probably one of boredom, but in fact it was one of total absorption, for she needed to know that every bit of her love and trust and softness was being taken away from her – not just her present and her future, but the whole of her marriage, for if he now loved another man's body, then he must always have hated hers.

'You ruined my life,' she said now.

'Jesus Christ, Janey,' Frank said. 'Nobody's life is perfect. Gay people come out all the time.'

'They do now,' she shouted. 'They didn't then. They didn't in Dublin.'

'I remember. Dublin in the sixties was full of those poor fucks. Desperate to find a wife, to have two-point-five children so no one would guess. Making jokes about queers to make themselves more normal. You could spot them a mile off. Grey-faced and furtive, wrapped up in rosaries, eyes on a permanent circuit for some place to sink themselves so that no one would see. And the wives – they always knew.'

'What was I supposed to do?' Jane whispered.

'Put on some make-up, get out and find someone else. Get on with your life.'

'I couldn't. My confidence was gone.' This came out as a suffocated murmur.

'Oh, Janey,' he sighed.

'Anyway, there was no point. You were the one I loved.' It was odd to be saying this to an aging man who had not shaved in days, but the whole point of her life and what had become of it belonged to him.

'Janey. Janey.'

She got up and began to clear away dishes. 'Why did you come back?'

'Now sit down, honey,' he soothed. 'Now don't be mad at me. I have something to say to you.'

She stayed standing, continued to stack the dishes very carefully so that their porcelain clink tiptoed through the silence.

'We're old now. We don't really have a gender any more. The thing that blew us apart isn't in the picture.'

'What thing?' She sounded cold and confused.

'Sex,' he said. 'I told you, I lost interest in sex. We're past it.' He chuckled. 'We're like two old suitcases that have travelled the world, stuck all over with labels that don't mean anything any more – queer, straight, male, female. We're into clear water now, Janey. We're just us.'

No, you're you, she thought. She could feel panic rising again. *I'm not anything I once was.* 'So what, Frank?' she said.

'Look how easily we talk,' he said. 'We're interested in each other in the way that really counts. The thing I thought was, now that sex is out of the way, we could be together again.'

'In a pig's eye, Frank.' Jane now reached for the whiskey bottle and gave herself a drink.

Her husband took it as an invitation to refresh his own glass. 'You know what, Janey? We furnish this lousy room.'

She said, 'I don't want my lousy room furnished. I gave things away on purpose. I chose to live in an interior world.'

'What the hell rubbish are you talking now?'

'Faith,' she said. 'My faith is what's kept me going all down the years.'

'So you've got religion now?'

'Don't mock me.'

'I'm not. It's just like you, Janey. You thought you had a little plateful of stars and when they stopped twinkling you said, well, fine, I'll have the moon instead. An ordinary man turns out not to be perfect – you say, right, I'll have God, He's perfect.'

Jane sat down slowly. And spoke slowly. 'If you believe that He made us – and I do – then the point of every single thing that happens in our lives is to lead us to Him. Saint Augustine said: "God fashioned us after His image and we cannot rest until we rest in Him."' She fell silent and looked at her lap.

'If you believe that, Janey' – Frank's voice was low. He was calculating his way into this serious chess game – 'then you have to accept that God made me the way I am. Whatever the hell His purpose was.'

Janey looked up again. She smiled – a narrow, bleak smile, he thought. 'I do accept that, Frank. It's just that you took me aback. The past is still a perilous place. I like my life. It's not a dry or empty existence. I'm sorry I got angry with you. I know we both had our separate paths. You found your kind of love and I found mine.' She smiled at him. A part of her meant it.

'Now listen, honey,' he said. 'Now don't get mad.' He saw her warning eye again. 'You're not some saint on a mountain. Don't tell me you're at peace with yourself. You've more prickles than a holly tree. You did your damnedest to work things out with yourself but instead you got stuck in an argument that's lasted thirty years. You're still locked in there with yourself, reasoning away.'

'Get the hell out of here!' She stood up. Only years of restraint and the fact that she was too old for that sort of thing stopped her throwing her drink at him.

Frank put up his hands in mock terror. 'Look at us!' he laughed. 'We're both has-beens. You think you're better than me because I'm a shambles. I'd throw myself on anyone's mercy. But you – you've got dignity. You've made a life of your own. You keep to yourself. No bother to anyone! Who are you kidding, Janey? You've just made a virtue of necessity. You've turned yourself into a recluse because you're not going to beg for ordinary human love. Well, I think I'm better than you. I'll beg. I don't care. I still think love is worth begging for.'

She felt anger rising inside her like a tornado. In a moment it would blow her head off. 'Well, go and beg elsewhere,' she said. 'I'm not begging for love because I don't want sub-standard love.'

'So what did you think you had before I came out, living with a queer? Was that what you wanted? For me to stay and then sneak off to toilets to make my peace with myself? It was a lousy deal but there was no way I could make it better. Sub-standard! You said it.'

'I should think a lot of what you had in the years since you walked out was sub-standard. Perhaps it was better than what I had. I had to learn to do without love a long time ago.'

'You're wrong, Janey,' he said. 'I meant it when I said I never stopped loving you. We could have been friends. We could have shared the kids. You wouldn't even talk to me. You turned the kids against me.'

'You're blaming me!' She felt breathless now. 'You ruined my life and now you come back to condemn me.'

Frank gazed at her with his sad, baggy eyes. 'You know, I haven't had a really good row in years. Guys can't talk to guys. It's still cock to cock with men, no matter what the relationship. Women go straight for the truth. Men are either vicious or bitchy.

I was only ever queer for sex. I was straight as far as conversation went. You need a woman for a real conversation.'

Jane blinked, unable to respond.

'You know,' Frank smiled, 'I used to go into bars just to sit beside a couple of girls, just to hear their conversation. When women talk to other women it's like getting into a warm bath.'

She sat down. Her knees felt weak. 'I never really cared about sex.'

'I've upset you.' He put an arm on her shoulder. She was astonished again, to feel some echo of familiarity. 'This is the row we should have had thirty years ago. Things would have worked out better if we had. I'm not blaming you, Janey. I made a mess of everything.'

'You made me feel ashamed,' she said. 'You made me feel that there was something wrong with me – the kind of woman a man like you would hide out in until he got what he wanted.'

He shook his head. 'I wanted to be like my mother and father – have a nice house and raise kids, be with a nice girl for the rest of my life. You were the one, Janey. I was so proud when you said you'd marry me. Think of it, Janey. In those days to be gay was to be a pervert. Normal meant heterosexual. Anything else was abnormal. If I had any feelings for guys I just slapped them down. Then when I met Keith the whole thing blew apart. I was crazy for him. Just plain crazy.'

'And now he's left you.'

He filled up his whiskey glass to the brim and drank it down. 'Keith left me twenty years ago. He was never faithful anyway. That's a shock, after living with a woman like you. Gays are even more promiscuous than straight guys.'

Suddenly he stood up. He administered a little confidential kiss to his wife's cheekbone and put on his battered overcoat. 'You know what you are, Janey? You're a moral hypochondriac. I think you really do like your life but you like your little aches and pains as well. Anyway, you're right. It's not fair of me to come back and start shaking things up. I'm sorry I said things about your faith.'

'Frank…' She wanted to say that it was a good thing to have

things shaken up, that the shaking up was marriage. Instead she said, 'Are you all right for money?'

He laughed. 'Fine, honey. I'm better for seeing you, Janey. You make me see sense.'

He moved quickly now that his mind was made up. When he was at the door she said, 'I've got a chicken for dinner. If you'd like to come and share it…'

He looked different now. He no longer looked like a half-derelict old man. When his eyes shone he looked young. The banishment of dejection peeled away the layers of seediness. 'I'd love that, Janey. I'll bring a bottle of wine.'

It was only after he was gone that she wondered why he had not simply stayed and talked to her until it was time for dinner. Had he just come home to lick his wounds, to test his power over her, to put a marker on his old territory? Now that he was happy again, he might go to a bar, find some gay man to chat to and then go off with him.

She sat by the cooling fire and waited for anger to set in. She found its path barred by a line of little memories that crept across her vision – children, pets, conversations, visits to the sea. Frank had given her back her marriage. She had the odd feeling, as she surveyed the room with its rakish remnants of whiskey and tea and cake, that it had been visited by an angel. She cleared it back to its normal pleasant bareness, banked up the fire and went out to church.

Geronimo

Helena Close

The Atlantic suits my boy. It churns and splutters and crashes like any teenager. Gregarious. Precocious. Alive. I stand on a shelf of flat rock watching him dive into the sea.

My son, flesh of my flesh, pauses to make that elusive perfect dive, form silhouetted against a dusky sky. He turns and waves at me and screams, 'Geronimo!' His body makes a huge splash against grey sea water.

I tense every muscle in my body and force myself to smile. He's dead, I know he is. He splits his head on the rocky sea floor and drowns quietly amidst the noisy playful screams of his peers. I stand here and watch and do nothing. I watch other children play and run and scream while my own child is dying. But then he appears, and climbs up the ladder out of the churning water and gives me the thumbs up. 'Geronimo!' As if that incantation will protect him.

And then I think of him, Danny, aged four, sitting on a supermarket ride – a spaceship. He's wearing a Batman suit with a cowboy hat and it's Halloween. I can see fat orange pumpkins in the fruit-and-vegetable section of the supermarket.

'Mom, it won't go. Make it go, Mom, please, please.'

His voice is tiny, a baby's voice. His eyes are huge, brown, sad. His eyes are always sad, even when he is laughing. I don't like brown eyes and wish his were blue, like mine or his small brother's.

'It's broken, honey, I can't make it go. I know what we'll do; we'll go on Postman Pat. How's that?' I say.

He looks straight at me. 'This one.'

'It's broken, honey, it won't work. We've already put coins in and it just won't work. Come on, we'll try Postman Pat.' I take him by the arm. He pushes my hand away.

'*This* one.'

'Now, Danny, keep it up and we'll go straight home.'

'I WANT THE SPACESHIP!'

'Oh, Danny, stop.'

He climbs down from the spaceship, the cowboy hat tilted at an angle on his small head. He looks at me once, and then walks ahead towards the exit doors.

I shudder now as dusk gathers. My son dives and splashes and screams, accompanied by a crowd of teenage friends. Boys and girls with faces like half-finished paintings, bare sketches of the people they become years from now. I walk closer to the diving rock to watch them play. Their screams and antics make the cold grey Atlantic seem like a good, kind place.

My son is wearing a snorkelling mask and treads water as he pushes the mask from his face.

'Can we get a take-away?'

His voice dips up and down in that classic teenage sing-song way. He smiles at me and I feel a sudden physical pain right in the centre of my heart. The pain is like a contraction and I breathe my way through it as I sit down on the hard surface of the rock. My son looks at me curiously, holding the mask in one hand and treading water with the other. His smile is gone and my pain eases instantly, as if I have just taken a magic pill to stop it.

'Take-away it is,' I say in a voice that sounds tinny, a voice that echoes around the cove. I imagine everybody is staring at me. My son nods and swims away, mask held high in one hand. I close my eyes and squeeze back tears.

Danny's eyes stare at me. He's six, his face is thinner than at the

Halloween of Batman and the cowboy hat. His eyes are browner, though. He stands in the hallway in his underpants, skinny little legs on soft green carpet. The door of his room is open. The walls are painted a rich yellow, the colour of the sun, and they glow light into the windowless hall.

'I won't go, I hate him,' he says, and crosses his arms on his bare, narrow chest.

'But it's his birthday and you like Tommy, you always play with him at school,' I say. Danny's younger brother, Peter, is crying in another bedroom and Danny is making me really mad. 'Get dressed. You're going and that's final. You told him already that you'd go, so now you must.'

Danny stares with those big eyes. I think he's going to cry. I look down and he is wetting himself. A stain has appeared on his underpants and urine is dribbling down his legs toward the carpet. It forms a little puddle on the floor before it soaks into the carpet, turning it black.

'Danny, it's all right, you don't have to go. I'll ring Tommy's mom. How's that?' I say.

But I'm really mad at him, too. I know he has beaten me. He has won and his brown eyes tell me that he knows. He walks into his sunny bedroom and I stare at the stain on the carpet. Sometimes I don't like Danny, not one bit.

'Mom, Mom, did you hear me? Is there anything to drink?'

I shake myself and blink. My son stands in front of me, dripping pools of water on warm stone. He smells briny, like some kind of sea animal that has come to bask on the rocks. He grins and bends down to root in the gear bags.

'I'll get it,' I say, but he has found the drink and is gone before I even reach down.

'Watch my somersault,' he shouts but doesn't turn around, just waves the juice bottle in the air. I laugh and watch him drink from the bottle and lean it against a rock. He stands then, waiting his turn to dive, a perfect form in dimming light. Love courses through me and I fight the urge to cry out, I love you, I love you, please watch out.

He does his somersault – an awkward graceless dive – a blur of arms and legs. I cheer him on and his friends laugh and follow him into the sea. Another parent smiles at me and I nod at her and move away a little, avoiding conversation.

It happens on a Monday. An ordinary Monday that begins with the radio and cereal and a light mist of rain. Danny is fourteen. There is a fresh crop of spots on his forehead and he sees me noticing them as he eats toast at the kitchen table. The song on the radio is a low familiar hum, *I am a lineman for the county.*

'What?' he says, his face screwed up in a scowl.

'Nothing,' I say.

'So why are you looking at me?'

I don't answer. I know the name of the song on the radio but it will not come to me.

He munches toast and I call his brother. Their father has left for work already.

'Hi, Mom, did you see my gear bag?' asks Peter, his blue eyes crinkling at the edges. He smiles at me. I smile back. 'Wichita Lineman', that's the name of the song.

'Ask your brother,' I say and we both roll our eyes at each other, behind Danny's back.

'Did you see my gear bag? I left it in the hall yesterday.' Peter butters toast while he speaks.

Danny grunts in reply.

'I take it that was no,' I say, and I and my second son laugh. Danny scowls again and storms out the door.

'Hormones,' I say, but the kitchen is empty. There's just me now, and the Wichita Lineman.

I go to pick them up from school at half past three. The rain is heavy and lashes the car, drowning out the sound of the radio. I park opposite the school gates. The first group of noisy youngsters is just emerging from the school. Their high voices carry over the torrential rain. I relax for a few minutes; my boys are always last to come out. *A family trait*, I think, and smile to myself. I turn up the volume on the radio. It's playing soft ballads. I call this rain music.

Peter comes first, his hair slick from rain. He throws his schoolbag into the boot and sits in the passenger seat next to me.

'Good day?' I ask.

He smiles and nods his head. 'I got ninety-eight per cent for my project.'

'Well done, Peter Moran!' I say and mock-punch him in the arm.

He flicks through the radio channels and finds one he likes. The last stragglers are leaving the school. There's no sign of Danny.

'Did you see Danny on your way out?'

He doesn't answer.

'Peter, are you listening to me? Did you see Danny on your way out of school?'

He turns down the radio. 'God, chill out, Mom. I couldn't hear you over the radio. And no, I didn't see him. We don't come out the same way.'

He shakes his head and turns the volume back up. Minutes pass. I drum the steering-wheel with my fingers. I'm getting mad. I know this because my thoughts become irrational. I believe that Danny is sitting somewhere, watching us wait for him. He's trying to torture me; he knows that today is Monday and I teach violin in the afternoon. He knows I do that every Monday. I grip the steering-wheel. My knuckles are white. I want to swear. I sigh loudly and grind my teeth instead. Peter looks at me and then looks out the window, searching for his brother.

'He's coming. I see him, Mom,' he says.

'About bloody time too,' I say, and start the engine.

There is a sudden screech of brakes and a faint thud that sounds like distant thunder. Peter is screaming. I turn to see where the noise comes from. A yellow car the colour of the sun has swerved to a stop in the middle of the road. Peter is still screaming so I scream too and push open the car door. I kneel on the wet ground. The driver of the car is standing over me, blood dripping down her face. A baby cries somewhere and traffic noises fade away.

Danny's eyes stare up at me. I call him and call him but he won't answer. His shirt collar is open and his tie is pulled loose. His eyes keep staring. They look black now, as if the brown has deepened and deepened until there's no other option but to turn black. A tiny trickle of blood comes from his ear. I touch the blood and look at it on my finger as the rain washes it away. My heart feels like it's going to burst and I scream, but something else screams louder. An ambulance pulls up beside us. The paramedics come and crowd me out. The driver of the car is crying. She holds a toddler in her arms. A little boy with blond curls, damp from rain.

Then I see Danny's pencil case. *DM loves AT* is scrawled on the case. Rubbers and pencils and a brand-new compass spill out on the road. Books are scattered everywhere. *Understanding Science. Business Matters. The Catcher in the Rye.* I start to pick up his things. He'll need them tonight to do his homework and they won't be much good if they are all soaked.

Somebody calls me by my name. I look up and a man stands on the pavement with Peter buried in his chest. I know his face but the name just won't come. All I hear in my head is *I am a lineman for the county.* 'Wichita Lineman', over and over and over. I stand up and watch as they put Danny in the ambulance. I must go with him and I reach for Peter to take him too. When we're finished in the hospital the three of us will go to McDonalds.

'He thought he could do it. He thought he could beat the traffic, and he nearly did. He nearly won, Mom, I saw him, he nearly beat it …'

I smile at Peter. 'Everything will be fine,' I say, and pat him reassuringly on the arm. The man, one of Peter's teachers, asks me if there's anything he can do.

'Not a thing,' I say. 'Everything is fine, all under control.' I smile at him and Peter. Both of them are crying.

Weeks later I wander into Danny's bedroom, the sunny cheerful walls mocking the empty, perfectly dressed bed. I almost run out but I smell him in here and I open his wardrobe. I can't resist the smell of him. I stroke his clothes. A newish tracksuit bought on a lovely warm Saturday. A grey sweatshirt with his smell so strong that it makes me gasp and tears come to my eyes. I run my hands over his things and it's as if I'm rummaging through the rooms of his short life. His football jersey, his karate suit, a too-small pair of Simpsons pyjamas. I bang the wardrobe door with my fist and something slips out. Danny's skateboard. I take it and rub the smooth wood of the deck. I twist the wheels so that they spin round and round. They seem stiff, like they're suffering already from lack of use. Danny's gone. I say this out loud to make it real.

'Danny's gone.'

'Mom?' Peter is standing in front of me, drying himself with a red Liverpool towel.

I smile at him.

'You said something … Were you talking to me?' says Peter. He stops towelling himself and runs a hand through wet hair.

'Hurry up, you'll freeze if you don't get dressed soon,' I say and move away a little to give him some privacy while he puts on his clothes.

'I'm starving. I mean seriously hungry,' Peter says as we drive away from the cove.

'Are you ever any other way, Pete?' I say. I turn onto the main road. The sun is low in the sky and is the colour of a blood orange. Fingers of transparent orange cloud drift lazily over it.

'Isn't it just beautiful,' I say. The orange glow makes the inside of the car shimmer.

'Mom, I've a great idea. Let's try to reach the cliff; you know the one where all the tourists go, at the top of the hill? Let's try to get there before the sun sets. Come on, let's go,' urges Peter, his face animated in the light.

'What do you want me to do, Pete?' I ask, but already I'm

gathering speed and we race up the hill, straight into the bloody glory of the setting sun.

'Faster, Mom, faster,' shouts Peter, 'It's sinking fast, we won't make it. Come on, we have to, like, beat it, we have to win.' He rolls down the window and shakes a fist at the sun. The wind whips his hair around his face. He looks like Danny. Cold air fills the speeding car and my heart pumps with adrenaline.

We turn the last corner and park the car at the side of the road. We must climb the hill to the edge of the cliff before the sun comes back into view. Peter runs ahead, screaming and shouting. A bus-load of Japanese tourists stares at us. Peter reaches the top and I draw level with him. Our breathing fills my ears and I'm aware that other people who have come to watch the sunset are looking at us.

'We did it! We beat the sun,' Peter says, and smiles at me. His eyes are the colour of summer sky.

'Geronimo!' I say, and we both laugh and watch the sun sink slowly into the sea.

The Sound of Twin

Evelyn Conlon

When we were young I know that people tended to like me more than they did my brother. I was quiet, a thing people like in a child, and I learned to play on that. I also picked up manners easily and never tired of practising them.

'Now what would you like, Damien?'

'Bread and jam, please,' I'd say, if that's what was on the table.

'And Darragh, I suppose you'll want something different?'

Sometimes Darragh would force himself to say, 'The same thing, the same thing,' but I could tell it was killing him. He was bursting to be different.

'Are you sure?' they'd ask him, never letting him be, needling him to be difficult.

I felt sorry for my brother, but couldn't help if I was better liked. Loved, in fact. We were twins, are twins. Identical. But only in looks. By the time we were nine years old people tuned to the trappings of civility could tell us apart because of our manners. I cultivated a voice that went smartly with my obsequiousness. In contrast, Darragh's accent roughened and toughened.

In the playground, when boys started to fight with me, by mistake, Darragh always came running and they scattered, either to leave us completely to our own devices or to return suddenly, as if they had forgotten something serious, to get stuck into him, with a particular viciousness, because they hated the mistake of mixing us up. Darragh learned to fight really well. If they left us alone, he would stay with me for a few moments before scarpering off to his important business of football. I had said the word before he did, but that's as far as my expertise shone. If I had rescued him the way he saved me, I would surely have said, Are you all right now? But Darragh never said a word.

I remember myriads of incidents from our childhoods. But they don't seem important to me. I can call them up, as you would a file, to check proofs of things that I have just thought. Yes, that's Darragh, that fits in with such and such a day. I knew that my childhood was merely a waiting room. From the day that I sat in Low Infants, making words with my chalk, and learning to respond properly to praise, I knew that there was something waiting for me.

We grew at the same rate. Even our teeth were the same. Our mother did her best. She dressed us in similar clothing, but not exactly the same. I think she got discounts in draper's shops because of the twin element in the transaction, but she would add some little flourish to the new clothes to differentiate between us – change the buttons, sew an extra pocket on a shirt, that sort of thing. But it made no difference, people still mixed us up; no one noticed her endeavours except herself. And me. Although, as the days after purchase and alteration moved on, I too forgot.

I was better at school than my brother, although it was hard for the teachers to tell. They had to put us at the opposite ends of rooms, or sometimes, that having failed, beside each other, where they would stare at us for a few moments. I knew what they were at, sinking in some formula that they had just worked out to tell us apart. My proficiency at lessons went with my general demeanour. Even if I'd wanted to, I would never have had the nerve not to do my best. Darragh, on the other hand, developed different skills – copying, bluffing and lying. In later years, due to these skills, girls left him after a few months because they discovered that he was not the person they had thought he was. With me they got no surprises. At school I did what I was told to do. Of course, I didn't relish doing what didn't suit me, I'm not a complete dodo, but I did it anyway. Darragh, never. How I envied him. And he thought ahead. He asked me what subjects I had chosen for the Leaving Certificate. 'Right, then, I'll do three the same and three different. You can do my last three exams.'

He'd even worked out the timetable so that the examination times of his last three subjects would not clash with mine. It never occurred to me to argue, it seemed a little enough thing to do for all that saving from all those kicks and thumps on the face. And there was no risk attached – unless they fingerprinted us on the day, no one would know the difference between us. By now our acne, which had appeared in almost symmetrical spottiness, was gone. In the school holidays we had tried beards, but the same streak of squiggly red had appeared in each one. Even Darragh thought this too ridiculous.

Darragh did better in his Leaving Certificate than he should have. We did not take the same subjects when we went to university. More Leaving Certificate strategy. It was because of this that I know the degrees of knowing something. I know that just because a person appears to know something does not mean that they do. The girls still left him after a few months. But he did begin to learn things, not from books, and not deep down, he was too busy for that, but surface things that would get him by.

We got our holiday jobs. I got shifts at a newspaper and Darragh delivered post. I believe that this is when our ways geared themselves up for a real parting. I became involved in the serious matters of news, the ins and outs of how decisions taken thousands of miles away come home to roost, the historical patterns of our lives, the similarities of divergent cultures. Darragh became allied with the bits and pieces of the letters he delivered, the things that people think are news, bills, aunts dying, babies being born, Dear Johns, football results. The link broke. How could I possibly, particularly now that I could see a serious future before me, care less about the foibles of lives that were just going to repeat patterns ad nauseam, day by day, year by year? No, I was not going to be suffocated by trivia.

The Sound of Twin

I did become even more solicitous of Darragh, because if I hadn't, the truth might have rolled out and drowned us. There was one last thing, in our final year, that saved us. We played the part of Gar in *Philadelphia, Here I Come!* Audiences flocked to see it because of our likeness, it gave new life to the play. People understood split personalities by looking at us; the curling of my lip, our lips, made people aware of the viciousness of secrecy. Our production won every medal going. Directors would be reluctant to put it on again for a number of years, until they could get the picture of us out of their heads. The author slipped in one night, and apparently left mesmerised, not having known until then what he had written. At the end of each evening's performance even our separate friends mixed in pubs. It was harder on mine than on his.

We got away from each other not a moment too soon. I learned to breathe properly, not in shallow gasps. It seems to me that the break could have been, and should have been, equally beneficial for Darragh. But he chose to squander it and became even more deeply dug into the frivolities of life. He tried to keep in touch with me, but as I travelled the world and the world of minds I really had no interest. I was still meticulously polite in our telephone conversations. I could always tidy my desk while he spoke. Rabbited on. By then I was a war correspondent, which was, of course, incongruous if one considered the schoolyard. Darragh was a salesman. He got as excited about his gadgets as I got about retreating armies. He showed his excitement; I didn't show mine.

During the six months that I spent in the Near East I did not speak to Darragh at all. I sent one postcard explaining the impossibility of communication, even postal. I didn't want a reply, because our writing looks exactly the same. I wanted no reminders. I didn't want to get envelopes that looked as if they were self-addressed. I relished the lack of phone calls, the absence of intrusion. There was no one to talk of resemblances, so I began to develop an image of my own. I lightened up a little, which is not the easiest thing to do when one's work involves body counts. By the time my Christmas visit began to approach I had built a whole persona for myself.

I arrived in Dublin airport amidst the ferocious buzzing of islanders returning home. I was as pleased as anyone else, although the war job had added an extra wariness to me, other, that is, than the one that I had deliberately refined. I met Darragh for drinks in a pub. I fell in with the general excitement of the season and thought that perhaps a new, appropriate phase of our adulthood had arrived. But he insisted that we meet again the following evening and, despite my reservations, I agreed.

It was a disaster of a night. There were some old mates there, still belonging to him. He jumped from conversation to conversation, pronouncing widely on everything, loudest on that about which he knew nothing. He told endless stories about past things that I had purposefully forgotten. He and the mates seemed to relish my discomfort. It proved that they had dragged me down a peg or two. I began to hate his voice and to worry that I too might sound like him. Surely not possible. *This will never happen again*, I swore to myself in the toilet, the only place I managed to grab back bits of my life. The holiday stretched interminably in front of me. I have no idea how I put up with him, them all. The gadgets, the stories. In order to escape early, I invented a resurgence of the war, without a trace of guilt or worry about being caught. There was no fear that they would check. I saw something in Darragh's eyes but looked away quickly. By the time I got to the airport I wasn't sure if I liked myself. But the check-in restored my confidence.

In the five years that followed, some normal semblance of sibling civility was established. On my travels I even spoke about my twinhood, my view of it, naturally. I didn't mix with the sort of people who might question my analysis. We had more serious matters to discuss. My dreams were usually clear. And, as I've always been away, I had no trouble meeting women. Enough to keep me going. We were in a fleeting world: they took their pleasure, I took mine. Then I met a particular woman, an Irish woman. In truth I would have preferred a woman of different nationality but we cannot control everything, I suppose. She was an aid worker on leave. She threw herself into the holiday as aid workers will. They carouse in direct contrast to the horrors they have seen. I was fascinated by her. The shape of her, the movement of her, the Cork sound of her, the electricity in her hair, the whole look of her. She told me that she was in love with me too. But on her fourth visit she dropped me. Said I was too serious, that she couldn't knock out fun with me any more. I believe that she enjoyed the journey to places better than the arrival. I told her as much and she said, 'See what I mean?'

Whatever that woman did to me, my luck changed with others. Perhaps I got hesitant, perhaps they smelt fear and failure from me, I don't know, but my luck certainly altered. It had to be luck because my manner was the same, as was my outward appearance, more or less. The more I was refused, the more I was refused. Despite my better judgement, I listened to love songs on the radio to see if they'd give me any clues. Not a chance. It would have been good to speak to somebody, but what should I say? A heaviness worked its way down my body from my shoulders to the flats of my feet.

Then a letter arrived, unexpectedly announcing Darragh's engagement. I'm the person who thought it was unexpected. It was because of my own woman trouble that it startled me. Him! Him who was always being left. Not any more, it seemed. And here I was making comparisons between us! They were having an engagement party, just a bit of a thing, nothing very formal, a few drinks really, that was all, and they, he and Maighread, would be delighted if I could make it. There was no need to let them know if I couldn't. Somehow he had managed to make the informality of the few drinks very formal indeed. I bet that woman had been talking to him and now he would have a completely different take on me. Well, I would be there, by God I would. And they wouldn't know a thing about it until I turned up. Surprise as weapon. Surprise as disruption mechanism of weekend plans. I arrived in Dublin the night before the drinks. It was an interesting thing to do, to re-enter one's own country unannounced. It felt like slipping through the back door. I checked into a hotel – again, an interesting thing to do in one's own city. I had a great desire to be bossy at the reception desk. This came from the relief of knowing tones of voices, the fact that I wouldn't be letting my country down if I was unmannerly. It was my country. Darragh would have laughed at me. There he was again, Darragh, Darragh, Darragh.

I went to a nightclub. And my luck changed. Marion was a nice woman, may indeed have been a lovely woman for all I know. I was too preoccupied in relief to engage in normal noticing. She came to my hotel bedroom easily, as is the way these days, as has in fact been the way for a long time. Hotel managers of the sixties didn't get those nosy eyes out of the blue nor overnight. And our night together was a lot more than competent. Abstinence had made me careful and appreciative. She had to leave, but would meet me tomorrow evening. I had decided to bring her along with me to the informal formal. Arrive unannounced and with a woman as usual. She dithered a little, having apparently had a previous sort of arrangement, but then decided that she could cancel it. That was a good sign for my luck.

When Marion and I met the following evening we were discreet in our pleasure at seeing each other afresh. As we arrived at the door she said, 'That's funny,' but I was too busy preening myself for the effect of my arrival, and taming my vindictiveness, to notice the hesitancy in her voice. I ushered her in and pranced proudly two inches behind. In the three seconds that it took for the scene to register itself on me, Darragh and his fiancée had unfortunately turned around to face me. There he was, my double, with his arms draped confidently over the bare shoulders of his wife-to-be, a woman bearing every single physical feature of my date. There must have been some silence, then the women erupted into uproarious laughter.

My brother recovered his jauntiness and said, 'Good God, what a surprise, brother mine.'

Brother mine! Where had he found such an absurd expression?

Some fool, who obviously had not seen Marion yet, hollered, 'Great to see Damien and Darragh together.'

Damien and Darragh.

Our names rolled off his tongue together as if they were the same breath of air. My face boiled over. The heat spread down my chest much in the way I expect the menopause travels on the skins of women. My head bobbed lightly on my shoulders, making me look, no doubt, like an ornamental dog in a moving car. My saliva seemed to have disappeared, one of my knees began to twitch. I wished that the other one would also contract so that I could have some sense of balance. And still the women laughed. Now Darragh joined them. And, as others realised what had happened, they added guffaws and giggles and baritonal snorts, until a landslide of mirth and hilarity flooded the room. The noise was overwhelming.

As Darragh moved towards me I could think of only one thing, how to get out of there. Easy, lift one foot and put it in front of the other. My desire for escape pumped into the farthest reaches of every sinew in my body. It was not just because of embarrassment that I wanted to leave, it was also because I was afraid that the murder I felt might be seen in my eyes. But Darragh was only two feet away from me, one foot, six inches, and he threw his arms around me in the most overdone rugbic crush I have ever felt. I was trapped, lost, with no war to save me. There was nothing for it but to stay, pass the night in beer time, call up the reserves of manners that I had assiduously performed since being a young boy. It may have been the worst night of my life.

That was two years ago. For obvious reasons I didn't go to the wedding. Marion was the bridesmaid. I'm thinking of them tonight, here in Kosovo, because I've just had a letter telling me that Maighread was safely delivered of identical twin boys on the first of April. So here it is, that thing that was waiting for me. May God help the one who is most like me.

Flower Child
June Considine

Across the road from the bookshop, the Liffey flowed on an incoming tide. The water rose so slowly it was hard to know that anything was changing until it crept above the dank brown steps. Then Ally could no longer smell the rubbish on the river bed. In its place was a freshness in the air she had learned to recognise. Seagulls swooped low over the walls, their eyes glittering, searching for food. She remembered the way they used to descend on her granny's garden, flocks of them screeching as they ripped plastic bags of rubbish with their sharp beaks.

'Dirty scavengers!' her granny would shout, rapping on the kitchen window to chase them away. Scavengers, living just to eat someone else's leftovers.

Last night Ally ate a hamburger that had been dumped in a litter bin. It was still warm, but hard, as if it had been fried in too much grease. Even now, to think about it made her stomach queasy. At Ricky's diner the chef was her friend. His name was Jack and he sounded like Daniel O'Donnell, soft and easy when he spoke. At the back of the restaurant so much food was dumped from plates she couldn't believe it. Steaks and chicken legs and spare ribs with meat still on the bone. Sometimes, Jack brought her into the kitchen and gave her food with no one else's teeth marks on it. He said she was a disaster waiting to happen. A daft wee thing, as daft as she was pretty, which was probably a nice thing to hear, but she wasn't sure about anything any more.

Last week she'd told him about the house in the country. 'Wake up, child, and smell the coffee,' he'd said. 'There's no house.'

'Yes, there is.' It was important that Jack believe her. 'Lots of holiday houses. Clara says no one bothers with them except in the summer.'

'And you think you'll be able to stay in one of them?' He forced her to look at him. 'That no one will see you? I know about such places. Even the stone walls have eyes and you'll be booted out so fast you won't see the mountain for dust.'

'No one sees me here and there's millions of people about,' she replied. She didn't mention the night of the Telethon when everyone was raising money for charity, and how, since then, she'd known that her old life could still reappear suddenly, tapping without warning at her elbow.

He wrapped chicken in tinfoil for her to take back to Clara. 'Don't pay a blind bit of notice to that old biddy,' he warned. 'She stopped living in the real world centuries ago. The only house she has is tucked inside her mind.'

Outside the Wordy Cause bookshop a barrow was filled with second-hand books. A red canopy protected them from the sun. 'Can I help you, Miss?' The man inside the bookshop came out and stood beside her.

'Just looking,' she said, turning away from him. He had black curly hair and tiny glasses perched high on his nose that made him look snooty.

'I'm just looking too,' he warned, going back inside to serve a customer.

The first book she opened smelled musty. It had yellow, brittle pages, a broken spine and tea stains on the cover as if someone had used it for a saucer. *All the cardinal sins*, she thought, listing them the way her English teacher, Miss McCarthy, used to do. *Don't*

*make dog-ears. Don't bend back the spine. Never put your cup down
on a book, which is a precious thing and must be respected.*

When Miss McCarthy talked about books she gave them a
personality, as if they were real people. Some were uplifting, she
said, and thought-provoking. Some were full of negative energy
that made you depressed and angry without understanding why.
Some were good bed companions. When you couldn't sleep at
night it was a pleasure to hold a good blockbuster in your hands.
The class howled when she came out with that one and Miss
McCarthy laughed too, knowing she'd walked right into it.

Ally was surprised at how easily the memory came back. As if
it was stored somewhere dark and safe until the right moment
came to set it free. She couldn't remember when she'd last read a
book. After her granny died she read so much she never seemed to
have time for anything else. No time to think about Granny or the
house on Barry Parade where the two of them lived together for
fourteen years. Rose, her real mother, would get annoyed when she
found her reading, even though Ally sat quietly, tucked into the
corner of the sofa. She said Ally was copping out and she'd be
better occupied making herself useful around the place.

Ally placed the musty book back on the barrow and began to
search for one about flowers. 'Knowledge is power,' Miss
McCarthy used to say. Ally thought about the future, when she
would move to the country with her friend Clara. She'd need to
know the names of all the wild flowers that grew along the
hedgerows. Nothing was real unless it had a name. Her granny had
named her after a flower. Alyssum, like the little white plants that
grew in rock gardens. People always thought her name was Alison.
Not that it mattered really. For as long as she could remember
everyone had called her Ally.

At last she found the book she wanted. Heavy and thick, full
of knowledge. Paintings of flowers, each one with a name and a
description. The man in the bookshop watched her, waiting to see
what she would do. She began to read, whispering the words to

herself. Wood Anemone: deep-cut leaves, long stalks, grows in drifts on the edges of woods, poisonous. Irish Spurge: medium-sized perennial, yellow-green leafy group, grows prolifically in Kerry, poisonous. How strange. She had never thought of flowers as poisonous. They grew wild in the crevices of the disused dock-side warehouse where she lived with Clara, green banks of flowers with white heads like trumpets. She supposed they were really weeds but it still amazed her that anything could grow in the crevices and cracks of the walls.

When Ally first ran away Clara took care of her. They met under a bridge when Ally tripped over her in the darkness. At first, in the confusion, she thought Clara was a mummy, one of those Egyptian ones wrapped in sheets, but the sheets came alive and a raspy voice ordered her to have a bit of respect for other people's privacy. If she wanted to lie down and be quiet there was a spare blanket to wrap around herself. In the morning Clara shared peaches from a tin with Ally and told her about the streets. She was like a fierce watchdog, barking at men if they stared too long at Ally or made suggestions. They called Clara a wino and an alco but, more often, they just said she was crazy, especially when she started shouting, her grey witchy hair hanging over her shoulders.

Ally's granny never believed in grey hair. She dyed her hair with Red Hot Sizzle and made Ally check the roots so that not a single grey hair escaped. She had an old face, puckered like an accordion, but, until the day she died, her hair was the colour of ripe raspberries.

On the first Saturday of every month they used to visit Ally's mother Rose, who lived in a terraced house with her husband Sam and their five children. But Sam wasn't Ally's dad, and the children were her half-sisters and brothers, younger than her, and always staring as if she was an unwelcome stranger. Rose never seemed to remember they were coming or to thank them for the Teatime Express cake they'd brought with them.

'You could have rung to remind me,' she'd say, looking cross. 'I'm up to my eyes with the kids.'

Sam stared at Ally from hard button eyes and pulled her close to him when no one was looking. He said she was pampered, a prize doll, full of herself. When he was out with his friends in the pub Rose would hug Ally as if she was really sorry to see her go. Granny said Sam was jealous because Rose had loved someone else before she married him. Ally hoped her real father had been nicer than Sam.

'Oh, he was a proper dreamboat, all right.' Her granny rolled her eyes in admiration. His name was Patrick and Granny had taught him to jive to her collection of Buddy Holly records. It used to embarrass Rose to see her mother acting like a young one, but Patrick thought she was a raver with her Red Hot Sizzle hair and fancy feet. He jived out of their lives after he'd promised to marry Rose. Granny believed he'd jived all the way to Australia and was probably still there, jiving with the kangaroos. When Ally asked her mother what he was really like, Rose snapped, 'Ask no questions and you'll be told no lies.'

After Patrick left Rose gave her wedding dress to an Oxfam shop. She gave Ally to her mother when she was born five months later. A wonderful gift, said Granny. One that could never be taken back. Ally was glad she didn't live in a house that smelled of babies and boiled-over milk, with a man who barked 'Salt!' if it wasn't sitting on the table in front of him.

After her granny died, Ally slept with her half-sisters, four of them together in the one bedroom. They got along OK but she always felt like they were in a club that didn't include her. Sam said there wasn't enough money to feed an extra mouth. Ally's granny was a miserable old skinflint who left nothing but expense behind her. Ally called him a liar. What about the money from the sale of Granny's house? He said he'd take a fist to her lip if she didn't put a zip on it. Instead, without warning, he hit Rose. She looked small, as if she'd shrunk into an old woman's body. Ally wanted to run between them. She wanted to hit him back, the same hard smack of flesh on bone, but Rose shouted at her to go upstairs. She'd caused enough trouble since she arrived.

After Ally ran away she became clever at spotting people she knew and fading out from the crowd before they noticed her. 'A slippery fish,' Clara called her. 'Slipping right through the net.' Until the night of the Telethon.

What a mad night it had been. People in fancy dress singing in groups, marching in bands, walking on stilts. They looked so happy because this was the one night of the year when everyone came together to raise money for charity and go on television waving enormous cheques. She stood on the edge of the pavement as the people flowed past on a wave of noise and laughter. They rattled their collection boxes, bullying everyone into giving money. She felt anonymous on the crowded street until Miss McCarthy touched her arm.

'Ally, how are you?' Instead of a pile of English copybooks Miss McCarthy carried a guitar. 'I've been worried sick about you.'

Ally was ready to run but the teacher's voice made her stay. Living rough solved nothing, she said. There was only one way to go – down. It was time to go home.

'I've got no home.' Ally was determined not to listen. 'Not since Granny died. I can't go back to them … I won't.'

Miss McCarthy looked as if she was going to cry. 'There are people who can help you make a new home.' She wrote her phone number on a piece of paper and handed it to Ally. 'Think about what I've said and ring me … trust me.'

She was still talking when Ally ran towards Clara, who was watching a group of men dressed as women, all glitzy pink hair and big boobs and spangles that flashed as they danced.

'The lunatics have escaped from the asylum.' Her laughter had a wild sound that frightened Ally. It wasn't a safe sound and she knew she could do nothing to make it different. When the men stopped kicking their legs and opened hip flasks, Clara shouted, 'Have you a drop of the hard stuff to spare, lads?' They turned away, embarrassed, when they saw her. Their laughter scratched against Ally's skin.

The squat where she lived with Clara had once been a warehouse used for storing cargo. Soon it would be turned into apartments and the white trumpet flowers would die, rootless under metal girders and marble floors. Clara's breath wheezed when she spoke too fast. She moaned in her sleep, her body twitching and shaking. If she wet herself it did not embarrass her because she never realised what she'd done and Ally had learned to block it out.

Clara talked a lot about the sixties. 'Make love. Not war.' When she lived in America she'd worn flowers in her hair and a kaftan with purple embroidery. She'd marched in protests, demanding civil rights for black people and an end to the Vietnam war and famine and bombs and everything else that was wrong in the world. 'We really made a difference,' she said proudly. 'We really made it happen.'

Ally liked it best when Clara lit a fire at night and told her about her childhood and the cottage where she'd lived. Outside her gate a river splashed over stones before disappearing into a ditch of hawthorn and fuchsia. Slí na hAbhann was the name of the village. The way of the river, she said, and it was so beautiful that people from the city came every summer, opening up their holiday homes, drinking pints of mountain air, spaced out on turf smoke and the roar of the river making waterfalls. She described the meadow after the rain, ladybirds on the stems of wild flowers, the scent of heather on the breeze. In the city you couldn't smell flowers because there was no stillness, she said. When the holiday homes were empty again and the only things moving on the horizon were sheep with black faces, they'd move to Slí na hAbhann and Ally would understand what she meant.

Some nights when she waited for Clara to come back, Ally

imagined how different it would be out in the countryside. When she grew frightened to be by herself, she'd repeat the names of the flowers she knew, whispering them over and over again until her eyelids felt heavy: violet, cowslip, bluebell, primrose, buttercup, foxglove, daisy, forget-me-not.

The man in the bookshop had stopped watching her. Quickly, Ally shoved the flower book under her anorak and sprinted across the road and over the Halfpenny Bridge. The sound of her footsteps drummed in her ears, almost as loud as her heartbeat. She ran through Temple Bar where the boys who sometimes stayed in the warehouse asked her about Clara. They had sharp faces and eyes that only noticed what was necessary for survival. Like the seagulls scavenging on the Liffey. It always amazed Ally how word on the street spread. As if the news was being sent out in vibrations, under the noisy layers of the city.

Late last night Clara fell to the ground and gathered her knees into her chest. Backwards and forwards she rocked, her face slack, her lips moist and blue. When she lay still her eyes were flat, as if someone had switched off a light inside her. Ally ran out along the quays until she came to a phone kiosk and dialled 999. Men came with a stretcher, clambering over the broken walls and glass, and lifted Clara gently from the ground. They covered her face with a blanket and carried her from the shadows. The fire was still burning. Sparks fluttered like luminous moths in the dark. Ally stayed out of sight, invisible.

The flower book was heavy in her arms. She left the boys and walked along the Liffey bank, passing the ships with foreign flags and the cranes that lit the skyline at night. A man walked out in front of the traffic. He ignored the angry drivers who blasted their horns and shouted. He spotted a traffic cone by the edge of the wall and lifted it. He raised it above his head and dropped it into the water. He just let it fall, not even looking over the wall to see the splash. From the expression on his face, Ally knew he'd stopped thinking long ago. She'd seen him with Clara a few times, the two of them sitting on steps, not talking, just looking straight ahead, sharing a bottle.

She came to a bench and sat down, suddenly so tired she didn't think she'd ever again have the energy to move. She opened the book and stared at the pictures. So many flowers. How could she ever remember their names? The tears came suddenly, streaking her cheeks as she thought about the mountain and the houses and the empty spaces waiting to be filled. She smelled the Liffey and the yeast from the brewery and the smell of Clara, the flower child, who had decided a long time ago that her mind was the only safe place to live. Ally hoped there was a heaven called Slí na hAbhann and that Clara was there, running as free as the river. The crumpled piece of paper with Miss McCarthy's phone number was still in her pocket. She allowed her fingers to rest on it for a moment. She imagined the weight of the telephone in her hand. The voice at the other end of the line. The moment when she had to make up her mind to speak her name. Alyssum … a small white scented flower growing in rock gardens. Above her the clouds formed a daisy chain, casting shapes on the Liffey, streaks of violet, the bluebell sky and the sun, as yellow as a buttercup, touching her hair.

Jack and Emily
Judi Curtin

Emily liked ironing. This was probably just as well, as her husband, Jack, liked to wear a clean white shirt to work every day. Each week Emily washed, dried and ironed five shirts. This, allowing for holidays, worked out at around two hundred and forty-five shirts for every one of the twelve long years of her marriage.

This foggy September day, she had uncharacteristically allowed the shirts to mount up. There were fifteen of them piled up in the linen basket – her own small Everest. Still, she was looking forward to a few hours of undemanding work. She found the sleek, repetitive motion to be rather relaxing. Sometimes she felt it was the highlight of her week.

It was early afternoon when she heaved the overflowing basket into the kitchen. She hummed to herself as she set up the ironing board and fetched the iron from the utility room. She switched the radio to the classical music channel. Jack didn't like music, so it was a treat to listen to the soothing melodies without the risk of incurring his displeasure.

She laid the first shirt collar on the garish flowered fabric of the ironing board, and waited for the iron to heat up. Soon the red light went out with a small click, and she smoothed the stiff collar and the yoke in three easy strokes. She rearranged the garment, and reached for the starch. The spray made a mottled pattern and the fabric became briefly transparent. Then, at the touch of the iron, the starch hissed into a sweet-smelling cloud of steam, as she ironed the right sleeve of the shirt, just as she had been taught in domestic science class many years earlier.

Those were easy days, her schooldays, as she giggled at her teacher's fussiness, not caring if she ever knew the correct way to iron a shirt, or stuff a tomato, or neaten a machine-stitched seam. Emily had sighed her way through the endless, boring classes, dreaming of the wonderful world that lay outside, just waiting for her to come and partake of its joys and excitement. Back then she had had so many hopes and dreams. Strange, really, all those hopes and dreams were now gone, and she couldn't recapture them, even in her most wistful moments. She couldn't pinpoint exactly what it was that made those times so special, why the days had slipped by in sunshine and wonder. She could remember dressing up on a Friday night, ready for the disco, but she couldn't quite recall why she felt so good, why she had that delightful tingle of anticipation. She could remember countless afternoons when she ran along the street with her friends, laughing as they raced to catch the bus into town. She no longer had any clear idea of how they spent their time once they got there.

One of the few things she *could* remember in any detail from those distant days was the correct way to iron a man's cotton shirt.

She finished the first three shirts and hung them carefully on their wooden hangers. If she had been counting, she would have realised that by now she must have been approaching the three thousandth shirt of her marriage. Emily wasn't counting, though. She had other things on her mind.

As she reached into the basket for the next shirt, she wasn't aware that a half-smile was lurking on her lips.

Jack wasn't a bad man. It was just that he was arrogant and cold and unfeeling. He couldn't help it. He'd had a difficult, lonely childhood. It wasn't his fault. It was only recently, though, that Emily had begun to wonder if it was fair that she should suffer too.

In the early days, she foolishly thought that her love could change everything. She kept the house warm and welcoming. She greeted him every evening with aromatic casseroles, or luscious roasts. She planned walks and films and cosy nights by the fire. She baked cakes and made raspberry jam. She made a little cross-stitch sampler reading, 'Home, sweet home' and hung it in the hall, where he could see it as soon as he stepped through the front door. In winter she laid Jack's pyjamas on the radiator at night, so they would be warm when bedtime came. She thought that her love could make everything right. She was wrong. Nothing she did made any difference. Not only did Jack not change, but as the years rolled slowly by, he seemed to become even more set in his distant, chilly ways.

How she would have loved a child – someone small, warm and cuddly. She could have wrapped it in snowy white towels, fluffy and soft from careful washing with mild powder and fabric conditioner. She could have given it a wonderful, frivolous name – Sebastian or Savannah, perhaps. She could have taken her baby for walks in its pram, and chatted with doting old grannies in the park. Together they could have fed the ducks with the crumbs from her home-made bread. She could have nourished the child with organic vegetables, carefully chopped and steamed and mashed. She could have tenderly wiped the soft, pink little mouth, and tickled the damp toes, and laughed at the sweet, gummy smiles.

But there was no baby, and there never would be. Jack didn't want one. He couldn't see the point. He didn't see why they should bring upon themselves all the mess and inconvenience, and ultimate heartache. He didn't want anything to do with smelly nappies and green noses, and porridge on the pale cream kitchen walls. And weren't they happy enough, anyway?

He had made up his mind, so there was no use in arguing. She didn't know how to, anyway. She had no words for her loneliness, her silent grief, and her boredom.

Instead he gave her foreign holidays and money for clothes, weekly trips to the hairdresser and the beautician, a subscription to *Hello*. It didn't compensate.

She took in a stray kitten once, unable to resist its piteous cries as it huddled in the driveway. She bathed it and dried it and gave it warm milk in a cracked saucer. She stroked it and smiled at its contented, squeaky little mews. She made a bed from old rags, and hid it in the back of the garage. She was childishly afraid of Jack's reaction. Because she knew what he would say. He would half-smile an indulgent, patronising smile. Then he would reel off a list of perfectly rational reasons not to keep the kitten.

He didn't get the chance to air his views, though, as she found the stiff, cold body on its raggy bed one morning before Jack ever knew it existed. She'd only had the little waif for six nights, but she grieved deeply, unnaturally at his loss. When Jack left for work that morning, she wrapped the skinny creature in an embroidered linen tray-cloth Jack's mother had given her for Christmas. She buried it at the far end of the garden, and planted snowdrops on the grave. The snowdrops threw up straggly leaves every year, but they never blossomed.

By the time she was on the left sleeve of the sixth shirt, she had settled into a comfortable rhythm. Her mind began to wander, and as the fine, white cotton slid easily under the iron, she thought she could see her precious life slipping away before her eyes.

One evening, some years earlier, she and Jack had sat together on the cream-coloured couch, watching television. He liked documentaries. Even though he hadn't much clue as to what was going on in his own living room, he liked to know what was happening on the other side of the world. That night, there was a programme about homeless people in San Francisco. A thin, scruffy twenty-year-old cuddled up against her feckless, boozy lover, who rubbed her cheek affectionately with his scratched and dirty hand. Jack wondered aloud how any human beings could allow themselves to sink so low. Emily found herself dreaming of being there, living in a cardboard box under a bridge – poor, but accepted; good enough. These thoughts, like so many others, she kept to herself.

Jack and Emily

*

Jack insisted that his shirts be starched. One day, in the early years, she was in a hurry, so she didn't bother, hoping he wouldn't notice. She was wrong. He never made a scene, of course. That wasn't his way. He just looked at her as if he was scarcely able to contain his disappointment. After that she was more careful. She couldn't bear his cold looks.

Once, after she'd had a few glasses of wine, she tried to talk to him about his lack of affection towards her. She tried to tell him how lonely she felt. He looked at her in genuine astonishment. He answered her in a few clipped, well-constructed sentences. As far as he could see, he was a perfectly dutiful husband. A perfectly dutiful husband wasn't quite what Emily had had in mind when she had sailed up the aisle in foolish hope, eleven years earlier. She didn't know how to tell him that, though, and she didn't bring up the subject again.

There was a button missing from the cuff of the thirteenth shirt. She switched off the iron, fetched her jar of white buttons and a needle and thread. She always replaced buttons as soon as she noticed the need, afraid that if she delayed she would forget. She stitched carefully, and then wound the thread around her stitches, making a stem – another skill learned many, many years earlier. Then she put away her sewing, and returned to the ironing board.

She checked her watch. Jack would be home at six. He always was. But Emily never liked to stop ironing until the last shirt was smooth and wrinkle-free.

She finished the fifteenth shirt with a little sigh. She folded up the ironing board and set the iron on its wall holder in the utility room. She put the starch in the cupboard under the sink. She went upstairs and hung the shirts in his wardrobe, buttons facing towards the right, the way he preferred. The wardrobe door closed with a sharp, satisfying click.

She packed a small canvas bag. She didn't need much, and didn't want to be burdened with a heavy weight. Anyway, she knew

Jack would be perfectly civilised. She could come back any time she wished to get more things. He'd probably even have her back to stay, if she asked. He wouldn't beg or cry, though. He wouldn't offer to change. He still wouldn't understand why she had left in the first place.

Emily knew perfectly well why she was leaving. What puzzled her was why she had stayed so long.

The evening before, he had brought home a holiday brochure to show her. He had booked a trip to Tuscany. They would travel in three weeks' time. He had researched it carefully. September was the best month in Tuscany. It would be warm and quiet. They would stay in a five-star hotel – good value in the off-season. The service would be impeccable. Emily wouldn't have to do a thing.

As he ate his parmesan-crusted salmon, Jack had talked with his usual authority about the history of Tuscany, its art and architecture. He didn't speak enthusiastically – Jack didn't do enthusiasm – but as he spoke, there was a certain cold fire in his eyes. As his words washed over her, Emily closed her eyes and pictured fourteen days and nights in his company. Fourteen days without his work to come between them. Fourteen days without even the ironing to distract her. She and Jack would share fourteen breakfasts, fourteen lunches and fourteen long, lingering dinners.

Half an hour later, her plan had taken shape. Though, as plans go, it has to be said that hers was rather shapeless. Leave. Get a flat. Get a job. Start a new life. That was about it.

She had a cousin who lived alone in a large apartment on the south side of Dublin. She would allow Emily to stay for a few weeks, and wouldn't ask too many prying questions. If the news bulletins were anything to go by, there was a labour shortage, and there would surely be work for one as willing as she. The flat might be more difficult. Emily wasn't fussy, though. She could live anywhere. Anywhere would be better than her beautiful, clean, cream home.

As she carried her bag downstairs, she noticed some crumbs on the stone-coloured carpet. She found herself vacuuming them away. It was going to be very hard to change.

She thought about leaving a note to explain. It would be rude not to, and Jack couldn't abide rudeness. But she couldn't decide what to say. She hadn't much experience of this kind of thing. In the end, she got a yellow Post-it note and wrote, 'I'm leaving.' Not much of an explanation, but it would have to do. She stuck the note to the remote control for the television, where she knew he would find it.

There was a bus at 5.30, so she'd be well away before he arrived. A more imaginative woman might have echoed the old song, and pictured her escape in a sports car, with the warm wind in her hair. Emily was content with the prospect of the 36A into the city centre, with diesel fumes in her nostrils.

She watered the plants in the sunroom. She took the stew she had made earlier out of the fridge, and placed it on the hob. She stuck another Post-it note to the saucepan lid – 'Simmer fifteen minutes.' She checked that the back door was locked. She double-checked that she had unplugged the iron. She keyed in the code for the burglar alarm, and closed the front door as the electronic beeps played their forty-five-second chorus behind her.

She had left the upstairs windows open. The house would be cold when Jack got home. Just the way he liked it.

Checkout Girl
Denise Deegan

Christmas Eve, 1989. Eighty-three years of life end in one split second. I feel no pain, just shock. My last thoughts are not profound: *He broke the lights! I had the green man!* My life does not flash in front of me. Someone else's does. Someone I don't even know. A checkout girl at the supermarket I was in, a little earlier. I don't understand. What has a stranger to do with my dying moments? Shouldn't they be about me? Not that I'm a selfish person, you understand. I'm just confused. I'd have thought God might have been here by now, or, at the very least, an angel.

I don't like surprises at the best of times. Or change. It's most unsettling to find myself being whisked back to a supermarket at a time like this. I was planning on heaven. I've never been one for detours. The time (I see by the clock and calendar on the white vinyl-finish wall of Walsh's Stores) is just over an hour before my life, as I knew it, ended. I hover now, invisible, above busy Christmas shoppers. Hovering, I am pleased to relate, is a big improvement on hobbling. Being invisible, though, is something I began to get used to around the age of seventy.

Ah, there she is, the checkout girl. Only she isn't at the checkout now. She's standing beside the deep freezers, taking instructions from a man in a cheap suit. Without looking at their name-badges, I know that she is 'Debbie', he 'Mr Casey'. I know that he is a manager and that when he asks her to 'face off' the freezer, he wants her to tidy its icy contents. I know that Mr Casey enjoys being called Mister, that using supermarket terminology makes him feel important and that giving Debbie freezer duty, once again, gives him a unique sense of satisfaction. He walks away, smiling.

After five minutes of sorting frozen peas, carrots, broccoli and pizzas into neat lines, Debbie can't feel her hands. She tucks them under her arms, watching for Casey, prepared to resume work if his weedy body rounds the corner. At the end of the aisle is one of the part-timers, taken on for the Christmas rush. She is humming along to the carols being pumped out over the tannoy as she 'faces off' Jaffa cakes, unaware of her luck, not just in terms of her location in the supermarket, but in terms of the lottery that is life. This girl has a college place. Her job here is temporary, her future full of possibility. The boys she dates don't need to be good with children. She and Debbie are the same age: nineteen. Yet they live as though a generation apart. Having a child can make the world a much more serious and grown-up place.

The supermarket gets busy. Debbie and others are called to the checkouts. In the future – my goodness! – I can see that technology will revolutionise this job, bringing such things as 'scanning' and 'bar codes' and computers that work out what change to give customers. But today, things are as I know and love them – simple and straightforward, like they've been for years. I close my eyes and listen to the sound the till makes when the buttons are pressed.

My peace is disturbed when I begin to sense what Debbie is feeling – the urgency of the shoppers waiting in line. Everyone is in a rush to finish last-minute jobs, get home, get ready. Only a day to go! The checkout is a barrier to progress. Debbie hurries to pick up a pound of butter. Though there's no label on it, she knows the price. One pound twenty-nine. It's been the same for years. The next item is a tiny plum pudding. She looks up from it to smile at the customer.

Oh, Lord, that customer is me! I am watching myself going

93

about my business an hour before my old life ended. It's a bit of a shock, seeing myself from outside. Especially from above. How tiny I am! Like a little bird. A sparrow. I am telling Debbie that my son will be home for Christmas.

'I haven't seen him in five years. He's a surgeon, you know, in New York. Very busy.'

Debbie smiles and keeps pressing in the numbers. Tat-tat tat.

The woman behind me is jigging about. She pushes the divider right up behind my little basket of things. She checks her watch and sighs. I stop talking, keep my head down, take out my purse and have it ready, my knotted fingers on the brass clasp. *There's that shake I've been noticing recently. I suppose something has to start shaking at eighty-three.*

Debbie tells me the total.

I grip the counter, thinking it must be a mistake. *I always add everything up as I go around. I'm so careful never to go over budget.* I look up at her, too ashamed to say that I am short five pounds. I look back down at my groceries. There's the pudding. The impulse buy. I reach for it. My voice almost inaudible, I say, 'I think I'll have to put this back.'

The woman behind me snorts.

Blood is pumping in my ears like a heartbeat.

Debbie looks at the pudding and then up at me. She hesitates for a moment, then seems to melt. 'It's Christmas,' she says. 'Why don't you pay me back the next time you're in?'

'Really?' Oh, the relief. 'That would be marvellous. I will be in next week. On Tuesday. I always shop on Tuesdays. I'll give it to you then. I'll make a little note when I go home so I'll remember.'

As she packs the bags, I begin to have second thoughts. What if this young girl gets into trouble for doing this? What if she doesn't have the authority? 'Are you sure it'll be all right? I mean, you can do this?'

'Oh, yes.' Then she adds, conspiratorially, 'But only for our best customers.'

I smile. 'Thank you.'

When she hands me my bags, I wish her a really *wonderful* Christmas.

She smiles. 'Have a lovely time with your son.'

She knows not to make small talk with the next woman, just work fast.

The last hour of my old life is almost up. Outside, I must be heading for those traffic lights. Here, someone comes to relieve Debbie. She checks her watch. Half an hour for what she has to do. She has permission to leave the store (from another manager, not Casey) to buy her daughter a baby doll for Christmas, not just any baby doll, a very specific baby doll – one that cries and wets and says Mama. Debbie got paid last night and finally has enough. She hopes that the toy-shop is still holding the doll she asked them to set aside. Quickly, she clocks out.

She turns up her collar against the cold and rushes past a group of carol singers outside McDonalds. She doesn't even see them. She is focused on the pedestrian crossing up ahead – the lights have just changed. She might just make it if she hurries. She does – in time to witness my little accident. Recognising me, her gloved hands go to her mouth. A sturdy woman pushes past her, through the gathering crowd, calling, 'Stand back, I'm a nurse.' Biting her pink-and-green-striped fingers, Debbie prays that I will be all right, that my son, the surgeon, home from America, will have contacts, will get the best care for me, will look after me.

Oh, how could I have lied about Rory like that? It wasn't as if someone I knew had asked me a direct question about my son. I had volunteered this falsehood to a stranger. Why? Yes, I wanted to be proud of him. But more than that, I wanted a better life for him. If only he was a surgeon in New York, not a prisoner in Mountjoy. Think how happy he'd be. My son, my little boy. Where did I go wrong? No. I have to stop thinking like that. Rory has to take some responsibility for what he did. And I have to stop blaming myself. Oh, but it *is* good to know that someone, even a stranger, and even for a brief moment, cares what happens to a little old woman who had nowhere to be on Christmas Day.

The ambulance comes quickly. Debbie looks at her watch and rushes to the toy shop. She is in luck. They have the doll. She makes it back to the supermarket just in time. With the shock of all that has happened, she forgets all about the five pounds she has to return to the till on my behalf, five pounds of her own money, to balance her act of kindness.

It is only at the end of the day, when the amount in the drawer does not match that on the paper roll, that she remembers. She tries to explain to Mr Casey, who is standing over her, looking like a member of the Gestapo. She dreads this time of the day, every day, when the customers have gone and the checkout girls have to sit at their tills in a long line, drawers open, waiting for the managers to supervise the count. Anyone who is out by more than five pounds on three occasions is fired. Oh, yes, that is the kind of trusting environment we have here at Walsh's Stores, the kind of environment that has managers checking the bags of the staff as they leave work, to make sure they haven't walked off with any of the merchandise. God knows what you'd get for a tin of beans on the black market!

Debbie is out by a little over five pounds. Thirty-seven pence over – the result of a miscalculation with a money-off voucher produced by the woman behind me in the queue. Debbie has always had a problem subtracting voucher amounts from the total bill. Not that that's the way she is supposed to work the maths. She can never remember the right way. Especially when under pressure.

Debbie looks up at Mr Casey now, her pale face drawn and worried, knowing too well that this is her third mistake. He is enjoying the moment. He will show this jumped-up little bitch. The nerve of her, turning her nose up at him. He's a manager, for Christ's sake. It's not everyone he asks out. She should have been thrilled. The little tart – he's heard she's a single mother. Well, he'll show her now …

I am so *annoyed* with myself. It was just a pudding. If I'd known what it would have led to I'd have insisted on putting it back. Oh, there must be something I can do. If only I weren't invisible. I could just tell him, explain that he is treating her like a criminal because of a simple act of kindness, because of excellent customer service. Is there any way I can salvage this wretched situation? Am I not here to make amends to this poor girl for getting her into trouble? Apparently not, because instead of being allowed to intervene, I feel myself being pulled away.

I am in a tiny but cosy Council house. Fairy lights blink on and off on a fake Christmas tree in the corner. One big red stocking is hanging on the mantelpiece by a thumbtack. The name 'Jessie' has been printed on it. Two people are dancing – a little girl of three and a woman of forty-two. Who are they? What am I doing here? They are wiggling their bottoms, pointing their fingers in the air, singing and laughing to a song that must be called something like 'Keep on Rocking in the Free World', because that seems to be the chorus. I've never heard this song before. It's not exactly seasonal, but I have to admit it's catchy. The woman lands down on the couch, out of breath, still laughing.

'Hiya,' the little girl says. To me!

Can she *see* me?

'Hiya, Ginki.'

Ginki?

'Ginki, will *you* dance with me? Nan's always getting tired.'

'Who're you talking to, Jess?' asks the woman, leaning forward.

'Ginki. My new fwiend.' She looks at me as if to say, 'There she is.'

The woman smiles to herself, remembering a time when her daughter, Jessie's mother, had an imaginary friend. Skooki did no harm at all.

'Nan, will you put on the Keep on Wocking song again? Ginki likes it.'

*

I haven't danced in years. But I'm dancing now. My joints feel free, all stiffness gone. No aches. No pains. I can move like the wind. I can jump on the couch. I can fly. The child is laughing at me. I am laughing at myself. Whee! I had better come down, though. It wouldn't do to frighten the woman by making her grandchild look up as if at a flying thing. A ghost. Or an angel. Could that be what I am? An eighty-three-year-old, wingless angel called Ginki?

The woman's daughter arrives home. She hides a doll at the top of a press in the hall. She is Debbie.

'Hiya,' she says, more cheerfully than she feels.

'Mam, Mam. I've a new fwiend. Her name's Ginki. She's a gweat dancer.'

Debbie looks at her mother.

The woman mouths 'imaginary'.

Debbie bends down and hugs her little girl. More tightly than usual. Later, when the child is in bed, Debbie tells her mother what happened.

'They want the uniform back or else I'll have to pay them eight pounds.'

'Eight pounds? For that piece of shit? Anyway, it's fuck-all use to them with the hole in it.'

'That's the problem. If I bring it back, they'll see the hole and I'll still owe eight pounds because I've wrecked it. If you wreck a uniform or don't give it back, you have to pay for it. That's the rule.'

'Well, d'you know what I think?'

Debbie looks at her.

'Fuck 'em. They've too many rules. Don't bring it back.'

Despite the language, I'm inclined to agree.

'But my reference …'

'You think that in a big place like that they'll notice if you don't bring back one shagging uniform? And it's their fault the hole's in it. Sure the minute you landed the iron down, the material melted onto it. Crap stuff, you wouldn't put it on an animal. Didn't cost *them* eight quid, that's for sure. You know, someone should remind them they're selling food. That's all they're at. Jesus, the way they go on, you'd swear they were selling diamonds or something.' She lights up a cigarette and takes a long drag.

'What'll I do, Ma? Where'll I get another job?'

'Don't worry. We'll think of something … after Christmas. Come on, I'll make you a coffee.'

It's not real coffee. It's some kind of cheap substitute, retailing at thirty-nine pence a jar in Walsh's Stores. Dinner was sliced pan and beans.

It is the first Christmas in years that I am in company. It's very exciting. Jessie has set a place for me at the table. Now she pulls my crackers for me. I look around at this little family and wonder why I never knew people like this when I was alive. My life was so small, really, so *limited*. Might as well have been in an enclosed order. It does not bother Debbie, Jessie or Janice that the Christmas crackers are from the pound shop and full of rubbish. Or that the turkey is, in actual fact, chicken. They wear their best clothes and their paper hats at an angle. They chat and laugh and have a few drinks. Maybe this is heaven.

Days later, Jessie is playing Mammies, clicking around in her nan's high heels, Debbie's handbag over her shoulder and her new baby doll in her arms. She puts the baby to bed, lying her on the couch and covering her with a tea towel. She then has a rummage in the handbag. She pulls out a wrinkly five-pound note and hands it to her mother.

'Here, Ma, buy yourself somethin' nice.'

'Thanks very much,' says Debbie, smiling and taking it from her. She rests the newspaper down on her lap. There were no jobs in it anyway, at least none to suit her. She looks at the note. Five wrinkly quid, the exact amount meant for the till. Technically, it still belongs to Walsh's Stores. She could bring it back. Or she could treat it as a redundancy payment. She knows what her mother would do.

'Get your coat,' she tells her little girl.

At the corner shop, she buys Jessie a packet of onion rings, herself a Bounty and her mother a Curly Wurly – all their favourites. Thinking she'll never be able to repay her mother for everything she's done for her and Jess, Debbie buys her a pack of Silk Cut. Gold dust to her. Now, there should be just enough left for a Lotto ticket.

When Jessie sees her mother pick up the slip of Lotto paper she begins to jump up and down. 'Ginki wants to pick the numbers. Ginki wants to pick the numbers.'

Debbie is getting tired of Ginki. Already the imaginary friend has had them wait at the traffic lights until they got the green man, despite the fact that the road was empty. Then they had to continue to wait to make sure that the cars that had actually appeared by then were going to stop. Now Ginki wanted to pick the Lotto numbers. What next?

I stoop down opposite Jessie. I look straight at her, then slowly hold up one finger.

'One,' she calls to her mother, not taking her eyes off me.

I hold up two fingers.

'Two,' she says.

Three.

'Three!'

Let me guess, thinks Debbie. *Four, five and six? We haven't a hope.*

Meanwhile, I'm trying to work out how I'm going to get Jessie to select twenty-six, twenty-eight and twenty-nine. The child can only count to ten. And I've only so many fingers. So, I try to will the numbers into her mind.

'Twenty-six, twenty-eight and twenty-nine,' she says confidently.

Debbie stares at her daughter. 'How d'you know them?'

Jessie shrugs. 'Just do.'

Two days later, they will be watching the telly, all three of them. The Lotto draw will come up. Debbie will have the ticket on her lap, holding it with both hands. In the split second when the last ball, a pink one, drops into its container, their lives will change forever. Debbie will stop breathing. She will check it again. Not trusting herself, she will call to her mother to write the numbers down, *write them down*. Her mother, cool customer that she is, will take the ticket from Debbie. She will look up at the screen, then down at the ticket, then up and down, and then she will scream. They will both scream and grab each other and jump up and down together. Then they will stop and look at Jessie. Debbie will say, 'Ginki was right. Ginki was right.'

The child will look up from feeding her baby. 'Who?'

Because I will have gone. I'm on my way now, in actual fact, my job done, numbers selected. It was that simple. And now it's time for the next step, the big one. It's the first time I ever remember a detour being the best part of a trip.

Fortune Cookies
Martina Devlin

Clodagh Ferguson shivers beside an empty fireplace in the front sitting room of her imposing Georgian home. It is a high-ceilinged chamber, splendid with architraves and cornices which visitors coo over – but they should try heating the place.

The house has been in her family since 1807, when a six times great-grandfather made a fortune in the fur trade in the United States. Returning home to Barry's Point, he built a gentleman's residence and married a girl not yet born when he had sailed steerage in an emigrant ship. He lived there in considerable style, but his financial acumen was bequeathed to none of his descendants and each generation grew successively poorer. The land surrounding the property was sold piecemeal for building developments, so that now the house is fenced in by housing estates and struggles for air.

Clodagh has attempted to rent out the house but nobody wants to take it on. Not when the roof leaks and the wind howls through cavernous bay windows. She realises that she is post poning the inevitable: she will have to sell up, settle her debts and hope there may be enough left over to buy a modest place. Her six times great-grandfather will spin in his grave and the children are sure to be inconsolable, but what else can she do? Since her husband absconded, her finances have steadily declined.

James never contributes anything to their daughters' upkeep.

He telephones the girls sometimes, and once he sent them rag dolls with waist-length plaits, but the cheques he promises never materialise. A hotel manager when they married, he was sacked three years ago for fiddling the books. 'It wasn't stealing,' he explained; 'I was going to repay the money with my winnings from the 3.30 at Leopardstown. Stupid nag let me down.' James packed his bags a fortnight later, emptying Clodagh's purse to underwrite his air ticket to Leeds, and from there he travelled to York, Doncaster, Chester … anywhere with a racecourse.

The family's sole source of revenue, apart from social security, is the negligible amount Clodagh earns by selling the jewellery she designs. This income is not up to the responsibility of maintaining a two-hundred-year-old house. Only a few days ago, the bank bounced a cheque to the firm that patched the valley in her roof. Which means it will also decline to honour her cheque for semi-precious stones. Without stones she can't make jewellery, and without jewellery to sell she can't raise their living standard above subsistence level.

Clodagh sighs. Can she really be the woman who sipped pink champagne from a crystal flute on her twenty-first birthday, candles flickering in every room and a throng of well-wishers helping to celebrate her coming of age? In two decades the future has dimmed from rose-tinted to grey. Such a weary shade.

Tonight she will phone the developer who has twice made her an offer. P.J. Quinlivan is aching to bulldoze the house and build a shopping centre in its place. The acrid taste of defeat twists Clodagh's mouth; she is supposed to be the chatelaine of her home but instead she is its executioner.

A series of raps on the front door intrudes on her gloom. Clodagh startles, nervous of roofers brandishing a dud cheque. Or an aggrieved salesman from the jewellery suppliers. She crosses to the window and peers out. Nobody visible. The knocker rat-a-tat-tats again. She hesitates. There is something insistent about it, although not in an authoritarian way. It's almost an enticement.

Should she? This is madness; another problem probably lies beyond the heavy crimson door. Yet she turns, even as common sense and experience urge her to stay her hand, and opens the door.

Whatever she may have expected, it is not this. A stooped oriental woman waits on the granite steps. Her only luggage is a silk bag with an elaborately carved handle shaped like some exotic bird's head. Clodagh raises a questioning eyebrow but the woman is silent.

'Can I help you?'

'Perhaps I can help *you*.'

The English is accented, the voice pipes like a schoolgirl's. The stranger's eyes dart upwards and fasten on Clodagh's: they are opaque and the jeweller in her classifies them as jasper.

'I don't see how.'

'I could rent a room. I imagine you have plenty – this would house my entire village.' The woman's eyes flicker briefly with amusement, before a veil descends.

Hope flares in Clodagh: perhaps there might be a solution to their financial problems, after all. She tried taking in paying guests before but it never worked out – they tended to expect hot water, always in short supply, and were forever complaining about draughts. Still, perhaps this elderly woman in her Mao suit and buckled slippers might prove less demanding than her predecessors.

'I have no money.' The newcomer's tone is casual, not a hint of apology.

Clodagh feels aggrieved for having allowed herself that misguided glimmer of optimism. 'Well, then, I don't see how we can do business. Goodbye.' She attempts to close the door but the woman scans her face in a motion that, while unhurried, conveys a sense of purpose.

'I could pay you in kind.'

'How? I need cash, not help with the housework.'

'Fortune cookies.'

Clodagh allows herself the luxury of a snort. 'It would take a mountain of fortune cookies to cover your rent. My sweet tooth isn't that far gone.'

'Nobody bakes them like me. People will trade for them.' She pauses. 'They may give you stones. Tiger's eye, perhaps, would sell well for you.'

Clodagh is taken aback. How does the stranger know about her jewellery business? Oh, this is ridiculous, anyone in town could have told her. And then a thought strikes Clodagh, a possibility so tantalising that she catches her breath and studies the patient figure more closely. A nest of wrinkles clings to each eye, not a hair strays from place in her grey bun. But it's the demeanour that impresses her – the woman's air of tranquil certainty. Clodagh's favourite film is *Chocolat*, it even inspired her to read the book. Suddenly she has a vision of their community being swept by cookie fever, and of the mysterious stranger solving everyone's problems with a clap of her stubby hands. A fairy godmother could be standing on her doorstep!

She has nothing to lose, and there are rooms to spare in this beached whale of a house. 'You can stay until the weekend.'

The children are thrilled with their guest.

'She made me a goldfish from an envelope.' Eight-year-old Pearl is reverent.

'It's called origami, my kitten, the Chinese are marvellous at it,' says Clodagh.

'I got a dragon to guard me in bed at night,' chimes in Ruby, who's six. 'Goldfish are no good at guarding people.'

'Goldfish bring you luck, May Lee says so,' Pearl retorts.

When the children are sleeping, Clodagh wanders into the kitchen, where the newcomer is cooling her first batch of cookies. She offers one to Clodagh with a courtly bow. It doesn't smell particularly appetising. Cookie fever is never going to bubble up in Barry's Point if they taste as powdery as they smell.

'Like this.' May mimes breaking it open.

Clodagh does as she's shown, and a slip of rice paper flutters out. Aha, it's not the taste of the cookies but the messages inside that are going to transform the community. Good, she's first in the queue for May's cookie magic. She pops a corner of cookie into her mouth. Sugary communion wafer. It will never sell. That's all right, there's always the note, penned in lavender ink in exquisite calligraphy, which she squints to read.

My father's bicycle is his gift for me to cherish.

What on earth does that mean? 'Can you translate, May?'

'The fortune cookies speak with their own voice. It is not for me to interpret.'

Clodagh mulls it over. Is she being advised against selling the house? Handing it over to a developer doesn't count as cherishing it; that much is clear. But she has no choice. Still, maybe she should wait a day or two. Tomorrow might bring a reprieve. A legacy in the post from a long-lost relative would be a head start – that could be the reference to a gift. More cheerful than she has felt in months, Clodagh lifts the kettle. 'How about a pot of tea? You must be thirsty after all that baking.'

The next morning's post brings a clutch of bills Clodagh can't pay. Her shoulders sag; when will the fairytale start working? Everyone knows if you take in a mysterious stranger you'll be rewarded for it. She needs her reward right now. Oh, she's building castles in the air; if she had any sense she'd ring the developer and get it over with. Clodagh decides to wait until after the girls have gone to school.

She waves to the children at the playground gates, and they look so trusting that she cudgels her brains for ways to avoid selling the house. Maybe the fairy godmother needs time to find her feet. Turning her key in the lock, she decides to make an appointment with the bank manager and ask for an extension to her overdraft. She notices a frosty thread in his voice when they speak on the telephone. Still, he'll see her in two hours' time: it appears the bank manager is even more anxious to meet her than she is to meet him. Quailing, Clodagh trails about the house and finds May Lee packing cookies into light card boxes donated from Pearl's art kit. Her nimble fingers have fashioned them into pagodas, and now they are counting in three cookies per box.

'It's not very many. People in these parts like value for money.' Clodagh is dubious.

'My fortune cookies offer something more important than value for money.' May's jasper eyes are expressionless.

She intends to tour the housing estate that is built on paddocks that once belonged to Clodagh's family, selling her wares. Clodagh suspects hardly any of the houses are occupied during the day, with everyone working to pay mortgages. But May seems adamant. The diminutive woman smiles, and although her teeth are yellow and curve inwards, there is a rare sweetness in her expression.

'Right. I'll walk as far as the first house with you; I have an appointment in town.'

The meeting with the bank manager is unpleasant. He warns Clodagh that she can expect no more credit, and suggests – in a tone far removed from suggestion – that she should realise her assets and meet her debts. There is only one asset, as they both know.

'You mean, sell the house?' she asks anyway, murky with misery.

Magisterial, he steeples his fingers and nods.

Back home, Clodagh finds that May has left a single cookie roosting beside the kettle. She breaks it open.

The phoenix always rises from the ashes.

Clodagh is pensive as she turns her feet in the direction of her studio. It's about time she tried making something more adventurous. Passing the back staircase, she sees May's bag dangling from the newel post and notices the carved bone handle again. Of course, it's a phoenix, and it would look magnificent as the template for an occasion-piece necklace. Her work engrosses her until it's time to collect Pearl and Ruby from school.

Clodagh thinks the necklace might be good enough to offer to the hotel for sale in its gift-shop. The same hotel that booted out James, admittedly, but she'll have to overcome her mortification – it secures the highest prices for craftwork. Now all she needs is for the manager to fizz into raptures over her necklace and place an order for a dozen more exactly like it. She does a swift calculation: if she could pull that off she might be able to avoid calling on P.J. Quinlivan. The time frame is tight, but this phoenix necklace is her finest work yet.

The sky has dimmed to twilight before May returns.

'Make me another dragon,' demands Ruby. 'Shane Andrews at school pulled the head off the one you did yesterday.'

'Give May a chance to catch her breath,' scolds Clodagh. 'Sit down. How did the fortune cookies do?'

'I sold one box.' May's legs dangle from the kitchen chair.

Clodagh is surprised. This isn't in the script – people are supposed to be enchanted by the cookies. 'Maybe you'll have better luck on Saturday when more people are at home.'

'One box did not displease me.'

Maybe it's about quality, not quantity. 'What did you get for it?'

'Three cinema tickets. I thought you could take the girls. They told me they never go.'

'We weren't complaining, honest, Mum.' Pearl is defensive. 'I just said you always told us there was no money this month, but you'd see next month.'

Clodagh feels her throat constrict. She knows treats are in short supply for her daughters, but has convinced herself they love the house and are happy to swap living there for seaside holidays and Barbie dolls. 'This Saturday afternoon we'll be first in the queue. It's a date, kittens. Now, homework time.'

Clodagh and May are drinking chrysanthemum tea, which, to Clodagh, tastes no better than the fortune cookies. It's already a week since May's arrival, and there has been no dramatic upgrade in her fortune. Nor in May's. She has made four more trips around the housing estates and sold half a dozen boxes. As for Clodagh, yesterday she trotted off to the hotel gift-shop with her pride and joy nestling inside an elaborate paper boat concocted by May. The phoenix necklace was duly inspected, the manager even conceded that it was unusual, but she declined to stock it. 'Too Eastern.' She touched its tiger's-eye beak. 'We find Celtic lines do best.'

Clodagh bowed to the inevitable and paid a visit to P.J. Quinlivan this morning. He welcomed her with open arms and she was nearly grateful – it has been so long since anyone made her feel wanted. She has racked up too many debts, credit extended long after it made commercial sense, due to her family's association with Barry's Point. Try as she might, Clodagh can foresee no imminent improvement in her fortunes. The house is Quinlivan's as soon as the paperwork goes through.

'What brought you to Ireland?' Clodagh swills the yellow liquid and looks at the woman she already considers a friend. Even if she isn't proving much of a fairy godmother.

'I came to work in a Chinese restaurant owned by my cousin's cousin.'

This sounds too prosaic – it must be a cover story. 'And then?'

'I married him and we had a son.'

Fairy godmothers don't get married, they arrange other people's weddings. Star-crossed lovers and so forth. 'Where are they now?'

'Running the restaurant, of course.' Her face shuts down, its planes realigning, and Clodagh knows from experience that it's futile to ask more.

She wonders about May Lee, all the same. She seems so self-contained, as if she has no past or future and only the present matters. She has never seen her wear anything but the Mao suit, yet one night she studded her hair with ornaments and sang to the girls. Such caterwauling! 'It's Chinese opera and it's thousands of years old,' Pearl informed her, but Clodagh was relieved when the performance ended.

Clodagh accepts she probably can't rely on a fairy-godmother cure, however enigmatic her guest, and thinks instead about where she and the children will go. It would be odd to be living in Barry's Point but not in the house where she has spent her entire life. Should they make a fresh start somewhere new? Does she have the courage for it?

Sensing her distress, May patters to the worktop and lifts a batch of cookies. She presents them with her customary bow.

Surely now some cryptic counsel from the Orient will improve everything. It's not too late, P.J. hasn't paid up yet. Clodagh is perennially hopeful as her hand hovers over the pile.

The stork's long legs lift him out of the water.

No point in asking May to translate that. Clodagh squares her shoulders. Fair enough, it isn't rocket science; it means she has the equipment to cope.

And maybe May Lee could use her help too, instead of the reverse. 'May, selling your cookies door to door isn't the way to make a success of them. Tomorrow I'm packing you off to the supermarket on George's Street. The manager's name is Denis Reynolds; I played with him as a girl. Give him a sample and say I sent you.'

Denis Reynolds agrees to take the entire stock, after some timely advice from his complimentary cookie.

A bridge can be built across the widest river.

He and his wife are debating buying the store, which has just gone on sale, but are nervous of the responsibility. He slips home to discuss it with her again in his lunch-break. 'Nothing ventured, nothing gained,' they decide.

'I was sure they'd sell like hot cakes.' Clodagh is perplexed when Denis tells her the cookie boxes are gathering dust. Her forehead wrinkles: she still can't understand why Barry's Point isn't awash with cookie fever.

'It's disappointing,' Denis admits. 'It was probably a bit impet-uous, snapping up all of them, but now it's down to me to shift them.' He realises he has to be more adventurous about promotions if he's going to own the store. His wife suggested that a pair of cute, pigtailed girls in those high-collared Chinese dresses, offering tasters to customers, would soon move the cookies.

Denis mentions this idea to Clodagh. 'I don't see why not, Pearl and Ruby love dressing up. Just for an hour or so on Saturday – I don't want to be accused of child labour,' she laughs. Imagine laughing when she's about to lose her home, she thinks in the next breath. Life goes on. May should bake that into her cookies.

'I'm not sure where we'll find the dresses, though,' Denis adds.

'If you supply the material, I'll ask May to make them. She's so clever with her hands.'

Pearl and Ruby are enchanted, just as their mother predicted, but May is nowhere to be found. She has vanished, but a pearl-pale and a ruby-red cheongsam are lying on the girls' beds. 'Where's May?' they wail, when they race home from school, but Clodagh has no answer to give them.

'I thought we were friends.' Clodagh swallows another mouthful of chrysanthemum tea, still wincing at the taste, but it reminds her of May Lee. The house resonates with a rattling emptiness in May's absence. Her life seems to be unravelling – no friend, no husband and soon no house. Her wallow is arrested by the sight of a solitary fortune cookie beside her row of cookery books. May Lee hasn't abandoned her after all! The cookie will be her route map to coping.

She breaks it apart, twirls the rice paper between her fingers and inhales, breathing in the essence of this house built by her grandfather six times removed. Tense with expectation, she reads the lavender script. Momentarily she is deflated, then Clodagh feels the ghost of a smile bud on her lips.

People make life worth living, not houses.

The Long Field
Margaret Dolan

The worn-out moon is no more than a milky whorl in the low-slung muslin sky. Dew quivers in mist-curled fields as Noreen drives from Cavan to Dublin airport. Honeysuckle in her nostrils. Imagined? Probably. Hopefully on the way back the sun will have broken through, painting the fields yellow with glossy buttercups.

That summer, the summer of '96, the summer of the big row, the summer she left, the meadow was covered in cowslips and smirking daisies. She, the shy good child. She, who wouldn't say boo to a goose, said it all that day. Every held-back word. Leaving her mother diminished. Her power lines cut like a snipped puppet.

This year is the year of the pure yellow buttercups. She wants to lie down in the dazzling yellow with Billy and make love. There will be nettles, though. Always nettles.

Don't get stung, she tells herself, recalling Billy's face when she mentioned the site.

'Play your cards right and my da will give us a site,' she said to him. Her tongue fluttering with happy talk.

'A site?'

'Yeah, a couple of acres to build a house.'

His brow jerked and scissored and the veins in his forehead pumped in thick ropes.

'Joke!' she laughed, frightened.

His brow smoothed and the pink panic left his face.

Last night she lay poaching fuchsia-pink in the big Victorian bath with claw feet, her legs razored smooth, hair shampooed and conditioned, dreamy bubbles popping on her shoulder, thinking of Billy. He says her hair is like kitten fur. Even wrote a song about it.

Billy is tall and gangly and plays a neat guitar. Massive teeth, like a toothpaste ad.

When Noreen first saw him performing in Sin É, in the East Village, his songs ripped up her heart. She went back again and again, arrowing him with her dark-blue eyes until he sang to her. For her.

They had hung out together for six months before she cleaned out the roaches from his apartment and moved in with him. Soon he'll arrive in Ireland.

It's 6.35 a.m. The plane, flight 524 from New York, has landed. Noreen has positioned herself right opposite the glass doors. Neck at full tilt. Heart whispering the words of his song. Their song.

Only a week earlier she herself stepped through those glass doors. As she waits she remembers her own arrival. Same flight. Same time. Heart jiggling. Wondering what she would find after nine years' absence. Nine years since she'd seen her parents.

She stepped through the glass doors and they were there. Smiling. Welcoming. Her mother, short and square, pearled and powerful, elevated by her high heels, hadn't aged or changed in all that time. Exactly as she was before the row. Even more so. Now having righteousness on her side. Her father, bent on his crooked frame, was looped over a walking-stick. She was full of pity for him and when he gave her an awkward embrace, tears in his tired eyes, love for this quiet man surged through her.

All the way home her mother talked. Her father tried a few

words but his sentences faded out, overtaken by his wife. She spoke to him in a cruel voice. Growling. Blaming him for their near miss when their standing in the community was almost toppled.

'Eight years without insecticides or artificial fertilisers or anything else. Much in demand since the mad-cow scare. I even lecture on organic farming,' her mother said, suffused with her own importance.

She looked Noreen in the face. 'That little business was a misunderstanding. All a silly mistake.'

Noreen looked her straight in the eye and said, 'What about the beast set aside from the herd for our own consumption?'

'That's all in the past,' her mother shrugged brazenly.

'You were dead lucky,' Noreen couldn't resist adding.

There is no one more moral than a converted whore, Noreen thought, but didn't say.

Instead she turned and feasted her eyes on the wild poppies fluttering scarlet on pale-green stalks on the new motorway, knowing if she missed anything her mother said, it would come around again and again.

It is 6.45 a.m. Glass doors glide open. Passengers trickle through. Relatives with sandbanked eyes unwind and come alive with squeals of recognition. Noreen joins in the communal well-being. Her smiles have aimed at the un-met. She wants to hug them. More and more pile out, stuttering with trolleys and bags and bottles. She examines faces surging towards her, looking for Billy. Her eyes lean down the passageway for a preview. A glimpse of Billy's sun-streaked hair.

The surge thins out. Glass doors open and close. Her breathing catches, coming in little darts. No Billy. Her feet set in despair, remain anchored long after the last straggler.

She should have waited, come with him, but she had to suss out the situation at home. Nine years is a long time. She wanted to smooth his path, protect him from her mother. Stop him leaping at her like a friendly puppy or, worse still, drawling, 'I'm just white trash, ma'am.'

Her mother has already quizzed her about his seed and breed.

'He's a musician, day job bussing tables,' Noreen tells her mother.

'What's that when it's at home?'

'Clearing tables in a café.'

A shut-your-trap look from Noreen halted her mother's disgust but not her lip-curling.

'Billy has great potential, brilliant songwriter.'

'Your father had potential, only a few acres but great potential,' she said, pretending to equate the two but not believing it for a minute. Noreen neither; she had seen the lip.

Noreen asks at reception.

The girl, cool, polite, says she can't give information regarding passengers. Not allowed. Suggests he might be in Shannon.

'Shit!' Noreen says, causing the clerk's lips to knit.

She turns to the screen, rolling and stopping, disappearing and reappearing.

A plane from Boston stopping over at Shannon will arrive in Dublin at five past nine. Two hours. Two more hours. She'd like to strangle Billy. She told him to make sure to get the direct flight to Dublin. Now she'll have to ring home. Break the news to her mother.

Listening to the purr of the phone, she visualises her mother, who will, even at this hour, be preparing to be the personification of Ireland-of-the-welcomes, fussing around the scrubbed kitchen, spreading the starched linen tablecloth with bone china, glinting blue and white, for a real Irish breakfast with brown bread and strawberry jam, home-made of course. Bossing her husband into changing his clothes. He muttering he's a working farmer and if the bucko doesn't like cowshit he shouldn't be coming to a farm. But conforming. He always does. Her mother waiting to boast to

115

Billy about their pure rashers and black and white pudding. Their own. Organic. No addictives.

Noreen tries to make her voice light.

'Everything's ready. And your father's anxious to get on with his chores.' Her mother's voice is vexed and as starched as the linen tablecloth. 'But I suppose it can't be helped,' she said in her lecturing tone, implying it very well could.

Noreen imagines her father's ruddy face blazing over a whiter-than-white shirt.

'Let Dad get on with it; Billy knows the score. Raised on a farm,' Noreen barks.

'Of course, of course he does,' her mother says in a soft flurry, placating.

Noreen knows she is trying. She has always been trying. But now she is trying not to be trying and succeeding in being more so.

Noreen puts down the phone before words are said. Inflammatory words, words that cannot be retrieved, like the words that preceded her departure in '96.

Words that took nine years to resolve.

Noreen's mother burst into her bedroom unannounced as she was rolling a joint.

'Drugs, drugs!' She screamed, scandalised. 'I'll give you drugs.'

'That's very civil of you,' Noreen quipped. 'Mine's a tab of E, thanks very much.'

A clout across the face sent her reeling.

'How dare you bring disgrace on this house, make a holy show of us, you, you drug addict.'

'It's only a bit of hash, for God's sake.' Cheek stinging.

'You're a Gallagher. We have a reputation.'

'We do indeed have a reputation: land-grabbers, that's our reputation. Greedy, grabbing Gallaghers.'

'There you go, dragging up that old chestnut again,' her mother said scornfully.

'You don't know what it was like. The whole class called me a greedy, grabbing Gallagher.'

Noreen remembers fingering the present under her desk. It was her last day in primary school. The day after her father had bought the long field. The present was a floaty Indian scarf. Rippling with colours, wrapped in gold and black, it was for her teacher with the cloud of golden hair. Áine had perfume for her and Cliodhna, chocolates. They had bought the presents on a school trip to Dublin. Had them gift-wrapped.

Her teacher was young. Her name was Miss Tobin. She said they could call her Alison. Alison had cornflower-blue eyes and wore a gold chain on her white ankle. Her long hair swished with her long skirt. Noreen emulated her, tossing her hair like her, walking like her. Alison had been everywhere. Seen everything. She told them about exotic places with strange-sounding names. She taught them new words. Words like 'ethereal', 'translucent' and 'ephemeral'. Noreen floated them around her head. The Indian scarf was all those words. Noreen was dying to give it to her. Watch her drape it around her neck.

Before Alison, Noreen's hand had never waved among the hands that flew up with answers. Too shy. Tongue-tied. Alison had encouraged her and she had felt special under her blue gaze and soon her hand fluttered with the rest.

'Acquisitive?' Miss Tobin asked. 'Anyone know the meaning of acquisitive?'

Hands waved and voices chorused, 'Miss, Miss!'

Noreen didn't know.

'Acquisitive, what is acquisitive, Noreen?'

'I don't know, Miss,' she answered in a warm blush.

'Come, come, Noreen, you of all people should know. It's part of what you are.' The soft blue gaze had a hard marble glaze.

Noreen's throat locked.

'Miss, Miss!' someone said.

'Greedy, Miss. It means greedy.'

'Dead right. Another word?'

'Grabbing, Miss.'

'Good. Another?'

'Gallagher. Greedy, grabbing Gallagher,' Seamus Burke shouted.

Everyone laughed. Even Alison. Although she pretended to admonish him.

Noreen couldn't look up. Her stomach was puffing hot with bile. Hot tears moved behind her eyes.

They followed her home, a big gang of them, chanting, 'Greedy-gut, greedy, grabbing Gallagher.' Even Áine and Cliodhna, her best friends.

She lay in the long field in the nettles to purge herself from Gallagher greed. Her arms, legs and face swelled and itched, making her feel like a martyr in exquisite pain.

'You don't understand the effect it had on me. My heart was crushed,' Noreen said.

'Nonsense. Oversensitive. That blow-in wanted the long field for herself. We gave a fair price for it and she wasn't prepared to outbid us. It's ancient history, ten years at least, so don't try to use it as an excuse for your drug-taking, missy. It won't wash.'

Her mother rocked dismissively on her high heels, twiddling her pearls.

'At least I'm only putting myself at risk, if there is any.'

'You are putting us all at risk, sullying our good name.'

The sting on her cheek and her mother's silly high heels made her punch her with the truth.

'What about the stuff you pump into the poor beasts in the fields? Up to their eyeballs in growth promoters. Everyone knows that. You are the drug barons.'

Her mother diminished before her eyes. Noreen couldn't take the words back. They were said. They were true.

She left. No contact for years, then last Christmas she sent a card. A letter at Easter. Her mother replied. Gone organic. No herbicides. An invitation to come home.

She hunkers down with her Walkman waiting for the Boston flight, filtering her loneliness, listening to Billy's songs. His songs liquefy her bones, leaving her in a puddle of passion and sorrow.

As the tape ends she begins to fret. What if he didn't get the flight? What if he was mugged on the way? What if he chickened out? Chickened out! She shouldn't have mentioned the site. What possessed her? She should have been satisfied. He was a great guy, even picked up after her. Swallowed her scrambled eggs, grey and sloppy as poultices, and said they were great. And she had to screw up by mentioning the site.

She wanders through the airport. Time to kill. Fractious kids, yanked out of bed at this ungodly hour, bawl and scream. Mooching through the bookshop, stomach rumbling, attention fragmented, feeling she could easily walk out with magazines or books unpaid for, unaware of her actions till a hand fell on her shoulder. Her legs wave at the thought and she returns magazines to their shelves and slinks into the ladies' to be confronted by her mirror image. A worried, whiney face with a dragged-down mouth.

A nosey smile, which Noreen tried to ignore, collides with her eyes.

'Delayed?' the woman, track-suited in lemon, asks. Little fans of wrinkles twitching at her eyes.

Noreen gives a distracted smile intended to deflect further conversation, but the woman is on a roll.

'*There's a kindred spirit,* I said to myself, *waiting for her man.* Am I right or am I right?'

Noreen nods.

The woman's clothes are coordinated, from the lemon stripe

on her trainers and the cute little matching bobbins on her socks to the band holding her gilded curls. Even her bag is trimmed with lemon.

'I'm Rose,' the woman says, snapping her bag shut.

Noreen grudgingly says her name.

'Coffee?' Rose asks.

Noreen shakes her head. 'Afraid I've only enough money for the car park.'

'My treat,' the woman says, leading Noreen by the arm as if escorting a prisoner.

If she thinks she's getting anything out of me for a coffee and scone she's mistaken, Noreen decides, but as the coffee hurtles through her, she becomes animated in a serious caffeine-induced rush. Her mind is throwing up images of Billy like flashbacks of a film. She wants to tell this fizzy lemon woman all about him but Rose wants to talk about her own man, her Jimmy who is coming back from Rome. A man of distinction. A real big spender, like in the song.

Noreen halts a snigger. Rose looks at her watch.

'I have to go. His plane has landed. He's such a big baby, gets upset if he comes out and I'm not there,' Rose says, laughing.

Noreen watches the woman meeting her man. Tears squeeze over Jimmy's pudgy cheeks as he reclaims his yellow rose. And Noreen feels an ache in her throat.

Fifteen minutes later she is standing in the same spot as Rose. Heart zipping along in a frenzied beat. Again the crowd. The surge. The expected. Again the met and un-met. No Billy. His absence echoing in the lonely squeak of the last trolley.

Neither her mind nor her feet are firmly anywhere. She moves as if through heavy water to the rack of phones and rings their apartment. It rings five times. What if Billy picks it up? What if he's still there? What'll she say?

At the sixth ring the answering machine whirrs on. 'Gone fishin'' croons Billy.

She rings again, listens hard, even hears the metronome

keeping a steady beat. She waits for the beep. 'Pick up, please pick it up if you're there, Billy. Please, Billy.'

She rings around New York. Sleep-laden voices. Words muffled and not knowing scatter like roaches at the flick of a switch. She lets the phone drop. She wants to put it back in its cradle but stands moored, watching it dangle. Her body seems to be plunging in a downward spiral with the hanging phone. People are looking at her. Concerned. Embarrassed. Automatically the dimmer switch goes on in her head and she closes down her reaction. Replaces the phone and moves slowly away. Her mouth sets hard with betrayal. Dumped on her own doorstep, and he hasn't even met her mother. What's more, she'll have to drive to Cavan into her mother's doomed expectations.

And then he is standing there before her, jet-lagged and strip-searched, jerking life into her. She lunges at him, thumping him with murderous relief. He shakes his head and his earrings jangle like wind chimes. And she wilts, folding into him like an origami flower.

Driving down the lush boreen garlanded with fronds of creamy, lacy devil's cheese, Billy says, 'What was that your daddy said about a site?'

Expecting
Emma Donoghue

I thought I saw him last Friday, stooping over the grapefruits in my local supermarket. Without stopping to make sure, I put down my half-full basket beside the carrot shelf and walked out the door marked 'Entrance Only'.

It might not have been him, of course. One round, silver head is pretty much like another. If I'd seen his face, if the strip of mirror over the fruit counter had been angled the right way, I'd have known for sure: soft as a plum, as my mother would have said, if she'd ever met him. But it was probably someone else, because he never shopped on a Friday, and why would he come all this way across town to a perfectly unremarkable new supermarket? Besides, I never told him where I lived.

We only ever met on Saturdays, in the windswept shopping centre I had to go to before the supermarket opened down the road. That first time, I was toying with an angora jumper on the second floor of the department store when I caught his eye. I figure they're safe to smile at if they're over sixty. He moved away with something long and green over his arm; I shifted over and browsed through five kinds of silk dresses before realising I was in the maternity section. Not that it mattered much, of course; anyone can wear any old shape nowadays.

The elderly gentleman held the heavy swing door open for me to go through first. 'Best to take things easy,' he commented, and

122

I smiled, trying to think of something original to do with pasta for dinner. As we emerged into the shopping centre he asked a question that was half drowned out by the clamour of the crowd. I said, 'Mmm,' rather robotic as usual among strangers. Thinking back, later that afternoon, I did remember hearing the word 'expecting', but I presumed he meant rain.

I bumped into him again in the charity furniture shop ten minutes later. Gallant, he insisted on lifting a table for me to look at the price. I only clicked when he said, 'The dress is for my daughter, she's due in July. And yourself?'

I shook my head.

He must have thought I was rebuking his curiosity; his face went pink from the nose out. 'Pardon me.'

'No, no, it's all right,' I flustered.

'Early days yet, then,' he said confidentially.

It suddenly seemed like far too much trouble to explain; we could be standing here all day. Besides, this garrulous stranger would think me a fool, or worse, a wistful spinster-type given to browsing through maternity dresses. So I said nothing, simply grinned like a bashful mum-to-be, as the magazines would say.

It's not the first mistake, but the first cowardice, that gets us into trouble. Why was it so hard to say that I hadn't heard his original question as we came out of the department store? If only I'd said, 'I'm afraid I'm not expecting anything!' making an awkward joke of the old-world euphemism.

And of course when the following Saturday, cup in hand, he edged over to my table in the shopping centre's single faded café, it was impossible to go back to the beginning. He told me all about his daughter's special high-calcium diet. I saw now that clearing up that first misunderstanding would have been child's play compared to this: how could I admit to having lied? I tucked my knees under the table, nodding over the pros and cons of disposable nappies.

He was lonely, that much was clear. I was a Saturday shopper because it was the only day I had free, whereas since his retirement he had developed a taste for the weekend bustle at his local shopping centre. But not a weirdo, I thought, watching him swallow his tea. All he wanted was to chat about this cyclone of excitement that had hit the year his only daughter got pregnant at thirty-three. 'Me too,' I said without thinking. Thirty-three, really? He thought that was a wonderful coincidence. And from amniocentesis we slipped on to living wills and the judicial system, his small mobile face shifting with every turn of conversation.

For a few weeks the office was a bag of cats, and I forgot all about him. Then one Saturday, rushing by with a baguette under my arm, I saw him staring bleakly into the window of what used to be the Christmas Shop. For the first time it was me who said hello. When, after pleasantries about crocus pots, he began telling me about his daughter, and how the hospital said it was nothing she'd done or not done or overstrained or failed to eat, just one of these things that happen in most women's lives, I wished I had followed my first impulse and walked right by. I didn't want to spare the time to sit beside him, making fork-marks in an almond slice.

He fell silent at one point and, as some kind of strange compensation, I began to rhapsodise about my own phantom pregnancy. I'd never felt better; it was true what they said about the sense of blooming. Instead of wincing, his face lit up. He said he would bring me a cutting from last Sunday's paper about pre-natal musical appreciation. I promised him I was drinking lots of milk.

Walking home with a box of groceries on my hip, I began to count weeks. If I had met him just after payday, which was the fifth of the month ... I realised with a spasm of nausea that I should be beginning to show.

At this point the ludicrousness of the whole charade hit home. Since it was clearly impossible to explain to this nice old man that I had been playing such a bizarre, unintentional and (in light of his daughter's miscarriage) tasteless joke, I would just have to make sure I never saw him again.

But I didn't manage to make it to the huge supermarket in the town centre after work any day that week. Come Saturday, I crawled out of bed late and pulled on baggy trousers. His steel-wool head was before me in the queue at the flower stall; when he looked around, I waved. Yes, his daughter was back at work, the daffs were for her, and wasn't a bit of sunshine wonderful? Only when he had walked away did I realise that I had my hand in the small of my back, my belly slumped over my loose waistband.

The next Saturday I did my hand-washing and baked scones with the end of the cheddar, then sat knotted up in an armchair and read some papers I'd brought home from work. My mother dropped by; when I offered her some tea there wasn't any milk or sugar, so I had to justify the empty shelves by claiming not to have felt well enough to go out.

Afterwards I lay on the sofa with the blanket she'd put over me, watching the sky drain. I was heavy with a lie I couldn't begin to explain. If I'd made a joke of it to my mother, she'd probably have called him a nosey parker.

My ribs were stiff; I shifted to face the rough woollen back of the sofa. If it was true, would I be throwing up in the mornings? Would I be feeling angry, or doubtful, or (that old pun) fulfilled? I grinned at myself and went to put on my make-up for a night out dancing.

The following Friday I managed to sneak away from work early enough to shop in town. I had packed my briefcase full of papers, then shoved them back in the in-tray; it was important to have a life.

I spent Saturday hoeing the waking flowerbeds outside my basement flat. Some friends arrived with *Alien* and popcorn. One of them noticed me holding my stomach after a particularly tense scene, and raised a laugh by warning me not to throw up on the sofa.

Truth was, I'd been trying to remember at what point it would start kicking. For a few seconds I'd believed in it.

It was time to call a halt. The next Saturday I trailed up and down the shopping centre for an hour and a half in the spring chill. Every time I went into the library or the pet shop, I was sure he had just left. When the tap on the shoulder did come, as I was reading the list of prices in the window of the hair salon, I jerked so fast he had to apologise. But looking shocked and pinched did suit my story, I supposed.

As we neared the top of the café queue, his bare tray shuffling along behind mine, I rehearsed my opening line: 'I'm afraid I lost the baby.' It sounded absentminded and cruel. I tried it again, moving my lips silently. The beverages lady cocked her ear, thinking she'd missed my order; I cleared my throat and asked for a strong coffee. It was all my fault for having let a tiny lie swell into this monstrosity. I should have cut it out as soon as it was planted.

Before I could begin, he placed his carrier bag on the chair between us. 'I'm glad I caught you today,' he said happily. 'I brought it along last week, but I didn't run into you. I was going to return it but then I thought, *who do I know who'd make good use of it?*'

Under his bashful eyes I drew out the folds of green silk. 'Wouldn't your daughter wear it anyway?' I asked.

He shook his head hastily.

'You shouldn't have,' I said. 'It's beautiful.' I slumped in the plastic seat, my stomach bulging.

He folded the dress back in its tissue paper and slipped it into the bag.

Though I didn't even know his surname, I felt like I was saying goodbye to a lifelong friend, one who had no idea that this was goodbye. I insisted he have a third of my lemon tart. We talked of Montessori schools and wipeable bibs, of our best and worst childhood memories, of how much had stayed the same between his generation and mine but would be different for my baby. We decided it was just as well I was due in August as the weather might be mild enough to nurse in the garden. When I looked at my watch it was half two, the coffee cold in the pot.

As I stood up I had a hysterical impulse to say that if it proved to be a boy I'd name it after him. Instead I mentioned that I was going off on an early summer holiday, but yes of course I'd be home for the birth.

The new regime was a manageable nuisance. On Saturdays now I went straight from karate class to a shopping centre twice as far away in the other direction. An old friend of mine, meeting me laden with bags on the bus, mocked me for being so upwardly mobile, to go that far in pursuit of walnut and ricotta ravioli. One Saturday in May my mother asked me to come along to the old shopping centre, to help her with a sack of peat moss, and I had to invent a sudden blinding headache.

The dress I wore as often as the weather allowed; it seemed the least I could do. The leaf-green silk billowed round my hips as I carried my box of groceries close to the chest. There was room under there for quintuplets, or a gust of summer air. When August came and went and nothing happened, I felt lighter, flatter, relieved.

That was five years ago, but always I keep one eye out for him, even on the streets of other cities where my new job takes me. I have my story all ready: how I shop on Sundays now when my mother can take the children, two boys and a small girl, yes, quite a handful. He's sure to compliment me on having kept my figure. And his daughter, did she try again?

I felt prepared, but last Friday when I thought I saw him among the grapefruit I backed out in panic. What do you say to a ghost, a visitor from another life?

It occurs to me all of a sudden that he may be dead. Men often don't live very long after they retire. I never thought to ask how old he was.

I find it intolerable not to know what has become of him. Is this how he felt, wondering about me? On Saturday when I woke in my cool white bed, I had to fight off the temptation to drive down to the shopping centre and park, watching through the windscreen for him to walk by.

The Ziegfeld Girl
Clare Dowling

Mavis was talking to the food again.

'Four lovely donuts! Oh yes, you'll go down a treat. And a nice plump melon. All the way from Africa, too!'

She patted the melon lovingly as she passed it through the supermarket scanner and smiled at the satisfying *blip*.

Trish Martin had been listening to Mavis's conversations with edibles since half past eight that morning and it was doing her head in. At least there were short periods of blessed quiet; Mavis wasn't half as interested in the washing powders and household detergents and scarcely gave them the time of day.

Trish reached down for another tin of beans, trying not to dislodge the fat brown envelope she had hastily tucked inside the waistband of her blue-and-white overall. Chloe at Customer Services had handed it over an hour ago, very curious. 'This has just come in the post for you, Trish.' But what else could she have done? It wouldn't have fitted through the letterbox at home, and so the doorbell would have been rung, and Noel would have had to come down to take it off the postman, and it would have been poked and prodded and held up to the light, and then put in the middle of the kitchen table, waiting for her to come home and explain it. Which she couldn't. Two hundred and eighty-five euro? Noel would faint.

She reached down covertly and adjusted the envelope, hoping

the CCTV camera was pointing the other way. She hadn't reckoned on the weight of it, or the bulk, and it was beginning to slip. Still, only another five minutes till her break and she could sneak into the toilets and—

'Mrs Martin!'

She bolted upright guiltily, her hand automatically clutching her midriff and the concealed envelope nestling there. The assistant manager bore down on her, flat brown eyes glinting accusingly from behind bottle-bottom glasses.

'Someone told me you were on drugs.'

Trish was quick to set the record straight. 'No, Mr Riordan. Jennifer's on drugs today.'

He looked at her suspiciously before raising his squat frame on steel-tipped shoes and glancing past a couple of shoppers to where Jennifer was listlessly stacking shelves with Anadin, Paracetamol and various cough mixtures.

'I'm on peas and beans,' Trish added.

'Well, I wasn't informed,' he said, peeved at not having caught her out. 'Oh, things will tighten up around here very shortly, Mrs Martin. You can count on that.'

It was difficult to know whether this was a reassurance or a threat. But Chloe – who listened in to all the telephone calls from her desk – said that he was virtually a shoo-in for the top job when the general manager left next week. In a separate telephone call, he had been heard ordering two hundred hairnets, which was very ominous seeing as only ten people worked on the deli.

She waited for him to move on but he didn't budge. Blast! Under his watchful gaze, she was forced to bend and fish another tin of beans from the box. To her horror, the envelope began a downward slide.

'Indigestion, Mrs Martin?'

He was looking at her oddly; her legs were buckled, her back hunched and one hand clamped fiercely around her middle.

'No, no, I'm fine,' she blustered, jamming the tin onto the top shelf too quickly. The effort dislodged the envelope further until it was halfway down her generous thighs and threatening to make an appearance at any second beneath the hem of her overall.

In a desperate stab at damage limitation, she clamped her knees together like a vice and squatted over the box of baked beans.

'Mrs Martin?' Mr Riordan took a step backwards, astonished.

It was too late. Slowly, inexorably, she gave birth to a piece of stationery.

'Well!' said Mr Riordan, looking at the new arrival nestling among the beans.

Trish snatched it up. 'Can I go on my break?'

'I think you'd better,' he said. 'And Mrs Martin? We encourage staff to read their mail at *home*.'

'Yes, Mr Riordan.' Clutching her precious bundle to her chest, she scurried off up the aisle.

All this had started two weeks previously on eBay. Trish had been trawling the memorabilia section looking for a signed Nirvana poster for Gavin's sixteenth birthday – he was obsessed with dead rock stars at the moment and had solemnly told Trish that he himself probably wouldn't live to see thirty. 'Oh, do try, love,' she had ended up coaxing, even though she had quite wanted to tell everybody about Mr Riordan's new rules about staff mobile phones and 'in-store romance', as he called it.

It was unlikely a poster of a dead man would cheer Gavin up, but it was worth a try. Then she had seen it: *Ziegfeld Girl, Red Slippers, Sequinned. Size UK eight and a half.* Imagine a Ziegfeld girl, one of those glorious, glamorous, prancing creatures, having feet that big! Feet exactly the same size as Trish's, Trish who trekked miserably into the foot equivalent of an outsize shop once a year to be kitted out in sensible brown slip-ons and navy flatties. 'I suppose they're OK for work,' Noel said – Mr Practical, Mr Down-to-Earth! Imagine if he found out that she had blown a whole week's wages – recklessly outbidding two others – on a pair of old red dancing shoes that bore the brown marks of someone else's sweat.

She locked herself in the staff toilets during her break, the padded envelope on her knees. Her mouth was slightly dry. She had never bought anything off the internet before and it would be just her luck to be conned. But no: the red shoes spilled out onto her lap, having survived the journey intact. The first thing that struck her was that they were in a need of a good wax. And look, poor things! Patches of sequins were missing in places, and something sticky had attached itself to one heel. Still, nothing that a little care and attention wouldn't fix. When she held them up in her hands the light seemed to shimmy and bounce off them as though they had a life of their own, and would at any moment hop down and tap dance across the toilet floor. These were shoes with a history. Shoes with a *past*.

She thought of their previous owner – Fanny perhaps, or Bessie or Bee. A glorious girl with piled-up curls and swinging hips, kicking her sequinned feet into the air and belting out 'Be My Little Baby Bumble Bee'. Oh, Trish could see her laughing now! Having stuck two fingers up at convention and respectability and social norms, and plumped for fun instead.

A woman with whom the likes of Trish wouldn't in a million years have a thing in common, except big feet.

She wore them only in her bedroom at first, when Noel was downstairs drowsing in front of the TV, and Gavin was in the garage tussling with mortality. Impatiently she would kick off her brown slip-ons – how she had come to despise them – and ease on the red dancing shoes. How she was transformed! Her big, lumpy, square-toed feet immediately became smaller and neater. They twinkled, for heaven's sake. And her ankles took shape, instead of sitting there all dull and dimpled. Her calves suddenly *tapered*. She would sit on the bed and cross and recross her legs like she was a movie star, watching herself all the time in the full-length mirror.

She stopped being embarrassed by this behaviour very quickly, and took to thinking that there really wasn't enough glamour in the world.

But the effect didn't end at her knees. A peculiar kind of lightness would work its way up and spread out all over her. She was giddy; she couldn't sit still. She took to walking to the bathroom and back in them: not with her usual *plod plod*, but with a cheeky, light sashay instead. When she got there, her face would be flushed with the thrill of it all and the danger of being caught by her husband or son, who would think she had gone mad. Then she stopped being embarrassed about that too.

'Trish?' Noel said over his cornflakes one morning, cautious. 'What are those on your feet?'

'What?' Trish said, pretending not to notice.

'Those shoes.'

'These? Oh, yes.' She rinsed a dish, humming.

Gavin slowly raised his chin from his chest to see what the fuss was about. He looked at the shoes, and then turned to meet his father's eyes for the first time in about six months. His eyebrows went up.

'Will we go to Jury's tonight?' Trish said to Noel.

'Jury's?'

'The cabaret.'

'The *cabaret*?' His eyes popped. A night out usually meant two halves in Murphy's pub.

'Why not?' she said, and walked – no, sashayed – out of the room.

Mavis was at the checkout nearest the supermarket door the day she wore them to work. 'Six cans of Coke. Don't drink them at once! Oh, and a couple of lovely soft rolls…' Mavis paused, mid-caress, as the double door swished open and a pair of red glittering shoes walked in.

'Morning, Mavis,' Trish said.

Mavis just gawked. Well, it was hard not to. Chloe on

Customer Services blinked her mascaraed lashes in a double take. The new clock-in machine was at the very far end of the supermarket, at Mr Riordan's instigation, and Trish set off down the personal hygiene aisle towards it. With each step, her heels hit the grey tiled floor with a sharp, attention-seeking ring. The sequins glittered under the fluorescent lights. Shoppers looked up, startled out of their early-morning stupor. Jennifer, adjusting her hairnet, drew in, wary.

'Morning!' Trish said.

She was on pasta and sauces that day. She piled her cart high with spaghetti and penne, and some large seashell shapes, which the bag said were conchiglie. And look at that – a jar of Dolmio had cracked, and tomato sauce oozed across the top shelf. She found a stepladder and a wet cloth, and that was how Mr Riordan found her a few minutes later.

'Mrs Martin?'

She looked down at him. 'Yes?'

Her red shoes were almost on a level with his nose. He kept very still, as though they might spring forward and attack him at any moment. 'Could you come down, please? I'd like a word.'

'Certainly.'

On level ground, she still topped him by at least an inch in her new shoes, and he was forced to surreptitiously raise himself onto his tiptoes to compete.

'Staff are required to wear a uniform at this store,' he said.

'Yes,' she agreed.

'You're not adhering to it.'

'Am I not?'

'Mrs Martin, let's not pussyfoot about things here.' He reddened, and hurried on brusquely, 'Your shoes.'

They both looked down. The shoes twinkled back up at them.

'Yes,' she said. 'Aren't they beautiful?'

'Well, I … Look, the point is that they are not part of the uniform!'

134

'That's very true,' said Trish. 'The supermarket didn't provide them, after all.'

'We certainly didn't,' Mr Riordan said, casting another swift, appalled glance downwards.

Trish said slowly, 'So I'll just go and take them off, if you'll give me whatever shoes you'd like me to wear instead.'

He blinked twice – a trap! He pushed his glasses up his nose, the better to glare at her. 'We don't give staff shoes, Mrs Martin.'

'So in other words I'm free to wear my own?'

'You're free to wear your own *suitable* shoes.'

'Who decides what's suitable and what's not?'

'The general manager!' he sang back (his inauguration cere-mony had taken place the previous week in the staff room, over tea and a packet of damaged mini-rolls from the shelf).

Trish said, 'That's written down, is it? That you inspect and pass shoes?'

His face turned white. 'I don't know. But I will check. Oh yes, Mrs Martin. Rest assured that I will seek clarification on this imm-ediately.'

'I'd appreciate it if you would,' Trish said.

She went back to her pasta. After a moment, he turned and left.

The discovery that it was *not* in fact written down unleashed some kind of madness that week. Maybe the rules had been too stringent for too long. Maybe morale was so low that rebellion was inevitable. Or maybe, like Trish, the staff at ShopSaver simply understood the importance of shoes.

For three wonderful days, Chloe manned Customer Services in a pair of white cowboy boots with tassels at the sides – and just dared those delivery guys to give her any cheek. Jennifer stacked shelves in the most extraordinary platform trainers that made her look like she should be dancing in a music video on MTV – and, indeed, was inordinately pleased when this was suggested to her. Mavis shocked everyone by producing a pair of black, high-heeled

135

strappy sandals, and wore them with fishnet tights. Fishnet tights! Two of the regular old boys started chatting her up, and never had the food got less of her attention. Pumps, mules, stilettos, espadrilles, even a pair of Dr Marten's – Mr Riordan said he had never seen such an appalling assortment of footwear in all his life. It quite ruined the cut of the uniform.

'You'll lose your job,' Noel fretted. His head was still spinning from the salsa class they'd gone to last night. The lads down at Murphy's would fall over if they knew. But he was developing a nice turn of the hip, he had been told.

'Do you think?' Trish said hopefully. Her head was full of dreams. There were training courses in London. She'd looked them up on the internet. You could do flamenco, jive or contemporary – anything under the sun. There were options to go on and get qualifications. There were grants. The very thought of it made her body go into a fluid-like trance.

But she didn't want to leave the girls. Not after starting this whole thing.

'What are these?' Gavin asked, poking at his plate cautiously.

'Stuffed conchiglie.'

'Oh,' he said. He was quite open to new things, these days.

The next morning, there was an emergency staff meeting. Mr Riordan, rocking back and forth on his nasty steel-tipped shoes, announced that there had been a review of procedures at Head Office – in *Bristol*, no less – and it had been decided to issue all staff with 'additional uniform requirements'. New, black, rubber-heeled shoes would arrive within the week.

'Will we go on strike?' Chloe asked. She had assumed great authority in the last week and people expected her to take the lead. She had contradicted Mr Riordan on several things recently and he had become slightly afraid of her.

'I suppose,' said Mavis, whose mind was on her forthcoming date.

'Do you want to, Trish?' Jennifer asked anxiously. 'Because we'll stick by you, you know.'

In the event, the decision made itself. When fifty-nine pairs of black shoes arrived by special delivery a few days later, there wasn't a single pair in size eight and a half.

'Oh, thank God,' Trish said, and danced out.

The House of Pleasure
Rose Doyle

'She saw you coming,' his neighbours said to him afterwards, hindsight making geniuses of even the fools among them. 'She saw you coming and she used you.' They were wrong, of course, altogether wrong. What they didn't see, even with the benefit of twenty-twenty vision, was that he'd been the one to see Marigold coming. A mile off.

He'd been in a bad way at the time, lonely and waiting for death and lacking the heart to do anything about it. But he'd known, the second he laid eyes on Marigold, that she could change things. That she would.

No point explaining any of this to his neighbours. Most of them wouldn't believe him, the rest wouldn't understand.

Marigold's first words, on a wet day in March outside the pub, were inauspicious enough.

'Cold today, isn't it?'

She smiled as she spoke, planting herself next to him and taking cigarettes from the pocket of her thin, white coat. Her hair was a shade of red that frightened the gulls.

'Got a light?' She had a raspy, smoker's voice.

He found his lighter and held it to the cigarette between her polished lips. She was well practised in the way she thanked him with her eyes. He liked that. He'd never had much time for women who pretended to be something they weren't.

He'd seen her get out of her car, also white, nonchalantly dropping the keys into her bag as she scanned the group at the door of the pub. He'd seen her pick him out and head his way.

He'd been flattered, of course. What man wouldn't have been? She was lovely, in her odd way, and if she wasn't all that young, mid-thirties maybe, she was a couple of lifetimes younger than he was. She was pale, and too thin. There were other men in the group outside the pub, smoking cigarettes like he was and looking out over the sea. She could have chosen any one of them to stand beside and have her fag.

She'd chosen him because of his age, he knew that, because he didn't pose a sexual threat. Just another of life's sad realities, but he didn't care. He needed her.

'There's rain in the wind,' he said as her white hand cupped the flame. Her throat stretched like a chicken's when she sucked on the smoke.

'Isn't there always,' she said, and shrugged.

'True,' he said, 'but you hardly came here for the sunshine.'

She smiled at that, and dragged again on the cigarette, looking out over the sea.

'It has other things,' she said. 'It's a long way from anywhere.'

'True,' he said again. It started to rain. The smokers threw down their cigarettes and went back inside. 'I'll buy you a drink,' he said, the words out before he could stop them. She turned, her eyes widened by surprise.

'All right,' she said.

She asked for a beer and sat looking out the window while he went to the counter. He ordered a pint for himself.

'Everything all right, Charlie?' the barman asked. He was looking at the woman in the window, his eyes hard. Her hair and her coat were the only bright things in the room.

'Why wouldn't it be?'

Charlie put the money on the counter. The barman reminded him of a constipated donkey he'd once owned. He'd never noticed the resemblance before.

'You've got company,' the barman said.

'You're right about that,' Charlie said, and took the beer and the pint.

They drank the first drinks in silence. When Marigold would have thanked him and got up to go, Charlie asked her to keep him company for another.

'Is it my sparkling wit you're after' – she was caustic – 'or my body?' She laughed, not unkindly.

'Your company's enough to be going on with,' Charlie said and, when she hesitated, went to the bar and got them two more drinks. She was still there when he got back.

'The barman thinks you're a fool,' she said, 'buying drinks for someone like me.'

'The barman's the fool,' Charlie said.

She opened the white coat and crossed her legs. Her high-heeled boots came to her knees, her skirt covered just a few inches of thigh. The gap between was covered in flesh-coloured tights.

'Are you married?' she said. He could see her instinctively calculating. He didn't mind. He had nothing to lose.

'No,' Charlie said.

'Why not?'

'I was, once, but my wife died giving birth to our child,' Charlie said. 'The child died too and I squandered my chances with women after that. Then I grew old.'

He stopped, liking the way she had of putting her head to one side when she listened, surprised to hear himself talking so much.

'I was a teacher for a while but I wasn't much good at it,' he went on. 'Mostly I worked on the land. I'd an ailing sister to look after for a long time. She's dead now too.'

'What age are you?'

'I'm seventy-five,' Charlie said, and saw her eyes widen again in surprise.

Her eyes would always give her away. They were black velvet with the bruise-coloured half-moons of the non-sleeper underneath. What they told him now was that she'd thought him even older. He couldn't blame her for that. He felt older.

'I don't think,' he said, 'that I was ever a young man. Never joyful in the way I saw others could be.'

'Never a bully and a bastard either …' She was staring out the window again, speaking more to herself than to him. 'Or were you?'

She turned suddenly, fixing the penetrating dark of her eyes on his, the rest of her face a lifeless blank. Everything he needed to know about her was in that look. He shrugged, and smiled.

'Drink up,' he said.

She half drained the glass before she said, 'You live alone now, do you?'

'Alone, yes. You can see my place from here. The last house on the way up the headland. The rain has it obscured a bit at the moment …'

'I can see it. Don't you get lonely out there?'

'I do.'

'Why don't you sell and move on, then? I'll bet there are developers itching to get their claws on a house with views like that …'

'There are.' He cut her short; he didn't want her talking about the developers. 'Plenty of them. I've never lived anywhere else.'

'I've only ever lived in the city but that didn't stop me getting out of it …' She drained her glass. 'I'll buy you a drink.' She was businesslike.

'Why did you leave the city?' Charlie said.

'I got tired of it. You can be lonely in a city too.' She signalled to the barman, who ignored her. 'Bastard's not going to serve me,' she frowned.

'Where do you live now?' Charlie said.

'No fixed abode.' She took a purse from her bag. 'I'm going to nail that shite of a barman. Same again?'

'Let it go,' he said gently. 'Tell me, Miss No-fixed-abode, what brought you to our delightful hamlet?' He smiled.

'I needed a drink. This place was open. Is that a good enough answer for you?'

'It'll do. Where are you headed for?'

She seemed not to be breathing, she had become so still. Charlie had had a child in a class once who used to hold her breath in the same way when she was anxious. She was dead now. Took a deep breath and jumped into the sea one day.

'I don't know ...' Her voice was very small. It got stronger after she gave a half-laugh and said, 'I'm on the road to God knows where. Not for the first time.'

'The house is too big for me.' He turned to the window. It was impossible now to see anything of the headland through the rain. 'My sister is dead six months and the rooms are filled with her echoes. My wife's too. I hear them in the kitchen sniggering together, and rightly so, every time I set about cooking something for myself.' He kept his voice neutral. 'You're welcome to a room, if you need a place to stay. The house is warm and the ocean's beautiful to look at on a fine day.'

'I'll stay the night,' she said, and let out her breath.

They got on well. She moved into his sister's old room, turning the mattress and changing the bedclothes herself, not letting him do it for her. She slept a lot in the beginning, in the day as well as at night. He got used to her being in the house very quickly, to her toiletries in the bathroom, her coffee cups everywhere, her overflowing ashtrays, even to the habit she had of standing, looking at him, when he was reading or writing or listening to the radio.

'You're a loner,' she said once, and he nodded and agreed he wasn't much good in company.

But for the most part, in the beginning, they kept out of each other's way. At the end of a week, by which time she'd brought everything from the car into the house, there was an unspoken agreement between them that she would stay as long as she liked.

After another week she announced that she found the house

dreary and set about brightening it up. She bought curtains in the town and threw cushions about the place. Charlie had to suppose it looked better. She brightened up a lot herself too; there was colour in her face and the jumper and jeans she bought for herself gave her a more substantial look. She watched television and seemed happy enough. But Charlie knew this would be temporary and was prepared. During the third week she offered him rent.

'I've always paid my way,' she said.

'I'm glad of the company.' Charlie waved away the money. She didn't insist.

She came to his bedroom that night. He wasn't asleep and by the light of the high moon filling the room he watched her walk towards the bed. He lay very still when she slipped in beside him. She was wearing something thin and silky and through it he felt the length of her fragile, woman's body against him, her breath on his neck. His regret was a terrible, aching thing.

'Charlie,' she said his name softly, 'I know you're awake, Charlie. This is what you want, Charlie, isn't it?'

When her hand moved across his belly and under the waist of his pyjamas Charlie sighed a slow sigh that was full of wasted years. He took her moving hand in his and held it quiet.

'Go back to your bed, Marigold,' he said, and let her hand go.

She lay still for a minute and then brushed the tears from his face. 'Don't cry, Charlie,' she said, 'please don't cry.'

He let her hold him then, for a short while, and let himself feel what he recognised as joy in her closeness, in her arms around him. When she felt for him again it was from the depths of the loneliness in both of them. This time he didn't stop her.

After she had excited him, expert and quick with her fingers and tongue, she lay carefully on top of him. She supported herself with her arms, careful not to put too great a weight on his old bones, and directed his awakened penis inside her. Her eyes were closed and she still wore the thin, silky garment.

They rocked together for a minute or two and, just before it ended, he thought he saw a silver, moonlit tear roll down her face. When it was over he moved her gently off and away from him.

'Go back to your bed, Marigold,' he said again, kindly.

She kissed him on the forehead and left.

They never talked about what had happened in the night. He didn't care to and she knew this. They understood each other very well. But things between them had changed. He'd lost the high ground, given her control. Whatever happened from now on would have nothing to do with him. He could hardly wait.

Marigold continued to treat him very kindly, even doting on him a little at times. But she didn't consult or ask permission when she got down to setting up business. She did give him a week's notice of the arrival of her associate, Della, however.

Della was a blond-haired woman, pretty enough and younger than Marigold. She had a mobile phone she never stopped using and music she never stopped playing. Charlie thought at first that she would put him out of his bedroom, she took such a fancy to the view. But Marigold intervened firmly and Della, for her trouble, got the smallest bedroom in the house.

'Della and me have a few friends calling tonight,' Marigold told him, in her kind way, a couple of days later when everything was ready. 'Do you need anything taken up to you in your room before they arrive?' Her smile was complicit.

'I have everything I want already,' he said, kindly too, in the way of loving friends with one another. 'I have my books and the radio. What time should I take myself out of the way?'

It was to her credit that she winced at his bluntness. 'Oh, Charlie …' She took a breath and looked away from him. 'It'll only be for a while. Until I get back on my feet.' She turned and smiled at him. 'It's just business, Charlie. A job like any other.'

This was not true but he let it go. 'What time?' he said.

The house, overnight, became a brothel. Men came and went, not every night but for five and sometimes even six out of the seven. They seemed to Charlie to be business types for the most part, though he made sure never to actually come face to face with any of them. He had no idea where they came from, nor how Marigold spread word of her business. He didn't ask. Things got noisy in the night, sometimes, but he wasn't much of a sleeper anyway. He simply tuned in to a music programme and went on reading. The men were always gone in the morning and none of them ever came in the day. Marigold's days were for him.

Della, obligingly, stayed in her bed but Marigold was up every morning by ten, no matter how late her night, and was good-humoured company the day long. They walked together, sometimes, and talked a great deal; about her childhood in a city and his on the headland. They didn't talk at all about their adult lives. Charlie forgot what it was like to be lonely.

But his neighbours, who had pitied him when Marigold first moved in, were beset now with moral outrage. He was being used by an evil woman who'd seen his loneliness and taken advantage. It was disgusting, at his age, but because he was an old man, and lonely, and they were, after all, a Christian community, they had been inclined to let him at it.

Now he'd become every bit as debauched and sinful as his whore, allowing in another like her, helping them both bring pimps and criminals, as well as God alone knew what diseases, into the parish. He'd clearly gone mad and would have to be saved from himself.

Meetings were held and Marigold spoken to.

'I won't let them destroy you, Charlie,' she said as she packed her belongings, which included Della, into the white car, 'and I won't let them destroy me. Hypocritical shites.' She slammed the lid of the boot. 'My time's up here anyway.'

'It is,' Charlie agreed. She'd done what he'd wanted her to do. She'd changed things.

When he shook her hand she kissed him on the forehead.

'Sell the fucking place,' she said. 'You don't have to stay here.'

'I know that,' he said.

'See you sometime,' she said.

'You never know,' Charlie smiled.

He had closed the front door before the car disappeared around the bend in the road. There were no echoes in the rooms now, no echoes anywhere. The house was altogether different. There was life in it.

Catherine Dunne
The Four Marys

It wasn't signed in blood, or anything. Not really. When the wine bottle fell, rolling and staining its way across the beige rug, Claire said it must be a sign: we should make a pact. She said it breathily, like a revelation; her eyes were huge, red hair like a startled halo around her small face. We nodded. We were at that intense, hazy stage of the evening. Maura did her usual housewife stuff, pouring salt onto the wine lake, which had acquired the contours of a slightly tipsy Australia. Maggie smoked thoughtfully, long red fingernails gleaming. She smoked a lot in those days, said it kept her weight down.

And so our monthly meetings were born, nights that have a certain mature predictability after twenty-one years. Maggie christened us 'the Four Marys', grey eyes lighting up with mischief when she thought of it. Maura was mystified by our shrieks of delight. Even kindly Claire laughed at her. She said afterwards that Maura was the only one of us who had never read *Bunty*. I replied that she was the only one of us born old.

Tonight, we settle ourselves around the table in Claire's house, anticipating dinner, wine and gossip. Hers is the most restful of the four houses: she is not married, doesn't share her space with spouse and messy progeny. Years ago, she'd entertain us with tales of the latest man in her life. She doesn't bother now – and we don't ask.

There was some unpleasantness a long time back with Maggie's husband, Ray. In the nature of these things, Maggie blamed Claire, and Ray blamed Claire, and Claire protested innocence before finally blaming herself. Maura was silent and disapproving for six months – as if it had anything to do with her. I said nothing. Tonight, Claire pours the wine, Maggie tosses the salad and Maura checks the progress of the lasagne. That always annoys me: the way she takes ownership of other people's houses.

It was Maura, too, who was doubtful at first about our having such *organised* meetings. She was the first to get married, and she always took Frank into account before agreeing to anything. The night of the pact, I could see that she was far more concerned about the state of her rug than the state of her friendships. She scrubbed and mopped vigorously, using up a full roll of kitchen towel. She kept glancing nervously towards the door in case we had disturbed her sleeping husband. Maggie caught my eye, raised one finely arched eyebrow and grinned wickedly. I smiled back, impatient even then at the safe, predictable contours of Maura's life. I hope she came to realise that something was bound to rock her boat, eventually.

Over the years, we've watched each other's sons and daughters grow up. Claire has always been a wonderful surrogate auntie. I've often wondered whether she regrets not having had children. Sometimes, I regret never asking. Perhaps she doesn't – perhaps all of our children are enough for her, or else they've put her off for life. For my part, I've always envied Maura and the uncomplicated maleness of her three sons. My two daughters drive me to despair: closed, sullen creatures with their eyebrows, noses, chins, tongues all pierced like pincushions. Navels glinting metallically midway between the quarter-yard of fabric described as a *top* and the half-yard below, stretching towards mid-thigh. My husband, Pete, often gloated that Lycra was twentieth-century man's most delightful invention – until he saw Carla wearing it. 'You're not going out looking like that!' Our younger daughter simply turned away, raising her eyes and her middle finger when she thought he wasn't looking.

Pete doesn't know, because he is never here, that this is still a Friday-night ritual. 'Ah, Mum,' and the front door slams. It's the same in Maggie's – the ah-Mum slam, followed by the slight trembling of cutlery and glassware on the table, the shivering of china in cabinets. I often wonder about the state of foundations laid in the seventies. If one snotty teenager can rock them, what does that say about durability, safety, solidity, now that all the debts are paid off?

Anyway, last year I ended up hosting our Hallowe'en dinner. It was a time of year that always made me feel a bit shivery. I didn't like sending my friends out into the darkness, with so many holy souls wandering around. I went to a lot of trouble that night, made a really special meal to celebrate our anniversary: exactly twenty years as the Four Marys. The other three knew that cooking was never my strong point. Especially Maggie. She'd often help me cheat, arriving at my house long before Maura and Claire, with some already prepared main course. But last year I insisted. I wanted to do it by myself, the others were to bring only wine.

Pete was fuming that I was hostess so close to a bank holiday weekend. That made me dig my heels in further. I figured that a whole eighteen years of fitting in around his plans was quite enough. He left in a temper that afternoon, car door slamming. When the doorbell rang a few minutes later, I assumed he'd forgotten his keys. Instead, standing in the porch with a huge cardboard box was Paul, Maura's eldest son. I glared at him, already guessing what the box contained.

'Can I put this down?'

I watched him struggle. Such a long body. Dark-blue sweatshirt, jeans that went against the current trend of widely flapping legs. Nice, neat fit. He dumped the box on the kitchen floor and, in my angry silence, began putting things onto the table. His hands looked competent, pale in the fluorescent light. He kept his back to me, lifting and unwrapping. A grinning pumpkin, candle ready to be lit. A crystal bowl of winter compote. Individual ramekins of colour-coordinated nuts and sweets. I couldn't help myself, I burst into tears. Maura could never trust me. She always refused to believe that I could surprise her.

Tonight, Maura brought her home-made petits fours to Claire's. Maggie grins, hands me a large glass of wine. In spite of myself, I start to smile. Maggie makes a face behind Maura's back. Claire is, as ever, gracious. I'm glad it's not my house. But the other three are suddenly in great talking-form and my silence is not commented upon. There has always been a tacit agreement that everyone is entitled to an occasional off-night. More than one brings forth the solicitous phone calls, the sympathetic ear, the unannounced dropping-in for coffee.

Although we aim for full attendance, as Maggie calls it, three still go ahead on occasion if it can't be helped. This has led in the past to a certain wariness on the part of the missing guest. I'd love to say that we respect the absent one, that we don't talk behind her back, but I'm afraid I'd be lying. That's why I've always tried to make every meeting, up to now. I've missed fewer than anyone. I used to be afraid of what they might say about me, their criticisms lingering in the air, ready for me to pick up on the next occasion. We've always talked, all of us, behind one another's back.

My Hallowe'en dinner was really the beginning of the end.

I couldn't help but feel keenly Maura's insult to my party-making skills. Poor Paul was mortified at my outburst, and handed me a none-too-clean hanky to dry my eyes. I made him promise to say nothing to his mother, already embarrassed by my tears. Still, the whole thing stung. I couldn't let it go.

Maggie was distracted that night too, great dark rings under her eyes, falling asleep straight after the starter. She sometimes did this, she wasn't a good sleeper, but, on that occasion, natural insomnia had little to do with it. Ray was in phase two of his mid-life crisis: apparently he'd just acquired a two-seater sports car and a secretary. To be honest, I think Maggie was more angry about the new car than the new woman. We all made sympathetic noises anyway, even Claire. Maura was highly indignant on Maggie's behalf. But, frankly, we were all rather tired of Ray.

I knew Maggie had been nursing hopes of a weekend cottage in the country, now that her career was soaring and the kids had flown. But I also understood that Ray was not a man for the charms of village life or the peace of a deckchair on Sunday afternoons. That evening, Maggie wept and Claire left early. Maura went on and on about 'my Frank' and his solid devotion to family values. I wanted the night to end.

Watching Maura on that occasion made me feel suddenly terrified: was this how we were all destined to end up? In a squeaky-clean home like hers, filled with the smug smell of home baking, watching as the universe narrowed to a slipper of sky outside the window? I made sure I kept Maggie's wine glass full for the rest of the evening. She stayed overnight in Carla's room and we chatted into the small hours, once we got rid of Maura.

Maggie and I were sipping tea at the kitchen table the following morning when Paul called again to collect his mother's dishes. He made us laugh with his wry observations about both his parents. As he was leaving, his shy, hesitant concern for my feelings touched me. I laughed it off, assured him I was fine. Maggie marvelled at how two dry old sticks like Frank and Maura had managed to produce such an attractive and witty young man. I agreed.

Before we finish up in Claire's tonight, we have to scribble down the date of the next meeting. It's my turn, but it doesn't matter any more. I sit quietly, afraid that any movement, any unguarded comment of mine will give everything away. I feel something suspiciously like a lump in my throat as I look around the table at the three women, warts and all, who have kept me company for over twenty years. I wonder at how everything has changed.

I reflect now that the past twelve months have been more eventful than any I can remember. Maggie has gone ahead and bought her cottage, without Ray. She still works in Dublin, Monday to Friday, but we all know that real life now happens in Leitrim at the weekends. Pete and I have really nothing left to say to each other. He was absent for so much of my life that I simply ceased to miss him. It happened so gradually, so long ago that I don't know any more what it was like to be close to him, to feel part of him.

The only thing we fight about these days is what he sees as Paul's inappropriate presence in our house: Carla is much too young for him; even Paula, at seventeen, is too young for him. Whenever he's home, Pete becomes overzealous in protecting his daughters. 'My girls.' As a result, they lie to him, sneaking out when he's dozing in the chair, changing into their party clothes and make-up in their friends' houses. They're hardly ever here now.

Maura has got herself a part-time job. In some obscure way, that makes me feel better. I don't feel so *responsible*. Paul says that I shouldn't anyway – he's a grown man, makes his own choices whom to love.

I suppose it is fitting in a way that they'll all find out together next month, at my empty house. I wonder what Maggie's reaction will be. Will she think– *Good for her – she deserves to be happy*? And will Claire, perhaps, be more shocked than anyone? Running off with someone else's husband is one thing, but their twenty-year-old son!

And Maura?

Mop your way out of this one.

Teatro La Fenice
Christine Dwyer Hickey

We walk together, Clare and I, across the lawn that leads down to the riverbank and down the smooth stone steps that will take us there. We pass Mr Fleming who keeps the grass laundered, drawing green stripes, light and dark, with the machine that goes before him. Behind him the house is tall and red with forty-two windows in all, each one just like the others. Except, of course, for the window in the turret, which curves slightly towards the gable.

When we reach the steps we stop for a moment, Clare organising her hand in mine. Then slowly we take them one at a time, one foot leading, the other joining and a little rest in between each stride. Clare tells me this is because I am nervous.

The grass is tougher here on the riverbank, not so nice to the touch, and Clare lays out a Foxford rug on our usual spot so we can be more comfortable. She guides me down to sit on one corner of the rug, moving my legs so that my knees face the centre. Then she sits herself down, on the opposite corner, in the same manner, her knees facing mine. And that's how we are, Clare and I, two old biddies really. That's how you find us. Like a brace of china dogs on either end of a mantelpiece.

Clare's fingers begin to move, slowly clawing the back off an orange. When it is naked she hands it to me and I hold its body loosely on my palm. I wait for her to encourage me to eat it and I

153

am listening to the noise the orange makes as I roll it in my hand when Clare begins to speak.

'I suppose they were good enough to invite me. But at the same time … they've a lovely garden, though. Such a nice garden. And a patio, if you don't mind.'

'A patio! Imagine.'

'Yes, a patio. For cooking sausages outside. In the summer, like. Though why? By the time they cook – would it not be quicker to fry them on a proper cooker, then bring them outside? Giving herself work. It's called a bee-bee-queue, you know.'

'Imagine.'

'It's a lovely garden all the same. Though do you know? – not a flower in it. And I mean to say, what's a garden without flowers? I always insisted on looking after the flowers in our garden. "No, Jack," I'd say, "let the gardener see to the orchard and the lawn, but the flowers are mine." Jack used be livid.'

'Livid?'

'He liked me to look after my hands, you see.'

She stretches out her fingers.

'And there's my daughter-in-law with not a flower.'

'Not a flower?'

'Ah, daisies, sometimes, for a while. But she cuts them. You know, with an electric lawn mower.'

'Cuts them?'

'Yes, you have to plug it in.'

'In the garden?'

'Ah, no. In the house. Then you have a big lead that you bring outside.'

'Now.'

Clare continues on about the garden. She only stops to dab juice away from my chin, or to pull a cardigan that is already there across my shoulders. She is always fussing but it rarely bothers me. And she doesn't demand much. Except my company and the odd little word or question just to show I'm minding her.

And you'd have to be minding what Clare says. That memory – where she puts it all!

I can't recall things on demand. What day did I come here? Who brought me? Was it fish or stew for dinner yesterday? Was it dinner or lunch? Was it yesterday at all?

I can't remember those details. I only see things in a block, one picture at a time. What comes before or what happens after – well, I'm just not in charge.

The river twitches. The river comes all the way from the city, Clare once told me. In the city it's big and wide. By the time it gets to us it has shrunk, small and narrow. On the other side of the river there is a thick, tall wall.

'That's the park over there,' Clare says, 'the Phoenix Park. That's where we're not allowed go.'

'I know that.'

'Oh. I thought, the way you were staring up at it, that you might have forgotten.'

'Ah, no, Clare, I didn't.'

There are times when I want to say more but I don't want to risk it. How can I say, for instance, 'Yes, I was the same about my own garden, my own flowers,' when I can't be sure? And she'd be bound to trip me up. Bound to ask me name, rank and number of every last flower. No. I'd never be able for it. And she's happier with things as they are. I like her being happy too. We're great pals, Clare and I, great pals. Everyone says so.

'Besides,' she continues, 'they don't even have a fry of a Sunday morning. Not a sausage. And I do love a rasher of a Sunday morning, a bit of puddin' too.'

'Ah, Sunday.'

'I could never face the golf course until I'd a rasher inside me. That's the worst about going continental, I always say. The breakfast. No rashers.'

155

'Is that right?'

'And then there's Mass. I know full well they never go except when I'm there. And, well, to tell you the truth, I'm not that keen any more. All those strangers trying to shake your hand.'

'Strangers?'

'I'd just as soon walk in the garden, talk to God in my own way, there amongst the flowers.'

'Except there aren't any.'

'What?'

'Flowers. There aren't any flowers.'

'Oh, yes, except for that.'

Now, there you are, for example. I'd like to say something at this point. Not about God or strangers. Not so much about the rashers either. But, well, going continental. Clare is always telling me what it's like going continental. And for all I know, I might know just as much about it as she does. I see this picture of myself so often. Well, my hands, really. Younger than now, of course, but the same ring is on the same finger and that's how I know it's me. And every time I look down on this part of the river or every time I look up at the big old stone wall of the Phoenix Park, I see it. This picture.

What I mean is, this hand (that belongs to me) is holding another hand (that doesn't belong to me). It's a hand with wider fingers and a lick of hair just under the knuckles. Yes, a man's hand. No doubt about it. And we are walking through streets, so narrow that the hands have to split and my hand creeps up and crawls around his arm instead. We cross this bridge, a baby bridge, so small. And I can hear the sound of the water slapping and slurping off stone. Then we come out into this big square and the steps on the opposite side grow bigger as we approach them. We climb, then enter a marble hall. There are voices speaking foreign all around our heads. More stairs now, but different this time, red as lipstick and polished at the sides. My hand (the one with the ring on) slides upwards and the man's hand follows it. And then. Oh, then, the magnificence! The beauty! The beautiful magnificence! We sit on the edge of a tier halfway to the ceiling. Below us an orchestra hums and haws in preparation. Above us angels. Angels fat as pigeons, skirting the ceiling of blue and gold. And a thousand lights winking out of chandeliers. And I feel like – like a currant in a wedding cake! A great big blue-and-gold wedding cake.

But how can I say that to Clare? How can I tell her that my hand is happy somewhere that might be foreign and that I feel like a currant in a cake?

Oh, that would be lovely all right for her to take back to Matron. Why, in no time at all it would be the geriatric unit for me.

'And supposing,' Clare says now, 'supposing the weather's bad? I'll be stuck indoors watching telly. They don't even go out of a Saturday afternoon. Would you believe it? And I used to love it so. A bit of shopping and then a stop off at Thompson's or the Green Door, maybe, for tea. Oh yes, the Green Door was *the* place. Best hat and gloves for the Green Door. Nothing less would do, you know.'

She turns slowly and stares into my face. 'Besides,' she goes, 'what will you do? All weekend. All on your own. Friday, Saturday and Sunday – you know it's a long old time.'

'Oh, me? I'll be as right as a raindrop!'

People say I'd be lost without Clare. But I wouldn't be lost, how could I? There's nowhere to get lost except the Phoenix Park and I'd never be able to find my way there. You'd have to go out the front, through the main gate. Then through the little housing estate that leads to the main road and the West County Hotel. You'd have to turn left then and walk all the way down to the village. You'd have to cross the bridge and find the sneaky little turnstile gate in the wall beside the cottages, you'd have to get yourself through the turnstile and then go left up a steep path with trees on one side, the wall on the other, steeper and steeper until you can see the river from the far side and you can see across it, to the house, the turret, the riverbank and the Foxford rug with only Clare on it. Clare and the orange. I wouldn't have a clue how to go about it.

I couldn't get lost here in the house. There are no more than three or four routes to be considered and there's always someone you can follow. No, not once in all the time I've been here have I forgotten. Not once. Except for … But that doesn't really count, because that time I did it on purpose. But, well, Matron got so cross, I had to let her think it was an accident. But I was just curious, that's all. That's why I followed her.

I wanted to see what was behind the door that needs the two keys. It's a green door too, but not Clare's green door. And do you know what was behind it? Not gloves or hats, nor pots of silver tea. But Purgatory. That's what.

The name came into my head the minute I set eyes on it. 'Purgatory!' I said it out loud and that's how she found me. Nobody belonging to this world or the next. The people inside all crying and moaning and trying to rock themselves back to this life or on to the next one. And ahh, the smell!

Clare says they're all in there on account of having eaten the aluminium off the bottom of the pans. Well, I ask you! They must have been mad in the first place. Luckily for Clare she never had aluminium in her house, only copper. Only copper would do.

Anyway Matron dragged my arm back into the main room and I followed it, and sitting back down in my place I made myself a promise. That I was never going to end up behind that door. Behind that door in Purgatory. And how was I going to do that? By keeping my mouth shut as much as possible, only saying what I had to say.

And was I glad to be back in our own main room! Our lovely own main room. They call it the Chinese Room, you know, because of the designs hand-painted on the wall.

A very important man used to live in this house. Just him and his family. He was the man who sold Parnell up the river. That's how important he was.

This was his Chinese Room. It is a large room, each foot of space taken up by a chair and on each chair a ginny-jo, who nods away the time between meals.

'What a beautiful room,' people from the outside always say, looking around it, up and down, as though they'll be asked to recite every inch of it before being allowed go home.

And silence, always silence. Here only the radio speaks. Except, of course, for when the doctor comes. Then it's a different matter. As soon as he walks through that door it starts. Like lepers in the desert as he passes, their chorus reaching out to him: the sore this, pain in me that, and not a bit well today, whatever is the matter with me at all …

Then, as he goes out through the door again, silence like a bird flies in over his head and flits from chair to chair. Until all is quiet again. And the heads are bent again, murmuring *pishpishpish* to the bells of the Angelus that call out from a radio on top of the long-locked piano. Clare used to have a piano in her house too, same colour, only bigger.

Clare is particularly animated today and I know there will be few moments of peace. She's been on about this weekend for such a long time. But of course that's the thing: I can't be sure how long exactly. I seem to remember her speaking of it when the river was green. And it's grey today. I also feel I've heard it when I was wearing my blue tweed and, yes! that red skirt like the colour of the rug she is now tucking around my legs. Definitely red. Perhaps that was a different weekend.

'You see, the thing is,' she says, 'if I say yes, then Gerard will have to drive all the way up from Cork to collect me. And he's so busy, 'twouldn't be fair. Though he has a beautiful car, I must say. Twenty thousand, it cost him. Twenty!'

'Now. Imagine.'

'Sure, I don't think my own house cost that when we bought it.'

'It must be very big.'

'Oh, yes, even the boot is—'

'No, your house.'

'Oh, yes. My house.'

She says nothing now for a while. I can hear the river whisper and mumble all sorts of secrets and Mr Fleming's machine wheezing back to it. And it's all so very pleasant.

'He has a phone, too, in his car,' she starts again. 'He speaks into it while he's driving along.'

'Has he?'

'Oh, yes, they have several, you know. All over the house.'

'And in the car, did you say?'

'In the car. A real one. A real telephone.'

'Plugged in at the house?'

'Ah, not at all. These things have their own way of working.'

Now what I think is this: if he has so many phones, why doesn't he ever ring Clare?

Even I get the odd phone call from – well, I don't quite know who. Not that I really want it, having to cross over to the phone with all the staff grinning at me and making boyfriend jokes.

The next time he phones up I know what I'll say. I'll say, 'Would you like to speak to Clare? She loves an old chat.' Yes, that's what I'll do.

Clare stands up and I know it's time for her foot-dip. Clare thinks there's nothing like river water for chilblains and corns. But we must never tell anyone about it. First she walks to the end of the bank, to the little ornamental bridge put in by the very important man who used to live here. Then she climbs down to the little ledge under the bridge and sits herself down and dips her feet in.

The water curls around her legs and cuffs her ankles. Sometimes it tickles her and you can hear her laughing.

Clare is getting herself ready now. And off they come, rolling down her legs in little creases and turning them from brown nylon sticks to purple poles. She's let the pants slip down as well by accident, and I thank God Mr Fleming can't see this far, her bare bottom, like two pork chops. And I notice too that her pants are soiled. Oh, only slightly, but enough to cause shame. And I could easily do it too. Like she did to me. Tell, I mean. Say, 'Clare is not wiping herself properly.' After all, who told on me when I had that little accident with the sheets?

She stands before me now, pulling her skirt down carefully over her knees. 'No,' she says, 'I've decided. I'm not going. No, no. That's it. I've made my mind up.'

'Your mind?'

'Yes. At the end of the day I just couldn't have it on my conscience leaving you all alone all that time. Well, supposing you were to have another accident? Who'd cover up for you?'

She flops the hands Jack liked her to look after backwards and draws her cardigan like a shawl over her head. Old Granny Grey.

'Gerard will be furious. And it's not as if I'm not disappointed myself.'

'But your granny flat!' I say, delighted with myself for having remembered. 'What about your granny flat?'

Well! You'd think I was after saying something terrible. You'd think I was after insulting the living daylights out of her.

'I thought I told you never to mention that to me? What sort are you, mentioning that to me? What sort of a,' – and she steps forward then and gives me such a puck in the arm that I nearly fall over – '*bitch*!'

And what did I say? What was it again? Granny flat. But I thought she'd like to see the granny flat they built her. Wasn't that why she sold her own house in the first place?

Clare walks away from me, her funny long feet leaving photos of themselves in the muck near the edge of the river. Soon she is there at the end of the bank. She steps down into the water but she doesn't sit down on the ledge. She stays standing, her back to me, her face towards the distant wall of the Phoenix Park.

Can she see pictures too? I wonder. A big piano; copper pots, the flowers that made her husband cross, the granny flat with no granny in it?

I would love to ask her. But I'm afraid her answer will tell me that the wall is only a wall. A big stone high wall around a park we're not allowed into.

The Cycle

Laura Froom

The pain began almost as soon as she boarded the train. Usually, she planned these things so well. How could she not, after all these years? Today, though, had just been one of those bloody awful days, when nothing went according to plan. She had intended to get the five o'clock train, which would have seen her safely tucked up at home with the doors closed and a whole weekend of privacy and quiet to get over the curse. Instead, a crisis in the office meant that Dominic, her boss, had been forced to call an emergency meeting. Two days before a deadline, one of the agency's most important clients had decided that elements of the new ad campaign were 'inappropriate' and needed to be re-examined. That meant a brainstorming session which lasted until after seven, the beautiful autumn day outside slowly descending into shadows by the time she left.

She could feel it approaching, even as she left the building and headed for the station: a sense of unease, of dislocation, and a tenderness to her belly and her breasts. Her already short temper contracted still further, so that she almost bit off the head of the lazy clerk behind the ticket counter, the idiot apparently more concerned with picking his lottery numbers than ensuring that she made her train, the closing of unseen doors already signalling its imminent departure. She was forced to sprint to make it, and that had not helped matters at all. Running, fretting and snapping at morons seemed only to accelerate the cycle.

She took a seat in the next-to-last carriage. The toilet was in the last carriage, right at the end, but the lights in that carriage were malfunctioning, flickering off and on with an angry buzzing sound, as though masses of bees were trapped within the fluorescent bulbs, so she had been forced to sit a little further forward than she would have liked. Still, perhaps it would be all right. It hadn't started yet, although it was close. The train crawled slowly from the station. Her fellow passengers read books and newspapers, or talked nonsense loudly on their mobile phones, their lack of consideration annoying her still further but providing a momentary distraction, an outlet for her frustration. She had a phone herself, of course, but she kept it switched off on trains and buses unless it was absolutely essential to leave it active, and even then she left it on vibrate and would step out of the carriage to answer it. She was very conscious of her privacy, and it constantly amazed her that people were prepared to discuss, at high volume, the most intimate details of their lives among strangers. Her father and mother would sooner have died than engage in a conversation upon which others might eavesdrop. In fact, her parents had rarely discussed anything of consequence on the telephone. They were resolutely old-fashioned in that sense. If something was important, then it was worth discussing face to face. Their telephone conversations, except in exceptional cases like bereavement or illness, rarely lasted for longer than a minute or two. Their daughter had learned from them the importance of discretion in certain matters.

The raised voices were nagging at her hearing. Her senses always seemed to be more acute at this time of the month, so that even moderately loud noises became difficult to tolerate, and she was more aware than usual of distinctive smells and tastes. She wondered if others experienced it the same way she did. She could only assume that she was not unique in these sensations, although she was not the kind of person who could discuss such matters with another, even if she were not so solitary by nature.

Towns flashed by. They were making good time. She allowed

herself a little sigh of relief, and breathed in deeply. As she did so, something rippled inside her. She grimaced, and shifted on her seat. *Hell.* The train slowed, disgorging passengers at another station. Others rarely got on to replace them at these provincial towns, and she was used to spending most of her journeys in empty carriages, especially as her destination was the last stop on the line, her house a mere stone's throw from the station. It allowed her to sleep a little later than most in the mornings, and made the trip home a little easier to bear.

She closed her eyes. Sometimes she felt lonely, living in the little village where every face was familiar to her, where every name was echoed dozens of times in the form of cousins, brothers, uncles, grandparents. Her parents had always kept themselves slightly aloof from the life of the community on the principle that good fences made good neighbours, and she was grateful to them for that. The round of meetings, charity drives, garden parties and festivals was not for her, but her desire to remain at one remove had given her a reputation around the village, particularly since she also chose to politely deflect the attentions of its menfolk.

She had no intention of ever dating a man from the village, of permitting him access to the little secrets of her life. She knew these men too well, and was not anxious to become one of their conquests. She had enjoyed some relationships in the city, but none that lasted. She liked men who were prepared to let her keep her distance when she chose, who wanted their own space as much as she wanted hers, but such men were harder to find than one might think. The demands that she made led her to attract those who were merely seeking casual one-night flings, or those who claimed that they appreciated her desire for independence even though, as time went on, they inevitably grew more and more uncomfortable with it, and tried to impose their own rules on her. She had quickly learned that when a man said he valued a woman's independence, what it really meant was that he valued his own, and would only indulge her desire for independence when it suited him to do so.

Another station passed, bringing her another mile nearer to home. The gnawing pain was stronger now, and she had a coppery taste in her mouth. She hated the cycle, the inescapable inconvenience of it. It really was a curse, but, as her mother had said to her in those first awkward months of adolescence, 'What cannot be cured must be endured.' Looking back, she remembered the shock and amazement that her own body could do this to her, wound her from deep within, bring her discomfort, pain and embarrassment, even as her mother had instructed her on what to do and how to prepare for it so that she was not taken by surprise. It was always easier to put up with in your own home, her mother had said, surrounded by familiar things, but you could not let it dictate how you lived your life. Yet, for the first few months, that was precisely what had happened: she was grateful and relieved once it had passed, but the relief only lasted for a week or two until it commenced, once again, its inevitable approach. It was different for the other girls: they seemed to take the changes to their bodies in their stride, and she envied them that. It was simply beyond her own capacities to do the same.

The train arrived at Shillingford, the last stop before home. Soon she would be able to lock the door and remain within the walls for the entire weekend. By Monday, it would all be over, and normal life would resume.

The door at the head of the carriage opened as the train moved off, and two young men entered. They were probably still in their late teens, although one wore a ragged line of scruffy facial hair on his upper lip, a nasty little excuse for a moustache that made him look shifty and untrustworthy. His companion, taller and bulkier, had acne pimples on his chin, bloodied where he had picked at them. They were dressed in cheap leather jackets, and jeans that were baggy and flared.

'All right, love?' one of the boys said. She did not look at him, but she could see him reflected in the glass. It was the one with the moustache. Neither of them had taken their seats. They stood, craning their necks to catch sight of her face and body. She drew her coat a little more tightly around her.

'Aw, don't do that,' said the spotty one. 'Give us a look.'

She bit her lip. Something contracted inside her, and she jerked slightly in her seat. Her skin began to itch.

'Go on, smile,' said the one with the moustache. 'It can't be that bad. I've got something that will make you smile.'

He sniggered.

'Lezzer,' said the other. He smirked at his wit.

'Nah,' said his mate. 'She's not a lezzer. They're ugly. She's not that bad.'

He pointed his chin at her. 'You're not a lezzer, are you?'

'Get lost,' she said, despite herself. She didn't want to be drawn into an argument with them, but they had just picked the wrong evening to confront her. It was only after she had spoken that she realised how dangerous it might be to antagonise them, to draw them upon her.

'Touchy,' said Moustache to his friend. 'Must be her time of the month. They all get a bit like that.'

He returned his attention to her. 'Is that it, darlin'? Time of the month? The old curse?'

His smile slowly faded, to be replaced by something infinitely more unpleasant.

'Don't bother me,' he said, so softly that she thought she might have misheard, until he repeated himself. 'Don't bother me one little bit …'

Suddenly, the train ground to a halt. For a moment, there was only silence, and then a voice came over the public address system.

'We would like to apologise to all passengers for this slight delay. This is due to a temporary signal failure on the line ahead of us, which means that we have to wait for the southbound train to pass before we can continue. Again, we would like to apologise for any inconvenience caused, and assure you that we will be on our way very shortly.'

She couldn't believe it. She pressed her face to the window and thought that she could nearly see the lights of the station in the distance. She could almost walk to her house from here, but the old manually operated doors were long gone and she, like all the others, was a prisoner of new technology. She felt nauseated, and the coppery taste in her mouth was growing more pronounced. It was now dark outside. She looked at the night sky. There were no stars visible, although a telltale edge of brightness had begun to show in the north as the clouds began to thin. This was bad, very bad. She could hear the boys whispering, and she risked a glance at them. The one with the pimples was looking over at her, and she could see the lust in his eyes.

'Unnnhhh.'

The groan of pain caused the boys to stop their conversation. She winced. The delay was just unbearable. What a bloody nuisance. She almost howled in frustration. There was no other choice: she rose, grasped her briefcase, and headed for the last carriage. If she could get to the toilet, she could do whatever was necessary and wait things out until the train got into the station, then slip away unnoticed through the back door, avoiding the two young men and the stink of their desire. She stepped into the space between the carriages, opened the door, and entered the empty compartment, the buzzing unbearably loud, the flickering of the lights paining her eyes.

Behind her, the two teenagers exchanged a look, then stood and followed her into the carriage.

Their names were Davey and Billy. Davey was the older one, the smarter one, and he was proud of his carefully cultivated facial hair. The moustache was sometimes the difference between being served in a bar and being refused, and he was very proud of it. Billy was bigger than his friend, but dumber and more brutal. They often saw women on the trains late at night, some of them a bit the worse for wear and unlikely to put up much of a fight, but somehow the opportunity they sought had never presented itself, until now. The woman was alone, the train was stopped: even if she cried out, no one would hear her. It was perfect.

They entered the carriage. The fluorescent lights flickered and buzzed, then finally gave up the ghost, artificial light yielding to the moon's luminescence as a great disc of white cleared the cover of the clouds and shone down upon the woods, the fields, and the silver body of the unmoving train. The toilet was ahead of them, at the far end. It wouldn't have much of a lock on it. On trains, they never did.

They were halfway down the carriage when the noise came from behind them. Something moved in the space between two seats, previously hidden from the young men by the shadows, the moonlight not yet penetrating its reaches. They turned as it unfolded itself, slowly rising up before them, taller than they were, and infinitely more powerful. There was a sharp animal smell in the carriage, and they heard a sound like a dog might make if someone threatened to remove the bone from between its paws. As Davey's eyes grew accustomed to the gloom, he saw clawed feet, longer than a human's and covered with fine dark hair that shone in the moonlight, and muscular legs that bent sharply at the knee, rising up to a flat crotch, a taut stomach, and small, pale breasts. Even as he watched, more fine hairs erupted from the pores of the skin, colonising the white spaces and turning them all to black. The tattered remains of a dress hung from the figure's arms and back, and as its fingernails curled in on themselves Davey thought he saw traces of purple varnish upon them. The hair on its upper body was thicker than that upon its legs and belly as the breasts slowly disappeared beneath it: it was denser, and tinged with white and grey, as though a great cape had been placed across its shoulders.

Then it emerged from the darkness, slowly advancing upon them, and the moonlight shone upon the woman's face. It was still changing, the features transforming before them, so that she remained clearly recognisable to Davey, like a figure glimpsed in a funhouse mirror, distorted yet still familiar. Her face was lengthening, the tips of her ears extending and tufting with hair, her nose and chin elongating to form a lupine jaw, the teeth within growing sharper and shining whitely, thick strands of saliva and blood dripping from the tips. Her hands, the fingers, now elongated, the nails sharp, gripped the back of the seat before her as her body shuddered, the change now almost complete. Davey heard four words emerge from deep in her throat, their meaning almost lost to him as she the animal overcame the woman.

Almost.

'Time of the month,' she said, and Davey thought that the words were followed by something that might have been laughter before that too was transformed, becoming a growl filled with hunger and the promise of death. Her eyes turned to yellow, and the full moon was reflected in their depths. She raised her head and howled just as, too late, the boys tried to run. Davey pushed Billy out of the way, using his size to squeeze past him before Billy even realised what he was doing. A splash of warmth struck Davey's hair and back as Billy's life ended with the rending of claws, but he kept moving, never looking behind him, his gaze focused on the rectangle of glass ahead of him and the silver handle of the door. He was almost close enough to touch it when a great weight landed on his back, forcing him to the ground. The train jerked into motion as Davey felt hot breath upon his skin, and sharp teeth upon his neck. In his final moments, he was struck, oddly, by the realisation that he had always been afraid of women. Now, at last, he thought that he understood why.

And then Davey screamed as he took his place in the great cycle of living and dying, and the world was filled with redness.

Hair

Karen Gillece

I am losing my hair. The knowledge of this returns to me in the morning as I wake, my head still swimming with sleep, and raise myself up to examine the pillow. A network of long red strands weaves and sweeps its way menacingly over the cool white cotton. At this early hour, when dreams still cling in my memory, I'm fascinated by these strands that curve and bend, forming shapes – I imagine the crescent of an ear, the whorl of a snail's shell, a treble clef – clinging like static; they are majestic in their spread.

Raymond stirs next to me, his inner clock ringing. I flip my pillow to reveal the innocent white underbelly and sink my head into it as he swings his legs out and steps into his slippers, scratching his chest and yawning. He shuffles blindly towards the bathroom, and a few minutes later I hear the hum of the shower starting, the hiss of water bursting from the jets, slapping against the cold, hard enamel. He doesn't sing in the shower. A brief silence after the water stops is broken by the buzz of an electric razor, which in turn is chased by the sibilant hum of an electric toothbrush. Raymond is a modern man, a gadget man.

He returns to the bedroom and dresses carefully, conservatively, and quietly so as not to wake me. I spy him standing in front of the oval mirror as he combs his full head of hair. At forty-five, he's proud of his active follicles. Silvery grey and coarse with age, his hair is tightly cut and neatly combed.

171

'Are you awake?' he whispers.

'Just about.'

'You'll be all right for tonight, then?'

'Mm-hmm,' I respond.

'I'll drop around to the off-licence on my way home, stock up the supply.'

'There's no need,' I offer. 'I got the wine yesterday, and we've plenty of spirits.'

'We need some champagne, though. We're supposed to be celebrating,' he says grimly. 'And Stefano likes a Kir Royale, so I'm told. Best be ready to offer it, eh?'

He bends over me and delivers his kiss before straightening up and smoothing out his tie. On his way out the door he stops, hand on the door-frame, and looks back at me.

'And call a plumber today, will you, love? The shower is clogged again. Honest to God, the amount of hair you women shave off your bodies …'

His unfinished sentence hangs in the room after he's left it. Moments later I hear the front door close behind him as he leaves the house.

Once the children have been fed and sent to school, I stand in the bathroom, ready for what has lately become a daily examination. Poised in front of the mirror, armed with a handheld compact, I twist and squirm – searching, probing – my one free hand sifting and parting my hair. These contortions and persistent combings are rewarded with a glimpse of my bald spot. It peeks out tentatively, and with a quick flick of my wrist, it's revealed in all its glory. White, hairless, smooth, it's a perfect circle with a diameter that has reached a couple of inches. I'm fascinated by it in a morbid kind of way. Horror-stricken.

When I first discovered it several weeks ago, I was curious and strangely amused by the little patch of sunless skin that had appeared like a fingerprint on my skull. But as the weeks passed and the boundaries receded, the patch has taken on a life of its own, growing, enlarging, pushing through, demanding more territory, fearless and greedy for space.

Washing my hair has become an ordeal that I only subject myself to every second day. Standing naked in the bath, I'm increasingly alarmed by the strands of hair snaking through the threads of water, swishing about my feet before plunging down the plughole to join their counterparts in a mutinous clogging of the drain. I've become exceedingly careful about brushing my hair, avoiding any kind of pull on my yielding scalp.

When we first met, Raymond used to marvel at the length and texture of my hair – auburn tresses that hung freely down the length of my back. Lying in bed after revelling in the youth and vigour of our flesh, he would gaze at my hair draped in blankets over the pillows and over the soft white swell of my young breasts. He would sigh with pleasure, satisfied, replete.

'God, you're like Eve,' he used to say, lying back against the clammy sheets.

On our honeymoon in Paris, he found a new icon for a simile. Creeping around the Musée d'Orsay, holding hands and overawed by the surroundings, we stumbled across Bouguereau's *Naissance de Venus*. Side by side, heads tilted upwards, we watched the burgeoning beauty of Venus unfolding in the sea to the sound of trumpeting conches. Witnessed adoringly by nymphs and cherubs, she lifted and stretched, creamy full flesh, small shadowy breasts with tender pink nipples, and her hair – coils of thick, streaming russet and gold, heavenly ropes – framing her exquisiteness.

'That's you,' he whispered, his hand in the hollow of my back. 'My Venus.'

For the rest of our honeymoon I wore the moniker proudly and he bestowed it lovingly. And when we returned to our home and his new job, he continued to whisper it to me. For a while, at least.

*

I have alopecia. Self-diagnosed, as I'm too mortified to see a doctor. I look it up in the dictionary. 'Abnormal loss of hair,' it pronounces. Well, that's certainly true. I scan the text for a cure or at least a cause, but find only the stark, tight words – 'ORIGIN Greek *alopekia*, "fox mange".' My shame is compounded by the bestial nature of my affliction. Hair loss is for animals and aging men, not for a woman in her forties, wife, mother, dinner-party hostess.

I dress myself with care, paying close attention to the application of make-up and the choice of clothing, desperately trying to draw attention away from my hair. I take some comfort from the fact that it's long enough to draw back into a tight ponytail with only a few strands escaping. I'm faintly aware that the youthfulness of the ponytail is slightly ridiculous, but it covers and conceals, and I'm grateful.

Shortly after eleven, as I drag the shopping in from the car, the shrill ring of the phone erupts in the hall.

'Hello?'

'Where've you been? I've been trying you all morning.'

'Doing the shopping,' I explain.

'Did you get the champagne?' he asks.

'No. You said you were going to stop on your way home from—'

'Yes, yes, I remember what I said. I just thought you might have … but you didn't, so …'

I picture him sitting at his desk, shoulders hunched forward over the phone, body clenched, pen tapping.

'Is that what you rang for?' I ask.

'What? No. I meant to ask, what are you making for tonight?'

'Well, I thought for a starter I'd do deep-fried mozzarella fingers with—'

'No cheese. Amy's allergic.'

To hell with Amy, I think to myself. *She'll eat what she's given.*

'And then for the main, I've a shoulder of lamb marinating in rosemary, thyme and olive oil.'

'Hmm. Well, that sounds nice,' he offers, solicitous now. 'And for dessert?'

'Tiramisu.'

He's silent. I can tell what he's thinking. Stefano is Italian. My husband is pondering the merits of serving an Italian dish to a native. For Raymond, this dinner party is so crucial that he can't allow the possibility of an innocent pudding toppling all his hard work.

'Is that all right?' I ask slowly, my voice brittle.

'Yes … OK.'

He sighs deeply and rings off.

Did it begin with Stefano, this change in him? Perhaps. I can't remember now. But sometime over the past year, something has happened to my husband – my warm, loving, compassionate husband. A hardening. A corruption of something that had been gentle and soft. It's easier for me to blame it on Stefano, this elusive Italian I have yet to meet.

In the kitchen I consult the row of cookery books – Delia Smith's *Complete Illustrated Cookery Course*, *The Naked Chef*, *How to Be a Domestic Goddess* – a domestic Venus. Some of these books are old and well-worn, pages sticking together from years of use, from countless strokes of greasy fingers. And as I pluck one from the shelf and begin flicking through it for an alternative cheese-free starter, a memory washes over me suddenly, so clear and immediate that at once I'm back there in the tiny bed-sit in Ranelagh, a tight space plugged with the smell of stewing bacon, the windows steaming up with condensation and sweat forming on my body beneath my clothes as I struggled with potatoes sticking to the bottom of a pan.

It was the first time I'd cooked for him – an unmitigated disaster – and I remember how I tried to conceal my panic, the composure I tried to exude, that cool exterior masking the flaking distress inside. And all the while, Raymond sat there talking, a beer in his hand, oblivious to my agitation – or, in hindsight, politely ignoring it. I remember how he spoke, the levity of his voice, the passion in it. Nearing the end of his apprenticeship, he was already brimming with plans – to make associate by the time he was thirty, partner by thirty-five, managing partner by forty. A big house in the city, a villa in France and a portfolio of promising investments. His ambitions were real and palpable. I was captivated by the determination in his voice as he spoke with passion, fire in his belly. And later, as we made love, the dinner ruined and abandoned on the stove, I felt something stirring up inside me – hope, perhaps, or the sweet beginnings of love. But it felt like knowledge coming to me, clear and absolute, that whatever his ambitions, whatever his plans, there would be a place for me amongst them.

Things were different then. The days seemed lighter somehow, joyful. I think of Raymond and how hard he has worked, the way he used to throw himself into his career with passion and commitment, the satisfaction it used to bring him. But somewhere along the way his verve and enthusiasm and fiery ambition have twisted and morphed into a hardened, weary slog. He still has his goals, but it occurs to me that somehow his quest towards them is more arduous, weighed down with the baggage he has collected. Compromise has crept into his life and taken the edge off his fervour.

He's made partner, but not managing partner. He was close, really close, but then Stefano came along. Breezing into the firm with his European panache and brilliant mind, his flair and his genius, he left them all behind. It was daylight robbery, according to Raymond. I have yet to meet him, this thorn in my husband's side, but I've pictured him in my mind – tall, commanding, an imposing Roman nose, an arched brow expressing his confidence, his arrogance, his allure. And a head of inky black Mediterranean hair, slick, oily and dense.

*

Hair

My sensitivity to language has heightened since I've started to shed my hair. Words, phrases that seemed so innocuous before are now as pointed and punishing as hot needles pricking my scalp. When Ray Junior and Fiona were sparring with each other, playful punches escalating into violent exchanges, I screamed at them to cut it out, they were driving me crazy.

'All right, keep your hair on,' my son said to me.

When I became so tense a few weeks ago for reasons I couldn't explain or understand, and Raymond arranged for his mother to take the kids so that I could head away for a few days, in a moment of tenderness he said, 'Take the break. Go and enjoy yourself. It'll be an opportunity for you to really let your hair down.'

And when I returned, relaxed, back in the heart of my family, determined to be positive, flopping onto our bed and turning my head, I spied the hair trapped in the pile of the carpet – long, straight, icy blond, a foreign hair, glinting treacherously in the sunlight. What had I said? What words could I have used?

The guests have all arrived – all except one – and are sitting downstairs enjoying their drinks, laughing and chatting, oblivious to the panic that is gripping my body as I sit in my bedroom, running my fingers frantically through my hair.

I was all right at first. The dinner was under control, the house spotless. Raymond even seemed cheerful, although he has grown tense at Stefano's lateness. And I had managed to sleek my hair back into a clip that actually gave me an air of sophistication while covering my patch.

I wore my hostess's smile as I greeted our guests, Raymond and I standing side by side, presenting a solid front to the world. Phil and Anna, Ben and Elizabeth, Mark and Judy – all partners or associates in the firm, and their spouses. I've known these people for years without ever really knowing them. Our acquaintance has been mapped out through a series of Christmas parties and dinner parties.

And then there's Amy. Amy with the long, straight, icy blond hair. Amy who knows where the bathroom is without having to be told.

My body is shaking and my scalp itches uncontrollably. Something is welling up inside me. I sit on the floor with my head in my hands. The clip has fallen away and I scratch my skull viciously. I've been gone nearly fifteen minutes and my absence has been noted. I hear the footfall on the stairs and Raymond bursts into the room, his eyes searching me out, impatient, furious.

'What are you doing?' he asks, looking down at me.

I'm crumpled and shrivelled. My hair is a mess. I'm crouched down by the end of the bed, limbs shaking, hair shedding. I feel like a hunted animal. A fox.

'Jesus Christ, look at the state of you!' he exclaims. 'What's got into you? Stefano will be here any minute, so pull yourself together!'

I know, I want to tell him. *I know about you and her. I found the hair. In our house. Beside our bed.*

But instead I say, 'I'm losing my hair.'

I'm as startled as he is by the words that have been spoken, flung out onto the floor between us, sitting there now, expanding and filling the room, echoing around us.

'You're what?'

'I … my hair is falling out.'

He looks at me blankly, suspending his reaction. And then his eyes flicker over me, taking in every inch of me from my toes to my stinging scalp. And I recognise the look. It has been lurking in the background for some time now, skulking and stalking, avoiding perception. But I see it now as we regard each other coldly. It is a look of contempt.

The doorbell violently interrupts and grabs him back to the reality of the present. He withdraws from the room, watching me, wary of me.

I hear him in the hallway, greeting Stefano. Taking a deep breath, I adjust the clip in my hair, pat my dress down, compose myself. I must get through this night. My legs feel heavy, feet sticking to each step as I descend the staircase to meet my husband's nemesis.

Stefano is at the bottom of the stairs, his back to me. I look down at him and suddenly stop, my breath caught, suspended. His head gleams under the hall light – smooth, shiny, the contours of his skull pressuring the tight spread of skin. He is completely and magnificently bald. I'm transfixed by the roundness, the tautness, the utter starkness of it. It's begging me to reach out and touch it, to place the palms of my hands flat against the cool surface, to run my fingers softly over skin and bone, naked, clean, pure. And deep inside me something stirs – a pocket of lightness, a sudden levity, like a burst of laughter – a change in me, slowly rising to the surface.

The Winner

Tara Heavey

Ernest Horan never gave without expecting something in return. Everything was calculated. Many people had discovered this to their cost. Among them, his employees, his many and varied business opponents. His ex-wife. She could have got a pile of money in the divorce – her lawyers told her often enough – but, by then, she'd had all the fight knocked out of her. Not by Ernest's fists, but by his words. All those years of put-downs – twenty-five, to be exact – have their effect on a person.

The Marian who married Ernest was a very different Marian to the one who divorced him. It was 1965 when she waltzed down the aisle. What a beautiful bride. Everybody said so. But aren't all brides beautiful? Just like all babies. The difference was that Marian was as beautiful several weeks before her wedding as she was several weeks – several years – after. You wouldn't expect Ernest Horan to marry anything less. He was a winner. A man going places. He couldn't be seen with any old hatchet-head on his arm.

He was pleased with his latest acquisition – a fine figure of a woman from a good, middle-class family. Her father had built up his own very successful business, and might even have some useful contacts. And Ernest was fond of her after a fashion, as one might be fond of one's pet Labrador. But love? Love was a commodity for which Ernest had no use. It was unquantifiable. Incalculable. To all intents and purposes, it did not exist. Instead, he ran his marriage

180

like a balance sheet with well-defined debit and credit columns. It went something like this. He gave his wife money, she bought the groceries. She cooked the dinner, he ate it. She made the bed, he slept in it.

He was a good provider. She provided him with sex, hot meals and a daughter. In the beginning, she was more than happy with this. Because she hadn't started to add anything up yet. Because Marian loved Ernest with all her heart.

Sarah, the said daughter, was to be the first of many – children, that is, not daughters – and her birth brought genuine pleasure to her father. Until it became clear that she was to have no little brothers. Because, for some reason, the other children would not come. Maybe those virgin souls had their eyes on other families. Families where love was a gift freely given with joyful abandon.

So little Sarah grew up with the certain knowledge that her father would never fully forgive her for not being a boy. This was made clear on her seventh birthday when he bought her a fire engine instead of the Barbie doll she'd wanted. When she got older, he repeatedly tried to interest her in his property development business. When she announced her intention to become a holistic therapist instead, his derision knew no bounds. Was she stupid? She'd never make any money doing that. How could she throw his business back in his face?

As a result, Sarah seldom spoke to her father these days. And Marian didn't speak to her ex-husband at all. As a result, neither woman knew of his visit to the hospital.

'It's a simple procedure, Mr Horan. You'll wake up a new man.'

The surgeon was the first person that Ernest hadn't been rude to that day. At last, a true equal with whom to converse. A man, like himself, who was at the top of his profession. The premier heart man in the country. You wouldn't expect Ernest Horan to allow anyone else to perform his triple bypass operation. There were risks involved, sure. But these were only miniscule and had been explained to him in detail. He'd signed all the necessary forms – unnecessary, in his opinion. Because he was going to win this operation, just like he won everything else in his life.

He'd told no one about the 'procedure'. Not his two younger brothers who lived in England. Nor his handful of friends, who, in all honesty, were no more than business colleagues he had yet to shaft. He would admit this weakness to no one. It would be tantamount to a jungle animal parading its injury in front of its predators. It would be ripped apart in minutes. He wouldn't let that happen to him.

'Count down from ten to one, please, Mr Horan.'

The anaesthetist's tones were gentle, the pressure of a soft hand on either side of his head.

'Ten, nine, eight…'

Darkness.

Ernest woke up just a few minutes later, or so it seemed. And in a manner wholly unexpected. Somehow, he had managed to get himself up to the ceiling of the operating theatre, where he remained suspended. He could feel no wires, no supports. No wings. He looked down on the theatre below. The room was a chaos of activity. Surgeons, doctors, nurses – all milling around as if in a panic over something. Voices were raised. They all appeared to be working on a pale, inert body that lay supine in the centre of the room. Its chest cracked open. Its heart exposed for all the world to see. Hold on. It was him.

The shock of this discovery propelled Ernest upwards, into a kind of tunnel that had suddenly opened up directly above his head. The tunnel drew him upwards, yet at the same time he had the sensation that he was freefalling. It reminded him of that time he had done the parachute jump, ostensibly for charity, although it was really for publicity. He had been afraid then. More afraid than he had been in years. A fear that he had never admitted to another living soul. That fear had stopped him from letting himself go and giving in to the sensation. Trusting that the universe would take care of him no matter what. But he felt none of that fear now. He spun like one of those parachutes that fall from a sycamore tree in autumn. Faster and faster he went, propelled towards a destination he could sense rather than know. He became aware of a light – a brilliant, white light. A light brighter than any other light he had ever known, still it did not blind him. It encompassed him. Held him. Until, suddenly, he was there.

He landed upright, as if he had never been falling. He dusted himself down and checked out all his limbs. He was surprised he felt no dizziness. The only aberration was his chest. It remained open, as the surgeon had left it. His heart glowed from within like the image of the Sacred Heart that had shone down on the kitchen table every day of his childhood. But he didn't have time to dwell on such matters. Because Ernest was standing at the entrance to the most beautiful garden he had ever seen. The only barrier between him and this garden was an intricately crafted wrought-iron gate, with heavenly scented roses twisting between its bars. Ernest spotted a lock at the side of the gate. He looked down at his right hand. A key appeared. He placed the key in the lock and the gate opened easily and instantly. He walked into the garden.

It reminded him of a picture he'd once seen of the Garden of Eden. In a book of illustrated Bible stories for children, if he recalled correctly. It was nothing like his garden at home, with its neatly trimmed leylandii hedges and flawless lawns. Here, the lawns were lush and green, yet thick with wild flowers – bluebells, primroses and orchids. Each season was represented. The trees were heavy with blossom. Butterflies – of every hue imaginable – fluttered from one bloom to the next. A stream babbled throughout the garden, gathering into a great waterfall. Kingfishers flew among the reeds and hummingbirds hummed overhead. Here and there, there were benches, and Ernest wasn't in the least surprised to see his mother sitting on one. He went and sat down beside her and embraced the only woman he had ever treated with true kindness.

'It's lovely to see you, Ernest.'

'It's lovely to see you too, Mam. And great to come home.'

'Ernest. This isn't your home.'

'But I thought…'

'It's not your time yet, love.'

'But I want to stay here with you.'

'You can't. You have business to attend to.'

And with that, Ernest found himself hurtling through the tunnel again. Down this time. Once more, he was in the presence of the great, white light. The all-encompassing, all-embracing light. And he knew, in that instant, a love that was breathtakingly unconditional. Then he felt an incredible sense of loss as he felt himself pulled away from that light. Until …

Wham!

He was back in his body. And, oh, the pain. The excruciating, exquisite, white-hot pain of it all.

'He's back!'

Ernest stayed in hospital for fourteen days. A twelve-day stay is usually the maximum for such an operation, but when your heart refuses to restart – albeit temporarily – it's better to be safe. One of Ernest's minions visited him in hospital, to give him an update on his business concerns. But he was sent away again.

Ernest returned to the large, fancy apartment that he shared with himself. As he stared out of the large, empty window, he felt the emptiness. But he also felt the joy.

He put the apartment on the market the very next day. There was no more time to lose.

He arranged to meet her in a coffee shop they used to frequent. Together in the beginning. Later on, they were more likely to go alone. They were both overly fond of the coffee slices. He was already there when she arrived, fiddling with the laminated menu and glancing anxiously every few seconds at the door. He was more nervous than he'd been in the early days of their courtship, when he'd attempted to woo this beautiful young girl, with soft, brown eyes so full of innocence and trust.

She arrived several minutes late. He cringed at the look she gave him as she sat down opposite. Her eyes were so altered. Had he done that to them? Or was it just him she looked at that way? Maybe others still felt the benefit of her sweet, trusting gaze.

'I took the liberty of ordering a pot of tea and two coffee slices,' he said.

'It'll take a damn sight more than a coffee slice, Ernest. What's this all about?'

'I just wanted to talk to you.'

'About what? Afraid I'm going to look for more maintenance?'

'No. It's got nothing to do with that. Why? Do you need more money? Because I can arrange it if you like.'

'Oh, for God's sake.'

Marian got up to leave. Ernest reached out and held her by the forearm.

'Please, Marian. Stay a while.'

She searched his face, looking for a reason to stay. She must have found one, because she sat back down as the tea and coffee slices arrived.

'I asked you to meet me here today,' began Ernest, as Marian poured, just like in the old days – almost – 'because I wanted to say sorry.'

Marian's eyes were needling his face with uncomfortable precision. Ernest drew a breath and continued.

'I'm sorry for the way I treated you all those years. It was unforgivable. You deserved so much more, a lovely woman like you.'

Marian stared at him hard, her eyes now shiny and bright. She rose once again from her chair. This time he didn't try to stop her. He just watched her retreating back and felt the sadness of unquantifiable loss.

He would have eaten both coffee slices, but all that cream would have been bad for his heart.

Tom McGovern had once been the managing director of a successful property development firm. Until, that was, Ernest Horan – his arch-rival – stole it all away from him through a sustained campaign of dodgy deals involving heavily bribed County Councillors. Tom had subsequently taken to the bottle in quite a serious way.

Ernest made the phone call the day after his meeting with Marian.

'Is that you, Tom?'

'Speaking. Who is this?'

'It's Ernest Horan.'

A long silence on the other end of the phone. Finally: 'What do you want, Horan?'

'I'm selling my company. I thought you might be interested in taking it off my hands.'

'Is this some kind of sick joke?'

'No joke. I'm perfectly serious. I'm getting out of the business.'

'And what am I supposed to buy it with? I'm broke. You made sure of that.'

'I can offer you a very good price.'

'Go to hell, Horan.'

The following week, Ernest found himself sitting in a small, fragrant waiting room. Everything was lavender, from the walls to the cushions to the oil that was burning. Ernest knew it was meant to make him relax. He had booked himself in for an Indian head massage. The therapist, Sarah Horan, refused to see him at first but he was persistent. In the end she gave in to avoid a scene in front of the other customers and the notoriously nosy receptionist.

'What do you want, Dad?'

She had brought him into the inner chamber where she worked. All pinks and reds and muted lighting.

'An Indian head massage, of course.'

She prepared the oils for the treatment, not really knowing what else to do. He sat in the chair, his back to her, and she stood over him and wondered about how much hair he had lost since the last time she'd seen him. And how his scalp was so florid now and somehow gnarled-looking.

'What's this all about, Dad? Mum said you arranged to meet up with her too.'

She was massaging his temples now. He reflected on how she had her mother's hands. Gentle, healing hands.

'I just wanted to say sorry, Sarah. For all the hurt I've caused you over the years.'

Sarah was silent.

'You were the best daughter a man could ever want, and I hope that, somehow, you can let me be your friend.'

Sarah remained silent. But Ernest felt something hot and wet drop onto his head that he knew wasn't lavender oil.

Ernest died ten years later. His heart stopped ticking again. This time, it didn't restart. He was at home when he died. In the modest apartment he shared with his cat, Boss, who had adopted Ernest as a stray kitten.

Sarah – who in turn adopted Boss – delivered the eulogy to a packed church. Among the coffin-bearers were Ernest's two younger brothers, home from England; several men who had been former patients – Ernest had trained and worked as a counsellor in his remaining years – and had later become friends; and Tom McGovern, who had eventually purchased Horan & Co. for the princely sum of fifty euro. Only now that Ernest was dead did he truly believe that there was no hidden catch. Even Ernest couldn't trick him from beyond the grave.

And sitting at the back of the church, an attractive, middle-aged woman with soft, brown eyes wept bittersweet tears.

Reflection
Arlene Hunt

7.40 p.m.

Dante scrambled onto the garage roof and walked quickly to the lip overlooking the driveway. He crouched down, slipping deeper into the shadows behind the chimney-stack. From here he had a perfect vantage point, a clear view of the car as it pulled in.

He settled in to wait. The rain slapped against his frozen cheeks but he didn't mind. If anything, the discomfort was a reminder, an admonishment. He must suffer a little too, punishment for the atrocity he was about to commit.

'Take him out,' Joe had ordered earlier that day, his papery hands clenched into white-knuckled fists on the desk. 'Take that bastard out.'

And so, here he was.

His mother had named him Dante after the poet. Joe claimed she had recognised in him something otherworldly, poetic, something aloof and predatory. She had been a beautiful woman, his mother, erudite, bewitching. From her, he inherited his dark hair, full lips and sombre green eyes. These details he had learned from Joe, for he remembered nothing of her himself and his old man had never spoken of her. She had died when he was barely into his fourth year. He had asked Joe once about her death. Joe had shaken his head sadly and Dante had let it be.

The gun felt too heavy in his hand. He slipped it into the

pocket of his jacket. Maybe it would have been better if he'd waited in the house. He glanced across the roof at the darkened windows and disregarded them. Too many places the target could run and hide; locate a weapon; get to a phone. Every man knew his own house. No, it was better to do him in the garage, cleaner, no fuss.

7.45 p.m.
He checked his watch again. The target had fifteen minutes left to live. Dante shuddered. He wondered if it would make a difference if the target knew he was about to die. Would he run? Or would he try to reason his way out, plead for mercy? He'd known men, tough men, men without pity or empathy, men who would cut your throat as soon as look at you. Those men, when death was imminent, all begged for leniency. They reached out, searching for consolation in their final moments. They pleaded with him to be given a chance, any chance. They searched his green eyes for any sign of weakness, resigned and weeping when they found none. Only one man Dante knew would not balk at death: that man was Joe, his boss.

Joe Maguire was the reason he, Dante, was a man to be reckoned with; the reason he had a flush bank account; the reason he drove a flash car and wore a Rolex; the reason he had girls and as much action as he could handle; the reason men feared him.

The reason he was alive.

The reason he was lying on a garage roof in the pouring rain with a gun in his pocket and a heavy heart.

A dribble of icy water slipped beneath his shirt collar and ran down his back.

Dante rotated his shoulders one at a time, hearing the creak in the left one. An old injury made worse by the damp and cold. He had been stabbed in the back, literally as well as figuratively. The blade had buried itself deep into his shoulder blade, tearing muscle and tendon before finally coming to a juddering halt in his shoulder bone. He had almost bled to death – would have, too, if one of Joe's men hadn't found him collapsed on the path, two feet inside his front gate. Joe had taken care of him then. Joe had nursed him through the worst days. Joe had promised him that no one would ever lay a finger on him again.

He had been nine years old.

Joe had kept his word. Dante's attacker had been hauled out of bed two nights later. Dante wondered if his father had pleaded for mercy, for forgiveness. Had he even realised why he was about to die? Dante felt no sorrow at his demise. He felt nothing for him, not even hate. He owed Joe. He was indebted to him – looked up to him; loved him.

He leaned his face against the rough plaster of the stack and tried to ignore the ache in his shoulder. It stirred up too many emotions in him, the sensations of death, how it felt to watch his life force drain away and be powerless to stop it. See the blood as it seeped across the paving stones. He remembered vividly the heaviness of his limbs, the cold creeping into his extremities. That was how his targets felt, he knew it – he didn't rejoice in their misery. He wasn't a monster.

7.51 p.m.

The name of the target was Mickey Hegarty, a one-time business associate of Joe, now running a crew of his own. Mickey and Joe had grown up together, but money and power had gone to Mickey's head and he had made one transgression too many to be ignored. Joe Maguire had accorded Mickey a certain measure of respect over the past two years, seeing as how they had a shared history – even going so far as to ask Mickey to his grandkid's christening, playing the good neighbour. He had held his tongue and turned a deaf ear to the occasional muttering of his men. As long as Mickey kept to his end of town and their paths never crossed, Joe surmised there was room for two of them.

Dante never understood why men forgot just how ruthless Joe could be when crossed. Didn't they know how he operated? Didn't they know the moment they fucked him over they signed their own death warrants? Joe heard everything. He knew Hegarty had been mouthing off, moving his boys onto turf that had always been Joe's. Making the egregious mistake of thinking that Joe's advancing years had made him soft. Dante shook the rain off his head. Even then Joe had shown remarkable restraint – calling Mickey up, letting him know his trespassing wouldn't be tolerated, offering Mickey a chance to turn it around. Then, last week, a shipment of cannabis had been fleeced from the docks and some of the dockers reported seeing some of Mickey's men hanging around the trawler. After that there were no more calls; all bets were off.

Dante couldn't remember a time when he had seen Joe so angry. The old man had actually trembled when he summoned Dante to the front room where he sat day after day by the fire, the phone by his hand. No one robbed from Joe Maguire. Joe raged at Dante that Hegarty had forgotten the golden rule of the underworld. 'Don't bite the hand that feeds you. Don't shit where you eat.'

Dante closed his eyes. A headache was developing across the crown of his head. He was getting a lot of them lately. He had an ulcer, too, spent most of his days drinking milk and chewing antacids. His doctor said he was suffering from stress. He was twenty-six years old – he felt fifty.

7.54 p.m.

He rolled his neck, easing the cramp a little, and checked his equipment again. The gun was clean and untraceable. He took out the silencer from his coat pocket and fitted it on quickly, taking care to minimise the gun's exposure to the rain. He would dump it the moment he had a chance, toss it into the River Dodder. Everything was perfect. The car he was using was a ringer, imported from the North and fitted with false plates. He'd parked it three streets away just to be on the safe side. He didn't foresee any problems, but that didn't mean there would not be any. Maybe the target would be late or deviate from his usual routine. Maybe the gun would jam. Dante hoped that that wouldn't happen. He had a bowie knife he could use, but he preferred the cold impartiality of a gun. He'd heard guys bragging about knives being the ultimate sign of a professional, listened to plenty of boozed-up arseholes claim they could kill a man with their bare hands. But Dante knew it was all bullshit. Use the most efficient weapon and do it fast and clean, that was his motto. And nine times out of ten, a bullet to the back of the head was the route to pick. When you severed the spinal column no fucker caused trouble.

He eased back into the shadows and tried to concentrate on his breathing. He was feeling a little queasy. His stomach kept churning over and over. Maybe the duck he'd eaten earlier was off.

Truth was he liked Mickey: had grown up alongside him; had eaten many a meal at his family's table. Although Joe had been the one to pay his way and keep him in school, it had been Mickey who'd taken him out and got him shit-faced when he was fifteen and had passed the Inter Cert with flying colours. Mickey who'd brought him into town to Louis Copeland and fitted him out with his first proper suit for his debs. Mickey who'd tossed him the keys of the Jag that same day, just so he could impress Susie Cowen. It had been Mickey who had patted him on the back and told him not to be a stranger when he and Joe parted company a few years back. Mickey had been like a father to him, more of a father than the piece-of-shit father he'd started out with.

Dante rubbed his hand over his eyes. He needed to get a grip on himself. It wasn't like he had any choice in this. He had his orders. For all of Mickey's good deeds over the years, business was business, and Joe had been good to him too. And Joe was not the one who had broken rank, had trespassed on another man's turf. Joe had not stolen from Mickey.

But Mickey … Dante squeezed his eyes shut. But nothing could blot out the image of Mickey's craggy face, his short bristled hair, the huge smile that split his face when he clapped eyes on you. The Mickey he knew would give you the last red cent in his pocket if he thought you were short a few quid. He was generous, charming, ribald, a ladies' man, a singer of Irish ballads when he had a skinful.

Shit. Dante's eyes sprang open.

The rain lashed him relentlessly. Dante clenched his teeth and tried to stop thinking about the past. It was pointless and it was wrecking his head. He had a job to do and that was it. A job, the same as any other he'd pulled. Fuck Mickey. If he hadn't crossed the line, he wouldn't be in this situation and Dante wouldn't be lying in wait. It wasn't his fault. Everyone knew the rules. Joe called the shots – everyone knew that. He answered to Joe and no one else. So why was he questioning him? Why had Joe sent him of all people to carry it out? Who was this lesson for? Was Joe testing his loyalty?

7.59 p.m.

Dante cocked his head. He could hear the Jag coming down the street, even over the pounding rain. Mickey drove the big car like it was a dodgem: too heavy on the clutch; always in the wrong gear; always too fast. Dante lowered his head. He had dismantled the security lights earlier and doubted Mickey could pick him out with the headlights.

He heard the electronic gates open and seconds later the car roared up the driveway. It pulled up to the garage door directly below him. A moment or two later, the door juddered and rolled up. Mickey revved the engine and drove into the garage, clipping the wing mirror off the wall as he did so.

Dante was moving before Mickey had even taken his foot off the brake. He dropped down silently onto the waterlogged lawn, darted along the wall and slipped into the garage before the door lowered again. He pulled the gun from his pocket as Mickey shut off the engine.

8.00 p.m.

Dante raised the gun and stepped softly to the rear door. Mickey was facing the wall, his right hand resting on the steering-wheel. He was rummaging around on the dash, trying to locate his phone and keys.

Dante opened the door of the Jag in one swift motion with his left hand. He placed the gun behind Mickey's right ear and released the safety.

Mickey gulped air. 'What the f—'

'You shouldn't have taken his shipment, Mickey.'

'Oh, Jesus.' Mickey's bladder loosened. Dante could see the dark stain spread along the insides of Mickey's legs. 'Dante, don't fuckin' shoot, not in the head. Oh sweet Jesus, please.'

Dante gritted his teeth so hard they ached.

'I knew it would be you, I knew he'd send you,' Mickey said softly. 'Oh Jesus, please, Dante. Don't do it here. Don't have Angela find me like that.' He tried to turn his head but Dante wouldn't let him.

Dante's finger tightened on the trigger. From the warm interior of the car, a wave of Paco Rabanne rose on the night air and enveloped him. Dante's chest tightened and his hand began to shake. It was the only aftershave Mickey liked. He remembered buying him a bottle of it one Christmas when he was … what? Seventeen? Eighteen? Mickey had acted like he'd given him all the gold in the world.

'Make sure Angela's taken care of, Dante,' Mickey said, his voice choking with grief and fear. 'She's a good woman … tell her I love her. Will ya do that for me, lad? Tell her I love her. Will ya do that for me? And the kids … oh, Jesus.'

He bent his head forward, almost offering Dante a clean shot.

Dante swallowed. How many men had he taken out this way? How many more would there be? It would never end. The futility of it racked him. What happened when Mickey was dead? Who would move up the ladder to take his place? Was he to kill them too? There would be retribution – someone would try to take Joe out. It would never end.

He was sweating heavily despite the cold, his breathing was irregular and shallow. Mickey's hands were clasped hard in front of him. Dante shook his head and pressed the muzzle of the silencer harder into the pink skin behind Mickey's ear.

Images flashed. Mickey laughing, telling him to eat, that he hadn't a pick on him; Mickey smoking a cigarette outside the gates of his school, his overcoat flapping in the wind as he stood leaning against the bonnet of his Jag, waiting for Dante to finish his classes. He was ignoring the other mothers, who watched him warily. Mickey had picked him up and brought him to McDonald's. The reason? No reason, he simply had a few hours to spare and he thought the best way to spend them was with a lonely kid.

Joe and Mickey, two of the best parents a kid could ever have wished for.

Dante removed the gun and stepped back.

'Dante?' Mickey turned his head slowly and peered into the shadows, trying to make him out. 'Dante?'

'It won't ever stop, will it?'

Mickey blinked big, salty tears. 'What?'

'You, him … this.' Dante took another step backwards. His hip brushed against a set of disused golf clubs. They sat next to a disused exercise bike. Dante looked around him, his eyes floating over all the assorted junk accumulated over the years. He grimaced. They were killing each other over money – money they used to buy shit they didn't even want. He thought of his apartment; it was top of the line, brand-spanking-new with views of the city to make an estate agent whimper. He hated the place. It was soulless. It meant nothing.

'It will just go on and on until everybody's gone.' He lowered the gun. 'I won't kill you, Mickey. Not this time, not ever. But he has others who will. Remember that.'

Mickey wiped at beads of sweat on his forehead. 'Son, listen, wh—'

'I'm not your son.' Dante unclipped the silencer and slipped it in his pocket. 'And I'm not his son. I'm nothing. Just a thing … a weapon.'

'Dante, wait.' Mickey wanted to step out of the car but his legs wouldn't support him, not yet. He wished he could think of something to say to this young man who had spared his life, but for once his blather, like his legs, failed him.

Dante moved back towards the door and rolled it up. He stepped out into the night and lifted his face to the heavens. The rain beat at him, and he let it. He had deliberately disobeyed a direct order.

He was not free from his life, he never would be, but he would not kill another man. Joe would be furious and there would be repercussions. But he would meet them head on, and if Joe felt he was to be cut loose, then so be it.

Dante closed his eyes and felt the rain wash over his face. It was cold, it was harsh and it was purgatorial. His shoulders shuddered once and, without realising it, Dante began to weep.

Pink Lady
Cathy Kelly

Marilee sat at her desk and ticked off the last task on her list with her pink pen. Pink was one of her eccentricities. She dressed in shades of lightest peach to vivid cyclamen; her professional cards were embossed with fat, pink script proclaiming that Marilee Cray, handbag designer extraordinaire, had a shop in the very best part of London; and the pure cotton sheets on the vast bed in her Chelsea house were never pure white, but white with a tinge of rose, as if the laundry fairies had misted rose blossoms over the washing.

Idiosyncrasies were important, Peter always said loftily. The pink had been his idea.

'It marks you out, makes you special,' he said, pointing out that the business wouldn't be where it was today if Marilee had been a common-or-garden handbag designer.

Marilee's now-famous idiosyncrasies counted, Peter insisted. She didn't like to argue that surely the actual designing counted for something. Peter, who was not a man who liked being argued with, felt that marketing was a vital tool in their business. *The* vital tool.

Lagerfeld had his fan; Donatella had her mane of platinum hair; Marilee had the colour pink – and a reputation for being obsessive over every detail.

And it worked. Had been working for over fifteen incredibly successful years.

As one interviewer gushed: 'Who would not kill for a handbag designed by woman who spends hours working on the exact positioning of a faux peacock feather? Who could resist any design from a woman so sure of her own tastes that she develops a migraine if she has to endure tea bags instead of specially blended Earl Grey tea?'

Such exquisite details, combined with her personal charm, meant that journalists went home, after an interview with Marilee, drooling at her perfect lifestyle and feeling vaguely dissatisfied with their own ordinary tea bags, leaky Biros and boring handbags that didn't say anything special about them.

Sales kept rising.

One of Marilee's few friends, an avant-garde milliner, went bankrupt. MC Handbags recorded its best year ever.

A rival handbag designer had to fire half his staff. Peter started talking mistily about buying a yacht.

Marilee's handbags were shockingly expensive but a fashion must-have, because each perfect piece somehow encapsulated a different subliminal message for the purchaser – 'Going to New York', 'Cocktails with Rock Bands', 'Dinner at Whatever Exclusive Bit of the Caribbean Is *In*'. Mind you, such descriptions were not written on the price tag that swung on a pink silken cord from each bag. But the customers knew what their handbags said. *You are exciting, you are somebody, you have an MC handbag!*

Peter never reflected on the fact that the business traded on people's insecurities. He thought it was great that women were so hopelessly needy that they required the right handbag to make them feel better about themselves.

'Women want to be like you,' he'd say gleefully when he read the resulting glossy magazine interview, where the writer would invariably wax lyrical over Marilee's skill, reeling with gratitude thanks to the last-minute, biked-over gift of an MC purse (handbags only went to magazine editors). 'They envy you your fabulous lifestyle. They envy us.'

Peter was happy at the thought of being envied. When they'd

lived in that kip of a flat off Liverpool Street, nobody had envied them. People had thought they were two hicks off the boat from Ireland who were living in cloud-cuckoo land with their dreams of running their own business. It was a different story now, wasn't it?

Marilee, on the other hand, didn't want to be envied: she just wanted to be liked. And to be loved. Just like the women who bought her handbags. She understood them and their need to have the right possessions, because the right possessions helped, didn't they? They made you feel better about who you were, and then people loved you more. And Peter loved her. Hadn't he told the woman from Italian *Elle* that he couldn't live without Marilee?

'Darkly handsome Peter Cray can't stop talking about his talented wife,' the article had said. 'They are clearly so in love with each other.'

Peter was good with lady interviewers. Possibly better with them than he was with Marilee …

Firmly, she pushed that thought out of her head, not wanting to give it shape in her mind. Breathing deeply, the way her yoga teacher had shown her, Marilee focused on the positive. She was very lucky. She was rich, successful, fêted. Loved, obviously. Of course Peter loved her.

Marilee's office door opened abruptly and Sukey poked her sleek, blond head round it.

'Marilee,' she said briskly. Sukey was Marilee's assistant and always spoke in brisk, head-girl tones, except when she was speaking to Peter; then she spoke with the reverence of someone in the Prado gazing at the Goyas. 'The car's here. You have to be at the restaurant at one to meet Steve Reuben, don't forget.'

Marilee felt a rare stab of annoyance at the intrusion. She hated being nagged. She'd been working hard all morning and she longed for a cup of tea. Not Earl Grey, either. She loved good strong tea. Builder's tea, as her long-departed mother used to call it.

She also wanted to run upstairs to the flat and change her

outfit because the mohair trim on her cerise suit was making her sneeze. Now Peter's bloody number-one fan was nagging her to leave early. *And* she hadn't knocked.

There were days when Sukey's blatant twenty-something beauty made Marilee feel all of her forty-six years.

'I'll be ready in twenty minutes,' Marilee said firmly. 'I don't want to be disturbed until then.'

Sukey's eyes widened marginally. Marilee never spoke with even the slightest edge to her voice, and Sukey despised her for it. In Marilee's place, Sukey would have had minions running round after her like Duracell bunnies on acid. Sukey knew that the only way to keep people in their place was to bully them. But her time would come. Peter had promised.

'Fine,' she smiled, with just the correct modicum of deference.

When her assistant was gone, Marilee slipped off her shoes and got up from her desk. Behind a painted Japanese screen was another door, one that led to the luxury apartment she shared with Peter. They lived on the two upper floors, while the MC offices and showroom were on the ground floor.

The secret door opened to a staircase that led into the kitchen, a cosy spot and the one room in the house that had escaped the Italian-palazzo elegance that Peter adored. As Peter never set foot in the kitchen, Marilee felt it was only fair that she get to decorate it the way she wanted. And there wasn't a speck of bright pink or a gilt chair in sight. Reporters were kept out of there: imagine if they discovered that Marilee's favourite colour was really buttercup yellow.

'Hi, Marilee,' said Gloria, their Australian housekeeper. 'You want tea?'

'God, yes,' Marilee said, sinking into a chair. She was weary. She'd been feeling out of sorts lately and her energy levels were non-existent. Peter had told her to go to the doctor and 'get herself fixed up'.

She knew he meant pills of some sort. But Marilee didn't want pills. She wanted to get rid of the vague sense of disquiet in her soul.

Gloria snapped open a Tupperware box.

'Danish pastry?' she asked, knowing that Marilee's strict Peter-regimented diet forbade carbs.

The sliver of a smile lit up Marilee's face. 'Go on, give us half of one. I'll never look like Kate Moss at this rate.'

They both grinned at this ludicrous notion. Neither Gloria, with her big, athletic frame, nor Marilee, who struggled to remain a size fourteen, would ever resemble Kate Moss.

'Live dangerously,' Gloria urged. 'Have a whole one. What his lordship doesn't see won't harm him.'

Marilee was guiltily wiping pastry slivers from her skirt when the phone rang.

Gloria answered it. 'Yes, Peter, she's here. Do you want to speak to her…? No, right. I'll tell her.' She hung up. 'He's going early. He says he'll meet you in the restaurant bar and don't be late.'

Marilee got up instantly.

For the millionth time, Gloria wondered why her sweet, gentle employer leapt obediently to attention for Peter. *She* was the talented one, but the way Peter carried on, you'd swear he was the genius behind MC Handbags.

Her shoes in her hand, Marilee hurried upstairs to the bedroom. The effects of her nice, calm interlude with Gloria had vanished and Marilee was now anxious about being late for the meeting with Steve Reuben. Reuben's was one of the biggest fashion conglomerates in the world, an international company with a turnover in the billions.

'Marilee, we've won the lottery!' Peter had said with delight when Reuben's got in touch with a view to buying out MC Handbags. 'This is the big time. Serious money. We'll be on the pig's back.'

'Haven't we enough money?' Marilee had been about to ask before she'd stopped herself. Peter was the businessman, he'd always taken care of things in the past.

'Creative types shouldn't bother number-crunching,' he'd say fondly if she suggested visiting the accountant with him. 'Don't worry about a thing, petal.'

Funny, she couldn't remember the last time he'd called her 'petal'. Probably when the Italian *Elle* woman was around.

She changed quickly into a dusky-pink trouser suit, then hurried back downstairs. Opening the secret door to her office gently, she realised that Sukey was sitting at her desk, talking on her phone, and clearly not expecting Marilee to appear.

Some instinct made Marilee stop and listen. Hidden behind the Japanese screen, she could hear Sukey's side of the conversation quite clearly.

'I swear the stupid cow's pre-menstrual; she said she didn't want to be disturbed,' sighed Sukey in martyred tones. There was a pause as Sukey listened. 'I know, Petey, but she's driving me nuts. I can't bear working for her.'

Marilee felt the skin at the base of her neck prickle. Sukey was talking to Peter. She was bitching about Marilee to Marilee's own husband.

'I know, Petey,' Sukey wailed again. 'I just hate waiting, darling. I can't wait for us to be together, that's all.'

Behind the screen, Marilee had to cover her mouth with her hand to stop herself gasping out loud.

Sukey sounded petulant now: 'When are you going to tell Marilee about us? I can't wait much longer, you know. I've waited a year, I won't wait any more.'

Marilee slipped silently out the door and went back upstairs. She phoned their accountant. He was surprised to hear from her.

'I thought you hated all this side of the business,' he said. 'Peter said looking at numbers gave you a headache.'

Marilee smiled. It was amazing how many things gave her a headache, according to her husband. He'd invented the notion that ordinary tea gave her a headache ('Marketing, petal'). He'd probably told Sukey that sex gave her a headache too.

'Not at all,' she said gaily. 'I thought you could give me a run-through of the finances, and perhaps tell me what you think of the proposed Reuben deal?'

Peter looked marginally shocked when Marilee arrived at the restaurant dressed in a sharp black suit. He coughed into his martini glass but recovered enough to stand up and smile urbanely at her.

'Marilee, darling, how lovely you look,' he said loudly; then, when he was close enough to kiss her, he whispered, 'Why aren't you wearing your pink mohair?'

Marilee moved so his lips didn't manage to so much as brush her cheek. 'I'm so tired of pink,' she said loudly, and smiled at Steve Reuben.

She left Peter with his mouth open and greeted Steve, who asked her if she wanted an aperitif.

'I'd love a martini,' she told him, sitting down in one of the armchairs in the cosy bar area.

Peter didn't like Marilee drinking at business lunches – booze could make the façade slip – but he said nothing.

When her drink arrived, she sipped deeply and gazed at Steve over the rim of the glass.

'Steve, we're going have to shelve talks of any sort of deal between MC Handbags and your company, I'm afraid,' she said in a marvellously calm voice.

'Why?' demanded Steve.

'Peter and I are getting divorced,' Marilee added, 'and that changes everything.'

She didn't know which man looked more surprised. Probably Peter, on reflection.

'I'm sorry about that,' Steve said uncertainly.

'Me too,' Marilee agreed. 'You see, Peter has been having an affair with my assistant, Sukey.'

Peter went pale under his tan and his hand flew to his Windsor knot to loosen it a smidgen.

Marilee didn't stop. 'He's also been salting money away for years without my knowledge, which has lots of legal implications for the future of the business, you understand. My accountant and my lawyer are looking into it all now.'

'But ... darling, it's not like that ...' stammered Peter. 'The figures need to be explained to you, er ... that money is a little investment, a surprise for you. A bit of creative accounting,' he added, looking pleased at this explanation.

'And you and Sukey running off together afterwards was also a bit of creative accounting?' Marilee enquired sweetly. 'I'm not an idiot, Peter. Stop treating me like one.'

'I hope we can do business afterwards,' said Steve to Marilee, with an eye to the main chance.

'Of course,' Marilee said. She had another good slurp of her martini. It felt quite refreshing. 'Let's have lunch now anyway. We're here, the food is good – what do you say, Peter? One last meal? Or do you want to go home and pack your stuff? My lawyer says you can expect quite a reasonable divorce settlement. Not as much as you'd get if you hadn't tried to steal from the company, but still, not bad.'

Peter didn't look hungry any more.

'Your table is ready,' the maître d' announced.

Marilee rose elegantly to her feet.

'You look beautiful in black,' Steve said gallantly.

Marilee's smile widened. 'Thank you,' she said. 'I've gone off pink. It's so last year.'

This Charming Man
Pauline McLynn

My name is Leo Street and I haven't always been a private investigator. Like a lot of other people, I started life as a child. From then on I had a fairly traditional Irish upbringing, barring the fact that I always thought my parents were slightly madder than most (mad as in crazy rather than cross), and nothing over the last three decades has done much to make me change my mind. After four years of growing, learning new tricks and running wild I was packed off to the local primary school. It had been talked up something rotten in the house, although one crucial detail was omitted, and I set out on the first day naïvely thinking it would be my last. So I was somewhat bewildered to hear that I would be expected to go every day for the next eight years. Thus began my learning curve, which has a habit of, even now, becoming a vertical line from time to time. I quite liked school in the long run, but it was an inauspicious beginning and could have led to real trouble later in life. And I still harbour it as good ammunition for family rows.

My second-level stint was at the Holy Faith Convent, also in my neighbourhood of Clontarf on Dublin's north side. This came with an ugly uniform that got shorter by the year and suited no one, with the noble exception of Samira O'Sullivan whose mother is Indian. Again, the educational process failed to throw up any evidence that I would win a Nobel Prize for anything except being ordinary and happy, but there are times when this can be viewed as a blessing. Besides, the last thing I wanted was to stand out; being a teenager can do that to a gal.

A school reunion is something to be avoided, always. A sweeping statement – perhaps – but true. An invitation to celebrate 'A Decade of Freedom from the Best Years of Your Life' arrived a month before the do, and I spent the interim period pondering not only what to wear but whether to go at all. School days might best be remembered from afar, I reckoned, and after all none of us was getting any younger. I dreaded encountering fossils who were the same age as myself and having to submit to the notion that time is a cruel mistress and gravity the enemy of all ladies with one or more chins.

The invite had stated dress was to be 'up'. I needed something that smacked of understated success and *sex*. I accepted that, in the end, I would wear my one good black dress, so next the obsession moved on to shoes, which were certainly an issue. I tend to wear a pair till they fall apart, and my current demon-heels were in a sad state and needed replacing. It was a terrible shock to realise that I was leaning towards buying a pair of flatties, and was even prepared to take up the hem of the frock to accommodate them. I settled finally on a less-than-elegant slingback style, reduced from fifty notes to a manageable and foxy twenty-five. The shoes were neither high nor low and only left a small amount of black dress fabric trailing across the floor (too little to require alteration, I had decided).

Barry Agnew, my then-boyfriend, an actor, refused to attend (with or without me). As I recall, his chosen words were 'no fucking way'. This suited fine, because I reasoned that it was essentially a reunion of pupils, not pupils and partners (though it was a sure bet that a lot of my ex-classmates would be touting trophy husbands).

But, worried about looking like a Norma-no-mates, I consulted various 'types' of my acquaintance as to whether I was (a) too sad for words to be going alone and/or (b) dangerously close to making a complete eejit of myself. The answers were a horrid succession of affirmatives, but then I do surround myself with a shower of begrudgers. The one thing I did know was that I had the most exotic-*sounding* job of anyone who would attend, unless Imelda Phelan had actually completed her course in nuclear physics at Oxford. And even if she had, her presence at this gathering was surely proof that her career as an apologist for the arms race was in serious trouble. There was also the salient point that I wouldn't be able to tell anyone what it is I actually do, needing to maintain the 'private' bit of private eye. I was going to have to choose the age-old excuse that I work 'in insurance'. You have no idea how boring that can make a conversation. Everyone wants to talk about the time the slates blew off their roof and the company refused to pay up. Scintillating, as I'm sure you'll agree.

Even if I were to confess to being a private investigator, the honest truth about my job is that I spend an awful lot of time waiting around for other people to mess up. It can be the most boring work in the world. Of course, there are times when it can be a little too exciting and dangerous, but these are about as regular as times when pigs take to the air. The Irish private dick is not as rare a creature as you might expect, however; just look in the Golden Pages. There are lots of us, from the really good through to the woefully inept. I'm happy to tread middle ground in this rogues' gallery, and I hope that at least I give value for money.

I put the dress, good underwear and a ladderless pair of tights in a safe place at the back of the wardrobe, in a bid to prevent my cats getting fur all over them, even though they are supposedly barred from upstairs. But I didn't have much hope of my ruse proving successful. There was also the possibility that No. 4, the dog I had acquired on a case in Kildare, might dart up and sneakily cock his leg on the ensemble.

I got back to work and tried not to spend too much time day-dreaming of the oohs and aahs I would get for having stayed so young and hip in this soul-sapping world. Actually, I used to see a few of the old classmates around the town, so it was really more the wonderment at how those who'd got out of Dodge were faring that occupied me. So my days were busy with that and with following various types who were planning to part several insurance companies from their not-so-hard-earned cash in a less than sporting manner. To be honest, these cases bug me as much as if not more than any others because, underneath it all, I have quite a lot of sympathy for those who can successfully free the excess money held hostage by the multinationals by way of a gentle scam. However, these jobs also pay the bills and the liberators of such funds are, strictly speaking, breaking the law and so must be stopped.

I took on the pursuit of a man who had a huge claim in against a recycling plant and was supposed to require a neck brace at all times. I had managed a grainy photograph of him in his back yard *sans* neck brace, but was sure I could do better. He was a golf fanatic, so I reckoned it was only a matter of time before he broke out and took the thing off for the back nine in some out-of-the-way course. I looked forward to some tasty trips to the country or at least to the green and leafy verges of Ireland's capital.

Sod's Law inevitably got involved in proceedings, and typically my crucial day at work following Neck Man coincided with the school reunion. I was crouched by a furze bush, alternately checking my watch – which insisted it was time to go if I was to apply a proper gloss on my sorry self for later – and gasping at the guy's stupidity. He had the brace off and was jumping up and down and twirling with delight at his short game. I had shot some brilliant stills and a good deal of video footage when his partner noticed me in the bushes. I can only thank the god of golf that we were on the eighteenth, because if I'd had to run any further to my car I think I would have collapsed or wet myself, as my harried muscles began to surrender under pressure.

Later, I arrived in the Parkridge Hotel, where staff were hard to find and nervous when approached. From the front door I could smell the booze and hear a weirdly high-pitched murmur in the near distance. It was the unmistakable mark of women on a night out. I followed the trail and it led me to the lounge, where a goodly swarm of Holy Faith graduates were milling about with drinks in hand and attitude in mind. The first I collided with was Imelda, resplendent in a cream tuxedo. She managed to hold her glass of wine away from her body in time and didn't spill a drop on her luxury threads.

'It's OK,' she laughed, as I began my apologies. 'I'm asking for trouble wearing this. I'm like a giant target for red wine and Guinness.'

I kissed her on both cheeks, like the luvvies Barry hangs out with, and told her truthfully that she looked like a million dollars. 'And, while I'm about it, would they be Yankee dollars?' I enquired.

'In return for nuclear arms?'

I nodded.

'I only did a year at Oxford,' she confessed. 'Hated it. Met a farmer, settled down and had four kids.'

I gave a low whistle. 'You don't look like any farmer's wife I ever met,' I pointed out.

'He's a very rich one,' she confirmed. 'Owns land the size of County Clare, so he can keep me in style. It's not rocket science,' she added, with a shrug and a devilish glint. She began to pick twigs from my hair and I told her I was going for a windswept look. 'You have succeeded,' she said, just stopping short of spitting on a handkerchief and wiping some muck off my face. 'Now, a tiny word of warning as you go to get us some drinks' – yep, she's good – 'there's a lot of baby talk in the room so be careful not to get trapped.'

'How do you know I'm not engrossed in all that?' I asked, investing my voice with the tiniest soupçon of pique.

'I know stuff, Street,' she said. 'My mother talks to your mother and then reports to me. I know what colour knickers you're wearing most days.'

This was all too plausible a scenario, so I took it on the chin and made for the bar. Sure enough, as I passed a knot of my peers

I heard one say, 'I can't get his name down for a school anywhere so I'm going to try to pass him off as a Protestant and go for the little place in Sutton.' This cunning plan was meeting with approval. I needed a drink. I squeezed in by a man sitting on a stool at the edge of the counter.

'Do you have kids yourself?' he asked, obviously reading something in my expression.

'No,' I answered. 'I'm child-free. Both my brothers have plenty I can practise with, though. And you know, there are times when I listen to the youngsters and grow fearful. I get the feeling they're going to take over the world from us one day.'

He laughed and bought me a drink. We fell into conversation and I found him funny and personable. He was also something of a looker and I am partial to a nice man who's easy on the eye. I noticed the remnants of a healing scrape on his knuckles that looked like it had been a sore injury. He told me he worked as a builder and those were the perks.

It was like a first date, with flirting and the exchange of tall tales and positive signals. I didn't feel the time passing and suddenly the bell was ringing to call us in for our meal. I had forgotten to ask why he was here but I soon got my answer. An old friend, Katie, appeared at his shoulder and said hi. This was Bob, her husband. Ah well, it had been nice to dream, I thought, suddenly feeling slightly sorry for my lot. We were gathering our things when Bob raised a hand to attract the barman and I noticed Katie flinch. Alarm bells began to softly toll in my head.

I work a lot in the shadow-dance between the law and the wider community. I'm not a cop and don't have any powers beyond those of a normal citizen. I take up some of the slack that the Guards can't deal with, or don't want to. And I see a lot of nasty things: the dark underbelly of the town and the meaner side of the human race. But when my job is done I slip away to start another, or pass on what I have to the authorities if needs be. It can be frustrating but you get used to it. Above all, I don't interfere. But there are moments in every life when you are faced with choices whose consequences aren't all about you. You can choose to ignore these and reason that it's none of your business. Or you can embark on a journey of responsibility and shun the tiny moral cowardices that we all commit each day. I made a decision.

I announced that I needed a visit to the loo, to repair damage, and asked Katie if she wanted to accompany me. She did. The fluorescent lights of the ladies' told me all I needed to know. Under a good make-up job were the tell-tale marks of bruising and one unhealed cut to the upper lip. Katie was also walking with a slight limp. I was angered that a childhood friend I remembered as bubbly and fearless seemed so diminished and afraid now. There was no time to waste.

'How many kids do you have?' I asked.

'Two,' she answered. She wanted to talk and I let her. 'Actually, I didn't think we'd make tonight because Conor had a wee accident and I had to take him to the hospital. He's fine, though. All patched up now.'

There it was, sealed in my mind. Her voice was a study in control, but her hands were not quite in the same league. I felt the stirrings of rage but I had a plan to assuage it.

'Katie, I don't want you to say anything to me about what I'm about to tell you. OK?'

She sighed, a little relieved, I think.

'I know what's going on. Do you understand? I *know*.'

She nodded, still looking at me through the mirror.

I handed her a business card. 'Here's my number if you need to call me. But you probably won't. Ger Furlong will talk to you tonight. You remember her, don't you?' She did. 'She is the woman you need right now, and if I were you I'd take all the advice and help she has to give.'

'He's not much of a drinker or anything,' she said weakly. 'He just gets angry sometimes.' She shuddered as a tiny sob racked through her. 'I love him, you know.'

'That's the trouble,' I said.

We went back to the gathering and I went in search of Ger, a formidable woman who works for Social Services. She was queuing for the buffet supper; chicken casserole for the carnivores and quiche for the vegetarians. Any vegans in the room were remaining thin.

'I don't like the way you're looking at me,' Ger said as I approached her. 'And you've skipped the queue, which could get you lynched.'

I spoke in low, urgent tones. 'You need to talk to Katie, Hunter as was. She's now married to a builder called Farrell. They're at table five and I told her to expect you.'

Ger acknowledged the information with a slight inclination of the head and told me to scram. I knew she would never contact me again about the matter. Lives depend on her discretion.

I can't say I enjoyed the rest of the evening as much as I might have, but there were some laughs. I'm not sure what the staff of the Holy Faith would have made of us as a group, their contribution to Irish society by way of the education system, but we were out there and getting by as well as we could. You do what you have to. I avoided table five by getting myself deliberately and publicly stuck with a shower of harpies playing embarrassing party games. I heard a rumour later that our year is now barred from the Parkridge Hotel, but I'm hoping not to have to check that out any time in the near future.

I broke a heel of my new sandals, ripped the back of my trailing dress, and staggered home at three in the morning, drunk and disorderly. Even Barry noticed that I was a bit upset, or 'tired and emotional' as he put it. He sent me to bed with a litre of water and some aspirin, telling me I'd be better before I was twice married. I dreamt all night that I had to marry two men and each of them was Bob Farrell.

Life got back to its usual pace and Neck Man got done for his attempted deception. Then one day, out of the blue, I got an unsigned card with a fuzzy London postmark. It simply said, 'Thank you from the three of us.' I burned it immediately, grateful for the acknowledgement though it wasn't necessary. And when a man phoned the office shortly afterward and asked for Leo Street, I immediately recognised the honeyed charm of Bob Farrell. I pictured his easy laugh and injured hand.

'Sorry,' I said, 'wrong number,' and hung up.

Three Letters

Roisin Meaney

On Tuesday, 29 October, at 11.43 a.m., Mrs Cynthia Cunningham opened the wrong letter.

Her carelessness was hardly surprising, given that she was trembling with rage at the time. Her hand literally shook as she inserted a perfectly manicured index finger into the corner of the envelope and slid it across. The nerve of that little nuisance – only yesterday she'd warned him that if it happened again, she was going to the Guards. And then, first thing this morning … She slipped the flimsy sheets from the envelope, gritting her teeth and feeling a fresh flood of anger as she remembered hearing the *thump* outside the dining-room window, causing her to look up from her porridge and see—

She took a deep breath and forced the image away; she'd deal with him later. She smoothed the pages flat with a palm and read …

Dear Mam and Dad,

… and immediately realised her mistake. For one thing, this was not Thomas's writing, and he'd never use such nasty paper, or call her anything but 'Mother'. And, for another, her husband had died seven years earlier.

She picked up the envelope and turned it over. *Mr and Mrs Gardner, 12 Rosemount Hill.* Not Mrs Cynthia Cunningham, 10

Rosemount Hill. Lord, she'd got her neighbours' letter – and, worse, she'd opened it. Must be from that daughter of theirs, a mousy little thing, what was her name again? Mrs Cunningham lifted the top sheet and glanced at the bottom of the letter – Grace, that was it. Grace Gardner. Small, nothing to look at, her father's nose, God help her. She'd be about nineteen now; left school a couple of years ago and disappeared off somewhere. Mrs Cunningham had no idea what she was doing now – she and the Gardners weren't exactly on gossiping terms – probably working behind the counter in some shop.

Not like her Thomas, less than a year away from getting his Masters in Science from Trinity. So handsome, and such a brilliant student – his father would have been so proud …

The doorbell sounded suddenly, bringing Mrs Cunningham abruptly back to the hall, and to the letter in her hand. She hurriedly slipped the sheets back into the envelope and dropped it onto the hall table before opening the door.

And there he stood, brazen as anything. 'Can I have my ball back?'

She felt her face burning with angry colour as she looked down at him. Barefaced cheek, not a word of apology – the utter nerve of him. She took a deep, ragged breath. 'No, you most certainly *cannot*. I shall take great pleasure in bursting your ball, and any other balls that you insist on throwing into my garden.' Let's see what he had to say to that.

His face took on a petulant look. 'You took loads already – and I don't do it on purpose, they just go in by an accident.'

By an accident – he couldn't even string a grammatically correct sentence together. What were they teaching them in schools these days? Mrs Cunningham stood her ground, galvanised by her anger.

'Tell that to my shrubs – you've destroyed them.' She indicated the small collection of bushes to the right of the door. 'And why are you not in school?'

His sulky expression didn't change. 'Mid-term break.'

Typical – children had more holidays than they knew what to do with. No wonder they were always getting into trouble, particularly this little vandal. He might be young – about seven or eight, she judged – but he still needed to be taught a lesson. And his mother had been no help when Mrs Cunningham had approached her the previous week.

'Oh, dear, I'm so sorry. He loves playing ball, but I'll be sure and tell him to be more careful in future, Mrs Cunningham.' At least the woman had had the sense not to ask for any of the other ones back. As far as Mrs Cunningham was concerned, what landed in her property became hers.

But the very next day, into her shrubbery another one had come flying; Mrs Cunningham should have saved her breath. It was downright insulting, to say the least, to ignore her so completely the way that woman had.

The boy was spoilt, of course. Anyone could see that. Coming along so late, when the daughter was practically reared – probably a complete surprise to his parents. Mrs Cunningham wouldn't be surprised if they called him their little miracle, or something equally nauseating. Children like that were always ruined. She'd bet he got whatever he wanted – including *carte blanche* to destroy his neighbour's shrubbery.

But not any more; Mrs Cunningham was a woman on a mission. If the parents wouldn't enforce discipline, she would.

'That's all I'm going to say. Now kindly go back to your own garden – and shut my gate after you.' She closed the front door firmly, and then sped into the dining room to watch as he walked down her path and out the gate.

And he left it swinging open behind him. Mrs Cunningham stood looking out for a few disbelieving seconds, then turned and went back into the hall.

'Right.' She picked up the opened envelope, yanked out the sheets again and scanned the writing rapidly.

Three Letters

Dear Mam and Dad,
    This is the letter I hoped never to have to write to you. I have something to tell you that will probably make you very angry at first, but please read this letter to the end.

Mrs Cunningham settled herself on the telephone stool, crossed her legs at the ankles and continued reading.

A few months ago I entered into a relationship with a man I've known for a long time. He's a wonderful person, kind and intelligent and sensitive. To cut a long story short, I've recently discovered that I'm pregnant.

Mrs Cunningham drew in a sharp, satisfied breath.

As you can imagine, I was very distressed when I found out – especially when I imagined how hurt you both would be at the news.

Mrs Cunningham turned to the second page.

But when I told my boyfriend, he was very supportive and promised to stand by me. We are both deeply committed to each other, and intend to raise the child together and, in due course, when the time is right, we plan to marry.

Mrs Cunningham snorted.

Mam and Dad, I know this news will come as a big shock, but please try to look on the positive side. I'm very happy – we both are – and I'm looking forward to spending the rest of my life with the man I love.
    We're wondering if you'd both come up to Dublin soon, and we could all sit down together and talk about it? Please write back

and let me know what you want to do. I hope, when you've thought about it, that you'll agree to meet us.

Your loving daughter,
Grace

Mrs Cunningham read the letter through a second time. Then she folded the sheets and replaced them slowly in the envelope, and stayed sitting where she was on the telephone stool, thinking.

After a while she got up and walked to her bureau. Pulling a sheet of paper towards her, she unscrewed the lid of her fountain pen and began to write. And this is what she wrote:

I see your precious daughter has got herself into trouble. Frankly, I'm not surprised, seeing as how you have no idea how to bring up children. Let this be a lesson to you.

And how should she sign it? Hardly *a friend* – that would be hypocritical. Nothing, then. And no need to disguise her handwriting – there was no reason why the Gardners should ever see another sample of it. She folded the expensive vellum – let them know that some people have standards – and put it into one of her matching envelopes, together with Grace Gardner's letter. She didn't bother writing an address – she'd wait until it was dark, and put it through their door. Why should she waste her money on a stamp?

And then they might realise the necessity for a bit of discipline in the home. Clearly, this girl hadn't been taught the difference between right and wrong – just like her little brother, brought up thinking he could do what he liked. Mrs Cunningham could just imagine the mother, telling him not to mind that cross lady next door. *You keep on playing with your ball, dear – it's easy to get a new one if she keeps them.*

And his big sister, spreading her legs without a thought for the consequences – disgusting. Get married when the time was right, indeed. In Mrs Cunningham's day, the time was right long before any babies put in an appearance – and well after the parents had met, and approved of, the daughter's choice. Certainly not before they'd even laid eyes on him.

Mrs Cunningham waited until it was well after midnight. She rarely went to bed herself before one or two o'clock, only needed a few hours' sleep, like Mrs Thatcher. Now *there* was a woman who understood the importance of discipline. Pity there weren't more like her in the Irish government today – all this nonsense about the rights of criminals, when all those people really understood was good, firm punishment.

The house next door was in darkness. Mrs Cunningham sped up the path and dropped the envelope through the letter-box, hearing the soft *plop* as it landed on the floor of the hall. There; her duty was done. She returned home and slept soundly for four and a quarter hours.

The following morning, Mrs Cunningham glanced out the kitchen window as she stood at the sink filling the kettle for her elevenses. Such a lovely morning, more like April than October, with that beautiful, cloudless blue sky and brilliant sunshine. Mrs Cunningham hummed as she unfolded her newspaper and scanned the headlines: another tribunal, more corruption. And precious little punishment at the end of all that expense, as far as she could see. The only ones gaining seemed to be the barristers. Maybe Thomas should have—

A sudden, faint sound came from the front of the house. It was a sound Mrs Cunningham knew well – and it made her drop her paper and dart from the kitchen through the hall and into the dining room.

And there it was – a white ball, perched on top of her holly bush. Shaking with fury, Mrs Cunningham marched to the front door and threw it open. No sign of the little demon. She crunched over the gravel to the ball, grabbed it and headed back indoors, almost stepping on the envelope which sat on the hall floor, and which she hadn't noticed in her rush to retrieve the ball.

She bent and picked it up without looking at it, and practically threw it onto the hall table. She'd deal with it later; now she had work to do. In the kitchen she selected her sharpest knife and carried it out to her small back garden with the ball. She laid them both on the garden seat and went into the shed, coming out a moment later with a bulky black plastic bag.

It took less than a minute to burst all six balls, although the brown one – was it leather? – took more than a little effort on her part. She made as much noise as she could, ramming the knife into each ball and slashing through the plastic, or leather, or whatever it was, with loud grunts. Hopefully he was listening on the other side of the fence. Panting, she replaced the useless balls in the black plastic bag and deposited the whole lot in her wheelie bin at the bottom of the garden. There, that would teach him.

She had washed her hands and poured almost-boiling water onto the coffee in the cafetière before she remembered the letter in the hall. She picked up the envelope and scanned the front of it – better be careful she didn't repeat her mistake of yesterday. This time, though, it was addressed to her – and the writing was Thomas's.

Funny, he never wrote letters, always phoned. Every Sunday evening, regular as clockwork. Some children were very dependable. Mrs Cunningham brought the envelope into the kitchen and settled herself at the table with a cup of coffee before opening it. Then she pulled out the single sheet of paper and unfolded it and began to read.

Dear Mother,
    The news I have will come as something of a surprise …

Mrs Cunningham blinked once.

… and while initially you may feel shocked, I'm sure that with time, you will come to see it as a very positive event.

Mrs Cunningham's free hand slid slowly towards her throat.

The fact is, I've recently got involved with a girl I've known for – well, all my life, really. It's actually Grace Gardner, from next door …

With an anguished cry, Mrs Cunningham crumpled the letter and flung it away from her. Then she buried her head in her hands, oblivious to the coffee that was splashing from the toppled cup onto her expensive quarry tiles.

Leaving the Wedding
Lia Mills

A couple of months ago Charlie picked a fight with me in Mc Daid's. He didn't like my outfit: low-cut tiger-print top, black micro-mini, black tights. I left him in a huddle with his friends and went up to the bar to sulk.

A woman who wore a thick gold necklace on the outside of her polo-necked jumper opened her eyes wide when she saw me. Her tiny eyebrows crawled up towards her bleached hair. She said something out of the side of her mouth to her friend, who looked at me too and smirked. The two of them broke up laughing. I looked down and, wouldn't you know it, one breast had slipped free of my top and was on display.

'Disgusting!' the friend said, as clear as anything.

And then this guy Lar appeared, out of nowhere. He stood between me and them while I fixed myself. 'What'll you have?' he asked. It was my face he looked at.

'Beam me up, Scotty,' I muttered. I must have been puce. I looked around, wondering if anyone else had seen.

'Don't mind them,' he said, handing me a pint. 'Are you here alone?'

'I'm with Charlie.'

'I see.' Lar looked over to where Charlie sat in the middle of a crowd, the centre of attention. In his element.

*

Even when I'm furious with him, the sight of Charlie unnerves me. He could be a model for aftershave, with his tan and his short, wavy blond hair and those innocent blue eyes of his. There's not a freckle out of place on that man's face. But he has no time for that kind of thing. 'Modelling's for poofters,' he'd say, if I suggested it.

There's no question of Lar being a model for anything, ever. He's an ugly man. His nose makes a thick, crooked slant across his face, his hair is long and tangled red and he has a beard. He wears big jumpers with frayed sleeves, unhealthy-looking denim, bad shoes. Mind you, his eyes are a peculiar shade of green-and-gold. You have to look at them a second time, to make sure they're real. His irises are like fiery folded petals. They flare a little when he looks at you.

Lar often comes into the second-hand bookshop where I work. It was the best job I could find when I left college with a bad degree, four years ago. I stayed because I like it. There aren't many jobs where height is an advantage; I'm one of the few people there who don't need to run around looking for the ladder a million times a day. People bring boxes and suitcases full of tattered, unwanted books into the shop and I have to decide what to do with them. I love the way they smell, of all the time that's passed since they were last opened. That boggy, resinous tang makes me dizzy. I like going through the pages and finding scraps of paper with messages on them, or reminders; I've found letters, locks of hair, pressed flowers. Sometimes there's an inscription on the flyleaf. 'This Bible is for Cornelius, from his mother. Heed it Well.' Poor Cornelius. I'm guessing there wasn't much affection in that household. I'll tell you one thing I've learned – people's handwriting has changed in the last fifty years, and not for the better.

Every now and again I come across something valuable, like a set of journals published by some small, forgotten press, or a volume of poetry whose pages have never been cut.

'Look at this,' I said to Lar, the first time I spoke to him, holding out a first edition of James Stephens's poems. The pages were soft and thick, like blotting paper. They folded over themselves, uncut. 'Imagine owning this and never bothering to open it.'

Lar is a poet too, but no one has ever heard of him. He took the book from me, held it up to his face, closed his eyes and breathed in. I'd thought I was the only person in the world who does that. Then he bought the book, even though I'd have sworn he couldn't afford it.

He asked me to meet him for a drink one afternoon. It was a back-street bar, seasoned by years of smoke and the rich, spunky smell of yeast. Dark wood and dirty windows. Old men were parked at the bar on high stools, staring into their pints. I went into the back to splash cold water on my face and when I came out the place was filling up. Lar had come in while I was in the loo. He sat there, looking towards the wrong door. He'd cut his hair. His beard had gone and his face was soft and pale without it. Too open. I watched him scan the people who came in, looking for me. His shoulders had a hungry slope to them under the blunt stalk of his neck.

I slipped out. Later, I slid a note under his door. 'I'm sorry. I changed my mind.'

Soon afterwards, I found out that Charlie was going out with another girl, a friend of his sister's, from their yacht club.

'Are you screwing her?'

The shock on his face told me more than I wanted to know. I was the one he was screwing. She was a different kind of girl entirely. He'd probably marry her.

'I didn't know men like you still existed,' I said, not being able to come up with anything better.

Charlie was the first man I'd ever gone out with that my family liked. The trouble was, I liked him too. I'd begun to wonder what it might be like to live with him, to nudge him awake at four in the morning; to come in from work and find him waiting for me beside the fire, a bottle of wine already open, two glasses.

I should have known. I don't even like wine. It gives me a blotchy rash on my neck and a headache the next day. It would never have worked, but that didn't stop me thinking about it. It didn't help that my cousin Jenny was up to ninety with her wedding plans at the time. It was all she could talk about. At least she didn't notice my lack of interest in flowers and seating plans and menus.

'We'll have a vegetarian option for you,' she told me, being tolerant of one of my many peculiarities. Height, bookishness, unusual clothes are others. Jenny guards against peculiarity in everything she does.

'You don't want to end up like Auntie Bea,' she warns. Auntie Bea is our great-aunt, really. She lives with our granny and flirts with herself out loud all day long, no matter where she is or who else is in the room. She admires her beautiful hands and strokes her nicotined hair and tells herself how beautiful she is. She sits with her legs bent to the side, like a model, and smokes through a cigarette-holder made of ivory, narrowing her eyes at any man who appears on her horizon.

Jenny is the opposite of me. She's tiny, but she's always known exactly where she's going and how to get there. She's like a force of nature, the way she bears down on a target and engulfs it. Hurricane Jenny. She's always wanted to get married. She's been saving sheets and towels and plates on special offer since she got her first job in Dunne's, the summer that she turned sixteen and started going out with Tony. The poor eejit never stood a chance. Jenny and Auntie Marian have moulded him into the sort of man they want and he's gone along without so much as a whimper of protest, as far as I can see. They steered him into Dunne's as well and now he's a regional manager or something. Jenny left, ages ago. She manages a trendy restaurant in the suburb where they've bought a house. It's all part of her master plan. Marriage, house, job, kids.

'We're different, you and me,' Jenny says. 'I'm a people person, and you're not.'

Auntie Marian agrees. 'Jenny's such a people person,' she gushes, over the growing mountain of presents on display on her dining-room table. 'Everybody loves her.'

'How's Charlie?' Jenny asks.

I can't bring myself to tell them. 'Grand,' I say. 'Never better.'

'Make sure you bring him to the pre-wedding party,' Auntie Marian reminds me.

My family have high hopes for Charlie. They think I need a man to sort me out and give me a future.

I can't believe it when I get to the bus stop and find Lar there, looking bored. He straightens when he sees me.

'There you are,' he says, as if he's been expecting me.

'It's me all right.'

I take a place at the back of the queue, three people behind him. Our eyes meet above all those heads bent against the rain. He falls out of line and comes to stand beside me. 'Where are you off to?'

'A wedding.'

He looks at my raincoat, the black beret I've clipped onto my hair, my shiny black boots and blood-red lipstick. And smiles.

'What?' I say.

'You're not exactly dressed for it.'

'Oh, yeah? What am I dressed for, then?'

'Danger.'

His eyes crease at the corners. He really is one of the ugliest men I've ever seen. He leans closer and whispers in my ear. 'Trouble.' He says the word as if he can taste it.

The slow, patient file of people begins its climb out of the rain into the full, lit warmth of the bus. We squash up to the end and grip the handrail. Lar's eyes are on a level with mine. He's the first man I've ever met who's as tall as I am when I wear heels.

These boots have been under my bed since last winter. With

the coat and the beret, they make me feel like a spy in wartime. All I need is a cigarette and an accomplice.

The bus lurches along. Lar's jumper looks as if it was knitted by someone's half-blind aunt, in clashing shades of red and orange that waver across his chest in uneven rows. He's in his usual jeans. You could barely bring him to a jumble sale, let alone a pre-wedding party.

'Come with me,' I say. 'It'll be a laugh.'

When we get off the bus the air is heavy with the smell of bonfires and rain. The pavement is slick and I nearly lose my balance, not being used to the heels on my shiny boots, but I catch myself in time.

'Who's this?' Auntie Marian asks, frowning at Lar. Jenny emerges from a crowd of well-wishers.

'This is Lar,' I mumble, not looking at anyone. I wish to God I hadn't brought him. What was I thinking?

Jenny drags me aside. 'Where's Charlie?'

'We broke up.'

'When? Why didn't you tell me?'

I look over her shoulder at a group where Uncle Frank is telling a long joke. The women shift from foot to foot and look out from under their hair like people waiting for a storm to pass. Each of the men has a glass upended over his mouth, like legs in a chorus line.

'Who is he?' Jenny asks, her eyes trained, fierce, in Lar's direction. 'He's very … rough-looking.'

Lar bends down to light Auntie Bea's cigarette, then snaps the lighter shut with a flourish. She blows a column of smoke into his face and smiles.

'He's a poet.'

'On the dole, so,' Jenny snorts. She hurries off to greet the latest group of arrivals.

*

The walls of Jenny's house are lined with chairs borrowed from other houses on the street and a few from the parish hall. Young people crowd the stairs and the elderly relatives take the comfy armchairs and ladderbacks. All the doors are open, including the one to the back garden, where bottles of beer cool in buckets of cold water on the grass.

The singing starts. A few of the old people lift quavery voices in plaintive ballads. Auntie Bea struggles to her feet and leans on the high back of an armchair as if it's a piano. She belts out a blues song in her breathy, off-key voice. Everyone cheers. I hate the silence afterwards, the pressure of a gap that needs to be filled. I'm afraid I'll leap into that gap out of pure hysteria, even though I have no voice.

When Lar says that he'll sing, my toes curl against the leather of my boots. I'd hate for him to make an eejit of himself.

I needn't have worried. He leans his head back and sings a slow lament in a voice that sounds like golden whiskey, sliding over ice. I can't believe it: they like him. Even Jenny smiles at me. Then an elderly man in a tweed suit struggles to his feet and begins a rebel song. There are nods and groans of approval and people join in the chorus. It'll be downhill from here.

I slip outside. Lar follows me.

'I didn't know you could sing.'

He smiles and bows. I look away.

'I'm going home.'

'I don't get you,' he says. 'What do you want?'

'Why do I have to want anything?'

He laughs. 'Come back with me?'

I shake my head and walk past him into the house to say goodbye.

The next day, Jenny is a vision in a white satin sheath that clings to every curve and lift of her body. It suddenly dawns on me that this day is all she's thought about since she was sixteen. When it's over, what will she look forward to?

'You're gorgeous,' I tell her, and mean it.

'Thanks.' Jenny grins in a way that takes me back to when we used to hide behind the sofa and eavesdrop on the adults. She looks happy.

'Good luck,' I say. I mean that, too.

At dinner, I am put beside Uncle Marty, home from the States. I make an effort to be sociable.

'What's it like in America?'

'It's better here,' he says. 'It's good to see the old traditions still alive.'

'Why? Don't people get married over there?'

He dismisses this with a wave of a fat red hand.

Across the table, Marty's wife Bridge dips her heavily flowered hat in my direction. 'I wouldn't have known you!' She eyes me up and down. 'You were such a little girl, when we left.' Her eyes go round and innocent. 'I suppose you'll be next?'

Marty cackles his disbelief.

'I doubt it,' I say.

Bridge leans closer to me, all sympathy. 'There's someone for everyone, dear.'

I look at her husband. 'I'm fussier than most.'

The waitress knows nothing about a vegetarian meal. She goes off to look for some pasta when I ask about it.

'So, you don't eat meat,' Marty says. 'I like red-blooded things, myself. Raw.' He spears a slab of underdone steak with his fork. 'Tell me,' he leers, 'would you find this revolting?'

I nod.

'And would you feel like that about sex?'

'Sorry?'

'About the men you sleep with.' He licks his oily lips. 'You know. Meat. Does it disgust you?'

Bridge pretends she hasn't heard.

I clear my throat. 'I prefer my meat alive.'

Marty slaps his thigh, roars out a laugh. People turn to look.

'Prick,' I say, a little louder.

He stops laughing.

I push myself to my feet and make myself walk, not run, out of the room. I can't wait to feel clean air on my face.

Lar lives on a square that is famous for its violence and decay. The house is tall and old, its heavy front door crowded with bells.

'Why aren't you at the wedding?' he asks. 'What do you want?'

'Do you remember that night in McDaid's?' I ask. 'When I fell out of my shirt?'

I don't say that everything since then has just been a waste of time. I save my breath for the stairs. Lar lives at the top of the house, under the eaves. When we get there, he pours me a tall glass of water and watches while I drink it, greedy, water spilling down my chin. His sleeves are rolled up and I can see the reddish hair glinting on his forearms.

'Won't they wonder where you are?'

'Probably.'

'Don't you care?'

'Not much.'

'Come here.'

Here we go. My heart starts beating in my throat as if it's looking for a way out through my mouth. He takes my hand and I let him lead me towards the bedroom. Instead, he pulls a ladder down from a trapdoor and tells me to climb it. At the top, I have to duck through a skylight and then we're up among the slopes and angles of roofs, stacks of chimney pots like pillars in some crumbling, half-assed temple. Everywhere I look, the city glows under its rim of mountains. There's nothing as commonplace as stars in that sky, only a foggy, throbbing shimmer of movement and music above a swirling tide of people. In the distance, I can see the river and the broad street where the hotel is, where everyone I'm related to is currently busy making judgments, making plans.

I curl my arms into his sides, up his back, look right into his

230

face, those green eyes on a level with mine. He doesn't seem surprised. He presses the length of his body hard against the length of mine so that I can know how unsurprised he is.

From where we're standing, the city looks as if it goes on forever, full of promise. I'm happy to be part of it, leaning against the warm weight of a man in the dark, knowing what's going to happen next. I don't much care what happens after that. This is enough of a future for me.

Emma Jane

Éilís Ní Dhuibhne

We were having a cappuccino at the airport café; our flight had been delayed and there was no indication as to when it would leave. We positioned ourselves close to a monitor and prepared to wait, splitting *The Irish Times* between us. He took the sports section and I took the rest. It was Monday, not a good day for newspapers. I skimmed it all too quickly. My coffee cup was empty, the beige scum of cappuccino fluff already stiffening inside the rim. I can feel time passing sometimes, second by jagged second, and this was one of those times. To keep the panic at bay I resorted to doing the crossword puzzle. Actually I do it fairly regularly; it's one of my nasty little secrets. An old saying or a cutting edge. Saw. Spectrum ending in 'w'. Rainbow.

A print in the French Revolution. Third letter 'b'. It was bound to be something simple and obvious, since that was the ethos of this particular crossword, but somehow I could not find the word. This happens. I fly through most of the clues and then get stumped at one. Some sort of block enters my mind. I glanced at my boyfriend, whose English is in many ways better than mine, even though it is not his first language. He was absorbed in whatever he was reading. His face was tense with concentration, his dark eyes glued to the page. He is somewhat short-sighted, I think; he always holds the page very close to his face, but he insists that it is just a habit. 'Hey,' I called, 'a print in the French

232

Revolution. Middle letter "b".' He did not answer or raise his eyes. I repeated, 'Hello! Anybody home? I asked you a question!'

'Excuse me!' he said, with a smile. 'I am concentrating.'

We met in the Financial Services Centre where I have worked as an accountant for ages. He came in as an IT consultant about a year ago. We were introduced over lunch one day soon after he arrived. He struck me as handsome, which is indisputable, but shy and unapproachable, which is also true up to a point. It never occurred to me that I could have a relationship with him, because he was so stiff and distant and he didn't seem to have a clue as to how to interact socially with me or anyone else. His politeness was excessive. He had impeccable manners but they worked against him, rendering him almost a figure of fun, like a Japanese tourist in a racist Hollywood movie. He was not, however, a figure of fun when it came to professional matters; he knew his stuff and was really impressive at meetings. And I was wrong about his inter-personal skills: it turned out that he was completely confident and competent as far as relationships were concerned. His approach to them was as meticulously professional as was his approach to everything else.

A few weeks after we had first met he invited me to accompany him to the opening of an art exhibition. I accepted. As a matter of fact, I had seldom been invited to anything like that before, not by a man. The men I know – the young men, the boys, I am twenty-three – do not *do* art.

He was much older than them, of course, already twenty-six. He did not drink, so his idea of a date was not a journey to mutual oblivion in an all-night club in Temple Bar or a weed-fest in someone's apartment near the mouth of the Liffey. We had what seemed to me a thoroughly old-fashioned, thoroughly civilised courtship (that was the word): going to dinner, going to the film centre and to the theatre, once or twice attending formal dinner parties. He managed to acquire a wide circle of acquaintances rather quickly.

My parents were uneasy about his nationality and religion, but naturally they did not mention their worries to me, and they were delighted that I had a proper boyfriend after years of wild spinsterhood. I was now having the sort of relationship they had had themselves in their youth, no doubt, instead of what they regarded as the completely dissipated life of a young Dubliner. They knew I was in safe hands when I was with my new young man, as my father ironically called him, whereas when I was with my old friends they lived in fear of being called up in the early hours of the morning by the police – when I was at college I had once, just once, been admitted, comatose, to the A and E of a city-centre hospital, after having ten too many at a nightclub. Now, for the moment, their concerns were dispelled. I hardly drank anything at all. My new young man believed I was almost a tee-totaller.

I missed my wild life occasionally, but not too much. I took to culture like a duck to water, to everyone's great surprise. 'You're growing up at last,' Mummy said. 'Excuse me, I earn sixty thousand euro a year,' I said. 'How many grown-ups do that?' Mummy had worked for five years in some menial capacity in the Civil Service but went on a career break when I was born and never worked again, so any reference to my career puts her in her place.

When he asked me to visit his family, I accepted the invitation. I was not being bought into a marriage, it was just a visit; I could come back. In fact I had a return ticket. The holiday would consist of a week with his family, followed by some touring and trekking in the mountains, then back home to Stillorgan. He would be returning with me. His contract ran for another year. There was no need to pay any attention to the future as yet.

He apologised.

'Sorry, you know I hate to be disturbed when I am concentrating on anything, even Tom Humphries on the heroic flaws of the Irish rugby squad.' He smiled and took my hand. His hands are incredibly warm, hot even, and I have bad circulation. I love having my hand held by anyone with hot hands; it is like wearing a human glove, but no glove is as warm and comforting as good hands.

'Yes,' I said.

'It gives me a headache.' He squeezed. 'So what is it?'

'Nothing.' I discarded the paper. 'I'm getting impatient is all. I hate being delayed.'

He smiled quizzically.

'Would you like another coffee?'

'No, thanks.' I'd had four cups this morning already. I released his hand. 'What happens if we miss our connection in Frankfurt?'

He shrugged.

'We'll wait for the next flight. Perhaps we'll spend a night in Frankfurt. Have you ever been there?'

'No, have you?'

'Yes. Frankfurt is fine for a night. But we don't have to worry about that yet. There's plenty of time.'

'I'm going to the ladies'. I'll be back in a minute.'

You can't say loo to him. Or score or chick or even chillaxe. It's not that he doesn't understand slang. He understands everything. But he doesn't like it.

He lives in a palace. It is built around a courtyard; it looks a bit like the Alhambra. There are palm trees around a rectangular pool, cool white rooms with lovely latticed wooden shutters, dramatic flowers, hibiscus and frangipani and so on. His family look beautiful, dignified and kind; the girls and his mother wear traditional dress most of the time, at least when they are being photographed, but for them that means delightful silk things in bright colours, veils of gossamer in shades of peacock and pink, snowy lace draped seductively across their jet-black hair. The family is not old-fashioned at all. One of his sisters is studying medicine and the other is an engineer. I'll fit right in, he said, though not with his usual confidence.

'Will I have to wear a veil?'

'Of course not. They'd think that silly,' he laughed. 'The girls wear western clothes most of the time anyway, jeans and T-shirts. Stop worrying!'

The girls have been promised to men in marriage, men they have not seen, just like in *East is East* or that other lovely movie that teaches us how other ways of life work too and where it all ends happily.

They haven't promised him, not yet.

'How will they feel about me?' I asked this question, although he had not asked me to marry him and I had not asked myself if I wanted to. I mean to say, I am from Stillorgan. My mates don't do marriage. Or if they do it happens after they have become pregnant or even after they have had the baby – maybe making sure that it goes full term and that they really have one before they tie that indissoluble-unless-you-spend-a-small-fortune knot. More likely they just don't get around to it. And they usually have to work for about ten years before they can afford even the mingy house in Kildare or Kilcock or Kilballysomethingorother a million miles from civilisation. I have decided that I will never live further from town than the Sandyford Luas stop, which also happens to be the last southside stop of the airport coach, but even on my salary it won't be easy to buy anything you could swing a cat in there. If we took the plunge I'd probably have a palace the minute I plighted my troth. Of course that too would be quite a distance from the Stillorgan Shopping Centre, but can a girl have everything?

When I pushed open the heavy door to the loo I got a surprise. It was full of colours. When I saw the colours I understood that everything in the airport is a pale shade of grey, with the occasional dash of murky brown. Even people waiting in queues seem to wear safe, muted colours. This cloakroom, however, was a riot of green and red and purple. The reason was that it was full of a kind of person you tend to meet at traffic-light junctions or in the doorways of shops, but not usually at the airport. Gypsies. From Moldavia or the Ukraine or somewhere. Still, I suppose some of them must pass through as they come into Ireland. Maybe they don't wear those bright gypsy clothes when they're slipping past the immigration officer? But these women were in the departure lounge, they were obviously on their way out, so I suppose they could wear whatever they felt comfortable in. After a while I noticed another colour: navy blue. There were three female Guards in the cloakroom, placed at strategic points. They looked stressed, to put it mildly, and seemed irritated that I wanted to answer a call of nature. They hardly moved out of the way to let me through. Having made considerable exertions, I finally gained entry to a cubicle.

I had barely bolted the door and placed the sanitised paper cover on the seat when a hullabaloo started outside. A woman began to scream, 'I do not want to go back! They will kill me!' Suddenly I realised exactly what was happening. A deportation. How exciting! I had heard about this sort of thing on the news. It happened three or four times a year. The Minister for Justice would issue an order and the Guards would do a raid on various places, round up fifty or sixty illegal asylum-seekers and escort them back to where they came from on a chartered flight. It was all supposed to be handled with dignity and decorum. But the women in the red and green skirts were scuppering that. Restraint was definitely not their style. And it struck me that hearing a knock on your door one night before you go to bed, being ordered to pack and leave, might not encourage decorum. I imagined the knock. 'Open up, it's the Guards.' The tightness in the chest, the panic. 'Take a small bag. You are returning to Moldavia.' Is there such a place? Moldavia? Somewhere not in the EU, anyway. Whatever.

'I will not go, I will not go!' the woman screamed.

I came out of my cubicle. She was sitting on the floor, weeping, while the other women gathered around her, complaining in a sort of Greek chorus. One of the gardaí was trying to restrain the screamer and the other was on a mobile, calling for help. I wanted to see what would happen next. So I spent a long time fiddling with the tap and letting soft soap ooze its way very slowly from the dispenser in its disgusting, greasy little dribble onto my hands. Ugh, the smell of that soap, deliberately horrible, I suppose, to stop people using it. I spent ages at the hand drier too; you have to, anyway, to actually dry your hands. I saw it all. By the time I had got around to pulling my brush out of my bag, reinforcements had arrived – more Guards and somebody else, a doctor probably. He jabbed the crying woman with a needle, I kid you not. The shock probably sedated her before the medication had a chance to work. She stopped yelling straightaway and then they all left, the brightly coloured women surrounded by a phalanx of navy-blue Guards, female and male at this stage. In an emergency, the gender-segregation rule of the loo is dispensed with, apparently.

I brushed my hair very slowly. The cloakroom was empty now, drained of sound and colour and drama. It had reverted to being a meaningless airport loo, grey and drab and silent.

And at that moment something happened. A dark wave washed over my spirits. Everything sank – sank back like a wrecked ship to the bottom of the sea. I felt oceans tumbling around in my heart and I wanted to weep for weeks.

But I knew what I needed. A drink.

A short restorative brandy, to help me forget that screaming deportee, or a long cool glass of white wine, my favourite tipple before I mended my ways and started being a girlfriend.

That's what I would have done had I been stuck in the airport alone or with my mates, or with that boy I used to have a thing with two years ago, Ronan, who left on an Erasmus to do photography in Finland and never came back. I would have gone to the pub and had a glass or two of Chardonnay, and the time would have passed quickly and pleasantly, and I would not have worried about a thing.

The monitor still said 'delayed' when I got back to the coffee bar. He was sitting with his eyes closed, his head drooping slightly towards his shoulder.

'Still delayed,' I said brightly. 'We'll miss the connection for sure.'

'*C'est la vie*,' he said quietly.

For a second I thought of asking him about the crossword clue again. But the solution came to me as I stood there, grinning.

'I'd like a glass of wine,' I said.

He didn't say anything to that.

'We can go to the bar over there.' I indicated the bar that looks out over the runway. It was fairly crowded even though it was quite early in the morning.

'But, Emma Jane,' he said, 'you know I don't drink.'

'I don't either, most of the time,' I said. 'But I really want a drink right now. OK?'

'I am not very happy about this,' he said. He was in earnest, and quite upset. 'At home you will never be able to drink alcohol, my parents would die of horror if you did.'

'Would they?' I felt like giggling.

'Of course,' he said. 'They hate in particular to see a woman drinking.'

'Hmm,' I said, looking at his smiling face against the grey and brown backdrop of the airport.

'Another coffee?' he asked. He smiled and squeezed my hand again, in his warm grip.

'OK,' I said. 'I'll have a latte this time, just for a change.'

He went back to the counter.

I could see the arrested asylum-seekers lined up to go through the security check. They were quiet now, resigned to their fate or chemically sedated, about to leave Ireland and go back home, the home they had left whenever – a year ago, three years ago – perhaps in a container truck, perhaps in the goods carriage on a train, perhaps on a scheduled flight, I don't know how these people get here. But they do. They reach Ireland, land of the Dundrum

Shopping Centre, Temple Bar and Tesco and the points race. Land of the rich, Liberty Hall; the place everyone wants to be.

I got up and left the table. He was just ordering the coffee; I could see his back, the back of his new cream Armani jacket, the back of his lovely head, as I headed for the stairs. My bag had been checked through to our destination. The flight would be held up again when it was discovered that I was not taking the plane, in case I had put a bomb in it. Oh, well! He would no doubt call me on my mobile long before that discovery was made. I took it out and switched it off as I slipped through the automatic door. One of the blue airport coaches was waiting at its stop. I hopped on without paying, without even asking where it was going. Nobody stopped me.

The bus started. It pulled away from the terminals, down the winding dark airport roads towards the M1 and the M50 and the other little roads that led to familiar places. The bus was as blue as the sky, and in the real sky above, great white cumulus clouds tossed around like promises of pleasure. The silver planes soared upwards, carrying the hopeful and the despairing alike. Their roaring engines sounded like the confused cries of all the human race.

Having a Baby

Anita Notaro

'How are you feeling?'

'Nervous. You?' I looked at my husband. He looked tired, crumpled.

'A bit apprehensive. I'll be glad to get off this flight, though. These seats are tight.' He patted his stomach. 'And I am not exactly fat.'

He wasn't. Robert was tall and thin and lean. Lanky, they called him at school.

'I wouldn't care about the seats if the food had been edible.'

He gestured towards the pile of sweet wrappers. 'Want another?'

'No, I want a toasted ham sandwich and a mug of decent coffee.' I tried to stretch but there was nowhere to go. I clicked open the seat-belt and stood up. 'That's better. Want to get out?'

'In a minute. I need to get my bits. My teeth are coated with … plaque, I think it must be.' He swirled his tongue around his gums. 'Grit, anyway,' he confirmed, giving me one of those looks. 'Fancy a snog?' He winked at me.

'We've done the mile-high thing. Back when I could still swing my leg up on the washbasin if I wanted to.' I sat down again and pecked him on the cheek. 'Thanks.'

'For what?' He was puzzled.

'For all this … for going along with the idea in the first place. I know it hasn't been easy for you.'

'Hey, I wanted it too, you know. There was no way I'd have done all this otherwise.'

'I know. God, it's taken a long time. I hope it'll be worth it,' I sniggered to hide my nerves.

'It will be. This is the final hurdle. Stop worrying.'

'I wonder what she'll be like? Really like, I mean. That picture didn't really give us a clue.'

'Yeah. Well, we'll know soon enough, I guess.'

'She looked like a doll. And I couldn't see her eyes.' I turned away slightly, in case he saw the tears that threatened. I was just tired from all the travelling. That black-and-white, out-of-focus picture had kept me going for months and given me the energy to continue knocking down the last obstacles. And there are hundreds of giant boulders to wrestle with when you're trying to adopt a baby.

'How long more to go?'

'Less than an hour.'

'OK, let me out, then, before the queues start for the toilets. I need to freshen up.'

'Right, you go first. I'll mind the stuff.'

He ruffled my hair. 'You always say that.' He disappeared down the aisle, having freed his washbag from the mound of packages in the overhead bins.

I sat down to mull it all over again. It was hard to believe that we were finally on our way to get her. I sighed. God, the heartache we'd been through.

First, there'd been the expectation of our own baby and the joy that had brought to us as newlyweds – making plans, trying to conceive at every opportunity, giggling together in hushed tones as we anticipated our next soirée.

I felt young again as I remembered how easy it had been to embarrass Robert. I had taken full advantage of his shyness when it came to sex. I used to ring him in the office where he worked and tell him to hurry home because I was wearing my black lace stockings. He'd be mortified.

That kept us happy for a while, until we realised there was nothing happening on the baby front. Our GP had told us to stop worrying, give it time. Why is it that everyone wants you to be patient when you're young and impatient and six months seems a lifetime? A year on, we were back in the surgery. They suggested tests. I felt as though our image was being tarnished somewhat. Up until then we'd been bullet-proof.

Discovering that there was no medical reason why we couldn't conceive cheered us up – and made for long, lazy nights in bed, with a bottle of wine, trying to 'relax', as the doctor had suggested.

Three years further on, having discussed it to death, we were back in a clinic, this time for IVF treatment.

'What are you thinking about? Your forehead is all creased up.' Robert was back.

'Nothing much. Feeling better?'

'Yeah, a bit less grubby, anyway. So?'

'So what?'

'Something's going on in that head of yours. I know that look.'

'I was thinking about the IVF.'

'God, don't go there, love.'

'It was tough, wasn't it?' I rubbed his arm as he sat down again. He pulled me towards him and kissed the top of my head.

'To think I always thought that having loads of sex would be heaven. I used to dread you telling me we had to have it immediately.'

'And several times, too.'

'Talk about killing a man's erection …'

'Remember the evening I called into your golf club to meet you for a drink? The look of relief on your face when I told you we didn't have to have sex that night.'

'That was the worst time, actually.' He looked at me. 'Wasn't it?'

'I suppose. All the money we had to find, you working two jobs ...'

'That didn't matter, although the cost was a drain, yeah. It was the waiting each month and then having to watch your heart break every time you got your period. That was awful.' He rubbed my hand the way he used to back then, and I thought how close we'd become. I loved him more now than when I married him first, clichéd and all though it sounded.

'Anyway, what's brought this on?'

'Just thinking about how we got to where we are now, and how bloody stressful it's been.'

He nodded. 'Mind you, the whole adoption process comes a close second to IVF in terms of stress. Remember that social worker, what was her name again?'

'Marian. You nearly clocked her one night.' I smiled, but it hadn't been remotely funny at the time.

'It was the total invasion of our lives I couldn't take. It wasn't enough that they'd had us checked out by the cops, but then they grilled us over and over again. The same sort of stuff, week in, week out.'

'They had to, you know that.'

'Sure I do, but I still think they could have been a bit more sensitive. You only have to look at us to know we're not a pair of mass murderers.'

'I bet some people thought Fred and Rosemary West were angels.'

'Suppose.'

'Anyway, I'd better go and freshen up too. They'll be switching on the seat-belt sign shortly.'

Landing in Romania felt like another huge leap. Bucharest was beautiful. It was a cold, grey day. My stomach was fluttering.

Our driver and translator was Titus. He had kind eyes. He smiled; he'd seen plenty of couples like us before, I knew. I'd say he'd helped patch up more than one bruised relationship and made quite a few weary hearts soar again.

The journey to the orphanage was like stepping back in time. Think Ireland in the 1950s – everything brown and depressing. Shops in need of repair, empty windows, impoverished villages, the odd flashing neon Coca-Cola sign to remind us that Ceaucescu's regime was over and prosperity had arrived.

The building itself made Mountjoy men's prison seem like a miracle of modern architecture. They showed us into the cleanest part of the building, I suspected. It had more brown walls – just a different shade – exposed, gurgling pipes and windows with cracked, grimy panes. The cold was bearable. The smell wasn't, though.

Titus talked incessantly. Papers were exchanged. Men and women came and went. After two hours sitting on hard, plastic chairs Titus approached us. He wasn't smiling.

'You must go to hotel. Wait. Problem with papers.'

'Our papers? But there couldn't be, we had them —'

'No. The child's. I will take you to local hotel. You stay there. I must go back to Bucharest.'

We didn't understand. He shrugged. Told us it happens all the time.

We spent two days sitting on a damp bed in a local 'five-star' hotel.

Lots more brown. This shade reminded me of the conkers I used to play with as a child. At first we tried to be cheerful. We even went out for dinner that night. There was no choice of where to eat. None of our usual 'Indian or Chinese or Italian' bickering. No tossing of coins to see who got to choose. We ate meat and salad and bread in a local shack and drank cheap red wine to numb our brains. Anything, in fact, to stop us imagining that we might not get her.

All day we sat in the room, in case the phone rang. My nails were stubs. There was no Reception so no one, we reckoned, to take a message. Our spanking new mobiles were useless. No signal.

Titus turned up in person on the third morning, just as we were about to throttle each other. 'Come. We try again.'

Another four hours with numb feet and sore bums. More frustration as we tried to understand what all the raised voices were saying. This time, at least, we had something to drink. Another couple, leaving with their second child, had passed on their flask to us the previous day. They told us laughingly how hot coffee had kept them sane. A chance meeting outside the hotel had provided us with the best tonic ever. They assured us all this bureaucracy was normal. We took photos of their gorgeous daughter, Anna. Although they lived in Surrey, we promised to keep in touch – perhaps visit. We fantasised about how our daughters would become pen pals, best friends even. All that and we barely knew their names. They were rushing to catch a flight to London, but their smiles warmed us all day, and Robert and I were holding hands again before long.

We heard the turn of a key, and the big brown door in front of us opened. A woman came out carrying a child. The little girl was picking her nose. Robert stood up quickly and my heart began banging against my ribs. Titus was urging us forward to sign the papers. 'Ignore the child for a moment, please. This is important.'

He gestured at the woman and spoke to her roughly. I signed the papers, my eyes fixed on a tiny face with boxer-puppy eyes and inky hair. Her skin was sallow-meets-grey. She was nine months old. At a guess she weighed no more than the five-kilo bag of rooster potatoes that I bought each week in Superquinn.

The official said something to the woman. She handed me the child.

I looked at her and tried to let her know with one glance that I would love her and cherish her and protect her until the day I died. Her eyes were blank. 'What's her name?' I asked Titus. I was whispering, afraid to disturb her. So far, we'd been given three different names for her, so I wanted to be sure. I was definite about one thing, though: she was the child in the photo.

He consulted the papers. 'Daniela.'

'Hello, Daniela; hello, darling.' I breathed in. The awful smell disappeared. She smelt of something. No Johnson's baby lotion had ever been smoothed into her skin or silky talc sprinkled on her little bottom. Instead she smelt of – I tried to think. I sniffed again. Baby, that was it.

Robert came and hunkered down and smiled up at her. 'Hello,' he said in his best children's voice.

Her expression never changed.

'Will you take a photo?' he asked Titus, wanting to capture the moment for me. It was perfect. We hugged her, but not so that we'd scare her. The door closed again and the key turned.

Titus and the official nodded and spoke some more, but this time their chat was friendly. I felt my shoulders sag with relief.

'So, how does it feel having a baby?' Robert tilted my chin up and looked at me tenderly.

'Perfect.'

'You'll be a great mammy.'

'I love that word. This is all I've ever wanted.'

'What about me?' But he was grinning.

'You'll be a super dad. I'll give her to you in a second, is that OK? I just don't want to frighten her or anything …'

'Sure.' He tossed both our hair. 'Remember, we've got all the time in the world, now.'

All the time in the world. And a perfect daughter to share it with …

Come to Me, Maîtresse
Mary O'Donnell

Since Gwen's arthritis had worsened, every afternoon now began much the same. After lunch, she and Al took a nap. Gwen used the bedroom and her husband lay on the couch in the living area. This was because Al liked the shutters closed but Gwen preferred them slightly ajar. She enjoyed drifting to sleep, or, slowly waking at around half past four, being vaguely aware of a sliver of hot light as it edged through the day's predictable arc.

It was the light that had made them love Carla-Bayle from the moment they arrived as passing tourists, fifteen years earlier; the way it caressed the hot magenta and umber of the houses on the street, their slatted green and white shutters closed to the heat. The dream had always been to have what Gwen called 'a place in the sun'. It would be a reward for the thin years of country living as she and Al came and went to teaching jobs at the local, when nobody really expected her to make the break into full-time writing. But she did, though not spectacularly.

The house they bought the following spring stood at the south end of the village, near the bronze memorial with its long scroll of the dead of two world wars. Across the road from the back of the house, off the patio, ancient fortified walls were the last obstacle between Carla-Bayle and the plains. The land fell away to crops of sunflowers, barley and maize. Viewed from the ramparts, country roads meandered for miles until they joined with the *route nationale.* Finally, at that point in the distance where the eye relaxes, lay the Pyrenees, mauve-tinged at dusk, crevassed and fissured, the high peaks white and pink.

Today was a break in routine. Calista Stoney was in the region with her niece, who was, by Calista's account, a rising young poet. Joanna would love to meet Gwen, Calista had written, it would be marvellous if they could detour on their way to Auch. Gwen had written back that of course they must come for lunch, giving them a date and a time. Calista had sent a return postcard in her big, looped, forward-slanting hand:

> *Dying to have a chat. Let me know if there's anything you want brought out from Europe's Hottest Capital!?! Love, Calista XXX.*

Al's hair was nearly as white as her own, Gwen observed as he leant over the cos lettuce at the kitchen sink, separating the leaves for a Caesar salad. She took a selection of local cheeses from the fridge, loosened the greaseproof paper slightly, and left them to soften on the little wooden worktop. Sometimes she and Al drove to the far side of Toulouse to the market at Montauban. They always bought things they had not set out to purchase – rabbits, fowl, the local foie gras, which was different from the one they favoured at Carla-Bayle, and, in season, truffles.

'Oh, darling, there's a tear in the parasol,' Gwen remarked, almost as an afterthought. 'Maybe you could stick a pin in it or something?'

'For God's sake, Gwen, it needs to be stitched.' Al turned towards her, annoyed. 'D'you think we have a strong needle and some thread?'

Gwen turned her attention to the cheeses again, this time completely removing the greaseproof paper.

'Hmmm? Needle and thread?' She poked at one of the cheeses with her finger. Condensation and slight mould clung to her fingertip. She licked it. 'These cheeses look really good, Al.'

Al gave a quiet snort and went to the food cupboard.

'It's here somewhere, I know it is,' he said, his hands trembling as he felt his way in the cupboard's twilit space.

'Don't worry about it,' she said, relenting. 'It doesn't matter. Really it doesn't. Come here. Kissy-kissy-munchkins?'

He gave that stiff half-turn that had become so characteristic of him in his late sixties.

'Kissy-kissy,' he murmured, smiling. 'We'll sort out that parasol, you'll see.'

Soft-spoken, given to thought rather than swift pronounce-ment, her husband was regarded by Gwen as infinitely wiser than she, and infinitely wiser than many of the writers of her acquaintance who sometimes believed themselves to have a monopoly on wisdom. Giving up his teaching career at the school had been a major consideration. Unlike her, he had not had other aspirations.

'Have you done the croutons, dear?' Al called from the rough stone patio. He balanced on a white sun-chair, needle and thread in hand, squinting as he forced the needle in and out through the red-and-yellow canvas umbrella.

'Hell, no. Forgot.'

'Not to worry. Lots of time.'

Quickly, Gwen cut the bread into small cubes and tossed them into a pan of hot, seasoned oil.

'Mmmm,' Al sniffed as the aroma of oil, garlic and herbs wafted from the kitchen. He came in quietly behind her and nuzzled her neck, nipping at her earlobe.

'Now, now, baby, you know Cook doesn't like to be interfered with.' She turned and kissed the tip of his nose. 'At least not in the kitchen. Hell. Visitors.'

'What about 'em?'

'They mean work!' Gwen complained, wiping her brow with the front of her forearm.

'They'll be gone soon. Oh, shit!' He gulped his drink. 'I think I hear a car, do you? They're here, aren't they?'

'Shit. Yes. Nice to see Calista, though.' Gwen glanced down at her apron, then removed it hastily.

'You look fine. Anyway, they're here.' He breathed out ceremoniously. 'Calista and her young charge.' Al brushed at his loose shirt, then glanced quickly in the oval mirror in the little hallway.

They stood at the open door, beaming a welcome. They extended their arms towards Calista as she ran towards them, smiling shyly.

'God, you two haven't changed *a bit*!' she squealed.

'Oh, go on now,' Al laughed, pleased.

A plump young woman of about thirty stood waiting to be introduced.

'And this lovely creature must be Joanna! Ah, youth, youth!' Al took her hand and embraced her. 'Welcome, my dear,' he murmured gently, his eyes curious.

'Don't smother her, you old fool,' Gwen joked, then rolled her eyes conspiratorially at Joanna.

Joanna, dressed in a sleeveless blue serge blouse and a matching skirt that swirled around her ankles, met their attempts at welcoming humour with a little smile, nodding at Gwen. With her short, uncoloured brown hair, pale, unmade-up skin, and the blue outfit, she reminded Gwen of a newly laicised nun. When she shook hands with Gwen, her clasp, Gwen noted, was firm and cool.

'Welcome,' Gwen said, meeting the girl's eyes, which were also cool. Calista cornered Gwen immediately, enthusing about the house. She admired the wooden furnishings, running her hands over the surfaces of chairs and picking up vases.

'What intense light! And the curtains!' she cried, examining the drapes that separated the main living area from the galley kitchen. Joanna, ushered to the swing-seat by Al, sat out on the patio.

'Well, yes, I suppose it does look rather grand from the perspective of the school staffroom on a wet November morning,'

Gwen said gaily, 'but you must remember that we get the most *awful* rainstorms here too. And winter is hard. It doesn't help my arthritis one bit!'

'Even here!' Calista exclaimed. 'Well, anyway, you're well out of the stress-palace. The school has gone from bad to worse...'

'So I gather,' said Gwen, cracking an egg over the Caesar salad. Expertly, she tossed the salad leaves with her fingers until the egg was evenly distributed.

'I think we're ready to go,' she said in a sing-song voice, 'almost there. Calista, be a dear and carry out the bread. Two little baskets.'

They settled themselves in the shade of the parasol, close to a lemon tree.

Calista and Joanna made appreciative sounds when Gwen served the salad.

'*Magnifique!*' Calista kissed the tips of her fingers in her enthusiasm. 'Can't beat it, can you?' She looked to Joanna for a response.

'What? Oh – no, this is wonderful. Really regal,' Joanna spoke quietly.

'*Du vin pour les belles dames?*'

Al was really moving now, Gwen thought, playing the good host. He poured white wine for the three women, and then, as an afterthought, offered them water.

'Please,' Joanna nodded, pushing her water glass forward.

'So where do you live, Joanna?' Gwen asked, forking through her salad.

'Bray.'

'What's that like nowadays?'

'Oh, you know. Lively. Hurdy-gurdies. Sugarloaf Mountain. Local radio. That kind of thing.'

Gwen wondered if there might be more to Bray, but didn't say so. 'Have you always lived there?'

'More or less.'

Calista cut some cheese and pushed the plate towards Joanna, who shook her head and passed it across to Al.

'Now for the good news from home.' Calista spoke coyly, smiling at Joanna. 'Will I tell them?'

The girl shrugged, suppressed a smile. 'As you wish… '

'Jo-jo's first collection of poems has been nominated for a McLoughlin Award!'

'Oh, wow! *wow!*' Al cried, clapping his hands together.

'It's wonderful, dear, just wonderful,' Gwen said. 'If you win, it will be a great opportunity, and even if you don't actually win, it will still have been an honour.'

'You'll soon be able to keep a man in style, that's for sure,' Al chuckled, breaking his bread into small pieces.

Gwen could tell by Joanna's face that it was the wrong thing to say.

'Jo-jo's steering clear of men for some time to come, right, Jo-jo?' Calista intervened lightly, with a slight frown.

'Well, at least the world of arts and letters is in secure hands,' Gwen said gently. 'I trust you brought a copy of Joanna's book?' Gwen looked across at Calista.

'Of *course* I did, I said to Jo-jo that you'd be really interested in reading her work.'

'Good. I am.'

'Do you review in Ireland?' Al asked Joanna.

'Well…' Joanna was diffident. 'It's a tricky area. But yes, I like to review.'

'Tricky is right,' Gwen chipped in. 'Like a rabbit in a tank of barracudas.'

For an instant, Joanna almost smiled.

'I'd imagine it's especially difficult for poets,' Calista said then.

'Why?' Gwen's eyebrows shot up.

'They all know one another,' Calista said.

'The dunghill syndrome, you mean?'

'I beg your pardon?' Joanna was staring straight at Gwen, her face very serious.

'Oh, you know. Poets are like dung beetles. All that scrambling around in a mound of s-h-one-t, if you see what I mean.'

Joanna gave an irritated little laugh. 'It's a bit more compli-cated than that,' she said with sudden vigour. 'Poetry is' – she hesitated – 'the highest art form there can possibly be.'

Al and Gwen exchanged glances and smiled.

'And there was I, as a mere fiction-writer,' Gwen joked, 'imagining it was one of *many* high art forms!'

'No. Poetry is the highest art form there is.'

Joanna went on to list her hierarchy of significant poets, the ones who counteracted that free-verse patter that the washed-up hippies and feminists wrote during the Eighties.

'It's sad.' Joanna shook her head.

'Hmmm.' Gwen was thoughtful. 'Now I can't be certain of this, Joanna, not being a poet any more. I was one twenty years ago, but then I turned to fiction and found it altogether much more satisfying. An easier habitat, if you like.' She pushed her wine glass towards Al. 'Fill me up, dear.'

'Oh, come on,' Joanna countered.

'In my experience. For what it's worth,' Gwen said lightly.

'Yeah, but there are some really good poets coming along now,' Joanna went on.

'Well, if they're good, they'll be heard, won't they?' Al said softly.

'You're right,' Joanna nodded, 'and the consoling thing is that in each generation of writers, only the best rise to the top.'

'Oh, nonsense!' Gwen's patience snapped. 'In each generation *some* of the best are certainly there, but side by side with *some* of the mediocre!'

Joanna put her elbows on the table and folded her little hands beneath her chin, regarding Gwen with polite amusement.

'Don't you understand, Joanna, the mediocre is *needed*. It

broadens the cultural habitat. That's if you must think in those terms,' she finished with a smile.

They fell silent for a time, and sipped their wine. Al looked down at his glass. Calista gazed enquiringly from Joanna to Gwen and back again.

Joanna decided to hold herself at a remove, to at least signal disinterest in Gwen and everything Gwen stood for. As the three older people sipped their coffee, she wandered the small garden, examining everything with a fierce botanic attention, the deep-green shiny leaves of the lemon tree, the olive bushes, a row of ripening vines that Gwen and Al had optimistically planted after they bought the house. She also absorbed the conversation that drifted in scraps from beneath the parasol. All the time, new phrases ran through her head and displaced the words she overheard, snatches of poems she had yet to compose, colours of emotion freshly born from her encounter with these quaint expatriates. There was so much to do, to write, and, she thought savagely, they did not know the half of it.

At the table, conversation flagged. Calista and Gwen fell silent. Al sat rattling the previous day's edition of *Le Monde*. Joanna moved around with a small camera in hand, then hung over the fence in order to focus on something that Gwen could not see.

'Got it!' she cried jubilantly.

'Oh yes, our friends the lizards. All over the place.' Al gave a broad wave of his hand.

Eventually, it was time to go. As they stood up, Gwen felt the familiar twinges in her ankles, as the skin of her feet pressed up in little cushions of flesh between the straps of her flat sandals.

'We want to make Auch by nightfall,' Calista said.

Al chased Calista around the garden when she refused to give him a kiss.

'Come, come, Calista,' he laughed, 'for auld times' sake. Gwen understands these ancient staff alliances, don't you, *Maîtresse*?'

'Indeed I do, *mon capitaine*.'

She blew him a kiss, aware that Joanna was observing them. *Damn,* she thought, as her ankles throbbed again. She had been sitting too long.

As Calista and Joanna drove away, Gwen and Al waved, calling out long goodbyes. Joanna stuck her arm out the window and waved briefly, but without turning back to look at them. It was strange, Gwen thought, to feel as she did now, of so little interest to this young person that the most they merited was a disdainful backwards toss of the hand.

They cleared up, moving back and forth between patio and kitchen. Gwen lifted the tablecloth and shook it. The movement churned the air, raising aromas of warm lavender and oregano, stirring butterflies on flickering trajectories.

'Here. Let me.' Al took the cloth.

'Come to me,' he said, holding her, pushing her back into the shade of the lemon tree. He stroked her back.

'I'm a fool,' Gwen whispered, leaning on him. 'My knees hurt too.'

'I know your knees hurt, I know. But you're not a fool. Why should you be a fool?'

'Washed up. We are, you know.'

'Did she bother you that much? But she's an innocent! She knows nothing.' Al caressed Gwen's neck with his thumbs, then kissed her on the lips.

'Older people say that kind of thing. It's not always true,' Gwen whispered, her voice shaky.

'In this case, you know it is. In this case.'

'And we're not— we're getting—' Her lips trembled.

They made their way across the garden again, through the kitchen, across the living room and into the bedroom. She dropped heavily onto the bed.

'That girl needs slapping down,' she muttered.

'I daresay,' Al said, removing her sandals. He stroked her feet, cradling her heels, one by one, in the palm of one hand.

'It's all right, *mon capitaine*, they're too tender. Leave them be.'

'*Maîtresse.*'

He watched, his head to one side as he awaited her response. '*Maîtresse?* Let it go. Some things have always been the same. This is one of them.'

'Yes, but…' Gwen thought of the anticipation she had savoured earlier in the day.

'Don't struggle. Not this time, *Maîtresse*,' he whispered, kissing her forehead.

He leaned closer and kissed her again, on the nose, on each cheek, finally on the mouth. As they undressed, she grew less aware of the pain in her feet, and the pain that until moments ago had seemed to skewer her right knee.

Twenty minutes later, gasping and perspiring, they curled around each other, their lust still unsatisfied. But her courage had returned. She tilted her head back and kissed him yet again, to signal an end to hopeless frustration; she tried to tease and coax him back to good humour.

'It really doesn't matter,' she murmured, 'not the way you think.'

He sighed, his hand caressing the mound of her pubis.

After he dressed, she listened for a while to the clearing-up sounds that came from the kitchen. Outside, a light wind stirred. The long *cratch-cratch-cratch* sound of the crickets dipped, then rose again as the wind-current rolled, ghostly, along the village walls. Somewhere, a rooster crowed. A car drove across the place, braked noisily, the engine left running. Gwen listened as two men talked and laughed. Eventually, she dozed. The light lengthened to a tawny oblong in the bedroom.

Burying Joe
Sheila O'Flanagan

He died young.

We went to see him in hospital and I knew that it was a matter of hours, not days. He had already moved away from us. His body couldn't keep him here and he didn't want to stay any more.

Even though I knew that he was going to die, I didn't say any of the important things. People are supposed to hold each other's hand and murmur last words, but that didn't happen. I don't remember ever holding his hand. I don't remember what I said. Irrelevant things, I guess. Because I didn't want to be there. I didn't want to see him like this. I wanted him the way he was before.

When visiting hours were over, we left. I waved from the doorway but his eyes were already closed and he had an oxygen mask over his mouth. We should have stayed with him, but we went home and made cups of tea and I knew that he would die.

They phoned later that night when we'd gone to bed. Until the phone rang he was alive. Then he was dead. Seconds earlier, a living person. Now a body. It happens in a single breath and nothing is ever the same again.

The people in work were sympathetic. I sat at home and played solitaire – with an old deck of cards, not on a computer. It seemed a frivolous kind of pastime, but there was nothing else to do. It came out twice in a row and then I shuffled the deck and put the cards back in the box.

I didn't think about him because there wasn't any point. I made soup. I watched TV. I can't remember what other people did, but my mother went into town to buy something in black, and so she was out when a neighbour called to say how very sorry she was.

People I didn't know were at the funeral home. I hadn't wanted to go there. But they made me go. To say goodbye, they told me, but as far as I was concerned I'd said goodbye a long time before. I'd said goodbye to a person. I didn't want to say goodbye to a body.

Women I'd never met before carried wreaths and stood beside the open coffin peering in at him. Some of the women were crying and I didn't know why. It wasn't as though he was part of their family, after all.

I didn't want to see him. Not when his eyes were closed. Not when he'd never open them again. It seemed rude somehow, although everyone expected it of me.

One woman said he looked peaceful. When I eventually took my place beside the coffin, I thought he looked dead. And when I kissed him on the forehead, he was shockingly cold. I hadn't realised how cold a dead person would be.

They said prayers. Like a blanket around us, the familiar words filled the room. I didn't believe in it, of course. Nothing happens afterwards. You simply cease to exist. Anything else is missing the point of the coldness.

Do we cry because someone else is crying? Tissues were screwed into balls in people's hands. I didn't have any tissues so I didn't cry.

They formed lines in the church. They came up and shook our hands and told us that they were sorry for our troubles. That's all you can say. 'I'm sorry for your troubles.' I've said it myself since. I want to say something else but I can never think of any other words. A half-smile, a sympathetic hug, a grasp of the hand and sorrow for our troubles.

I hadn't bought anything black and I didn't have anything black to wear. I didn't have anything suitable for a funeral at all. I wasn't at a point in my life where I had funeral clothes. I am now. I've been to funerals and I have the right clothes. But I hadn't then. I wanted to wear something bright and cheerful. I think he would have liked that. But I didn't, of course. I wore brown corduroy trousers and a brown lambswool cardigan with cream stitching. One hundred per cent wool. I also wore a little make-up. But not mascara because that would leave black tracks on my cheeks when I eventually cried, as I knew I would.

The neighbours were there. We hadn't spoken to them for years but they sat in the church beside each other. She had the right funeral clothes. He wore a black tie. They looked solemn. Maybe they were remembering the last argument. Maybe they were thinking about something else altogether.

The people from work were in a group. They whispered to one another.

I wanted to be somewhere else. I didn't want to keep looking at the coffin, polished pine, covered in flowers and cards and with a little nameplate to tell us who he was. But I couldn't help looking at it. And seeing him inside. Cold. Weighing nothing because of the illness. Not the person he was before.

The priest talked about Lazarus rising from the dead. *God,* I thought, *don't do that trick on us here! I couldn't go through it all again.*

Then I felt guilty because I should want him to be alive.

I thought of other things. Of things that he never knew about. The bloke I'd been seeing when I wasn't at the hospital. There was no contest between the bloke and the hospital, though, to tell the truth, the relationship was already floundering. But it gave me a reason to be somewhere else. A reason to look forward. I thought about going out the next weekend. Would it be OK to do that? Was I supposed to be in mourning? Would people think it was wrong? I looked at my watch. Seconds were taking hours. I wanted them to get on with it. I wanted to be outside in the sun, under the blue sky and the white clouds. I'd never liked this church. Ever.

They'd asked me to do a reading but I wouldn't. I can't, I told them. I'll cry. No you won't, they said. You'll be fine. He'd want you to do it. But I shook my head. He wouldn't. He understood me. It wasn't a lack of respect. They didn't believe me. Other people could do readings. Why couldn't I? I shook my head again and wouldn't look at them. Actually, they were right and I was wrong. I should have done it. I could have done it. I mightn't have cried.

People chatted in the churchyard. Pink blossoms floated from the trees. The sun was warm through the hundred per cent lambswool cardigan.

I talked to someone I didn't know while they slid the coffin into the hearse and packed the flowers around it. The bloke – my bloke, for today, anyway – asked me how I was feeling. I told him I was OK. It didn't matter how I was feeling. Other people had known him longer. All his life. I'd known him all my life and that was only nineteen years.

We climbed into the Daimler. Comfortable seats. Grey leather. We all fitted easily. The sun poured through the window and was stifling. I was too hot in my cardigan and trousers. The car was so smooth that I hardly realised we were moving. Slowly out of the churchyard and onto the main road. I leaned my head against the window. I wasn't any help to anyone. I said that I liked the car.

The graveyard was in the country. He was a city man but we were burying him in the country. He was supposed to like it out here but I wasn't certain. It was a long way from the houses and the streets and the shops and the noise. Here, there were birds and trees and tractors. It was very beautiful. But lonely. Not the same as the city at all.

We drove along the twisting, winding roads. Still smooth, hardly jolting when we hit potholes. The other cars followed us, a long colourful snake. And behind them were the people who wanted to get somewhere in a hurry but couldn't get by. People fuming behind the wheels of their cars who didn't care about the funeral. Who had lives to lead and wanted to lead them now. I felt bad about delaying them. I wondered if it would matter, really matter, that they were late for whatever they wanted to do.

The driver of the hearse turned from the main road and we looked at one another in surprise. This was unexpected. He shouldn't have turned here. We followed him.

'I'm sure he knows where he's going.' I wasn't really.

'Maybe I should say something.' My mother looked worried. Black wasn't her colour, although it was a nice suit.

'Let's wait.' I didn't want to make a fuss and neither did she.

The road steepened and we followed the incline. The land dropped away from us as we climbed the hillside.

'He doesn't know where he's going,' she said.

'I know.'

We looked at one another. I turned around. The colourful snake followed us as the road narrowed even more.

The driver looked around when the road petered out in front of him.

'It was the last turn,' my mother told him.

I thought he looked shocked but maybe that was only because he hadn't looked anything until now.

'We'll have to go back the way we came. I have to tell the other driver.'

The valley stretched below us. Green and beautiful and, somewhere, a quiet country graveyard where people were waiting for us.

He flashed his lights at the hearse. The cars stopped. The drivers conferred. They gestured back down the road.

In a small car, it was a three-point turn. I couldn't see how we were going to accomplish it in the Daimler. A five-point turn. Seven points. Nine points, even. I had started to take driving lessons when he became really sick. I could do three-point turns but not here.

The hearse edged backwards and forwards. I wondered what

would happen if it went too far forward and slid over the edge. I could see it, tumbling over and over, spilling its contents as it went and then exploding in a massive fireball when it came to rest. I'd been watching a lot of American films on TV.

It didn't go over the edge. I lost count of the points on the turn, though. Lost count of the number of times the car had moved close to the edge and back again. I wondered if the driver was embarrassed at the mistake. If he'd sweated as he manoeuvred the car. If he was saving up the story to tell to his wife and children later. 'You'll never believe what happened…' he'd say as he walked into the house. 'You'll never believe the kind of day I've had.'

The rest of the colourful snake turned one by one. Nobody went over the edge.

I looked at my watch again. Time had caught up on us and passed us out. They'd be asking questions in the graveyard, the workers waiting for us to show up. Wondering where the people from the city were. Annoyed at our tardiness. And we were still driving slowly. I wanted to tell the driver to get a move on but he probably didn't know how.

He was always punctual. Dependable. He was never late. I would sit and wait for the car to arrive home and he always did. He was one of the most dependable people I knew. But today he was late. He was late for his own funeral.

I thought about that. I sneaked a glance at my mother and my sisters, who were talking about the unexpected detour. My mother was fiddling with her watch. She knew we were late too.

How many people are late for their own funerals? I wondered. It couldn't be a very common occurrence.

I started to smile. I couldn't help it. And then I started to laugh. Quietly. Inside of me. He would have laughed too. My father found life funny, even when it wasn't. He laughed a lot. I could remember him laughing. So I laughed and laughed until salt tears rolled down my cheeks and dripped onto my brown corduroy trousers. I'd been right not to wear any mascara.

Away with the Birds
Patricia O'Reilly

We watched through the lounge window as Rosemary moved about arranging the cushions on the sofa. There were ten of them in jade and cerise silk. We knew the exact colours and type of material because she'd told us. She peaked and tweaked and patted until she had the cushions standing precisely on their points, then she stood back, arms folded across her chest, as though locked in the wonder of her handiwork.

She was no longer the Rosemary we'd grown up with.

As we rang her doorbell, we knew we wouldn't say anything to her about what we'd just seen. But, as it happened, that was the afternoon she told us. Everything.

We knew Rosemary was different from the rest of us – a loner, never quite making it to the inner circle of any gang – not that she seemed to care. When we started going clubbing on Saturday nights, we'd invite her to join us.

She was a magnet for guys. By stretching our imaginations, which we did frequently, we could pretend that we were equally fancied.

Sometimes she came with us, other times she didn't. When she did, invariably she pulled. She loved to dance, but she never danced alone or in a group like we did. But then she didn't have to; guys lined up for the privilege of being seen on the dance floor with her.

Away with the Birds

She'd discovered boys at the age of thirteen and she fell promptly in love with their attention. She learnt to smoke like them, drooping a cigarette from between her index and second fingers, and to talk like them, in short staccato bursts about football and PlayStation. Though she always made sure to walk and to laugh like a girl – wiggly hips and throw back head.

We thought she was dead sexy, the way she inhaled and exhaled and continued to talk as smoke snaked around her words. Unlike us, she wasn't into dressing up or making up. She couldn't care less about clothes and said she hated the feel of lipstick on her mouth, and as for blackening her eyes ... But she took great pride in her hair, which hung almost to her waist, long and sleek and pale.

Her preference was for older, dark-haired, snake-hipped dancing guys. If she danced with them more than once, she'd let them leave her home. Next day, instead of going through the ins and outs of 'he said and I said and he tried this and I did that', the way the rest of us would explode with our meagre experiences, she would be annoyingly reticent.

That was until she met Johnny. And he wasn't even her type. He was blond and plump and didn't like dancing, though he was good fun and laughed a lot. She began to invite us around to her place for coffee and, between her mother and herself, they'd tell us what Johnny did and what Johnny didn't.

We thought Rosemary's bond with her mother odd – for want of a better word. Though we were jealous too. We had uneasy relationships with our parents and tried to get away with letting them know as little as possible about what was going on in our lives. Our primary ambition was to leave home, have our own places and live without parental input or involvement.

Rosemary had no such ambition. Why should she? There was only her mother and herself and they played amicable house together. Her father wasn't in evidence. Whenever the subject came up, she'd make a joke about an immaculate conception or a stranger in the night, which we thought amazingly romantic. Her mother, we decided, was made for romance. In an older-woman way. She was astonishingly glamorous – loads of make-up, very short skirts and enormously high heels – and she was always going away for weekends.

One Saturday Rosemary called me. The others were sitting around my – or rather my parents' – kitchen table, drinking coffee and talking booze, guys, sex and clubs. Though not necessarily in that order.

Would we meet her at the pet shop?

'What for?'

'I'm going to buy Mammy a canary.'

'Why?' we asked, half an hour later, surrounded by the pungent scent and soft sounds of small animals, as we mooched admiringly in front of a cage of long-eared rabbits.

'So she won't be lonely when I move in with Johnny.'

Our imaginations leapfrogged with the implications. 'We didn't know…' we began together.

Rosemary's hair shone like spun gold and she had that smug, in-love look that we only knew from the old movies we regularly and avidly devoured. It was a look that made her secure and mature beyond our years.

'I didn't know myself until recently,' she defended.

'So when did he ask you?' We were dying to know. At the very least we imagined a moonlit night with Johnny on bended knee. We were in our final year at school. Rosemary had left at the end of fifth year to do art.

'Well, he hasn't actually asked yet.'

By then we had our backs pinned to cages of white mice and there was a terrible intensity about her as she told us how much she and Johnny loved each other, how they were going to make a life together and have lots of babies. And she'd paint portraits.

We named the canary Buddy, wished her the best and kept waiting for the announcement that never came.

When I rang her home a few weeks later, a male voice answered and said that she'd moved out. I was too taken up with the fact that Rosemary had gone without telling us to wonder who owned the voice. I wrote down her new address and the three of us called around the following Saturday afternoon.

Rosemary's room was small and dark. It smelt of ammonia and was full of wire cages of yellow and green canaries making an awful racket. 'What are you doing?' we asked. 'Why all the birds? Where's Johnny?'

'So many questions.' She ran her hands through her hair, and tried to smile but it was a wobbly effort and the light had gone out of her eyes. 'I'm collecting canaries,' she said. 'They can be trained to sing, you know, and can live for fifteen years. Johnny is with Mammy now. So there.'

We said the usual things, like that's awful, what a rat and you're well rid of him. We weren't experienced enough in the ways of the world to know or say anything else. We thought of our mothers with our boyfriends – not that we'd ever had proper boyfriends … But suppose we did? We found the idea not only ludicrous but positively nauseating. Our mothers were ordinary and, for once, we were extraordinarily glad of that.

Rosemary went in on herself, spending her time in that horrible room with her discordant birds. Most weekends we visited, though usually we ended up chatting among ourselves while she stared into space. When we saw her mother and Johnny in the shopping centre, we stared coldly at them. But they were too wrapped up in each other to notice us.

Then the inevitable happened. Rosemary met a new some-body. Another canary enthusiast. And with it quite good-looking – tall and thin and Latino, the kind of guy who, given half a chance, we'd go for, but whom Rosemary would inevitably get. When Ron visited her, he brought his canaries in travelling cages and the two of them sat around and talked birds.

Despite Ron's looks, we thought their relationship spookily reminiscent of that old Hitchcock film, *The Birds*. Particularly when they let the canaries out of their cages and had them flying around, bickering and twittering and dive-bombing, landing with grasping claws on handy heads.

Not that Rosemary was miraculously cheered up by having Ron in her life. She was being cautious, she said. Once bitten, twice shy, and all that. Still she went ahead and married him, and it transpired he had a fine house with an aviary.

We often went over to keep her company while he was out. She'd show us what he'd bought. Things for the house. Clothes and jewellery. Make-up and perfume. While we were envious, we thought it funny; strange-funny, not funny-funny. Rosemary, who used to dress in tat, now wore designer gear – though always black, and only ever combat trousers, T-shirts and flat boots – and she had her glorious hair cropped short.

That afternoon she took a small key from an antique bureau and opened the third wardrobe in the master bedroom, which was a particularly impressive room done in all white with splashes of gold and had an outside balcony running its full length.

'What do you think of this?' she asked, standing back to allow us a full view.

Rails of pastel-coloured dresses. Racks of high-heeled, pointy-toed shoes. Shelves of hats and wigs. Drawers packed with frothy underwear.

We stood in a line looking from her to the open wardrobe, thinking, *Not Rosemary's style,* but saying, 'Wow,' and 'Cool.'

Rosemary sat on the edge of the bed and began to cry. 'Tell us what's wrong,' I think we said. We must have, because once she started talking, there was no stopping her.

In the beginning, as well as their joint interest in canaries, she was pleased that Ron wasn't pushing for sex as she was still hurting for Johnny. She'd gone off sex, she said, and was planning to be celibate for the rest of her life. We were so constantly preoccupied with the awfulness of not having sex that we couldn't imagine anyone choosing not to, particularly with a Ron on tap.

She knew Ron loved her – she was always going on about that, the way she'd gone on about Johnny. But for the first time, she explained that his way of loving was different. 'How?' we asked. In the circumstances, the only kind of love we considered was sex. 'Kind of controlling,' she said. 'And he seems uncomfortable in his skin.' We were both sad for her and mesmerised by her insights.

Their honeymoon was awful. Days and nights with huge spaces in them. It was the first and last time they had sex.

We raised incredulous eyebrows, but Rosemary continued as though she hadn't noticed, saying that afterwards she felt smothered, as though her spontaneity was for ever stifled. 'And it was, *I* was, never the same again,' she assured us earnestly, her eyes huge in her pale face. 'We went back to celibacy.'

When she found the nightdress, the only explanation she could come up with was that it was a present Ron had squirrelled away for her. She couldn't make out his expression when she thanked him, but she took it as disappointment at his surprise being ruined. 'He could be like that,' she said. 'Petulant on occasions.' That night she wore it uneasily, lost in its large satiny pinkness, and he sulked on his side of the bed.

When he finally told her, she knew nothing about such matters. But she could feel her fear. Pecking at her like the bad-tempered canaries she'd grown to loathe. Trapping her. And Ron was so pleased that the burden of secrecy was off him. That he no longer needed to pretend, to be tormented. The torment was now hers. He so wanted her to be part of his shadow life.

And we still didn't know what she was talking about.

She gestured to the wardrobe. 'They're not mine, you know. They're his – Ron's. He dresses in them.'

So that was it. Rosemary's words curled like blue smoke into the atmosphere, trailing our loss of innocence in their wake, welcoming us, I suppose, to the real world.

The information stretched the boundaries of our imaginations, lapped at our minds like an icy tide. We were silent, trying to picture Ron in women's clothes, wondering when he wore them. Under his suits and shirts? Out, masquerading as a woman? In the privacy of his home with Rosemary? Tending to his canaries?

When Ron made the appointment with a psychiatrist, Rosemary presumed it was to help her, but the psychiatrist thought she was there to facilitate Ron – 'facilitate' was the word he used – and she lacked the courage to correct him as he went on about *it* being a socially unacceptable condition. He said the words slowly, giving each one time to sink in.

If Rosemary knew nothing about *it*, she knew that. What sort of an eejit did he take her for? He went on about making *it* part of their life together, stressing Ron's vulnerability and her need to be strong. That psychiatric soothing was another nail in the coffin of her despair.

Ron loved shopping, particularly lingerie shopping, and she became his alibi. Pink-faced, excited like a child, his fingers stroked satin, caressed lace, fondled silk. His favourites were French knickers, along with matching suspender belts and flesh-coloured stockings, with seams, no less. In grandiose gestures he bought armfuls of everything for Rosemary too. Though she always insisted on black.

One evening he asked if he could dress up for her in his favourite frock and shoes. Maybe they'd even open a bottle of wine? Celebrate the new Ron. As he dashed upstairs loosening his tie, he called back that he was so glad she understood.

This vivacity, which up to now had been strictly confined to his birds, was new and unnerving. As Rosemary waited for Ron, she felt as though she was being pecked at by a whole family of canaries. Did she have to do this? Yes, according to the psychiatrist. Ron needed expression. Expression backed by her support.

She looked around. The lounge was perfect. Tidy. Not a thing out of place. It was the way Ron liked it. Then she spotted the cushions. All ten of them. Piled higgledy-piggledy. She knew they'd look better arranged. And she settled for standing them on their points, determinedly making diamonds from their square shapes, ensuring that each cushion snuggled into its companion.

Rosemary could hear Ron's careful footsteps coming down the stairs and across the hall. When he stood in the doorway, she composed her face into expressionless pleats and forced herself to look from the ground up. Black patent stilettos, pink belted dress. Scarlet lips, rouged cheeks, green eyeshadow. Crimson fingernails patting at curly brown wig. Now she'd a second reason for hating make-up.

When finally she met his eyes, in them she saw feminine vulnerability battling with masculine pride. Huge repulsion and small compassion clashed within her. For that night compassion won, but it didn't stop her loathing him for what he'd made her, and it confirmed to us that we knew virtually nothing of the ways of the world.

We wondered to ourselves why she didn't leave, but of course didn't ask. We would have gone, running down the perfectly gravelled driveway, without ever looking back.

'Come on, I want to show you something.' She was back in control of herself and we followed her from the bedroom, down the stairs, out of the kitchen, to the end of the garden.

Afterwards we couldn't agree on what we'd expected as Rosemary opened the door to the aviary. But it certainly wasn't Ron in a pink dress and blue rubber gloves calmly cleaning out the cages, surrounded by dozens of twittering green and yellow canaries.

Breaking and Entering
Julie Parsons

I'm not sure when I first began to hate my husband. I used to love him more than anything else in the world. I think I even loved him more than I loved my children. I certainly loved him more than I loved myself. I could always find a reason to be self-critical. I could never match up to my ideal of what a woman should be. But that wasn't how I saw Justin. Justin was the best. Plain and simple.

We had a very straightforward life, Justin and I. We met when we were teenagers. We got married when I was twenty-three and Justin was twenty-six. We had our first child, a girl, a year to the day later. I gave up my job as a national schoolteacher. Justin was made a partner in his father's legal practice. A second child, a boy, was born two years later. We moved up the property ladder. Life was good. We were happy. When the children started school I went back to work. Justin wasn't pleased, but I assured him I would continue to put him and the children first. And I did.

I always did. Even though I knew that I was slipping inexorably down his priority list. There was gossip. I tried not to listen. The other wives in the yacht club sniggered and smiled knowingly. I didn't rise to the bait. I kept my counsel. After all, a husband with a guilty conscience is a generous husband. Every birthday, every anniversary, was marked with a gift of jewellery. Justin had good taste. He chose the best pearls. The most flawless and beautiful. Earrings, rings, pendants. As I got older he decided that diamonds were more suitable. Again his choice was exquisite. I gleamed and sparkled and shone. And ordered a safe to be installed in the back of our wardrobe.

'And we'd better make sure the insurance premiums are index-linked,' Justin said.

'Of course,' I agreed. 'I'll look after all that. You've enough to worry about,' and I kissed him on his soft fair hair and breathed in his familiar scent of Wright's coal-tar soap.

I was looking forward to retirement. There would be so much time for us to spend together. Justin stopped working first. I followed suit a year later. Of course I swore I'd keep in touch with all my colleagues, and they with me. But somehow after the first couple of months the inevitable happened. They were all busy with their young families and soon we tacitly accepted that, without the school in common, we had nothing much to talk about. Having the pension was nice and I began to enjoy my indolence and laziness. Both our children were living away from home now. Our daughter was in Sydney and our son in New York. We kept in touch by e-mail. Neither had married. I waited in vain for grandchildren. Meanwhile, the more time I spent at home with Justin, the more I began to loathe him.

It wasn't his physical degeneration that I minded. After all, I was at least a stone heavier than I once had been. My hair was grey and lifeless, my chin sagging, my hands wrinkled and spotted. I was beginning to walk with a stoop, and the gaps between my teeth filled with food as I ate. I could have looked upon Justin's similar deterioration with tolerance and understanding. But I could see that he was revolted by me. He had begun to sleep in the spare room. He had used a bad bout of flu with night sweats and a persistent cough as the excuse, but when the flu had passed, and the cough was reduced to an occasional vigorous clearing of the throat, he still did not return to our bed. He seemed to spend most of his days in his study logged on to the internet. When I made a few friendly enquiries, he rebuffed me. So I stopped asking.

Instead I read the property pages. I couldn't believe how many wonderful houses and apartments were suddenly for sale all over the world. From Cape Town to the Czech Republic, there seemed to be incredible investment opportunities. I mentioned this to Justin; I thought he'd be delighted at the prospect of a new interest. But he muttered something about insecurity in the money market.

'But look,' I waved the *Irish Times* property supplement in front of his flushed face, 'look, here, beautiful old apartments in Budapest. Just think, we could spend the summer right in the heart of Europe. Wouldn't it be interesting? We could go to Vienna and Prague, we could get right inside an ancient and fascinating society. Spread our horizons a bit further than suburban Glenageary and Killiney.'

He stared at me for a moment, then his gaze drifted over my shoulder. He stood up and fished his car keys from his trouser pocket.

'Once it might have been,' he said, 'but now? I think not.'

I waited until I heard the car accelerate out of the front gate before I allowed myself to cry. I felt miserable for the rest of the morning and even worse after lunch. My head ached and a great weight pressed down on my shoulders. Justin was gone for the day. Lunch at the club followed by a commissioning run around Dublin Bay in his friend Roger's new cruiser. Or so he said. I walked upstairs. The house was clean and tidy. It was silent. I looked out the landing window. Our garden was a neat rectangle of lawn bordered by a box hedge. Just like our neighbours on either side. I longed suddenly for forests of silver birch and formal parterres with fountains and antique statuary. I opened the door to what I had once thought of as our sanctuary. The bed was neatly made. My nightgown was folded on my pillow. I moved to the wardrobe and took my keyring from my pocket. I pushed aside the row of suits that Justin no longer wore and fitted the small key into the safe's heavy door. I turned it briskly. The door clicked open. Once I had felt that all the love that Justin had for me was kept in pristine condition within the safe's metal walls, that no matter what happened I could count on that love to sustain me. But now I couldn't even bring myself to look inside. I turned away. I closed the curtains. I lay down on the bed and pressed my face into the pillow.

I must have been asleep, very deeply asleep, because I thought first of all when I saw the young man leaning over me that I was dreaming. It was hard to see him clearly in the half-light. But he was nice-looking, with black curly hair and a gap between his two front teeth, although he smelt strongly of cigarette smoke. When I began to sit up, he pushed me back down and held me firmly with both hands pressed to my shoulders.

'Don't worry,' he said, 'I won't hurt you. I thought there was no one in.'

'What do you want?' I asked, and I began to struggle. He didn't answer and I was suddenly very conscious of the wardrobe standing open and inside it the safe.

'How did you get in? I didn't hear anything.' I pushed my hair back from my face, thankful that I hadn't bothered to undress before I lay down.

'You wouldn't hear anything,' he said and smiled, almost shyly. 'I'm good at locks. Breaking and entering, it's my speciality. Still, if I'd known you were here I wouldn't have come in. I saw your old man leave in his car, and your car, the black Golf, wasn't here either, so I thought you both must be out.'

'My car? You know about my car?'

'Yeah, of course I do. I do my research. I like to suss out a job before I take it on. So where is it?'

'The car? If you must know it's having its exhaust replaced. I brought it to the garage yesterday.'

'Shit.' He smiled again and began to back away. 'I'd better be going. Do me a favour, would you? I haven't taken anything. Don't call the cops just yet?'

'I tell you what…' I stood up. 'One favour deserves another. Let me show you something.'

I was amazed how easy it was to organise the purchase of the two-bedroom apartment in the art-nouveau building just minutes away from the River Danube. High ceilings, parquet floors, tiled fireplaces with ornate wood-burning stoves. A small kitchen with a tiny fridge, an old gas cooker and a twin-tub washing machine. The bathroom had a mosaic of a dolphin in green and gold on the wall, a large, old-fashioned bath, and shower fittings that looked like something the Hapsburgs would have used.

I didn't rush into anything. I thought it through from start to finish. I consulted a nice young man called Zoltan in an Irish property company with established links in Hungary. He was only too happy to help. He praised my spirit of adventure and suggested I open an account in the Hungarian central bank. He told me about the wonderful spas and mineral baths whose origins go back to the time of the Romans, and the cafés where I would be bound to meet intellectuals and artists. People like his grandparents who had lived through the Second World War and the uprising of 1956. He suggested a solicitor and helped me through the legalities of the purchase. The time passed more quickly than I had anticipated. Justin didn't seem to notice my new-found interest in life, or the large brown envelopes that arrived for me in the post. He obviously had other things on his mind.

And then one day the letter came from the insurance company. It contained a cheque for €100,000.

'In settlement,' it said, 'of your claim for your jewellery, itemised below.'

I carefully prised the staples from the cheque. I counted the zeros. I took my mobile phone from my pocket. I punched in Zoltan's number.

The Guards had been so sympathetic when I called them that afternoon. I was in tears. I couldn't understand it. I'd been asleep. A bad headache. I'd taken my painkillers. When I awoke I went downstairs to make a cup of tea. There was glass on the kitchen floor. The back door had been forced. I couldn't immediately see if anything had been stolen. And then I remembered the safe. I ran up the stairs and into the bedroom. The safe door was open. My bunch of keys was on the floor. Everything was gone. A lifetime of memories.

'My husband will kill me,' I sobbed down the phone. 'He's always telling me I should put the alarm on when I take a nap in the afternoon. He says a huge number of burglaries take place when the house is occupied. I've never believed him, but now, what on earth am I going to do?'

They found no fingerprints. But they said there had been a series of similar robberies in the area. Jewellery was the thief's speciality.

'Funny,' one of the Guards said, 'that he broke the glass. He's usually more careful than that. He's pretty good with locks.'

He had been very careful when I showed him the safe. He inspected everything before he put it into his rucksack.

'No point in getting stuck with any of this stuff,' he said. 'My customers are very particular.'

'And will my insurance company definitely pay up?' I asked.

'Definitely. I'll leave a bit of a mess just so they know it was a break-in. You keep calm about it all. You were fast asleep. You didn't hear a thing. I used your keys to open the safe. OK?'

I nodded.

'And good luck with it. An apartment in Budapest, eh? Sounds great.' He turned to go. 'Now get back into bed. Take your pills and go back to sleep.'

I raised a toast to him, my burglar friend, that first night when I sat beside the Danube drinking a glass of Tokay. I still don't know what came over me, that afternoon in my bedroom in Dublin. A moment of desperation? Or was it inspiration? I love my apartment. Everything in it is just the way I want it. My pension is paid into my Hungarian bank account every month. I'm taking lessons in Hungarian and it's not as difficult as people say. I'm offering English lessons in return for conversation classes. When

Justin and I have been apart for five years, I will divorce him. I've already met a number of very interesting men. The Hungarians seem to appreciate maturity in a woman. So different from Justin. Or maybe, just maybe – since that afternoon it's me that's different.

One Mile and a Quarter

Suzanne Power

People cannot be avoided on piers.

But they give the illusion of escape from the world and into the sea. I have always believed the illusion.

At 9.15 a.m. on Friday I locked the door of my car. I do this every day, taking myself and my thoughts down to Dun Laoghaire West Pier. It's the little-used one – dog-walkers and natural loners prefer its mile-and-a-quarter round trip to the shorter East Pier. Grass ruts through the resilient stone, wildflowers and weeds have made a home in the crags and the benches are battle-scarred after ferocious winters. Still herons prefer the calm lee in the crook of the West's arm, while restless gulls stick to the litterbins that line the East Pier.

They say that the architect of these piers killed himself when his still granite walks into the roving sea were complete. One had to be built a quarter-mile longer than the other. The West, then, killed him. But they say that about any great endeavour that isn't perfect.

The difference makes perfection; it gives to each his own. There's an ice-cream van at the start of the East Pier and a bandstand halfway down it. An unhindered north-easterly on most days of the year is all that will welcome you to the West Pier. I love it. It means I don't share my pier.

Friday proved different. From the minute I set out he was there and instinct said he would represent intrusion. He wasn't a regular walker at this time. The few that are know to avoid me.

If someone else decides to walk a pier at exactly the same time as you, at the same speed, you have only two choices if you want to be alone – slow down or speed up. I sped up and so did he. I couldn't slow down. It was too cold a day for that.

'Not today,' I whispered. 'Today I need to hear.'

The sea talks to me, the mast bells sing, the wind catches my breath and lets all the words I have to use to get through a single day run away with themselves.

Off the pier I'm a nervous creature. I make life pleasant for my husband, mediating between him and my sons. *Your father doesn't mean it like that*, I say. *You shouldn't do that, it will upset your father. It would be best*, I smile my worn smile, *not to tell your father that. You know how he gets.* All these meaningless phrases to keep a peace I can't bear any more – of temporary ceasefire, the tension of battle to come. I form treaties with my other face, the one that forgot where it came from.

My youngest son calls this expression my bridge smile. He says I'm a full embodiment of petty, bourgeois hypocrisy, speaking the words as if they aren't clichés. He doesn't realise that everything he does is a cliché – drinking too much, drugs, failing exams, hating his parents. It's a cliché to break your mother's heart. I used to towel-dry his curls in front of a fire – now he's sixteen and has shorn them and any part of the loving we had. He hates me for not standing up to his father. He doesn't see how alike they are in their dismissal of me.

I share this habit with them, fostered and encouraged it in them. But for the pier I wouldn't exist for myself at all. I don't know how that happened exactly. I think it has something to do with always doing the right thing by a family. Is the right thing always to think of others?

So you see my need to avoid idle talk. I listen to the fairy tinkling of the yacht bells, the scraping cries of sea birds after the wake of the super-ferry that dwarfs harbour walls that for two centuries were high and proud protectors of the sea town I was born in and will die in. It's my only restoration.

My fellow walker kept step. I saw the shape of him a pace behind. Something in me tells others, *I will do as you say*. He would wear me down in the end, to polite response towards his need for company.

He was at least seventy by the look of his salt hair. His eyes were grey as the day, but I didn't see them at first. I slowed for a moment to let him come level, returned his half-smile. I was afraid. Like I said – people can't be avoided. Your only option is to turn back. But if I can reach the lighthouse at the pier's end, I've walked far enough away to feel life can't catch up with me. I breathe.

'Fresh weather.' His smile grew to full and rested well. He fitted his own skin.

'Yes. Even on the warm days you find cold spots here,' I said. I don't know what made me say the rest; I had only planned one word. His eyes encouraged more.

'That's the great thing,' he smiled. 'Keeps the hordes at bay.'

He understood.

'You're a regular, then?' I asked.

'Not at this time. I'm usually one of the dawn chorus. But I didn't feel up to it first thing today. I'm getting on, just a little.' The lines around his eyes creased more. He had tree-bark skin. 'Mind if I walk with you? I can see you're not one for talk. But company is nice.'

We shared this. The waters lapped at the kind old stone that held the weight of all those who had promenaded. I don't know how people can say stone is cold – it lives as surely as we do. Clouds knitted over a thin sky and spring sun. There was the prospect of arriving at the lighthouse ahead, the sense of arrival offered, though we'd only walked halfway. We paused at the breakpoint to watch the waves grow tall and out to meet their adult selves in the open, knowing sea. A yacht came through to moor, the crew waving because they could be themselves on water. In fine new cars, on land, they would cut you up.

The man looked at me and for too long. I kept my head turned to the sea. 'I had a wife,' he said. 'A son. We had a business, a house and a boat. All but the son are gone. I miss them all.'

'Who do you miss most?'

'Her.' He had water in his voice. 'But the pier gives her back to me. I watch the boats and she and I are on ours again.'

'I have one son at home still,' I said. 'He doesn't speak to me unless he has to.'

'What age?'

'Sixteen.'

'That's the age where they practise silence and betrayal. Be patient with him, he'll grow. What about you?'

I'm unremarkable. Three children. One husband. One mother. No father; he died some years ago. A job I don't dislike or like. Groceries to get. A carpet-shampooer to hire. A car key to cut after my youngest lost it down the shore outside our house. He was unapologetic. He's always like that.

Two of my boys have left home. I see them when their lives permit. I miss them and the part of myself that went with them since I gave myself in equal measures to my family. I drop the youngest at school and then drive to the pier. It's a silent journey but for my poor bids at conversation. When he has tired of them he reaches forward and snaps on the radio. I don't know the music and I don't care for it, but it's better than what's between us. I'm too soft with him, my husband says, I should harden. When we talk of our children he says 'you should'. They are my business.

He has a business that pays for our house. He pays for the car that I lock so carefully when I set out on my pier walk. So he was angry when my son started to drive – my car, of course – and bumped into things and lost the car key in the drain.

'These things,' he says, 'have to be paid for.'

'You haven't taught him enough respect,' he says. 'At least the other two knew how to respect things.'

When they lived at home nothing was right either.

My fellow walker heard all of this, without interruption. I didn't labour on any part – I listed.

'When I turn that key in the car door, I turn off the world,' I finished.

'And now you've been forced to share it with an old man who craves company.'

'No, please don't worry.' I smiled the bridge smile.

The old man laughed and said his name was John and asked what mine was. I told him.

'Now you, Helen,' he laughed on, 'have to learn to speak the truth. That's one of the freedoms of getting older.'

'How long have you had it?' My smile vanished.

'About twenty-one years. I'm seventy-one. And I won't ask you how old you are.'

'I should've had five years' worth of freedom to say what I want by now.' I didn't mind him knowing. I do most people.

'Fifty-five will do for a start, it's better than no start at all.' He rubbed his chin with his palm and creased his eyes to look out at the horizon. 'Why did your husband marry you if he doesn't want to speak to you?'

'I don't know. He thought I was pretty. Now I have no face at all.'

John didn't try to deny it for me. He let the morning interrupt us. We watched the businesslike joggers on the facing East Pier turn around and start back, wearing headphones to block out the music of the wind.

'Eejits.' He shook his head. 'Let them stay over there. This is our pier.'

We had some time to separate a little and watch the sea on our own, to follow it where it went. The horizon seemed close on such a day, with the heavy winter slipping off our shoulders and the light shawl of spring landing.

Quiet between us.

Then the wind got up and the chill demanded to know what we were going to do next, like an impatient, persistent child. I looked over at John, who was leaning against a balustrade, his eyes on me. He didn't attempt to remove them.

'You,' he pointed at me, a slow point with a crooked finger, 'are not pretty. There's more to you than that.' There was no threat of advancement, just kindness.

I sniffed. It could have been the salt spray landing on my numbed face, or it could have been what he had offered.

'What made you talk to me?' I asked.

'Ah, I'll talk to anybody. I'm only an old pensioner.'

'If you're asking me to speak the truth, speak it for yourself.' My anger was risen. My anger never rises, like my cakes – I was neither a baker or a shouter.

'Well done. It was your walk. I knew the way it was with you. This pier, we're all kindred on it.' He turned to look at the town. 'We've all had the same thoughts when we stand here. Shall we start back?' He offered me his arm.

I took it.

'Can I tell you my first truth?' I asked. 'I don't even play bloody bridge.'

I walked a mile and a quarter that day. I had only planned on half the distance.

Seashell

Deirdre Purcell

'There's a body—'

'Hmm?' Firelight played over the relaxed figure of the child's mother, who, lost in the comings and goings of her nightly soap on TV, did not turn around. 'What's that you said, honey?'

When she heard no answer, the mother looked over her shoulder. In the relative gloom of the doorway, the whites of the boy's eyes gleamed like candle wax. His maroon school jumper had turned black and his fair hair was darkly plastered. His mouth worked but no sounds came out.

'You're soaked!' She reached for the remote control and flipped off the TV set. 'What is it? What's wrong?'

'I told you.' The boy's voice rose in pitch. 'A body. There's a body—'

'Where?'

'In the back gar—' He swallowed the second syllable.

'What do you mean, "a body"?' Briskly. 'Don't be silly, David. It's just your imagination playing tricks. I've warned you about that PlayStation, you're spending too much time at it, it's bad for you.' Her fingers hovered over the remote. 'Anyway, there couldn't be a body in our back garden; we have a high wall all around our back garden. Nothing could get in unless it fell from an airplane!'

The attempt at humour fell flat. He continued to stare.

She sighed. 'Just tell me one thing. What were you doing out there on a night like this?'

'I needed a screwdriver from the shed to fix something' – the words came in gulps as he tried to control tears – 'and the door slammed and I got a fright and I dropped it and I was looking for it on the ground and—' Again the rest was cut.

Behind the heavy velour curtains, another rain volley rattled the window-frame, but as she pulled her cardigan tighter around her, the mother noticed he was shaking from head to toe. 'Go on upstairs and change your clothes before you catch your death. Have you your homework done?'

He stared.

'All right.' With some force, she threw the remote on the coffee table and stood. 'Show me! Show me what you think you saw – but honestly, sweetheart, you'll have to be sensible about those bloody games. They're not good for someone with the kind of imagination you have.' She attempted to brush a thick, wet wedge of hair off his forehead, but he ducked. So hard he hit his head on the door-frame.

'Are you OK?' She sprang to rescue him. To hug him. Again he ducked.

'I'm fine. Mum, you're wasting *time.*'

'Come on,' she said wearily, 'let's go and see what's what.' She reached for his shoulder to turn him, but he resisted. 'No! I'm not going out there!'

'Please yourself!' She was fast losing patience. Soap time was private time, the only half-hour in the day she claimed as hers, and it was ticking. She rationed herself to just one show every evening, switching allegiance between *Coronation Street*, *EastEnders* and *Fair City* when she became bored or irritated with a particular storyline. Tonight she was coming to the end with *EastEnders* – again. In fact, just before the intrusion she had been castigating herself for sticking for so long to the latest Den Watts saga. Truly, it beggared intelligence.

She cast a longing glance about the cosy, insulated room, slid past her nine-year-old, frozen now in the hallway, and marched into the kitchen, where she leaned over the sink, made a canopy of her hands against the condensation on the cold windowpane and peered outside. Behind her, the dishwasher hummed, the ingredients for tomorrow's lunchboxes and Owen's late supper were neatly assembled on a glass cutting board, while all around, the swathe of black granite worktop gleamed its compliments to her skills as a homemaker.

In the garden she could see nothing except tumbling darkness.

She sensed her son behind her and for his benefit went to the glazed back door, switched on the outside light and, face tight against the glass, gazed showily at the raindrops whirling in the illuminated cone and at the spidery branches of her cherry tree whipping the gale. The tool shed reared as a dense cut-out against the black sky and she silently cursed the feebleness of the light, which on a night like this illuminated a radius of not more than five or six feet. Margaret made a mental note – come the spring, she'd have Owen fix a bulb to the side of that shed. He would have to wire it so it connected to the one above the back door, enabling both to be switched on simultaneously.

'There's nothing out there, David,' she called as a piece of something white, fabric or a torn sheet of newspaper, gusted, wraith-like, across the wavery light. She made a second mental note to remind Owen that the recycle bin had to go out tonight alongside the ordinary one. He'd also have to make sure the lids were secure against this storm.

'But there *is*!' Her son's tone was close to panicked. 'I *told* you. There's no use just *looking* out. You have to *go* out there, Mum.'

Margaret turned away from her back door to contemplate this dismayed, agitated little boy who seemed to live permanently on the edge of some mysterious and desperate crisis. David was an IVF child, finally born to his mother in her mid-forties as a result, she often congratulated herself, of her own iron will and determination, inbuilt virtues that had always served her well and which

287

included the move to Ireland from New Zealand so she and Owen could make a fresh start. Sexual harassment? Owen? The charge was monstrous and the solution obvious – a fresh start in a prosperous, forward-looking country, away from lying reports and David's domineering family who had been less than generous in their response to the preposterous accusation.

Yes. Teaching for her, sales for him. The bonus was David.

At the age of fifty-five, however, despite all her years of dealing with schoolchildren, David was still an enigma to her. Only God knew how she was going to deal with him when he entered his teens. Which was why she had decided they should all have family counselling – when Owen could fit it in, of course.

As far as Margaret could see, though, the family sessions were having very little effect on the family dynamic.

Yet while she, being the primary carer, bore the brunt of the problem, she sincerely felt that their son's hypersensitivity had to be a trial for Owen too. It was hard to tell with him. He was busy-busy-busy, chasing one project after another, brain elsewhere, travelling, having meetings, morning, noon and very late.

She checked her watch. Her husband's flight should be landing about now. Why was he never here when he was needed …

She could see the tears beginning to gather as, with half his face covered by his forearm as though to ward off attackers, the boy stepped backwards into the hallway. He was hiccupping now. Should she indulge him by asking what kind of a body he thought he had seen? Male, female, grown-up, child?

Probably best to keep things light, she thought. The counsellor had explained that David had the type of personality that needed the security of having his parents accept him as he was. 'He might grow out of this nervousness,' she had said, making notes, 'but then again, he might not. We'll just have to take things one step at a time.' Margaret had been encouraged by the counsellor's use of 'we' and had decided there and then to throw herself whole-heartedly into the Help David Project. And looking at him in the state he was in now, she decided she would have to redouble her efforts to persuade her husband to knuckle down.

'All right, darling,' she said, 'just to put your mind at rest I'll go and check. You go get yourself dry. Where should I look?'

'Behind the shed.'

'Just let me get a coat, and while I'm doing that, you take off your wet jumper and I'll spread it out in front of the fire to dry when I come back in. OK?'

'Stop *delaying*, Mum!' He clutched his left ear with his right hand, a reflex when something frightened him that had persisted since babyhood. 'Go *now*!'

'I'm going, I'm going, calm down.' Abandoning the idea of getting her coat, she employed her bright, even classroom tone and braced herself to open the back door. Immediately, the ferocity of the wind snatched it from her so it crashed against her recently redecorated wall. Annoyed, she forced it closed again and checked the dent the handle had made in the plaster. It was on the tip of her tongue to remonstrate – *Now look what you've caused!* – but she managed to restrain herself and opened the door again, more cautiously this time.

Outside, the wind literally took her breath away. Snug in the double-glazed television room she insisted they refer to as The Den, she had not realised quite how fierce the storm had become. She took a deep breath as though poised for a dive and quickly, head down and hands flailing in a useless effort to protect her hairdo, made her way towards and then around the shed.

The body, face buried in the detritus that always seems to accumulate behind a shed, was whorled like a seashell around a briefcase. The face was pressed into his briefcase, one of those handy-dandy ones with separate and expanding compartments for laptop, toiletries, clean shirt and underthings.

The body was unmistakeably Owen's. Even in the noisy darkness, Margaret recognised the new camelhair coat she had bought him for Christmas. He had been wearing it when he left for the airport at 6.15 the previous morning. Outside it had been clear and starry. She knew this because she had got out of her bed to wave him off, as she always did when he went away on a business trip, no matter how early the hour. She had started the practice when he had left the safety of employment to go out on his own and, slightly despising herself for being superstitious but continuing nonetheless, had never missed a morning since.

After his taillights had gone from her view around the corner of the road, she had wandered into the kitchen and – *The hell with it, it's still Christmas* – had turned on the central heating an hour before it was due to click on automatically. She had made herself a cup of tea.

On her way back to bed, cradling the steaming cup between cold hands, she had looked in on David. Asleep. Curled around his bunched-up duvet.

Curled up just like this.

The rain, a forest of cold pine needles, stung her scalp and scalded her cheeks. 'Owen?' The storm crushed the name so it was entirely unimportant, one name in a world of names.

As if it was not hers, her right foot extended itself tentatively to touch the body. She was wearing shoes as soft as moccasins – David's Christmas present to her – and, through the suede, felt the hardness of her husband's body under the sodden wool. Appalled, she withdrew her foot and stepped back, squelching into mud and almost falling into her compost heap. *Thank God that didn't happen*, she thought, righting herself. *That could have totally ruined my new shoes.*

Seashell coils wrap themselves around Margaret's brain as she retreats through the days that follow. Through the arrival of police, ambulance and priest.

Through frantic combing for reasons, for signs or signals, an exercise that finds no one to remember or posit a single moment or word of significance ...

Through a funeral that twists and tightens around her as she attempts to grasp what is happening ...

Through crowds swirling around her house ...

Through finding Owen's car in the airport car park ...

Through merciful placement in a clean, hard bed where she is assured daily by kind, firm people that David is doing well in his temporary foster home and that his grandparents, Owen's mother and father, are on their way from New Zealand to take charge of the situation ...

Through the words of the note, found inside the pocket of the wallet, inside the inside pocket of the new coat.

I can't go through it again. You'll cope. You always do. Tell David I'm sorry.

Through the abruptly inimical screen of every TV, filled only with images of soft, sliding planks and hard, twisting water, piling bodies on bodies on sheds on Owen's body ...

She will not yield the note. The note is curled inside her curled fingers, fingers so tightly curled around the note that their flesh must eventually absorb it.

We'll Be Away in a Tumbrel

Trisha Rainsford

Cascading screams and dripping, slipping faces ran inside his brain. An eye, an ear, a nose. A mouth became a weeping, wailing wound. His mother's face.

'Oedipus! Oedipus! Oedipus!' a fat man screamed at a tall, thin boy lying bleeding in a ditch, and Henry heard everybody laugh.

'Mammy,' the boy said and his lips were white and the hands covering his bleeding stomach poppy-red. 'I want my mammy.'

'Oedipus,' the fat man said again. 'Bloody fucking Oedipus. Grow up.'

The boy cried. 'Please, Mammy, please.'

Henry woke. *It's-a-dream-a-dream-only-a-dream-a-dream-a-dream-only-a-dream.* Gradually he made out the wardrobe, the dressing table, his suit on a hanger for the morning. Máire stirred beside him as he reached across her for his cigarettes.

'Shh,' he said as she groaned in her sleep, 'it's fine. It's fine.'

He lit a match and a cigarette and his eyes stung from the smoke and the wakening. Not long now. The cigarette would do it. It always did.

At school next morning Henry slapped Frank Shinnors with his yardstick.

'Pup,' Henry said, whacking the stick hard across the boy's outstretched hand. Shinnor's eyes glistened and his face was red but he smiled and raised an eyebrow.

'Bloody ungrateful pup,' he said with the second and third slaps. 'Men gave their lives so you could be free and proud and not a bond-slave to an English master.'

Henry panted with exertion. 'Boys not much older than you died in ditches so you could have the privilege of sitting in this room and you don't care, do you?'

There was a loud banging on the door.

'Mr Cassidy!'

Henry looked up. 'Mr Fagan? Can I help you?'

'A word?'

'Certainly.'

Henry looked at Frank Shinnors, whose eyes were playground marbles but still not even one tear had wet his red cheeks.

'Let that be a lesson to you,' he said after a deep breath. Shinnors' lips quivered and Henry caught a brief glimpse of the blood-soaked palms in front of him before the boy closed his fingers and folded his hands in by his sides.

'Get back to your seat. Take out your geography books and study the industries of Munster. I'll be examining when I return – and not a word while I'm out of the room, mind. Not one single solitary sound.'

The door made a loud click as Henry stepped into the corridor and Pádraig Fagan looked away from the window.

'Henry.'

'Pádraig. What can I do for you?'

Pádraig Fagan adjusted his tie. 'Just wanted to let you know that the ceremony is set for Tuesday. Twelve o'clock – immediately after the Angelus.'

'It'll be announced from the pulpit, I presume,' Henry said.

'At all Masses.'

'And parents are invited?'

'Everyone is invited, Henry. Please God it'll stay dry during the ceremony.'

'With luck, Pádraig. Who is reading the Proclamation?'

'I was thinking of reading the Irish version myself, what would you think of that? Perhaps it might be better to get a boy to read it?'

'Not at all. It would be entirely fitting for the principal to read at the ceremony. Give it a sense of dignity.'

Pádraig smiled now.

'Perhaps somebody else could read the English translation?' Henry said.

Pádraig frowned as if he was thinking, though Henry doubted it.

'Good idea,' Pádraig said. 'Who would you think might be good?'

Henry's heart gave a thump. *Maybe somebody who risked his life for you, you half-baked jackeen? Somebody – who isn't running around the countryside going to dances every weekend and courting women in short dresses and white patent-leather knee boots?*

But he didn't say that. He just smiled as Pádraig struggled to come up with a plan. Behind him he thought he heard a voice from his classroom, so he thumped on the door and all was quiet again.

Padraig frowned. 'Do they know the national anthem?'

'Of course they do.'

'And do they know they must salute as the flag is being raised and the anthem is being sung?'

'Obviously,' Henry said.

'Good. Good. How about Eoin O'Brien? He's a nice boy and he has a good strong voice.'

'Eoin O'Brien?'

'To read the Proclamation in English, Henry. Keep the focus, man!' Pádraig laughed. Henry swallowed the taste of loathing.

'Eoin O'Brien isn't the best reader in sixth class,' Henry said.

'Yes, yes, but we can teach him to read that one piece by Tuesday, surely? I'll talk to his mother. His father paid for the flagpole. They'd be proud. Something to boast to the relatives about, eh? The eldest son reading at the fiftieth anniversary.'

'As long as he doesn't make a mess of it.'

'He won't, he'll be delighted to be honouring the men of 1916
– what boy wouldn't? I'll talk to his mother this afternoon and you
do a bit of work with him today during lunchtime and sure we'll
be away in a hack then, won't we?'

'As long as it's not a tumbrel, Pádraig.'

'Sorry?'

'A tumbrel. Instead of a hack.'

Pádraig frowned and shrugged.

Henry took a deep breath to stem the gush of annoyance inside
him. How could this half-educated corner-boy be principal of a
school?

'The carts that took the victims to the guillotine during the
French Revolution?'

Pádraig's face clouded and then he laughed. 'You're a gas man.
Very droll. A tumbrel, indeed. I'll talk to you later. Let me know if
you have any problems with Eoin.'

'I will,' Henry said as he stepped back into his silent classroom.
Henry almost laughed at the problems he could foresee with a
blushing, pimply Eoin O'Brien stuttering his way through the
noble words of men who knew they were signing their own death
warrants as they signed the Proclamation of Independence. It
would be funny if it wasn't so bloody disrespectful.

But everything was disrespect now, wasn't it? Nobody cared
any more. The young people sang and drank and the boys grew
their hair long like girls. Would those men have died so willingly if
they could have seen the Ireland that was destined to follow their
sacrifice? They should have left the bloody country to the English.
They deserved it.

Henry slammed the duster on the oak desk and looked around
at the faces in front of him.

'Padraig Pearse wouldn't cross the road for any one of you,' he
said. He looked at each boy in turn. 'Nor give up one drop of his
precious blood. There's not even one of you worthy to lick the
boots of the men of 1916. Get out your Irish books and learn off

the poem on page twenty-seven. Eoin O'Brien. Come up to my desk and bring the copy where you wrote out the Proclamation of Independence; I have no intention of working during my dinner break. Come on, come on, boy, what's taking you so long?'

Henry was surprised when Máire brought up the subject of the dream.

'Do you have that nightmare every night now, Henry?' she asked as she poured tea. He looked at the antics of the people who lived in the willow-pattern on his cup. 'Well?'

'Not every night,' he said, still not looking at her.

'But most nights.' Henry shrugged.

'Is it the same one?'

He buttered his toast and shrugged again.

'The one where Thomas is dying?'

Henry nodded.

'How is it possible for a man to dream the same dream for fifty years?' Máire asked.

'I don't know.'

'You've been dreaming and screaming and sweating that same dream for as long as I've known you, man and boy.'

'Is Fionnuala definitely going to be here for the ceremony?' Henry said.

'Yes, she is. John is away in England and Fearghal and Séamus are back at boarding school.'

Henry tutted. 'Boarding school.'

'I know – but that's the way of it.'

'At least it's a Catholic school,' he said, not that he cared. Henry had no time for the Church after what they'd done to the men who died to give them a leg up into power. But Máire cared and he knew it would move her attention away from the dream.

'Thank God for that,' she said, 'thanks be to God.'

*

It rained during the ceremony, a thick, drizzly rain that meant they had to crowd into the school hall after they raised the flag in the schoolyard and sang the 'Soldier's Song'. In the hall Henry listened to Pádraig Fagan and Eoin O'Brien read the Proclamation, rushing through the precious words of freedom as if they were reading a racing schedule.

Henry didn't care any more, though. The whole event was a travesty anyway. He just had to get through it and go home and have a couple of rashers and an egg, then walk the dog and go to bed and hope the dream was gone for a while.

Maud Ryan sang 'Faith of Our Fathers' as the rain stopped and the sun came out, and then Pádraig Fagan stood up once more in front of the packed hall.

'In our midst today,' he said, peering up at the sun that was streaming in a window, 'is a man who was deeply involved in the struggle for freedom. A man whose own brother, a mere boy at the time, was shot to death at the side of the road not two miles from here. Ladies and gentlemen, without further ado I'd like to invite our own most esteemed staff member, Mr Henry Cassidy, to say a few words to us on this historic occasion.'

Pádraig Fagan began to clap and the entire audience followed. Máire and Fionnula smiled at Henry from the other side of the maple-floored hall and he slowly made his way to the small wooden stage. The principal shuffled Henry in front of the microphone.

He looked at the people assembled in front of him. Tall and small, fat and thin. Boy-faces and man-faces and woman-faces. All looking at him. Waiting. For what? Did they think he'd tell them that it was worth it? Did they think he'd say it was all right that his brother had bled his sixteen years into a ditch a mile from home? A noble cause well served?

If only he and Thomas could have glimpsed the future. If they were old enough to shoot guns and blow up police cars they were old enough to leave home. He was fourteen, almost fifteen,

Thomas was ten months older. They could have gone away to England or America instead of staying and fighting.

Fighting. For what? Freedom? What freedom? The English were gone, but there was no freedom. Now the people he and Thomas thought they were freeing were slaves of other masters. Slaves to fashion and American films and music and greed. If that was the case, then what was the point of it all?

He'd given them his brother. Lived fifty years alone in the world with that picture of Thomas crying for Mammy stuck inside him like a half-staked vampire who can't quite die. He looked at the faces in front of him and wanted to tell them how he begrudged them every drop of his brother's blood. He wanted to say how sorry he was, how horribly sorry that his only brother had thrown away his life.

Henry coughed and the microphone rocked and crackled.

'Reverend fathers,' he said, coughing again. 'Reverend fathers, ladies and gentlemen. I'd like to take this opportunity to announce my retirement – effective immediately.'

Henry nodded his head once and walked off the stage and through the crowd that parted like the Red Sea must have parted in front of Moses.

One Small Step
Patricia Scanlan

I need assertiveness classes, I decide, as I stuff a turkey that I do not want to stuff, let alone eat. I'm annoyed at myself. Once again I've behaved like an absolute doormat. Mad as I am at my older sister, I'm even madder at myself.

My name is Jessie Ryan. I'm a forty-year-old wife, a mother of two, a freelance copy-editor, a finger-curling PMT sufferer and, right now, a doormat. Let me fill you in before we go any further. Monica, my eldest sister – married to flashy git, Andrew, who likes to be called Drew – is having her annual family barbecue.

Because it's family, and family is very definitely B-list, she doesn't bother with caterers. Why would she when the rest of us can bring an assortment of grub? I get a phone call from her four days before the event.

'Bring the turkey over as soon as it's cooked so I can carve it and plate it up before the others arrive. Lia can do up the salads. I'll sort out the ribs, burgers and chicken for the barbecue.' Monica issues her instructions like a sergeant-major.

'Do we really *need* a turkey?' I ask a tad irritably. 'I don't like cold turkey.' (PMT is really beginning to kick in and I'm way behind schedule for a deadline that is looming fast.) 'I don't have *time* to cook turkey!' I tell my sister.

'*What?*'

Monica is clearly taken aback by my lack of enthusiasm.

'Of course we need a turkey, we always have a turkey. All you have to do is bung it in the oven. You *know* Gran and Grandad won't eat barbecue food. You *know* how conservative they are. And neither will Marcus after getting the trots ... no, sorry, *salmonella* ... two years ago, at Susy Carter's charity barbie.'

Monica drips with sarcasm. She doesn't like Marcus, her brother-in-law. Mind you, I'm not mad about him myself – apart from being a hypochondriac of the highest order, he gives me the creeps. His hugs are revoltingly gropey, if you know what I mean. You don't want to be left alone in a room with him. I get the shivers just thinking about the time he snuck up behind me one Christmas.

Monica is still rabbiting on. 'He's such a wussie, honestly. He doesn't just get a headache, he gets a brain tumour, and as for ...'

I tune out and let her at it. Why does she bother having a barbecue when it seems such an ordeal? It's become a sort of family tradition now, though. She had the first one six years ago and between you and me – and I know this is a bitchy thing to say about my own sister – it wasn't for love of us all. It was only to show off her posh new house in Howth with the fabulous sea views and landscaped garden.

The first year she and Drew looked after the cooking but the following year, when she decided to do it again and get all the family entertaining out of the way 'in one fell swoop', as she rather crassly put it, our sister-in-law Lia suggested we all bring a dish. That year wasn't too bad – three dozen savoury vol-au-vents did the trick – but somehow over the years three dozen vol-au-vents have turned into a twenty-five-pound turkey! Maybe Monica feels a family barbecue is expected of her now, but, even still, why should I have to suffer?

'I could do a salmon instead,' I interrupt her anti-Marcus diatribe.

'Claire's doing salmon, you do the turkey as usual and bring a bottle of gin or vodka.'

I feel my blood boil. Monica and Drew like spirits. Matt, my long-suffering husband, and I prefer wine.

'Monica, Matt and I aren't mad about spirits, we prefer to drink wine,' I explain.

'Oh, for God's sake!' Monica can't hide her exasperation. 'There'll be plenty of wine here. Look, I have to go, Drew's entertaining some colleagues from New York and I have a manicure and hair appointment booked. Bye.'

She sounds distinctly tetchy, huffy even. My heart sinks. Monica in a huff is not for the faint-hearted. She does huffy better than anyone else I know and can stay frosty for weeks.

So that is how, this Sunday morning, I'm up at seven-thirty, stuffing a fine, fat, white-skinned, blue-veined turkey, with extreme bad grace. This year I've cheated. I've bought Superquinn's apricot and walnut stuffing instead of making my own. I rub the skin with lemon to crisp it up, swaddle the bird in tinfoil and manoeuvre the roasting dish into the oven.

I still feel hard done by. Resentment has multiplied in the four days since my conversation with Monica. That turkey is proof positive that I do not count in her eyes. She did not listen to one word that I said to her: a) I don't like cold turkey; b) I'm tied for time and am under pressure with my work (I was up until 1.00 a.m. this morning, editing, and am bog-eyed with tiredness); and c) even though I don't like spirits I'm still expected to bring a bottle of gin or vodka.

What is it about Monica that makes her feel that her desires are far more important than mine? Why are my feelings of no consequence and why do I put up with her bullying? Because, frankly, that's the issue here. Bullying and a lack of respect. Monica doesn't rate my copy-editing as a job at all. As far as she's concerned I'm at home all day so I don't 'work'. She feels perfectly free to ring up and ask me to collect her children from the crèche because she's been delayed at some very important 'strategy planning session'.

(She works as a PA to a stockbroker and likes to think she's at the cutting edge of high finance.)

Don't think I mind helping someone when they're stuck, that's not the issue. It's just that, week in, week out, I'm expected to drop everything and run to her assistance. What really bugs me is that she expects it of me and I find it so hard to put my foot down and say, 'No, enough is enough.' Matt, my kind, lovely husband, tells me that I have to draw my boundaries and make a stand.

Am I being super-sensitive? I ask myself over and over. I don't think so, and today I've made a decision. This is the last turkey I'll cook for Monica's bloody barbecue.

Bits of stuffing are caught in my rings so I rinse them under the tap and gaze out at my garden. It's a mellow late summer's morning (Monica is always lucky with her weather). The scent of sweet pea and roses drifts through the open window. My damson tree is heavy with ripening fruit. Soon I'll pick it and make pots of ruby-red jam that my children will spread on chunky slices of Vienna roll, thick with butter.

I hear the pitter-patter of feet on the stairs and my two-and-a-half-year-old daughter, Millie, bursts into the kitchen, blue eyes wide and clear, golden curls dancing.

'Allo, Mammy. I's hungry,' she declares.

I bend down and sweep her into my arms, nuzzling her neck, inhaling her delicious baby scent. I adore her, and my four-year-old son, Adam. I know I'm very lucky really (in case I'm giving the impression of all gloom and doom). I have an extremely happy family life. In fact, sometimes I think Monica is a little envious. She might have loads of money, a big house and a 'high-flying' career, but Andrew is not the ideal husband. His career is everything. He's a pilot and I think he plays away. Monica is very insecure about his fidelity. I know I'm being judgmental here, but I wouldn't put it past him. He thinks he's God's gift to women.

'I's hungry, Mammy,' Millie repeats indignantly. I kiss her

again and open the fridge to get her a yogurt drink, and milk for her cereal.

As the hours pass, the aroma of roasting turkey fills the kitchen. I'm reminded of Christmas. My mouth waters as I eventually lift the sizzling golden bird from the roasting dish.

'Looks good, Jessie,' Matt says as he slides the big dish underneath and carries it to the table for me. He and Adam dive on the crisp streaky bacon covering the breast.

'Yummy.' Adam grins, grease dripping down his chin. 'You're a brill cook, Mam.'

Matt and I smile at each other over his head and I feel a moment of happiness. How lucky I am to love and be loved. They are going to play football in the park, my precious husband and son. I warn them to be back before two. We're expected at Monica's for three. Millie is having her nap.

My men leave the house, still chomping on crispy bacon, and absent-mindedly I pick at the stuffing that is overflowing onto the big oval serving plate. It is scrumptious, and I'm starving. A wild recklessness overcomes me. I grab the carving knife and fork and slice into the smooth, succulent breast. Juices ooze out. I carve again and lay the steaming white slices on a plate. I pull some of the rich, dark meat from under the wings and place it neatly beside the breast. My fingers are sticky and I lick them, teasing myself with the taste of what is to come. I spoon out stuffing and take a jar of cranberry sauce from the press. I dress the slices of meat with scarlet cranberries and shake some pepper and salt over my feast. Exhilarated, I pour myself a glass of chilled white wine.

Sitting at my kitchen table I cut a portion of breast, add a dark piece, and, pressing some stuffing on top, ease my fork into the mouth-watering food. I eat slowly, savouring the contrasting moist flavours. It is *delicious*. I've surpassed myself this year, I think happily, taking a sip of cool, sweet wine. Tension evaporates. I feel perfectly at peace as the silence of the house wraps itself around me. This is the life.

*

It's the usual bedlam getting out, and we arrive at Monica's half an hour late. My sister is doing her nut.

'You're late! Bring the turkey into the kitchen until I carve it, before the others arrive,' she hisses at me as she ushers Matt and the children ahead of her.

She looks the height of elegance in her cream linen trousers and black sleeveless Dolce & Gabbana polo. I carry the tinfoil-wrapped plate carefully, reverently. Drew is out on the deck wearing a chef's hat and apron, presiding over his smoking barbecue. He salutes us in his hearty hail-fellow-well-met tones, which he reserves for lesser family mortals and those he feels superior to.

'Jamie Oliver, eat your heart out,' Matt murmurs, giving me a wink.

I laugh and Monica turns and glares at me. That makes me laugh even more. I'm a little tipsy. The two glasses of wine I've had have gone to my head. I'm not used to drinking in the middle of the day. I follow Monica into her state-of-the-art kitchen and place the turkey on the island. Monica is all business. Impatient, she pulls away the tinfoil, anxious to get carving. Her jaw drops.

'What happened the turkey?' she squawks.

'Oh, I had mine hot. It was delicious,' I say offhandedly as I pull a couple of bottles of wine from the tote bag on my shoulder. 'You might want to put these in the fridge to chill for later,' I add breezily.

I smile at her, before stepping out through the patio doors to join my family. This is one barbecue I intend to enjoy.

Awakening
Mary Stanley

It was early summer and freak wet weather had been my constant companion over the previous days. The rain appeared to have eased but the sky was still ominous and I couldn't wait for the long hot evenings that the forecasters on the news predicted.

I worked in a university in a German town – writing my thesis, doing a little teaching, translating for a professor whose forthcoming lecture abroad was in English – and despite the dull thud of a headache, it was of my work I was thinking as I drove home along the banks of the river, not noticing that the recent heavy rain had raised the level of the water to a worrying height. The river was flowing fast with branches being swept downstream, and it swirled and eddied with unusual force, but the road, my own thoughts and my need to get home absorbed me.

Professor Mahler's forthcoming lecture on alienation was preoccupying me on two fronts. On the one hand I was concerned about some of my translation and the precision of my vocabulary, and on the other I was thinking about the content of his speech. He and I had spoken about this earlier in the day.

'Sarah,' he had said. 'You and I are removed from reality, far removed from the hand-to-mouth existence that many people on our planet face. What do we know about harvesting grain, slaughtering cattle, fishing the ocean? What do we know about eking out a life close to the soil with barely enough to survive? We live in a world where we can indulge our minds. That makes us luckier than most. But we must not lose sight of the important things. We have created a gap between what we really are – what really matters – and what we have allowed ourselves to turn into. And we have let this gap become a canyon; a canyon so far across we can barely see the other side of it from here. We live our lives, day to day, forgetting that the other side is out there, maybe deliberately. Maybe we don't really want to remind ourselves of how far adrift we have wandered from reality. But then something happens, some moment in life that pulls us up short. We're born with nothing. Nothing has any meaning. We give things meaning and eventually become defined by them. Do we want that? Should human beings strive for that? To be defined by the clothes we wear, the clubs we are members of … the trivia we give meaning to? Is that the meaning of life?'

It was these words that occupied my thoughts and I supposed that the important things for me were my home and its contents – my work, my books, my notes – all the little things that put together made up my life, that had meaning for me and which over the years I had nurtured into significance.

Home was a two-roomed apartment, built in the cellar of an old farmhouse. It was situated just a few hundred metres from the river, the garden path sloping downwards and around the side of the farmhouse to my apartment entrance. On the other side of the building a stone stairway led upwards to the front door of the main house.

I crossed the bridge from the high road and came down into the village through the winding streets until I reached the farmhouse. I grimaced before opening the car door, swinging my feet carefully onto the footpath to avoid the puddles. Leaning back into the car, I lifted out my folders and my bag and then turned back to face what I had seen while parking.

My carefully tended vegetable and flower patch was muddied

from the rain, all growth washed onto its side, with even the vines on the trellis drooping from the battering they had taken from the elements. Soil had been swept from the beds onto the path and I groaned as I realised that my gardening and tidying from the previous weekend had been washed away.

I placed my paperwork on the dry surface of a stool in the porch before taking a carton of milk from my bag. I emptied the rainwater from the hedgehog's saucer, filled it with milk and put it under the patio table for my regular night-time visitor, carefully ensuring that the table would protect it from any further rain and silently promising that I would leave an egg for my prickly guest the following evening.

Even as I shut the door of the apartment and picked up the post from the mat, it began to rain again, and once inside I closed the shutters on the windows and pulled the curtains. Back in the tiny kitchen I took two painkillers with a cup of tea and opened the letter from my mother. The Irish stamp, my mother's sloping hand, the gentle smell of her perfume … somehow that scent wafting on the paper suggested a very different image of what a home could be. I found myself thinking of that home, that other life I'd had before I came to live in Germany – the warmth of childhood and a mother's love, of a kettle seemingly always on the boil, and someone there to pour it for me.

'My darling Sarah,' she wrote. 'There is nothing new here. Life goes on as normal …'

It was almost eight o'clock. I thought about cooking some-thing, but my head was throbbing, and I decided instead to go to bed. Dropping my clothes in a heap on the floor and wearing just a long cotton T-shirt for comfort, I slipped under the quilt, switched off the bedside light and closed my eyes. With the shutters fastened no light penetrated the darkness of the basement room, and the pounding of my headache eased as I drifted into sleep, with the sound of rain clattering against the window.

*

I woke several hours later with memories of a strange dream in which Noah was calling me into his ark. It was a bewildering moment, waking in pitch-blackness, sensing something was wrong, reaching for the lamp switch and no light coming on. The bed seemed wet and I wondered for a moment if I had perspired so much that the bed was sodden, but as I tried to get out of it I realised that there was water rising up the sides of the bed, then over the top.

I struggled to the floor in darkness to find myself thigh-deep in ice-cold water. In total shock I waded to the window. Opening the shutters, I peered out, but the electricity supply for the whole village was gone and there was nothing to be seen. I could hear the sound of water lapping against the glass. It was coming in, seemingly through the walls and under the floor, at an incredible pace. My thick double-glazed windows suddenly seemed wafer-thin, offering little protection.

The water was already at my waist.

With great effort I moved across the floor towards the kitchen. Fumbling in the dark and finding the door closed, I searched for the handle, but with the weight of water behind the door I could not push it open.

All the while I was in a state of disbelief. How could this be happening? Was I still asleep? What kind of nightmare was this? Could I possibly be awake? But the cold, wet flow of water was so real that some part of my mind kept telling me that I really was awake and that I had to act fast.

I pushed my way back to the window, panic coursing through me as images of the rising water that I had earlier ignored on my drive home now registered in my brain. I realised with horror that the river was flooding the valley. The water outside was higher than that in the bedroom and I stood there terrified, clutching the windowsill, my mind struggling to find a way out as it dawned on me that I was trapped inside.

Now swimming, I went back to the door and tried again and

again to push it open. Only by standing could I put any weight on it, but I needed one hand to hold the door-handle down, and I did not have the strength to push against the water on the other side. I suddenly realised that, even if I managed to get into the other room, I would have the same problem reaching the garden door. And with every moment the level of the water was rising higher and higher. It was now above my chest.

In the dark I could feel books lifting off the shelves, coming down around me – trapped just as I was – and papers, files and folders floating from their safety into the black water. I knew Professor Mahler's notes, my translation, the first chapter of my thesis, were sinking into the water in the kitchen. His work ... my work ... I blotted out the image.

I swam back to the window, frantically telling myself there had to be a way out if I could only keep afloat. My feet could no longer touch the floor.

Suddenly two men in wetsuits with lamps attached to their heads swam into view, their lights shining into the room and focusing on me. They banged on the pane, indicating I should open the window.

I could see them through the glass, above me in the water. I knew what they wanted me to do, but I was too afraid to twist the handle, knowing what would happen, what had to happen ... The river would pour into my room and I could not imagine how I would survive that. They hammered on the glass over and over, pointing to it anxiously and gesturing that I must open it. It was almost in fear of them leaving me in their frustration that finally, utterly terrified and with shaking fingers, I released the catch. I was flushed backwards by the incoming flood, which also carried them through the window into my bedroom.

I lost all sense of direction as the river washed over me. Something soft wrapped around me, possibly the quilt from the sunken bed, before it sank back down, entangling me in its folds. Somehow fingers reached me and I felt grasping hands lifting me from the deep. Then I was back on the surface spluttering, gasping for air, overcome by the roar of the water and the fear of being lost in that deluge of darkness.

I thought I heard voices shouting but did not know if they were speaking to me. I could only clearly relate to the sound of the river sucking and pulling while the men's hands struggled with me against its force. Their lamps lit up our way like two white streaks of light across the watery shadows and, fighting against the force of the river, they lifted and guided me back out through the window into the night. They swam on either side of me across the garden, and around to where the farmhouse steps were now submerged. Up above, willing hands reached down and lifted me to safety.

Candles had been lit in the farmhouse and I found myself among neighbours, people I had only ever nodded to in passing and who now welcomed me with cheering and with joy. I could see it in their faces, feel it in their embraces as I stood there shaken and frozen, unable to believe or assimilate what had happened. Someone wrapped a blanket around me and someone else thrust a glass into my hand.

Everything and everyone in the room seemed larger than life, clear-cut against the wooden beams in the room and the pale paint. The glass in my hand felt as if it had been etched somewhere far back in time; the bubbling liquid had a colour and taste that were clearer than anything I had ever drunk before. And it was as if I got drunk on that first sip.

As I drank I felt I should be celebrating something but I could not think what that something was. I could not disconnect from what had happened, even though I knew that in their own ways each of these people must have come to that room to find refuge and that maybe some of them had come like I had, with frogmen dragging them from their chambers of death. Like me, some were wrapped in blankets with their hair matted around their heads and splashes of mud on their faces. As they talked and laughed and embraced I slowly realised that the whole village had been on the move while I had slept, that warnings had been given and evacuation had started hours before.

I felt that if I were behaving normally I would scream or dance or sing, and instead I stood there wrapped in blankets drinking with them, trying to smile, trying to be normal. I did not know what was normal in a situation like this and for the first time in my life I didn't care.

It's funny how we behave in such moments. All the little things that we think matter, all the pretence of daily existence, all the barriers – all were washed away. We rejoiced in being there, talking as though there were no boundaries, finally falling asleep on the floor as if in a dream, and waking in the morning to find it was reality.

It was days later before the river subsided and the water drained away. In borrowed clothing I emerged with my new friends to survey the horror of what had happened. People came – people I hardly knew, some I had never seen before – to help shovel away the mud. In my basement home someone salvaged the books from the top shelves while others threw out the mud-covered notes and folders that made up my life. I worked with them as in a trance, wondering what was real, what could ever be real again.

My computer and all my notes were gone, the disks destroyed, my work washed away by the river, lost forever in the mud and the sewage. The folders in the kitchen had completely disappeared under thick layers of stinking filth.

But there was something there, something new, something that had not been there before. At first I was not aware of it, so overwhelmed was I by the sense of loss, of shock and horror.

Professor Mahler came to visit, dressed in boots and bringing a shovel to help. He had seen it on the news and recognised the village I lived in, and it was he who pulled me to my senses.

'Everything is gone,' I said. 'Everything.'

'Is it, Sarah?' he said in his incredibly calm voice as he looked around. 'I see you. I see friends helping out. I see that what you have lost you will recreate.'

'The files,' I said. 'Your work ... my work ...'

'And they matter?' he asked. 'Those things matter? I think that what matters is that you survived. You and the others in this village. You have one another to give and receive support. My work? Well ... I will rewrite my lecture. You will translate it again. Our lives will go on, very much as before. I am not belittling what has happened to you, but life will go on as before. You still have all the means of support you had before this happened. No one died. Everything can be rewritten. Trust me, this is not loss. Not loss as it could be, not loss on a grand scale.'

Not loss on a grand scale?

At first I could not see what he meant. I was still in a state of shock ... still learning that I had survived ... still learning that what they were drinking to in that impromptu party in the farmhouse was survival itself.

No one died that night. Professor Mahler was right about loss but that took me time to understand. The structure of my life was such that insurance policies paid for the things that had material value. With time, my car was replaced, as was my television, my computer, the electrical items in the kitchen, my clothing – and my job was still there. There was food when I was hungry, drink when I was thirsty. There were people around whom I now knew, people to whom I learned to relate and whom I learned to love. My life was not destroyed.

Yes, I was shaken to the core of my being, but the illusion of reality in which I lived was still there. Professor Mahler rewrote his lecture. I re-translated it. I travelled with him to Oxford and we stayed in the best hotel. We ate the best food, drank the best wine, talked the best talk. I flew on to Dublin and visited my mother. Then I came back to Germany and my life continued ... much the same as before.

Or so it might seem.

But something had changed. There was something new.

It took a while for me to realise that the light of day was brighter, the taste of life clearer and sweeter – I was lucky.

No, let me change that. I am lucky. I have learned to seize the moments of every day in a new and different way … every moment … every single moment.

Dancing

Kate Thompson

Yes, the cottage was available. No, they couldn't let it out for just one day, it wasn't financially viable. He'd have to pay the weekend rate even if he only stayed overnight, even out of season. 'That's fine,' he said. 'I'll be happy to pay whatever you ask.' It would be worth it, to be with her again.

The man who met him to hand over the keys was not the man who'd met them the last time, and he was glad of this. He wanted no questions asked, no remarks passed. 'Not necessary,' he said when he was asked if he wanted someone to escort him to the island and show him the ropes. 'I've been there before.'

'Are you expecting company?'

'Yes.'

'You know the mainland is inaccessible at high tide?'

'Yes, I know that. Thanks.'

The journey took ten minutes. The narrow road bumped him uphill and down before rounding a headland and petering out on a rocky foreshore. The sea was smooth as slate-blue silk now, but he knew that later today that silk would be torn to flitters by the wind that had been forecast for the evening. He stopped the car and let the engine idle for some minutes, regarding the white-washed cottage that looked back at him from the island at the other end of the causeway. It was the kind of cottage a child might draw: two windows, a door and a chimney. He remembered her reaction the first time she'd seen it.

'Oh – it's dotey! Perfect! Take me there now!' They'd rumbled across the causeway and the minute they pulled up by the garden gate, she'd climbed out of the car and had gone dancing up the path, the white silk of her dress shimmering round her. When she reached the cottage door she'd turned to him. 'Come *on*, slow-coach!' she'd called. 'I can't wait to explore.'

He'd unlocked the door, then lunged for her hand as she made to slip through. 'Wait! We have to do it properly,' he told her, scooping her up in his arms to carry her over the threshold.

'But it's not our home.'

'It is for the next fortnight.'

He set her down on the flagstone floor and watched as she moved around the room, emitting small squeals every time she came across something that pleased her. 'Oh, look – the fire's set with real turf! Oh, look – a rocking-chair! And fresh flowers and a bottle of wine! How kind. They've thought of everything!'

'They certainly have. Get a load of that.'

He'd indicated with a nod the window that framed a view John Hinde could have sold a thousand-fold. The seascape was dotted with emerald islands – drowned drumlins clustering at the foot of the purple, cone-shaped mountain.

'Do they really climb it barefoot?' she asked.

'They do.'

'I'll do it barefoot – suck up to God. That way he might answer my prayer.'

'I wouldn't dream of allowing you to climb barefoot. Think of the damage you could do to your precious dancer's feet!'

'Dancers' feet,' she told him, 'are as tough as old boots. They have to be.'

He set the car in motion now across the causeway, knowing that in less than an hour's time there'd be no going back. Water lapped on either side, and he wondered if he'd swim when the tide was fully in. She had swum naked that first day, emerging laughing and goosebumpy before getting back into the white silk dress.

'Shouldn't you put on something warmer?' he'd asked.

'No! It's my wedding day. I'm wearing this until bedtime. Sure, I can dance to get warm.'

And she'd done exactly that – danced barefoot on the patch of green lawn that fronted the cottage till the goosebumps disappeared, and he'd been reminded of the first time he'd seen her on stage. It had been in a production of *Swan Lake*, and she'd been in the *corps de ballet*. He'd been so captivated by her smile that he'd barely registered the other dancers.

The car slid off the causeway onto gravel. He parked it by the twisted fir tree where they used to leave it and reached behind him for his luggage. He was travelling light: an overnight bag and a suiter were all he had with him. Fishing in the pocket of his jacket for the key, he walked up the garden path and let himself into the cottage.

It was much the same, although the rocking-chair had been reupholstered. There was turf in the fireplace, the shelves were packed with the same books and board games to take care of bad-weather days, and the view beyond the window was as heart-stopping as ever. Only there was no celebratory bottle of wine this time, and no flowers on the table.

He went through to the bedroom, dumped his bag on the floor, then turned to the bed. It was covered in the patchwork counterpane that had, according to the owners, been worked by the old lady who had lived in this cottage until her death twenty years ago. Laying the suiter carefully on the bed, he unzipped it and ran a hand over its contents. They would sleep there together tonight, he with his beloved wife safe in his arms.

Practicalities next. He put a match to the fire and consulted the tide table, then fetched a coolbox from the boot of the car and stowed perishables in the fridge in the tiny kitchen. Butter, smoked salmon, champagne. He'd have preferred lager, but her tipple of choice was always champagne. Veuve Clicquot. He'd even gone for a pricey vintage. He knew there were no champagne flutes in the cottage, but such niceties had never bothered her. She'd drunk the stuff from tumblers and tooth-mugs and teacups. He recalled visiting her backstage one opening night, watching as she poured out the champagne he'd brought for her. 'Kinda sums up the life of the *corps de ballet*, doesn't it?' she'd remarked with a laugh. 'Drinking champagne from a polystyrene cup smeared with Makeup Forever's TO4.'

He checked his watch, then went to the door of the cottage and looked out. The sea had closed over the causeway. Nobody could disturb them now, unless they chose to arrive by rowboat or launch. The island was all theirs.

It took him twenty minutes to walk its circumference. In that time he glimpsed the sails of a yacht in the distance, swelling with the wind that was beginning to get up, but otherwise there wasn't a sign of human life. Cattle grazed stoically, oblivious to his presence, and in the field above the cottage daffodils grew rampant. He picked a great sheaf of them and didn't allow himself to feel guilty that the flowers would spend only one night adorning the table in the sitting room, because she deserved flowers.

The sound of a helicopter traversing the bay made him look up. That's how she'd love to arrive, in style, by helicopter! They'd done it once as a treat on her birthday – forked out for a chopper to a gig in Slane, then hung out in the VIP area, trying to look casual and spying on the real VIPs. He watched as the machine swooped over the island, then veered off in the direction of the mountain they'd climbed a year ago, on their honeymoon. They had vowed that if her prayer was answered they would come back and do it again on this, their first anniversary. But her prayer hadn't been answered – even though she *had* sucked up to God by climbing in her bare feet – and while he knew that they would never climb the mountain now, he knew that she would come back to the island. She had promised as much, and she always kept her promises.

Dusk was falling as he let himself back into the cottage. He prepared and ate his supper, then switched on the radio for the nine o'clock news. He didn't listen to it as he sat in the rocking-chair. He just stared at the fire, waiting for the weather forecast. It would be windy again tomorrow, but dry, with sunny spells. Perfect.

At half past nine, he set the fireguard in front of the fire and went to bed.

He woke early, as he'd known he would. He didn't bother with breakfast; he just showered, shaved, dressed, then packed the car. The causeway was a straight finger pointing towards the mainland, and would remain so for many hours until the next high tide. But he wasn't going to hang about. What needed to be done should be done soon – should have been done a long time ago, in fact. But he'd been selfish, and kept her to himself. Now it was time to let her go.

The dress lay crumpled between the bedsheets. Last night, as he'd wound it in his arms, he'd realised that it still bore traces of her scent. He retrieved it now and shook it out before hanging it on the cushioned arms of the satin-covered hanger she'd kept it on. The silly girly things she'd surrounded herself with – the padded hangers, the embroidered slippers, the lace-trimmed handkerchiefs – all these had used to make him laugh at her: but that girliness, that femininity was what had made him love her.

He hung the dress on a coat hook by the door, then went to the kitchen to fetch the champagne and a glass to drink it from. The last item needed to complete the ritual rested on the sill of the window that afforded that spectacular vista of the sacred mountain. He picked it up and went outside, locking the door after him.

The wind had picked up, as forecast. In front of the cottage he laid the dress carefully on the lawn where she had danced a year ago today. Then he undid the foil and the wire cage on the champagne bottle and drew the cork. A plume of vapour escaped like a sigh as he poured. He set the glass down on the sea wall, then picked up the dress again, pressing it to his face, inhaling her scent for the last time. He straightened the straps on their padded hanger – they had to be just so! – then hooked it onto a branch of the fir tree before taking a few steps backwards and watching the dress come to life in the wind. The hem lifted and a ripple ran over the white silk, and then a gust inhabited it, lending it a shape that seemed faintly human. She had kept her promise. She was here.

Against a background of tangerine-streaked sky the white dress danced in the dawn, insouciant, buoyant, until another gust plucked it from the satin arms of the hanger and propelled it into the air. The wind took it spiralling past him, over the sea wall, then sent it speeding across the white horses cresting on the surface of the choppy pewter water. It came to rest on the small island opposite, where it lay on the stones, eddying a little as if breathing, as if she were resting, summoning strength for her finale. And then the wind seized the dress again and carried it over the crest of the island and out of sight.

He reached for the urn that sat on the sea wall next to the glass of champagne and twisted it open. The ashes felt grainy to the touch, not soft and friable as he'd expected. Delving his hand into the urn and with the wind at his back, he hurled the ashes towards the sea. A gust snatched them as it had snatched the dress, scattering them towards where a watery sun was showing its bleary face on the horizon. Another handful escaped, then another, until virtually nothing remained. As he upended the urn, a trickle emerged, spilling onto his jacket, leaving a chalky residue. He didn't brush it away. Instead he reached for the glass of champagne and held it aloft. 'Godspeed, beloved,' he said.

One Perfect Day
Breda Wall Ryan

'Straighten your back, Denise, you look like a victim.' That was Mammy, always jabbing me between the shoulder-blades, for my own good. She could have given it a rest for Granda's funeral, a real family funeral, all aunts, uncles and cousins to the nth degree.

'Remember you're the hostess, Denise. Don't let the family down.' Granny rapped on my skull with her snuff-box.

Granda's old cronies gripped the handles of Granny's Spode teacups between finger and thumb, faces droopy with misery. I knew how Granda would have put them at their ease, so I said, 'Do ye saucer yer tay, men?' Straight away, they poured the tea into the saucers and blew it cool before slurping, then sucked the ends of their moustaches. Aunt Iris sniffed.

'Dear God! Does the girl know nothing? She'll be inviting them to take out their teeth next.' One of the men brightened at that.

'Thank ye kindly, ma'am. In that case, I'll have a cut of shop bread after all.' He angled out his denture and dropped it into his cup before sopping a sandwich in his saucer of tea to make it easy on his gums. I got another rap of Granny's snuff-box.

She ordered me to pass around crustless sandwiches and make myself useful. I was too *oimealach* to be trusted with a teapot.

'Ham and mustard?' I croaked. Aunt Iris pretended not to hear. I tilted the stacked plate towards me so the lot wouldn't slide

320

onto her black shiny lap, hawked the frog out of my throat and offered them again. 'Fancy a sanger, Aunt Iris?'

'Isn't there any cucumber?' I shook my head. Aunt Iris had notions, like cucumber sandwiches and Earl Grey tea. 'Don't flaunt your chest like that, child, it isn't ladylike,' she hissed, loud enough for the street to hear. 'I don't know why your mother doesn't bind your chest, or lace you into a bodice. Bosoms like a cow at ten years of age, it's indecent.' Her companion looked me over like a cut of beef at the butcher.

'She's a fine strong girl, God bless her!' she said to Iris. 'They'll have to put a rock on her head to stop her growing.' They tut-tutted together like cats lapping milk. Mammy heard the insult; it meant big lump. Another jab between the shoulder-blades warned me to straighten my back and not look like a victim.

I am *a victim. I'm a* fucking *victim. And Aunt Iris has bosoms like Daisy the Friesian;* she *can talk!* I thought to myself. I couldn't say any of it out loud, because Mammy would've mollafoostered me. 'Here!' I dumped the whole plate of triangles in Aunt Iris's lap, in front of her two big bazooms, ducked Granny's raised snuff-box, and clumped out to the toilet.

'Shan't be a mo.'

'Just powdering our noses, dearie.' Aunt Iris's two posh friends were in the bathroom. I could *hear* their puckered lips. They'd go on looking in the mirror, smathering on red lipstick for hours; they wouldn't care who was outside the door, legs crossed and bursting. I squeezed myself tight and ran to the toilet in the yard that nobody ever cleaned because nobody used it. I shut my eyes against the mouse-sized spider in the corner and let fly. If he went on the attack, I'd drown him. Instead of a loo roll, squares of ancient newspaper, threaded on a loop of twine, hung from a nail. Paper mites scrambled over Pope John's face on the top square. If I wiped with that, I'd end up with a holy tattoo on my underneath. That'd be a laugh; not that I could show anyone. I made sure the spider was still in his corner, flushed a whoosh of rusty water and hopped it, fast.

'You have a hearty laugh, Deenie.' My cousin Jamesy sprawled on the churn stand, dragging on a Player's, a large bottle in his hand. The tang of Guinness hung in the air, a yeasty blend of hops and grown men. 'Hop up.' He patted the sun-warmed concrete. 'Have a swig.'

People said there was a want to Jamesy Cotter, but he was my favourite cousin. He didn't stick burrs in my hair or tie cats' tails together or say something I understood, and then snigger because it meant something bad besides. Uncle Jamesy and Grandpa Cotter blamed Jamesy for their Stephen getting killed. Stephen, their white-haired boy, was playing chicken outside the pub when a lorry ran him over. Now he was practically a saint. The two men had been inside giving Stephen sups of whiskey, saying wasn't he the hard man, egging him on. They weren't responsible for what happened, on account of having drink taken; Jamesy should have had the wit to keep an eye on the child.

'Hey, steady on, Deenie. I said a swig, not a gollop. What do you think?'

'It's rotten, so it is. Why do you bother with it?'

Jamesy sighed. 'For the effect, chicken. The trick is to reach a state of perfect happiness, then keep topping up, so you stay there.'

'Like heaven in the catechism?' I winced at the bitter taste of porter that clung to my tongue.

'It keeps the black crow off my back, chicken. Here, have a fruit pastille to take away the taste.' He ripped the paper off the roll of sweets. I selected a green one. 'Sorry they're a bit soft from my pocket.' I didn't mind.

'I have a terrible sweet tooth. I'd suck anything you pulled out of your pocket if it had a sprinkle of sugar on it.' Jamesy laughed; I could see the porter was making him happy already. He struck the cap off another bottle against the churn stand and dropped the empty in a crate.

'Four dead soldiers, eight standing,' he said. 'Your Granda would've loved a couple of these. He must be happy now. He waited a lifetime to get a share of your grandmother's land.'

'What do you mean?'

Jamesy told me how my grandmother's father made a match for her with Granda because Granda Murphy had his own place and a couple of sidelines, too: one as a carter, and another as a pig doctor. She wouldn't agree to the match unless her father settled his own place on her, and not on Granda, which was the custom. Then after the wedding, when the time came for the hauling home, when friends and neighbours carry the bride and her belongings to her new home, she refused to go. Her father's place was hers since the settlement, and she wouldn't leave or let Granda move in. The couple had lived separately all their lives.

'Except, I suppose, for the four occasions that produced their four children,' Jamesy said, stowing another empty and wiping his mouth on his sleeve. 'The girls lived in town with your grandmother and went to the convent school, and your father lived wherever he liked and ran wild.'

'You're not making this up, are you, Jamesy? They've lived with us as long as I can remember.'

Jamesy said that after Granda's farmhouse fell down, he signed the place over so Dad could build a new house. Granny signed her place over to Aunt Iris when she had to get married to avoid a scandal, but Granny and Aunt Iris didn't pull together, so Granny came to live with us, too. I told him how they took up both sides of the fire. Granny read *The Irish Press* and the *Catholic Digest* all day and half the night, and Granda sat with one rheumatic knee pointing east and the other west, tapping his blackthorn on the hearth between his feet, in a black rage because she refused to read aloud to an illiterate ignoramus.

'She's a hard woman,' Jamesy said. 'They say she doctored a man during the Civil War; your Granda would have nothing to do with it. And your Aunt Iris is no better.'

I told him about the welts Granny raised on my head because I was too tall for a girl and I'd be left on their hands, and because red hair

323

brought misfortune on the family. He was lucky they weren't his relations. Jamesy was a cousin on Mammy's side, where Granny said my bad blood came from, when she wasn't blaming it on Granda.

Jamesy said wasn't that a holy terror. Granny was just like his own aul' fella, thinking he could change a person into someone they were never meant to be.

'You and me, chicken, were born into the wrong families. In any other house, we'd be stars.'

I told him about Aunt Iris and the chest-binding, and he said the twisted aul' bitch was jealous. Didn't her own daughter, the scrapings of the pot, have two crossed eyes and knock knees because Iris married her first cousin? Jamesy opened another bottle and passed me the rest of the fruit pastilles.

'Jealous she is, chicken. You're getting shocking good-looking, Deenie.' He put an arm around my shoulders. When I sat up straight I was only a half-head shorter than him. 'Will we run off together and get married?' I said they wouldn't let us, with me being only ten and three-quarters.

'Will we run off and get married when you're fifteen, so?'

'OK,' I said. 'Sound.' We shook on it. I reckoned on Jamesy sticking at twenty while I grew up to fifteen. 'Who will we marry, though?' I asked and he said each other, weren't we two of a kind?

'Jamesy?' I remembered he hadn't finished his yarn. 'What did you mean about Granda getting a share of Granny's land?'

Jamesy said Granny sold the field for the new cemetery to the council, and Granda was first in line to buy a plot in it. 'He holds the freehold on that six by three, nothing she can do about it.'

'She's always saying she'll be buried with her own people. Jamesy, how come you know so many secrets?'

'Ah, Deenie, chicken, haven't I been listening to the skeletons rattling for twenty years? When they send me away for the shocks, my concentration goes astray. Bits of conversations drift in and out of my head. To get a grip, I try to work things out, put bits and pieces together, come up with the low-down. It keeps me from going mad. Anything you want to know about skeletons in the cupboard, ask Jamesy.' He pulled me in close to his side and kissed me smack on the ear. My first genuine, non-duty kiss; it sounded like a gunshot.

'Why do they send you away, Jamesy? They say there's a want to you, but I think you're smart, so I do.'

'That black crow on my back takes over, so I can't see a bright spark anywhere. They send me away for the electric shocks.' I wondered if it was like getting a shock from the electric fence in the cow pasture, but I didn't like to ask. 'Electric currents through my brain. Imagine!' he muttered. I shivered.

'You could just drink a lot of large bottles, Jamesy. Then you wouldn't have to go away at all.'

'Don't look now, Deenie. We're being watched.' Of course I looked, but I couldn't see anyone, or feel any eyes on me. Jamesy said Frank Foley had his eye on us. He wasn't at the funeral because Granny despised him; he was a caffler when life ought to be serious. Frank had great time for Mammy; he gave her buckets of fruit every summer, to make jam. Jamesy said he was a man of many talents, we should be neighbourly and call him over, but we'd better not go drawing Granny Murphy on us.

Jamesy stumbled down off the churn stand. He sang, 'One for the money, two for the show …' He held the bottle close to his mouth, turned his toes in and made his legs wobble to the rhythm. He even flicked his red hair back like Elvis. Aunt Iris stuck her head out the back door and shrieked.

'Come quick. Jamesy Cotter is after taking a fit, he's shaking out of control.'

Jamesy sat back beside me on the churn stand, all relaxed. Uncle Jamesy and Granny and a whole bunch of oldies crushed past each other to get a look at the spectacle.

'Are you all right, Jamesy?' Mammy asked, and Jamesy said never better. 'Only Iris thought—'

'I know, Helen.' Jamesy nudged me. 'Half a bottle of medium sherry. Sad.' Mammy looked as if she'd seen the Blessed Virgin smoking a pipe. Jamesy flashed his full rack of film-star teeth at Aunt Iris. 'Don't worry, Iris, your secret won't go past the assembled company.'

Aunt Iris spluttered, but all she managed was, '*Aunt* Iris to you, Jamesy Cotter.' Jamesy laughed. Iris wasn't a real aunt to Jamesy, he didn't have to say 'Aunt'. She turned on me next. 'You, get inside, Miss.' Jamesy cut her off.

'Myself and Deenie are off to our place to do the milking.' We left Mammy saying what a credit Jamesy was, and Uncle James saying he wouldn't care if the flood swept the lot of them, Lola and Daphne and that Jamesy above all, if he could only have his Stephen back.

'Don't be upsetting yourself, pet, sure you don't mean it.' Mammy led him back inside. She liked him because he was her brother, and he hadn't always been contrary. Life, she said, had knocked the spirit out of him.

Jamesy lifted someone's car keys, to round up the cows. He drove over and back behind the herd while we both flapped the car doors like Stetsons, yelling, 'Yeehaw!' He pursed his mouth like Aunt Iris and said, 'How now, brown cow!' I said he could be an actor, if he wanted.

'What a coincidence, dear girl! I have recently become a valued member of the Ballygobackwards Amateur Dramatic Society, at the invitation of that illustrious thespian, Father Terence O'Flynn, P.P. Much to the chagrin of one's pater, don't you know!'

'God, Jamesy, that sounds great, though I don't understand half of it. You have a lot of big words for a fellow that left school at fourteen.' I promised I'd come to see him in *The Importance of Being Nobody Much*, a skit he was writing with Frank Foley in aid of the church roof. It was to have completely new gags each night, so people would go more than once.

Jamesy shovelled feed into the grain crusher, three parts barley to one of oats and one of bonemeal. The cows were supposed to get a measure of the meal, and another of chopped turnip. Turning a handle on a turnip machine was a mug's game, according to Jamesy. He had a better idea, as long as we didn't banjax the crusher; then we'd be up the creek. He unbolted the safety grid on the hopper and started tossing in turnips with the grain. We watched the revolving grinders chewing the turnips to bits. Then I ran down the loft stairs to see what came out below. The meal and turnip had mixed to a pulp on the barn floor.

'It looks great, Jamesy, only we should have stuck buckets under it.'

We scooped up the mush and fed it to the cows. Jamesy did the milking, then we fed the calves together. He had an easy way with him, but whenever we fell quiet, his face clouded over. I knew the porter was wearing off. We ran a scoop of grain through the crusher to clean it, so Uncle Jamesy wouldn't guess at Jamesy's latest labour-saving invention. Jamesy hefted a turnip in each hand, weighing them.

'Do you think, Deenie, a turnip would be about as hard as a head?'

'A head of cabbage?'

'A head of human.' He fake-laughed, acting. 'The head of a man.'

'Harder. Much harder, Jamesy. Wouldn't a man's head be like an egg, soft inside a hard shell? A turnip is hard right through.'

'Good thinking, Deenie, girl.'

He dropped me home and handed me the borrowed car keys. 'If you're asked, say you don't know where I am. I'll be at Frank Foley's, but what they don't know won't trouble them.' He walked away, whistling. He turned at Frank's door.

'Hey, Deenie! Today was one perfect day, wasn't it? One perfect day.' He pulled the keystring through the letterbox and let himself in.

*

I saw Jamesy from time to time after that, in plays at the parish hall or sometimes outside Mass. He'd wink and say, 'Fifteen, Deenie.

Don't forget!' or 'Didn't I tell you you'd get shocking good-looking?' From time to time, I'd overhear that he was away, bad with his nerves, or that he was giving the Cotters a hard time. Then I was sent to boarding school. I got to know first-hand what being sent away was like; I didn't like it, either.

Jamesy went headlong into the crusher my second year at school. I didn't hear until I came home for Easter. They said they poured him into the coffin. The death notice read, 'following an accident'.

The time for crying was long past, but I went up to the grave anyway. I knocked the cap off the large bottle against the edge of the headstone the way he'd shown me. I swallowed half the bitter porter in one long gollop. I poured the rest over his name, over the dates that were too close to make up a lifetime, over the space for the names that Uncle Jamesy would've sacrificed to the flood, if he could have Stephen back. I sat on the weedy mound sucking a fruit pastille, waiting for the state of perfect happiness. And I remembered that it took a full five minutes to unbolt the safety grille on the crusher, and that a man's head isn't half as hard as a turnip.

One Moment in Time

Sarah Webb

To Tanya Delargy

'Stop the car!' Rita says.

'What's wrong?' I ask, jamming on the brakes in response to the urgency in her voice.

'Look.' She points out the passenger window. 'Under the lamp-post. See?'

I peer out into the night. A girl is slumped on the pavement, silhouetted in the lamplight, bare legs and feet sticking out in front of her beneath an expensive-looking frothy green skirt. Her head is bent forward and her long blond hair falls over her face in two sweeps like curtains. Two dishevelled young men in tuxedos flank her, pulling heavily on their cigarettes.

'Do you think she's OK?' Rita asks me. 'We can't just leave her there, can we?'

I sigh and wordlessly switch off the engine, open my door and step out of the car. It's the early hours of the morning and we've been at a party in town with some of the work gang. I've just dropped a friend home to Bray and I'm dog-tired. Sometimes it's a curse being a non-drinker.

I walk towards the trio. The boys look at me with interest. One has a bottle of Jack Daniels hanging loosely in one hand. He takes a swig of it defiantly. He's built like a brick. The other boy is skinny and tall, over six feet. 'Everything all right here?' I direct the question to the tall boy, as he seems a little more sober.

'What's it to you?' the Jack Daniels boy asks.

The tall boy gives him a dig in the ribs with his elbow. 'Cool it, man,' he says. He turns towards me. 'Sorry. Everything's fine, thanks. We're just trying to get her home.' He nods down at the girl. I now realise that she's older than I thought, maybe in her late twenties, more woman than girl. The boys both look young, maybe eighteen or nineteen at a pinch.

We all stare down at the woman. Her mouth is lolling open, her lips flabby, and her head is resting rather ungainly against her upper chest.

'She's a bit drunk,' the tall boy explains needlessly.

'What happened to her shoes?' I ask, taking in her red, scratched feet. She also has cuts on her lower legs and around her ankles.

'She threw them into someone's garden,' he says. 'And then she climbed over to get them, but she couldn't find them.' He shrugs. 'We were at a twenty-first in the hotel up the hill.'

'Stupid cow,' the Jack Daniels boy adds.

The tall boy glares at him. 'Leave her alone,' he says.

The Jack Daniels boy puts his hands up defensively, sloshing some whiskey on the pavement in the process. 'Sorry, man,' he says. 'Sorry.'

'And how are you planning to get her home?' I ask.

'We'll carry her,' the tall boy says, looking at his friend, who nods assent.

'Finish this first,' the Jack Daniels boy says, tapping his bottle with his hand, then adds, 'I'm a prop.'

'A what?' I'm in no mood for all this.

'You know, rugby. I can carry her. No sweat.' He lurches sideways, banging into his friend.

'We'll carry her between us,' the tall boy says, steadying his friend.

'Where does she live?' I ask him.

'Sandycove.'

It's about forty minutes' walk from where we are, sober. I figure it will take them two or three hours to carry her in the circumstances. That's if they get home at all in their collective state. I sigh. 'Get her in the car,' I say with no further preamble. 'I'll bring her home.'

'Why would you do that?' the tall boy asks a little suspiciously.

'Yeah, what are you – some sort of social worker?' the other adds with an unpleasant kind of leer.

'Just get on with it,' I say. I'm too tired to explain.

They lift her off the ground and she moans a little. Her eyelids flicker but she doesn't open them. I walk ahead of them and open the rear passenger door.

'I'm dropping the woman home,' I tell Rita, who has turned to look at me. 'She's too drunk to walk.'

'OK,' Rita says, a little taken aback. 'And what about the boys?'

'Where do you two live?' I turn around and ask them.

'You can drop us at the same place.'

'Fine.'

The boys manage to lift the woman into the back seat and then climb in and sit on either side of her, keeping her vaguely upright. They all stink of alcohol.

'So, where are you boys in school?' Rita opens as we set off.

'School!' the drunk one laughs. 'We're in college. First year.'

'What are you studying?' Rita continues, unwilling to give up.

'Engineering,' the drunk one says. He takes a swig from his bottle.

'Law,' the other adds, then stares out the window.

Rita gives up. 'You're very good to do this,' she says in a low voice. 'Ungrateful brats.'

I shrug. We drive in silence for several minutes.

'Right, where exactly in Sandycove?' I ask as we approach the area.

'The road down by the sea. Down by the beach and then on a little,' the tall boy says.

'Near Joyce's Tower?' I ask.

He grunts. 'Near there.'

'Fine.' I'm regretting stopping the car at all. I tighten my grip on the steering-wheel and vow never to get involved again – an idle threat, I know, but right now I mean it. These boys are just plain rude. As Rita says, ungrateful brats.

As I drive down the coast road, the tall boy gives me curt directions.

'Turn right,' he says. 'Her house is up that laneway.'

We bump up a long, private drive and I pull up outside a large white single-storey Victorian villa. There's an original wooden conservatory to one side and wide granite steps up to the front door. *Lucky woman*, I think. 'Is this it?' I ask.

He mutters assent. By this stage the Jack Daniels boy is asleep, snoring loudly, his head on the girl's shoulder, his mouth wide open, a trickle of drool meandering down the left side of his chin.

I look at the house again. It's in total darkness, illuminated only by a sliver of moon. It doesn't look like anyone's waiting up. I open the door and step out. I can hear the gentle lapping of waves and smell the salt tang in the air. I look down towards the sea. The house has its own private jetty.

Rita gets out and stands beside me. 'Poor little rich kids,' she murmurs.

I smile. 'Better get rid of our load,' I say.

The tall boy is having trouble lifting his drunk friend out of the car.

'Get yer hands off me.' The drunk boy flails his arms. The Jack Daniels bottle is now lying empty in the well of the passenger seat. 'Leave me alone. Wanna sleep.'

I look at Rita and she nods back at me. 'We'll do it,' I say to the tall boy.

He gives a snort. 'Yeah, right! He's fifteen stone.' He steps back from the car and puts his hands out in front of him, palms up. 'But be my guest.'

I ignore his snide tone. 'Help your other friend out,' I say

332

instead, my voice letting him know that I'm taking no more nonsense. He flashes me a look, sees the steel in my eyes and then does so wordlessly.

'Ready?' I ask Rita.

'Sure.'

We reach into the car and drag the drunk boy's upper torso along the seat. He groans, but doesn't open his eyes. Then we stand to either side of him and put our arms around his body, our shoulders under his armpits.

'On three,' I say. 'One, two, three.' We both take the weight and lift him out of the car. Then we drag him towards the house, his black boots skidding over the gravel.

The tall boy looks on with interest.

We dump the Jack Daniels boy at the bottom of the steps.

'Man,' he mutters from his prone position, stirring. 'My head.'

We walk back towards the car. The tall boy is now carrying the blonde girl towards the steps.

'Are we going to go now?' Rita asks me. 'What about the woman?'

I sigh. Rita's right. We can't just leave her. I walk back towards the tall boy. He's now sitting at the bottom of the steps with two comatose friends.

'Get her inside,' I tell him.

'What?'

'You heard me. Look, *mate*, I'm not leaving her until she's safely inside. Understand?' I walk up the steps towards the door.

He swears under his breath. 'There's no one in. The old man's away. There's no point ringing the bell.'

I feel like screaming. I take a deep breath. 'Look, it's late and I'm tired. I've had almost enough of this. She must have keys. Check her pockets.'

He pulls a bunch of keys out of his own pocket. He must have taken them earlier, I surmise. I'm immediately on my guard.

'Is there an alarm, do you know?' I ask.

'No, it's broken.'

'Are you sure?'

'What's it to you?'

I don't like his tone. I grab the keys off him. 'Rita!' I shout. She's sitting in the car, keeping warm. She gets out and walks towards me.

'Can you carry the woman up the steps?' I ask her.

She nods. 'Sure.'

'And you stay here and look after your friend.'

'Why should I?' he snaps. 'And give me back the keys.'

'Just do it!' I reply sharply.

'I wouldn't argue with her,' Rita adds. 'Really. Not a good idea.'

He sits down on the bottom step, watching us.

I open the door and step back; Rita lifts the woman in. She's strong, Rita. You should see her at work. He's right, the door isn't alarmed. I walk in, Rita following close behind me, and I close the door firmly behind us.

'Hey!' The tall boy is halfway up the steps before he realises what's happening. 'What the fuck are you doing? This is my house! Let me in.' He starts banging on the door. We ignore him. We find a sofa in the first room we walk into and Rita places her on it. The woman doesn't stir. We place a throw from one of the other sofas over her legs and lower body.

As we walk back into the hall, the boy is still banging on the door.

'Step back from the door or we'll call the Guards,' I say calmly through the letter-box.

He does so. Rita and I walk out and I pull the door behind us. I post the keys through the letter-box.

'What are you doing?' he asks. 'Are you mad?'

'Quite possibly,' I say. He follows us to the car. His friend is still asleep on the steps, oblivious. 'You're fucking crazy, man,' he says. 'What the hell did you do that for? You stole my keys.' He hits the bonnet with his hands. 'How am I going to get in now?'

'Step back from the car,' I say, my voice icy. 'I'm warning you. Or, like I said, I'll call the Guards. I advise you to go home, and bring your friend with you.' He looks at me, his eyes flicking with anger, but he steps back. He spits a rather unpleasant swear word at me. I don't even wince. I'm well used to it.

We get into the car and drive away, the boy still throwing abuse at me. We can hear him right down the laneway.

The following morning I'm getting into the car to drive to work when I spot a red wallet on the back passenger seat. I reach back, pick it up and open it. The blonde woman and the tall boy smile out at me. His arm is around her shoulder and they look very pally.

I laugh.

Sandycove is on the way to work so I decide to make a detour to return the wallet. Not that I want to see any of the previous night's ménage a trois again, you understand, but I have to admit my curiosity is piqued.

I pull up outside the house once again and step out of the car, wallet in hand. A tall grey-haired man appears at the top of the steps. He looks familiar.

'Is there anything wrong?' he asks.

'Just returning this.' I hand him the wallet.

'It's the wife's,' he says, turning it over in his hands. 'Where did you find it?'

The woman from last night appears, dressed sedately in dark trousers and a cream roll-top jumper. I realise now she's in her thirties. 'Did you find it on the road?' she asks, cutting in. 'I was out collecting my stepson from a twenty-first last night. It must have fallen out of the car.'

'Something like that,' I say.

'Thanks,' she murmurs, then gives me a sly wink. 'See you, Officer.'

*

On the way down the drive I see a figure behind me waving at the car. I stop. The tall boy from last night is running towards me. I open my window.

'You never said you were a Guard,' he says, slightly out of breath. 'You don't look old enough. And I can't believe you shut me out of my own house. I had to sleep in the shed.'

'You didn't tell me she was your mum,' I say, stifling a grin. *Serves him right*, I think.

'Stepmum,' he corrects me.

I shrug. 'It was your own fault. I thought she was safer in the house on her own. You could have been anyone for all I knew. Why didn't you tell me the truth?'

'It's kind of embarrassing, don't you think? My stepmum being out of her head like that. She likes to party when Dad's away. Dad doesn't know anything about it. He only came back from Geneva this morning. You didn't say anything, did you? To my dad, I mean.'

'No.'

'Thanks.' He smiles but it doesn't reach his eyes.

I shrug. 'That's OK.'

'Were you on duty last night?' he asks. 'You know, under-cover?'

I laugh. 'No, I was on my way home from a party.'

'So you didn't have to stop?'

'No.'

He pauses for a moment, taking this in. 'I'm sorry if I was rude. I'd just had one of those nights. And the nicer you and your friend were to me, the more annoyed I got.' He looks at me curiously. 'So why did you stop?'

'You asked me that last night.'

'And?'

'That could have been me in a former life, drunk on the side of the road, needing a safe lift home.' I stop, unwilling to tell him my story. More than once during those dark days the Guards and the odd kindly soul had stopped to help *me*. But sometimes no one had, and I'd woken out of my stupor to find my wallet stolen and, on one occasion, my shoes missing. You see all sorts with this job, and believe me, I'd got away lightly. 'I think people should look out for each other,' I say instead.

'That's it?'

I look him in the eye. 'What else is there?'

He holds my gaze for a moment and then looks away, embarrassed.

I put the car in gear and drive away. At the end of the laneway I glance in the rear-view mirror. He's staring at my car. I turn left and focus on the road ahead.

Notes on the Authors

Cecelia Ahern completed a degree in journalism and media communications before embarking on her writing career. At twenty-one she wrote her first novel, *PS, I Love You*, which was sold to forty-one countries. Movie rights were bought by Warner Bros. It went on to be one of the biggest-selling debut novels of 2004, reaching number one in Ireland and the UK *Sunday Times* best-seller list, and it was selected for the *Richard and Judy* Summer Read campaign. *PS, I Love You* also became a bestseller throughout Europe and the USA. In November her second book, *Where Rainbows End*, also reached number one in Ireland and the UK, remaining at the top of the Irish bestsellers list for twelve weeks. Her third book will be published in 2005.

Catherine Barry is the author of *The House That Jack Built*, *Null and Void* and *Skindeep* and has had numerous short stories and poems published. She also works for OPEN, an organisation that helps lone-parent groups in Ireland, and has worked previously with the long-term unemployed. Catherine lives on the northside of Dublin with her two children, Davitt and Caitriona, and her two cats, Jacque and Billy.

Sara Berkeley was born and raised in Dublin and now lives in Northern California with her husband and small daughter. She has published three collections of poetry, *Penn*, *Home-Movie Nights* and *Facts about Water*; a collection of short stories, *The Swimmer in the Deep Blue Dream*; and a novel, *Shadowing Hannah*. She recently completed another novel and a collection of poetry due to be published in 2005.

Maeve Binchy was born in Dublin, where she worked first as a teacher, then as a journalist for *The Irish Times* and eventually as a novelist. She is the author of over twelve bestselling books, including *Circle of Friends*, *Scarlet Feather* and *Nights of Rain and Stars*. Her books have been translated into many languages and adapted for both cinema and television. She lives in Dalkey, Co. Dublin, with her husband, writer Gordon Snell.

Clare Boylan is the author of seven novels and three volumes of short stories. Her novels include *Home Rule* and its acclaimed sequel *Holy Pictures*, *Room for a Single Lady*, *Black Baby*, *Beloved Stranger* and *Emma Brown*. Her most recent short-story collection, *That Bad Woman*, was widely praised on publication. Her non-fiction works include *The Agony and the Ego*, a collection of essays on the art and strategy of fiction writing.

Helena Close lives in Limerick with her husband and children and writes full time. Her novel *Pinhead Duffy* has just been published by Blackstaff Press. Helena is co-author, with Trisha Rainsford, of the Sarah O'Brien novels *Hot Property*, *Gazumped!* and the forthcoming *Love Happens*. They have also written a TV series, which is in the early stages of development.

Evelyn Conlon, born in Monaghan, is a novelist and short-story writer. She has travelled widely in Australia and Asia, recently returning from a visit to Indonesia where she read and lectured. Her latest novel, *Skin of Dreams*, delves into the issues surrounding capital punishment. She is noted for the originality of her approach, being described as 'one of Ireland's most distinctive and energetic voices'. She has published three collections of short stories, three novels and edited three collections, including *Cutting the Night in Two* (New Island) and *Later On*, a memorial anthology of the Monaghan bombing.

June Considine has written extensively for children and adults. Her twelve books for children include the *Luvender* fantasy trilogy, seven titles under the popular *Beachwood* series for teens, and also V*iew from a Blind Bridge* and *The Glass Triangle*. Her adult novels, published by New Island, are the bestselling novel *When the Bough Breaks*, and *Deceptions,* released in October 2004. Her short stories have appeared in anthologies for teenagers in Ireland, the UK and US. She has also worked as an editor and journalist, and as a scriptwriter for children's television and radio.

Judi Curtin was born in London and brought up in Cork. She studied at UCC before training as a primary-school teacher. Her first novel, *Sorry, Walter,* was published in 2003. This was followed in 2004 by *From Claire to Here.* Her first children's book is due to be published in autumn 2005. She is currently working on her third novel. Judi lives in Limerick with her husband and three children.

Denise Deegan is a freelance journalist and the bestselling author of *Turning Turtle* and *Time in a Bottle*. She lives in Dublin with her husband and two children. Denise has worked as a nurse, china restorer, pharmaceutical sales rep, lecturer and public relations consultant, giving up her own PR business to write fiction. Her most difficult job was that of checkout girl. Denise's favourite short stories are 'Guests of the Nation' by Frank O'Connor and 'The Selfish Giant' by Oscar Wilde. Her third novel will be published in Spring 2006 by Penguin.

Martina Devlin has written four novels – *Three Wise Men, Be Careful What You Wish For, Venus Reborn* and *Temptation* – as well as a number of short stories. Her next book, *The Hollow Heart*, will be published in autumn 2005. Her website is www.martinadevlin.com.

Margaret Dolan, who lives in Meath, is a short-story writer, a novelist and a playwright. Her most recent drama (real life-and-death stuff) was performed in the hospital theatre, where she took the starring role: a double bypass with complications. She is seriously traumatised at sleeping through that dramatic event. There was an odd side effect from the operation: she went to the 'Far Side' and came back a gambler. Some blame the medication; others, the death and resurrection bit. Anyway, she is now a full-blown gambler who divides her time between writing and playing poker.

Emma Donoghue was born in Dublin in 1969. Her books of fiction include the historically based *Slammerkin* (2001), *The Woman Who Gave Birth to Rabbits* (2002) and *Life Mask* (2004); a book of fairytales called *Kissing the Witch* (1997); and two novels of contemporary Ireland, *Stirfry* (1994) and *Hood* (1995). She also writes plays, radio drama and literary history. Emma lives near Toronto with her lover and their son.

Clare Dowling began her career as an actress and co-founded independent theatre company Glasshouse Productions. She wrote and had produced six stage plays and went on to write two short films. She has written children's books, short stories and drama for teenagers and has had three bestselling novels published, *Fast Forward*, *Expecting Emily* and *Amazing Grace*. She is a scriptwriter for *Fair City* and is currently writing her fourth novel, *Divorcing Henry*.

Rose Doyle lives and writes for a living in Dublin, where she was born. She has published seventeen books, including novels for children, fourteen novels for adults and, as editor, two anthologies. The book of her *Irish Times* series on Dublin's long-time traders, *Trade Names*, was recently published by New Island and her most recent novel, *Shadows Will Fall* – a psychological whodunit that moves from Dun Laoghaire to Coney Island – was published by Hodder & Stoughton.

Catherine Dunne is the author of four acclaimed novels: *In the Beginning*, short-listed for the Italian Booksellers' Prize; *A Name for Himself*, short-listed for the Kerry Fiction Prize; *The Walled Garden*; and *Another Kind of Life*. She has also contributed to three anthologies: *A Second Skin*, *Irish Girls about Town* and *Travelling Light*. Her most recent book, *An Unconsidered People*, is a work of non-fiction that explores the lives of Irish immigrants in London in the 1950s. She lives in Dublin and is currently working on her fifth novel.

Christine Dwyer Hickey is an award-winning novelist and short-story writer. She is twice winner of the Listowel Writers' Week short-story competition and was also a prize winner in the prestigious *Observer* Penguin short-story competition, with the story that appears for the first time in this collection. Her trilogy, *The Dancer*, *The Gambler* and *The Gatemaker*, has received wide critical acclaim, and *The Dancer* was short-listed for the Listowel Writers' Week Book of the Year. Christine's fourth novel *Tatty* has been long-listed for the Orange Prize and was also short-listed for the Hughes & Hughes Irish Novel of the Year 2005. She is Honorary Secretary of Irish Pen and lives in Palmerstown with her family.

Laura Froom is a writer and journalist, with a particular interest in horticulture. She has written extensively on the organic cultivation of vegetables and roses, as well as promoting innovative fertilisation procedures. She divides her time between Britain and Ireland and is currently single. This is her first published short story.

Karen Gillece was born in Dublin in 1974. She studied Law at University College Dublin and worked for several years in the telecommunications industry before turning to writing full time.

Her first novel, *Seven Nights in Zaragoza* (2005), was published by Hodder Headline Ireland.

Tara Heavey was born in London and moved to Ireland at the age of twelve. She read modern English and History in Trinity College Dublin before studying law and practising as a solicitor for five years. She lives in Co. Kilkenny with her partner and son. Her novels so far are *A Brush with Love*, a number-one bestseller, and *Eating Peaches*. Her third novel will be published in September 2005.

Arlene Hunt is the author of two crime thrillers set in Dublin, *Vicious Circle* and *False Intentions*. She lives in Barcelona with her husband, daughter, three cats and faithful basset hound. She is currently working on her third novel.

Cathy Kelly is the author of eight novels: *Woman to Woman, She's the One, Never Too Late, Someone Like You, What She Wants, Just between Us, Best of Friends* and *Always and Forever*. She is a number-one bestselling author in the UK and Ireland and a top-ten bestseller internationally. *Someone Like You* was the Parker RNA Romantic Novel of the Year. Cathy lives in Wicklow with her partner and their twin sons. She is currently working on her ninth novel.

Pauline McLynn's latest novel is *The Woman on the Bus*. She has also written three novels featuring Irish private investigator Leo Street (*Something for the Weekend, Better than a Rest* and *Right on Time*) and contributed to the novel *Yeats Is Dead* by fifteen Irish authors (in aid of Amnesty International) and the short-story collections *Girls Night In* (in aid of Warchild) and *Magic* (in aid of One Parent Families). She is also an actress, probably best known for her role as Mrs Doyle in the sitcom *Father Ted*.

Roisin Meaney was born in Kerry and since the age of eight has lived mainly in Limerick. Her debut novel, *The Daisy Picker*, won the Tivoli 'Write a Bestseller' competition and was published in May 2004. Her second, *Putting Out the Stars*, hit the shelves in February 2005. She divides her time between teaching and writing and is currently working on a third novel.

Lia Mills is a novelist and short-story writer who also works as a freelance non-fiction writer, editor and arts consultant. Her first novel, *Another Alice*, was published by Poolbeg Press in 1996 and her second novel, *Nothing Simple*, has been published by Penguin Ireland (2005). Since 2000, she has worked on several Public Art commissions, most recently with Ballymun Regeneration Ltd.

Éilís Ní Dhuibhne was born in Dublin. She is the author of many books, including *The Dancers Dancing*, *The Pale Gold of Alaska*, *The Inland Ice* and *Midwife to the Fairies*. She has received several awards for her writing. She is a member of Aosdána and is currently Writer Fellow at Trinity College Dublin.

Anita Notaro is a television producer and journalist and worked for RTÉ for more than fifteen years directing *The Late Late Show*, *The Eurovision Song Contest* and the General Election as well as a host of other top-rated programmes. She started writing fiction in 2001 and her first two books *Back After the Break* and *Behind the Scenes* were bestsellers. Her third novel, *The WWW Club* will be published in Ireland and the UK later this year by Bantam Books and has just been sold to Morrow, a division of Harper Collins in the USA.

Mary O'Donnell is the author of three novels – *The Light-Makers* (1992), *Virgin and the Boy* (1996) and *The Elysium Testament* (1999) – and a collection of short stories, *Strong Pagans and Other Stories* (1991). She has also published four collections of poetry.

She is an experienced teacher and workshop facilitator who has completed residencies at University College Dublin, in County Laois and in New South Wales, Australia, and has taught writing in prison, schools and on the faculty of the University of Iowa's Irish Studies Program at Trinity College Dublin. She is a member of Aosdána.

Sheila O'Flanagan is the author of nine novels, including *Anyone But Him*, *Isobel's Wedding* and *Too Good to Be True* – all of which have been number-one bestsellers in Ireland and top-ten bestsellers in the UK – as well as a collection of short stories, *Destinations*, which also topped the Irish charts. She received the *Irish Tatler* Award for Women in Literature in 2003 and has twice been nominated for the Romantic Novel of the Year. Her novels have been translated into twenty languages. She lives with her partner and cat in Dublin.

Patricia O'Reilly's fiction books are *Time & Destiny* (2003), *Felicity's Wedding* (2001) and *Once upon a Summer* (2000). Her non-fiction books are *Dying with Love* (1992), *Writing for the Market* (1994), *Earning Your Living from Home* (1996) and *Working Mothers* (1997). She is a writer and researcher and has written extensively for newspapers, magazines and radio. She is a lecturer and trainer in various aspects of writing.

Julie Parsons, a former radio and television producer, has been writing full time since 1998 when her first novel, *Mary, Mary*, was published. She followed up its success with *The Courtship Gift* (1999), *Eager to Please* (2000) and *The Guilty Heart* (2002). They have all been translated into fourteen languages. Her fifth novel, *The Hourglass*, will be published in January 2006.

Suzanne Power has been writing since she was eight years old, when she received her first pay cheque – a princely three quid – for a poem

in the local paper. Now, a millennium later, her novels, *Lost Souls'*
Reunion and *The Virgo Club*, have been published to critical acclaim
and translated into Russian, Dutch, German, Greek and US English.
She has twin boys and lives with her partner in Wexford. Her third
book, *Love and the Monroes* will be published in June 2005.

Deirdre Purcell's tenth novel, *Children of Eve*, is the latest in a long
line of Irish number-one bestsellers. She adapted another, *Falling*
For A Dancer as a highly succcessful mini-series for BBC/RTÉ,
while *Love Like Hate Adore* was short-listed for the Orange Prize.
Her non-fiction work includes *Be Delighted*, a tribute anthology
she compiled and edited in memory of the comic actress Maureen
Potter, and *The Time of my Life*, a ghosted autobiography of the
broadcaster, Gay Byrne. She lives in County Meath.

Trisha Rainsford lives in Limerick with her husband and children.
Up until recently she taught Classical Studies to Leaving Cert.
students. Her novel *The Knack of Life* (2005) was published by
Penguin Ireland. Trisha is co-author, with Helena Close, of the
Sarah O'Brien novels *Hot Property*, *Gazumped!* and the
forthcoming *Love Happens*. They have also written a TV series,
which is in the early stages of development.

Patricia Scanlan was born in Dublin, where she still lives. Her
books, all number-one bestsellers, include *City Girl*, *City Lives*, *City*
Woman, *Apartment 3B*, *Finishing Touches*, *Foreign Affairs*, *Mirror*
Mirror, *Promises Promises*, *Francesca's Party*, *Two for Joy* and *Double*
Wedding. She is series editor of The Open Door Series, a
prestigious literacy project she developed with New Island, which
has become a critical and commercial success internationally. She
has written three books for the series and is working on a fourth.
She also works as an editorial consultant with Hodder Headline
Ireland and helps young people with creative-writing projects.

Mary Stanley was born in London and educated in Ireland. A graduate of Trinity College Dublin, she has worked in England, Italy and Germany. She is the author of *Retreat*, *Missing* and *Revenge*. Her new novel is *Searching for Home* (2005). Her website is www.marystanley.com.

Kate Thompson was once an award-winning actress but is now the author of seven bestselling novels. Her number-one bestseller *The Blue Hour* was short-listed for the Parker Romantic Novel of the Year in 2003 and all her books have been widely translated. Her latest novel is *Living the Dream* and an eighth, *Sex, Lies and Fairytales*, is due in October 2005. Her web site is www.kate-thompson.com.

Breda Wall Ryan has had stories short-listed for both a Hennessy Award and the Davy Byrne Award. She is currently studying for an M.Phil. in Creative Writing at Trinity College Dublin and is working on a novel and a collection of short stories. She lives in Co. Wicklow with her family.

Sarah Webb worked as a bookseller for many years and now writes full time. She lives in Dublin with her partner and young family. Sarah's previous novels *Always the Bridesmaid* and *Something to Talk About* were number-one bestsellers in Ireland. Her other novels are *Three Times a Lady*, *Some Kind of Wonderful* and *It Had to Be You*. Her sixth novel, *Take a Chance*, will be published in the autumn. She also edited a collection of real-life travel adventures, *Travelling Light*, in aid of the Kisiizi Hospital in Uganda. Her website is www.sarahwebb.info.

Acknowledgements

The efforts of many people and organisations enabled us to achieve our aim of donating every penny from the cover price of *Moments* to GOAL. Everyone involved donated their services entirely free of charge. We would like to express our full appreciation to all who made this project possible through their hard work and goodwill. In order of appearance:

THE WRITERS: Thirty-nine writers, listed in the contents page, kindly donated stories – many of them original – forgoing all royalties, for the collection. It was through their astoundingly swift and positive response when first approached that it quickly became clear that Moments would come to fruition.

THE PUBLISHER: CLÉ – Irish Book Publishers' Association kindly agreed to publish the book. Our thanks to Jolly Ronan, Administrator, Fergal Tobin, Director, and all the members of CLÉ.

THE COPY-EDITORS: Emma Dunne, Kristin Jensen, Eileen O'Carroll, Deirdre O'Neill, Claire Rourke and Mary Webb kindly donated their professional services.

THE PROOFREADERS: Eilis French kindly proofread the collection and Claire Rourke (at short notice) the prelims and endmatter.

THE JACKET DESIGNER: The talented Ms Fidelma Slattery gave us this beautiful cover, and also input the corrections on the galley proofs and designed ads.

THE SALES AGENTS: Thanks are due to Alasdair Vershoyle, Director of Compass Ireland, and Christina Ramminger of Compass Ireland, who sold *Moments* to the book trade, and to Patricia Prizeman who joined them in the sales drive.

THE PRINTER: Enormous thanks are due to John Harold and the following staff at ColourBooks Ltd, who donated 10,000 copies entirely free of charge, and a further 5,000 at cost price. David Alford, Patty Andrews, Tom Bolger, Tracy Brady, Vivian Brodigan, Mark Cairns, Teresa Clarke, Sharon Conway, Noel Courtney, Stephen Doheny, Peter Donnelly, Eoghan Farrell, Adrienne Foran, Paul Hayden, Tara Hayden, Kevin Heffernan, Paul Kavanagh, Fiona Kavanagh, Colin King, Mark Kinsella, Ian McCarren, Garreth McEvoy, Keith McDonald, John McMahon, Dessie Noctor, Adam O'Connor, Ronan O'Leary, Ciaran O'Neill, Martin Richardson, Ray Buckley, Lonneke Schutte, and also the suppliers: Graphocolour Ltd – Ink; Litho Supplies Ltd – Printing Plates; Celotec Ltd – Cover lamination; Arctic Paper – Text paper (part-sponsored); Uniboard – Coverboard (part-sponsored)

THE DISTRIBUTOR: Thanks to Patricia Lowth and all the staff at Columba Mercier Distribution who came on board to distribute *Moments* to the bookshops.

THE BOOKSELLERS: Our fulsome thanks are due to the booksellers of Ireland – from the wholesalers Eason and Argosy to the retail groups Hughes and Hughes (who also kindly agreed to sponsor the launch), Dubray, Waterstones and every single retail outlet throughout the country who have stocked this book.

Thanks are also due to Jeremy Addis at *Books Ireland*, Kathleen Murphy and all at Eason Advertising, Faith O'Grady for rights management, New Island for administrative support, Marie O'Malley for donating the cover image, Jolly Ronan and Henry

Tubritt at Spot On! for website design and hosting, Grainne Killeen for PR support, Roddy Flynn, Pfizer and RTÉ. A significant donation to print cost was made by Gill & Macmillan, and donations to the project were also gratefully received from the Irish Copyright Licensing Agency and Mercier Press. Many other individuals from across the publishing industry volunteered their services for the project. For further details see our website at www.moments.ie.

Ciara Considine and Joseph Hoban
Project Co-ordinators

Copyright notices